Next Exit, Dead Ahead

CW Browning

Cover design by Dissect Designs / www.dissectdesigns.com
Book design by Clare Wroblewski

CW Browning
Visit my website at www.cwbrowning.com

ISBN-13: 978-1500800406

Author's Note:

With all endeavors, artistic or otherwise, there will always be periods of uncertainty and doubt. There are times that, no matter how dedicated we are, we start to question ourselves and our project. For a writer, those times of self-doubt can be crippling. Without the unfailing love and support of our family and friends, it is easy to lose sight of the passion that drives us.

This book saw far too many of those moments throughout its creation. With each terrifying one, I reached for my phone. Next Exit, Dead Ahead would never have seen the light of day if it weren't for the two people who inevitably picked up their phone on the other end. My dear friends, Jacquie and Kristine, have been tireless in their support and encouragement, always there when I need them most. Answering random texts at even more random times of the day and night, their unselfish availability knows absolutely no bounds. I will always be thankful for their friendship and support.

Next Exit, Dead Ahead

"There is no deep shadow, no utter darkness, where evildoers can hide."

~ Job 34:22

Prologue

Alina Maschik hooked her bags over her shoulder so they fell across her body, first the rifle bag and then her satchel. Sliding the door of the helicopter open, she squinted against the onslaught of wind and watched as the roofs of the buildings below grew closer. Coming in to land was her favorite part of flying, and the noise of the wind and propellers didn't bother her one bit. Glancing at the man beside her, she met his brown eyes and nodded. He nodded back as she returned her attention to the door and swung her legs outside the chopper. The landing pad was still far off and Alina looked out over the city as the helicopter descended.

Dusk had fallen, cloaking the old city in deep shadows. Lights sparkled intermittently, illuminating the buildings and the Thames below, transforming everything into a glowing kaleidoscope of color. Alina followed the river with her eyes, the waterway winding like a snake through the city, and her mind went back to her history classes. She wondered if this was how the river had looked to the German bombers as they followed it during the Second World War, relying on it to lead them to their target. The city would have been dark then, blacked out, but the river led those pilots to the heart of London, where they dropped their bombs mercilessly. Not for the first time, Alina thought of all the abuse this London Town had taken over the years. Yet, here it still stood, stalwart and ageless. It never ceased to amaze her, this city that had endured so much and yet survived to remain the bustling international hub it was today.

Alina returned her gaze to the top of the building below. It was close now and the chopper was hovering, ready to land. The propellers whipped the air around them into a cyclone of wind, throwing up light debris from the tarmac below. Letting go of the side of the door, she dropped out of the helicopter, falling the last twelve feet or so. A familiar rush of excitement swept through her as she dropped through the air, her senses adjusting abruptly from the vibrating floor of the helicopter to the sudden emptiness and lightness of air. Alina ruefully admitted to herself that she probably should have waited until the chopper descended a few more feet as the tarred rooftop rushed up at her quickly. That twelve feet or so was actually slightly more, and Alina braced herself for a fast, hard landing.

Her boots hit the roof heavily and she winced as the shock jolted up her spine and through her body. She stumbled, regained her balance quickly, and ran out of range of the propeller blades spinning above her. Stopping just outside the landing space, she turned to watch as her companion followed, wisely waiting until the chopper was just above the landing pad to jump. He landed and bent over, running toward her as the helicopter settled on the roof behind him.

"You realize you're insane!" he yelled over the noise.

Alina just smiled, turning to head toward the steps that led down from the helipad. He joined her and they descended together, advancing quickly to the door being held open by a thickly-muscled man bulging out of a navy suit. Her companion nodded to him and held out his hand.

"Hello, Marcus," he greeted him. "How's the blood pressure?"

"Better now that you're home, sir," Marcus replied, his face creasing into a grin as he grasped the outstretched hand.

"Just a little detour." Alina's companion winked and smiled. "Nothing to be concerned about."

"That's good to hear, sir."

Alina continued through the open door, stepping into the building quickly. She found herself in a brightly-lit hallway and her companion joined her a second later.

"We can go along here to the private elevators," he told her, motioning along the hallway.

She nodded and fell into step beside him, brushing her hair out of her eyes. The hallway had the hushed, official feel of a government building and their footsteps echoed off the plain, white-washed walls as they moved toward a door at the other end.

"You're not very chatty, are you?" her companion asked, glancing at her.

Alina looked at him in surprise, her lips curving slightly.

"Why do you say that?" she asked.

"We've now been in each other's company for over twelve hours and I don't think I've heard you say more than a few phrases," he replied. "I don't even know your name."

"I know yours," Alina retorted with a quick grin, "sir."

"Yes, and that puts me at quite the disadvantage," he complained, coming to a stop before the heavy metal door. He laid his hand on a raised square screen beside it, waiting while a light scanned his hand print. When it was finished, he lifted his hand and waited expectantly. A second later, the door buzzed and he pushed it open, holding it for her to pass through. "How am I supposed to ask you to join me for dinner if I don't know your name?"

"Well, you could just say, would you like to join me for dinner?" Alina answered, stepping into a small alcove facing an elevator.

She watched as he pressed a button and stood back. He glanced down at her as the doors slid open, his eyes dancing. He was quite good-looking, his face lean and his chin strong. His brown hair was just starting to silver at the temples, and lines were forming at the corners of his eyes after years of laughter and sun. He stood around six feet and carried himself with the assurance of a man accustomed to being in charge. When he looked at Alina, she felt her lips tugging into a smile as his eyes met hers. Exuding power from his every pore, he also possessed a contagious air of reckless enjoyment that drew her to him. Her lips curved on their own as the elevator door slid open.

"Would you like to join me for dinner?" he asked as they stepped into the elevator.

The doors slid closed and Alina looked at him, her dark eyes meeting his. She was tempted. Oh, how she was tempted!

"I'd love to, but I don't think I'll have time, sir," she answered somewhat regretfully.

"Please. Stop with the sir," he said, turning to direct the full force of his charm upon her. "I think we've moved beyond that, don't you?" He held out his hand with a smile. "My friends call me Jack."

"Very well, Jack." Alina grasped the outstretched hand and his long fingers closed around hers. "You can call me Maggie," she added after a slight pause.

"You don't look much like a Maggie," Jack informed her, his fingers tightening on hers when she would have pulled her hand away. "Why don't you have time for dinner?"

"I have a plane to catch," Alina answered, her eyes dancing as her hand rested in his. He pursed his lips thoughtfully.

"That's easily solved," he decided with a grin. "We'll arrange for a later flight."

Alina felt a laugh bubbling up inside her. Oh, she was tempted all right!

"I'm afraid you would find me a disconcerting dinner date," she said gravely, pulling her hand away as the elevator came to a stop.

Jack reached out quickly, hitting a button and preventing the doors from sliding open. He stepped closer and looked down at her, his handsome face laughing inches from hers.

"I doubt that very much," he retorted. "Nothing could be more disconcerting than having a fearsome captor, with his head split half open, fall into the filthy pit where they were keeping me, and then looking up to see you."

Alina did laugh then.

"You handled it beautifully," she told him. "You looked as though you were terribly bored with it all."

"That was my good old British, stiff upper lip, my dear." Jack smiled into her eyes. "Join me for dinner. Let me thank you properly," he murmured softly, his voice rolling over her like soft silk.

Alina was sorely tempted. Jack was amusing her and it had been many days since she laughed. Her stomach rumbled, reminding her of how she hadn't eaten, and she was suddenly ravenous. Alina knew without a doubt that if she had the spare time, she would have accepted his invitation gladly.

"I really have to get back," she said regretfully.

"Then I suppose I'll have to content myself with a rain check...Maggie." Jack sighed, stepping back.

"Rain check it is," she agreed.

"Beware, I have every intention of holding you to it!" he warned her, hitting the button again.

The elevator doors slid open and they stepped into an underground parking garage.

"I'll look forward to it," Alina assured him.

"You have a car here, I presume?" he asked.

Alina nodded and held out her hand to him.

"I do."

Jack grasped her hand, his lips curving again.

"Then until next time," he said, his hand tightening on hers slightly. "God willing, we'll meet under more comfortable circumstances."

"God willing," Alina agreed with a laugh.

She turned to walk away and made it a few feet before he called out and stopped her.

"Maggie?"

"Yes?" she turned her head questioningly.

"You're sure you don't have time?" he asked, drawing another laugh from her.

"I'm sure," she answered.

"It's that important, then?"

"Oh, yes." Alina smiled faintly. "I have to go see about a hawk."

Chapter One

Viper rounded the corner, her eyes adjusting to the sudden darkness. What should have been a crisp, fall breeze was filled with the disturbing smells of gun powder and latex. She glanced to her left at the high wall and automatically gauged the distance to the top before looking to her right at a chain-linked fence. It ran alongside the narrow path, and whatever lay on the other side was concealed by impenetrable shadows. Stephanie and Angela were just disappearing around a bend ahead and Alina moved forward, conscious of her gun nestled in the small of her back. Her fingers flexed instinctively as she moved into the darkness.

A sudden, blood-curdling scream rent the air and the hair on Alina's neck rose. Her eyes narrowed and she moved around the bend quickly. There was no sign of Stephanie or Angela. Glancing around with a frown, she moved forward cautiously in the darkness. A low, faint growl rode on the breeze and her eyes cut to the right. The fence exploded suddenly with blinding white light and in the split second of brightness, she caught sight of what appeared to be a creature, moving parallel with her on all fours on the other side of the fence. In a second, the light was gone and she was thrown into blackness again.

Viper took a deep breath, bracing herself for the onslaught she knew was coming.

Seconds later, the darkness was shattered with another blaze of flashing white light. The fence rattled as the creature launched itself at her, hitting the chain-links with a crash and letting out an ear-splitting screech. Alina found herself facing a human, dressed in a white jumpsuit, with blood dripping from his mouth and a broken chain dangling free on his ankle. His eyes were wide and hideous, peering at her ghoulishly in the pulsing light, and his face split into a wide and terrible grin. A hand with talons for finger nails reached through a hole in the fence and swiped at her, a guttural noise emanating from deep inside his throat. Alina moved away quickly, but he followed her, hopping like a frog along his side of the fence. His eyes bore

13

into her and she had the uneasy feeling that she was confronting a beast instead of a man.

She was just turning away to go around another bend in the path when an all-too-familiar chill streaked down her spine. Viper turned her head swiftly. The beast-man was still staring at her, his mouth open, hanging onto the side of the fence. Turning around, she scanned the darkness behind her quickly, but nothing was there. She and the beast-man were alone. Alina turned back to continue on with a slight frown. Her spine was still tingling with awareness and Viper knew it had nothing to do with the man hanging from the fence, drooling blood behind her. This was a feeling she had felt many times before, and it was one she had learned not to ignore.

Rounding the bend in the path, Alina was plunged into darkness again. She could hear creaking to her left and she turned her head in time for another light to flash, briefly illuminating an operating room with blood smeared on the walls. The light went out immediately and Alina paused, looking into the plexi-glass fronted room. The light flashed on again, accompanied by an ear-piercing electronic screeching, and she was presented with a woman in a bloody hospital gown. She had something long and dripping with blood hanging out of her mouth and Alina's eyes dropped to the severed head, gaping neck-side up, in her hands. Behind her, on a gurney, was a headless body dressed in surgeons' scrubs.

Viper turned away, her lips twitching, and continued on, trying to ignore the persistent tingling on her spine. She glanced behind her again, but still saw only darkness. Intermittent creaks, loud bangs, and sounds of chains filled the air, making it impossible to listen for the sound of anyone approaching from behind. Another scream sliced through the night, this time coming from behind her, and Alina heard the fence rattling. She smiled. The beast-man had found himself a more receptive audience.

Alina watched fog rising from a decrepit and moldy graveyard to her left and wondered why she let Stephanie and Angela talk her into this. Haunted houses, haunted mazes, haunted prisons: they were all the same. Strobe lights, loud noises, and actors dressed up in blood and gore with the sole purpose of trying to scare people into screaming. Once upon a time, Alina would have jumped and screamed, succumbing to a racing heart along with the rest of them. Now, however, the only thing increasing her heart-rate was the lingering chill that kept sliding down her spine. Viper glanced behind her once more.

Something was there, and it had nothing to do with the haunted prison walk.

Motion in the graveyard snapped Alina's attention back to the crumbling tombstones and fog laying across the ground like a foot-thick blanket. She was surrounded by darkness again, but an artificial glow of moonlight illuminated the tombs, casting a bluish light over the area. There was nothing there, but Alina knew something had moved. She searched the graveyard curiously, looking for the hidden corpse sure to make a sudden, and appropriately terrifying, entrance. An owl hooted from hidden speakers and a cackle of crazed laughter followed. Viper shook her head slightly and moved on, following the path.

She had just passed the graveyard when there was a rush of sound and the corpse leapt out behind her with a gurgling groan that echoed around them. Viper swung around, her arm coming up instinctively to block his advance. Grabbing his outstretched arm, she clamped two fingers on his wrist, effortlessly forcing his arm down. He froze, staring at her.

"Tsk tsk," Viper murmured, waving her finger before his rotting face. "I don't know what you died from, and I would rather not catch smallpox this evening, if you don't mind."

The corpse grinned and a long worm slithered out from between rotten teeth. Viper arranged her face into an appropriately horrified expression and the corpse's shoulders shook slightly with laughter. He moaned and faded into the darkness again as Alina turned to continue around the bend, smiling in the darkness. As soon as she rounded the bend, strobe lights started flashing and she found herself surrounded by cells. Stifling a sigh, she did her best to appear startled at the gruesome occupants and the display of horror they put on for her benefit. After all, they were actors. She knew they fed off her reaction. It wasn't their fault she was impossible to scare.

When the lights suddenly went out, plunging her back into total darkness, she braced herself. A cell occupant launched out of the cell in front of her, landing directly in front of her. She was hit with the rancid smell of sweat and fake blood as he tried to corral her into the empty cell.

"Are you here for my conjugal visit?" he demanded, grinning and staring at the low V of her sweater.

Viper raised an eyebrow as he moved into her personal space.

A moment later, she was rounding the next bend in the walk and the hapless actor was back in his cell with no clear idea of how he got there.

Alina's amused smile faded when that persistent chill streaked down her spine again. She stopped, turning around slowly. She still couldn't detect what was causing her sixth sense to run riot and Viper slowly raised her eyes to the old, thick stone building looming over the haunted walk. Her lips tightened almost imperceptibly as she stared up at the imposing prison beside her. The walk was now running alongside the old structure and she scanned the wall with the barred windows high above her head. She glanced back curiously and saw stone steps behind one of the makeshift walls of the path. The steps led to a thick wooden door into the prison, and high above the door was a dark window. It was significantly smaller than all the rest, and Viper's eyes narrowed as they rested on the dark window thoughtfully. Without knowing why, she reached out and touched the side of the prison, her fingers resting lightly on the rough stone.

Icicles streaked across her shoulder blades and up her neck, causing the fine hair on her skin to stand on end. Viper frowned, shrugging her shoulders quickly, trying to rid herself of the cold. Instead of dissipating, it poured under her sweater and down her back, covering her with goosebumps. Catching her breath, she snatched her hand off the stone and turned her back to the prison, continuing along the walk. She rubbed her arms briskly, her heart pounding. The wind hadn't changed, but Alina was suddenly freezing.

And it had nothing to do with the haunted walk.

When she finally emerged from the thick stone wall surrounding the courtyard at the back of the prison, Stephanie and Angela were waiting for her. They were laughing as she stepped out and Angela waved from where they were standing.

"We lost you!" she called.

After the loud screeching and bangs in the walk, the sudden quiet outside seemed unnerving and Alina glanced around, memorizing the faces of people milling around her out of habit. She moved toward her old friends, her eyes adjusting to the semi-darkness illuminated by street lights.

"I was behind you," she replied, joining them.

Angela Bolan flipped her honey-colored hair out of her face, her green eyes glinting like a cat's in the dim, street lighting. Dressed in jeans and a fitted sweater, she looked like she had just stepped out of a Guess ad.

"We were going to wait, but then someone jumped out at us so we kept going," she informed her with a laugh. "Stephanie said you'd be fine."

Alina looked at Stephanie Walker with a laugh. Her brown eyes met Stephanie's, and Stephanie shrugged with a grin.

"I didn't think you'd be worried back there," she said and Alina shook her head.

"I was fine," she agreed.

Stephanie nodded and the three women turned away from the high prison walls. Alina took a deep breath, inhaling the fresh air gratefully after the humid heaviness of dry ice, smoke, fake blood and latex. She glanced at her old friend in the darkness. While Stephanie was trying hard to pretend nothing had changed, Alina was acutely aware of a subtle shift in their friendship. Stephanie regarded her with a certain level of wariness now, and there was an invisible wall of uncertainty between them. She supposed it was inevitable after what Stephanie had witnessed two months before in a remote clearing in Virginia. Stephanie had seen Viper, pure and unadulterated, at work in all her cold and emotionless glory. She had watched as the worst side of Alina emerged, the dark side. It was a side of her that, until that night, was only witnessed by people who didn't live to remember the experience.

"I thought it was fun!" Angela announced, drawing Alina's attention back from the past. "I'm so glad we came. I never even knew this place was here!"

"The prison or the haunt?" Stephanie asked.

"Both!" Angela hiked her purse more securely onto her shoulder. "I want to come back after Halloween and take a tour."

"It's just an old prison they turned into a museum," Alina murmured, coming to a stop on the sidewalk. "Why do you want to walk through an old prison?"

"You don't think it would be fun?" Angela demanded, looking at her. "They said the Boston Strangler was held here, before he became the Boston Strangler. I think that's fascinating. You don't think history is interesting?"

"I think it's over-rated," Alina retorted with a shrug as they turned to walk down the street, away from the old prison and toward the parking lot a few blocks down. "The present is bad enough without constantly looking over our shoulder to the past."

"I couldn't disagree more," Angela argued. "If we can't learn from the past, there's no hope for the future."

"There's no hope for the future now," Alina informed her, grinning at the look on Angela's face.

"Well, there certainly won't be for *you* if you don't stop baiting her," Stephanie interjected with a laugh. "You know how passionate Angela is about history."

"Killjoy," Alina murmured.

"Just for that, you're coming back with me," Angela said with a huff. "*Both* of you!"

"How did I get dragged into this?" Stephanie protested as they crossed a driveway emerging from the Mt. Holly Police Station behind the old prison under debate.

Alina looked up, toward the municipal parking lot further down where Angela had parked her BMW. The teasing argument in progress next to her faded into the night as her eyes lighted on the man. He was leaning against a streetlight about half a block away, watching them with his arms crossed over his chest. Standing well over six feet, he was intimidating even at this distance. Alina felt a little flutter somewhere deep in her belly and her breath caught in her throat. Sensing his slow smile across the distance, her own lips were already curving in response when Angela caught sight of him.

"Is that who I think it is?" she asked, cutting off Stephanie in mid-sentence.

"It depends on who you think it is," Alina murmured.

"Did you know he was coming into town?" Stephanie asked, glancing at her sharply.

"No."

Alina glanced at Stephanie in time to catch the quick frown that crossed her face. She bit back a laugh.

"Don't worry, Steph. As far as I know, this is not business-related," Alina assured her dryly.

Stephanie met her calm gaze and grinned ruefully.

"You can't blame me for being a little suspicious," she replied. "Every time you two get together, dangerous things happen."

"I didn't even know he was in the country," Alina said, unable to keep the sparkle from her eyes or the slight smile from her lips.

She looked back to the man waiting patiently, watching as they crossed the driveway. Damon Miles was every bit as dangerous as he appeared to be, dressed in black and leaning against the lamp, his eyes ever watchful. He moved with a lethal, jungle-cat grace that screamed a warning to anyone foolish enough to cross him. The last time she saw him, he was disappearing into the crowds at Heathrow Airport. He had been heading to somewhere in Europe, while she was on her way to the Middle East. They parted company with the same smile they always shared, wondering if they would ever see each other again. She supposed she shouldn't be surprised to see him leaning there now, watching them with that sharp blue gaze of his. Viper had bought the house in New Jersey so Hawk would know how to find her.

And he had.

"Well, if it isn't Mr. Hunk O' Mysterious himself," Angela said cheerfully as the trio grew closer. "When did you blow into town?"

"Not long ago." Damon straightened up with a smile and held out his hand. "How's the shoulder?"

"Getting better every day," Angela answered with a smile, grasping his hand. "The physical therapy is going well."

"That's good to hear." Damon nodded to Stephanie. "Ms. Walker, always a pleasure."

"Well, that depends on why you're in Jersey," Stephanie retorted with a laugh, holding out her hand. "As long as deadly assassins aren't right behind you, it's good to see you again."

"I think we're clear on that point," he said with a grin.

"Are you here for business or pleasure?" Angela asked him, smiling.

The sly look she cast Alina wasn't lost on Damon and his grin grew as he glanced at Alina. His deep blue eyes were dancing with laughter and Alina's eyes narrowed suspiciously in reaction.

"That depends entirely on Alina," Damon murmured.

"Of course it does," Angela said, laughing delightedly. "I think we just lost Lina for the rest of the evening," she said to Stephanie.

Stephanie looked at Alina and grinned.

"I think you're right," she agreed. "Let's go for a drink and leave them to catch up."

Alina watched her friends depart with a teasing wave before turning her dark eyes to the man looking down at her lazily.

"Hawk," she murmured.

"Viper."

Alina chuckled suddenly and turned to fall into step beside him.

"Are you really here just to say hello?" she asked, casting him a glance from under her long lashes.

"I warned you I'd be back," Hawk replied softly, looking down at her. "We have unfinished business, you and I."

Alina swallowed as her heart thumped painfully in her chest and her mouth went suddenly dry. Two months before had found them on a tropical island. They were sent there to relax while their boss cleaned up an inter-agency mess they had exposed in Washington. Alina still hadn't quite worked out in her head what exactly transpired on that island in August. Perhaps it was the sun, or the exotic culture that surrounded them, but Viper allowed the unthinkable to happen. She had allowed herself to feel and act like a woman for the first time in over ten years. Long relaxing days spent either on the beach or exploring the island outside the resort had culminated in insanity their last night there. Vague recollections of drinking rum and dancing in an outdoor tiki bar, wrapped in Damon's arms, came to mind and Alina felt her cheeks grow warm with the memory.

The entire evening was a blur in her mind, but she did remember going back to Damon's room only to fall into an alcohol-induced sleep, his arms wrapped securely around her. She had realized, even in her drunken state, that they had wandered into unfamiliar territory in their relationship. It was confirmed the next morning when she opened her eyes to find Hawk watching her, a strange look in those blue eyes of his. It was a look that at once filled her with both warmth and fear, and she had dealt with it the only way she knew how to deal with emotion. She ignored it.

They were both called back into the field that morning, vacation over. Hawk had flown as far as London with her. When they parted company in the airport, he made no secret of the fact that he intended to pursue this strange relationship they now found themselves in. Alina had disappeared into the crowds uneasily aware that, eventually, Hawk was going to demand a response from her.

And now here he was.

"I know I shouldn't be surprised, but I am." Alina didn't try to pretend ignorance. "I suppose I thought it would just stay on the island."

Damon stopped walking and looked down at her, his eyes glinting.

"It didn't start on the island," he retorted, his eyes meeting hers. "If it had, this would be much less complicated."

"Well, it wouldn't be us if it wasn't complicated," Alina muttered, her lips twitching. "We do have a habit of making everything difficult."

Damon laughed and motioned to a motorcycle a few feet away.

"We keep it interesting," he retorted, pulling his keys out of his pocket.

Alina grinned and watched as he pulled a spare helmet from a saddle bag, tossing it to her.

"That we do," she murmured, catching the helmet and putting it on.

"Are you sure?" the man demanded, his dark eyes pinning the messenger with a hard stare. "There can be no mistake. We already lost him once."

"I'm sure," the messenger answered positively. "It *was* the Hawk."

Jenaro Gomez shrugged off the arm of the woman draped over him and got up from the couch, striding over to stare out the window into the darkness. The woman frowned in displeasure and got up with a huff, stalking out of the smoke-filled living room and disappearing down the hallway toward the bathroom. Jenaro watched her go before returning his attention out the window.

"Where did you see him?" he asked over his shoulder.

"Outside the old prison on High Street," the messenger answered. "He met a woman there, possibly the same one he was with on the island. It was hard to tell."

"What would bring the Hawk to New Jersey?" Jenaro mused. "He must know we're here."

"How is that possible?" another man spoke up from across the room. "No one knows we're here."

"Do you have another explanation?" Jenaro demanded, turning from the window. "If so, tell me!"

The man was silent and Jenaro cursed, taking a turn around the living room impatiently. The other two watched him, loathe to interrupt his thoughts. Jenaro Gomez was a frightening man at the best of times, but when he got the look in his eye that he had right now, he could be downright terrifying. There was a good reason he was lieutenant and second-in-command of the Casa Reino Cartel.

"If the Hawk is here for us, he must know about the bank," Jenaro finally decided. "Increase the pressure on our boy and get him to move up the timetable."

"I'll see to it." The man across the room stood up and headed toward the door.

"Turi..."

The man stopped at the door and turned around inquiringly.

"Find out where the Hawk is staying," Jenaro said slowly, "and put Lorenzo on him. I'll contact La Cabeza and see what he advises. For now, just watch him and report back."

Turi nodded, disappearing out the door as Jenaro returned to the window, ignoring the messenger. He stared out into the night, his eyes narrowed. The Hawk was a formidable complication he hadn't expected, but it was not altogether unwelcome. They had lost him two months before, when he left the island and went into Europe. With nothing to go on but a picture sent by a dead woman and no name, they were unable to trace him again. The Hawk was a phantom. He didn't seem to exist, and those who must know of his existence could not be bought. Yet, if the messenger was correct, he had fallen into their laps here, in New Jersey of all places.

Jenaro smiled a slow, terrible smile.

He wouldn't allow the Hawk to get away again.

Chapter Two

Alina flipped on the kitchen light and dropped her keys on the marble-topped bar. Damon glanced around as he slid the door to the deck closed. The house was just as he remembered it. To his left, the living room was spotless. The chocolate brown couch and matching recliner were just where he remembered them, and the mission-style coffee table gleamed in the dim light filtering from the kitchen. The flat-screen TV mounted above the fireplace was dark, but Hawk knew it was linked into Viper's extensive security system. She could monitor her perimeter from that screen, as well as from several others throughout the house.

Damon turned his attention to the dining room in front of the bay window on his right. The gleaming, dark wood table and chairs were also spotless, looking like an ad from a furniture magazine. A black, marble-topped bar separated the dining room from the large, state-of-the-art kitchen and he moved forward to perch on one of the stools, watching as Alina reached behind her back. She pulled her gun from the holster at the back of her jeans.

"Water or coffee?" she asked him, setting it on the bar next to her keys and heading toward the fridge.

"I've been up since yesterday," Damon answered with a yawn. "I'll take coffee."

Alina pulled herself a bottle of water from the fridge and turned to look at Damon. The over-head light was bright and she got her first good look at him. His dark hair fell over his forehead in a careless wave and his cobalt-blue eyes were tired. There were lines at their corners and a certain grimness about his firm lips. Dark shadows under his eyes accentuated the five o'clock shadow along his jawline, giving him the travel-weary look of a man on the move. Her eyes narrowed as she sipped her water.

"You just got into the country?" she asked.

"This morning," Hawk told her.

"Does Charlie know you're here?"

"Not unless he has a tracking device on me."

Alina studied him for a moment. He looked exhausted, but he also had something in his eyes, a watchful glint that made her pause. It was a look she knew well. She saw it many times in her own reflection. Capping her water bottle thoughtfully, she set it on the island in the middle of the kitchen and turned to hit the power button on her espresso machine.

"How long are you staying?" Alina asked, turning to face him.

She leaned on the counter, watching him from under dark lashes, while she waited for the semi-automatic espresso machine to warm up. Damon met her gaze steadily, his face giving nothing away.

"That depends on you," he replied softly.

Alina's heart fluttered and her breath caught in her throat. Her lips curved slowly as her brown eyes met his blue ones.

"That doesn't sound like a very solid plan," she murmured.

Laughter leapt into his eyes and he grinned.

"It's more solid than you think," he retorted with a wink.

Alina grinned reluctantly and turned to the coffeemaker again, pulling a mug out of the cabinet and setting it under the spout. The bean grinder came to life as she pressed the button to brew eight ounces of strong espresso.

"I heard about an insane raid on a Taliban camp a few days ago," Hawk said loudly over the noise, changing the subject.

He hadn't missed the flash of uncertainty in her eyes, and he was too accomplished a hunter to startle his prey. He would give her time to adjust to him again. They had a lot to work out between them, and Damon wasn't about to scare her away.

"Oh?" Alina glanced over her shoulder. She encountered sparkling blue eyes that were penetrating even as they held a glint of amusement.

"Yes." Hawk's voice lowered as the grinder stopped and coffee started to brew into the mug. "The story I heard was that it all happened so fast it took the camp by surprise. Several Taliban were killed, and those left alive were badly wounded."

"Imagine that." Alina pulled the mug out from under the spout and walked over to set it in front of him. "Was it a SEAL or DELTA team?"

Damon pulled the mug of steaming coffee towards him, a laugh lurking about his mouth.

"Neither," he replied. "I heard it was a ghost."

Alina laughed and grabbed her water bottle from the island. She came around the bar to settle onto the stool next to him. As she passed him, she caught a whiff of spiced musk and fresh woods. It was a scent she would always associate with Hawk, and a feeling of contentment washed over her. Sipping her water, she shrugged the emotion aside with a slight

23

frown.

"I don't believe in ghosts," she told him.

Damon winked at her and sipped his coffee.

"Neither do I, but they say this 'ghost' blew into the camp at night while half of them were away attacking a military convoy several kilometers away," he continued. Alina lowered her water and encountered another sharp look from dark blue eyes. "This is where it gets good. While they were attacking the convoy away from camp, this ghost came in and picked off the ones who stayed behind one by one. The few left alive *never even saw him.*"

"Therefore, it *had* to be a ghost," Alina murmured, her lips twitching. "Just one person did this?"

"That's the story." Hawk set down his mug and turned his head to look at her. "He went in, picked off half the camp and made it to the center of the compound, where he rescued a high-profile prisoner from a pit in the ground."

"Good Lord, it sounds like a good, old-fashioned Stallone movie," Alina exclaimed, drawing a laugh from Damon.

"That's not all," he told her.

"Of course not."

"While Rambo was doing all this, the other half of the camp attacking the convoy walked into an ambush," Hawk said. "They were captured and taken by NATO forces. One of the captured has been on *our* Most Wanted list for three years."

"This ghost appears to have had extremely good information," Alina decided. "When did you hear all this?"

"Last night, on my way out of Tel Aviv." Hawk sipped his coffee again. "My source says everyone is buzzing about it."

"Buzzing about a ghost?" Alina scoffed, setting her bottle down. "Sounds like a fairy tale to me. You would have to be completely insane to even attempt something like that as a single person. Even the SEAL teams aren't dumb enough to try something that dangerous!"

"Hey, watch what you say about my brothers," Hawk warned her without heat and Alina winked at him. "But you're right. Someone *would* have to be completely insane to even attempt it."

They were silent for a moment, Hawk sipping his coffee and Viper staring thoughtfully across the kitchen. The silence lengthened and Damon glanced at her, his eyes glinting. She turned her head and her eyes met his, unreadable. After a moment, he smiled reluctantly.

"Whoever this ghost was, they certainly had speed and luck on their side."

"And a good plan," Viper answered calmly. "Never underestimate the power of a good plan."

"Oh, I don't," Damon murmured.

Alina grinned.

"And speaking of plans, what's yours?" she asked.

"Besides you?" Damon grinned at the sudden surge of color in her cheeks. "My immediate plan is to sleep."

"You look like you need it," Alina informed him, wishing her heart wasn't thumping so hard. "And if you're coming from Tel Aviv, you deserve it. That corner of the world isn't exactly restful."

"Mmm."

"Were you just passing through?" Alina asked, glancing at him.

Damon met her glance with a laugh.

"Viper, are you fishing for information?" he demanded.

"Maybe," she admitted, grinning sheepishly.

"You can do better than that," Damon murmured.

"Oh, I will," she promised.

Damon finished his coffee and set the empty mug down. He looked at her, drinking in the sight of her with a slight smile. A deep cut on her jawline, close to her ear, was healing and he reached out to trace the thick scab gently.

"It's good to see you," he said softly.

Alina's heart thumped heavily in her chest and she locked onto his dark blue eyes, drowning.

"It's good to see you too," she answered just as softly.

Damon smiled and stood up, his hand falling away from her face.

"Thank you for the coffee."

"Anytime," she replied, standing up and walking with him to the sliding doors. "Where are you staying?"

"Not far." Damon slid open the door and stepped out into the night. "I'm sure you'll find it."

"Of course," Alina said with a laugh, joining him on the deck.

They stood at the banister, gazing over the dark lawn. The house was buried in the outer reaches of Medford on sixteen acres of land, surrounded by thick woods. Alina breathed in deeply and sighed contentedly. The air was crisp with the scent of fall, and leaves covered the grass in the darkness. A cool breeze blew across the lawn, rustling through them in the darkness as an owl hooted in the trees. Moonlight filtered through the branches, casting silver shadows over the yard. The night was peaceful and another feeling of contentment washed over her.

"I hear you've been making friends in high places in London," Hawk said suddenly, glancing down at her.

Alina looked at him in surprise.

"You've been hearing quite a bit," she murmured.

He grinned, turning to face her.

"Only bits and pieces," he assured her. His smile faded and he reached out to rest his hand on the side of her face. "Be careful there. The higher they are, the less they can be trusted," he said softly.

"Oh, I'm well aware of that," Alina replied, smiling faintly.

Damon stared down at her for a moment before nodding. He lowered his head and pressed a soft kiss on her forehead. Alina ignored the sharp stab of disappointment as his hand dropped away from her face and he stepped back.

"I'll catch up with you tomorrow," he murmured.

Alina nodded and he turned to leave. Suddenly, a *whooosh* came out of the darkness and a large, black bird swooped out of nowhere. It skimmed over Hawk's shoulder, the tips of its talons inches above his jacket. He ducked with a startled curse and Alina laughed as the hawk came to rest on the banister beside her.

"For the love of..." Hawk glared at her. "Can't you stop him from doing that?!"

"He's just saying hello," Alina retorted, still chuckling.

She reached out her hand to the black hawk and Damon straightened up, watching as the hawk tilted its head to the side and allowed her to stroke its neck with her finger. It made a low sound suspiciously like a purr, and Damon realized it was cooing with pleasure. He shook his head slightly.

"I swear that bird has a twisted sense of humor," he muttered.

Alina's eyes glinted in the darkness.

"He likes you," she retorted. "If he didn't, you wouldn't have any eyes left."

"Well, that's comforting," Damon said, turning to head down the steps of the deck. "I'll try to remember that next time I see claws and a beak coming at me from nowhere."

Alina's laughter followed him to the motorcycle parked in the driveway.

Stephanie pulled her hair into a pony-tail and leaned over the sink to splash water onto her face. She was exhausted. Angela had dropped her off after a few drinks and Stephanie went straight upstairs to get ready for bed. It had been a long week at work and all she really wanted was to crawl into bed and sleep. Tomorrow was Saturday, thank God, and she had every intention of sleeping in as long as she could. Switching off the faucet, she grabbed a towel to pat her face dry. The only reason she had even gone tonight was because she promised Angela weeks ago. Otherwise, she would have spent the evening happily in bed with a book.

Stephanie dropped the hand-towel back onto its rack on the wall and turned to leave the bathroom, flipping off the light as she went. At the bar, Angela had been filled with speculation about why Damon had come back to Jersey. She spent two drinks rattling on and on about the unresolved sexual tension between him and Alina. Stephanie frowned now as she headed across her bedroom toward the bed. She didn't know anything about unresolved sexual tension, but she *did* know when Damon showed up, trouble was never far behind. He could deny it all he wanted, but she wouldn't be comfortable until he had been in town for at least a week without anything unusual happening.

Getting into bed, she reached for the book on her bedside table. She settled against the pillows and opened it, but found herself staring blindly at the pages. The first time she met Damon, she had become embroiled with a terrorist and an assassin. The second time she saw him, Alina was being hunted by her own government, and Stephanie and John were hiding in a safe house, their own lives in danger. Now, here he was again.

She lifted her eyes and stared at the wall across the room. Damon claimed he was just here to see Alina, and Stephanie hadn't missed the blush that stained Alina's cheeks under the street light. Alina hadn't been expecting Damon, that much was clear. Perhaps Angela was right. Perhaps he *had* come back just to see Alina. Perhaps it *was* just unresolved sexual tension. Damon had certainly been protective of Alina the last time she saw him, two months ago in a clearing in Virginia. He had been hovering over her like an avenging angel. At the time, Stephanie was struck with the thought that he was acting more like a lover than a business associate.

She sighed and turned her attention back to her book. Angela was probably right. He was probably just in town to see Alina. She lived in Jersey now. He would have to come here to see her. It would be silly for her to get suspicious each time he showed up, especially if Angela was right. If Angela's "senses" were accurate, they would be seeing a lot of Damon.

Stephanie was just focusing on the pages in front of her, setting Damon and Alina out of her mind, when her cell phone started vibrating on the bedside table. She sighed when her partner's ringtone started playing.

"I'm in bed," she answered the phone without preamble.

As soon as the words were out of her mouth, she regretted them. Her partner, John Smithe, was a teenager trapped in an FBI agent's body. There was a short silence and she pictured him trying not to laugh.

"Is that an invitation?" he finally asked.

"Not even close," Stephanie retorted. "What do you want?"

"I have information on Rodrigo," John told her.

Stephanie's eyes lifted from her book again, narrowing sharply. Rodrigo Frietas was an informant who had suddenly disappeared four days ago. He came to the FBI a few weeks before, claiming to have information about a cyber-terrorist hacking ring Stephanie and John were investigating. At the time, he offered information in exchange for protection. Stephanie interviewed him once last week. After reviewing his information, they set up another meeting, but he didn't show. All attempts to find him had failed. Rodrigo had simply vanished.

"Tell me."

"Remember Marcy? She works with Angela at the bank?" John asked.

Stephanie heard the sound of his car door creaking open and then slamming shut.

"Blonde bimbo, sure," she said with a grimace.

"You say that like it's a bad thing," John murmured. "I'm not sure why you hate her so much."

"I don't hate her," Stephanie replied. "I just think she should show less nipple."

John burst out laughing.

"Personally, I'm okay with the amount of..."

"What about her, John?" Stephanie cut him off.

"I just finished having dinner with her," John said.

Stephanie glanced at the clock with a raised eyebrow. It was just after one in the morning.

"Late dinner," she muttered.

"Dessert ran later than expected," John retorted.

"Of course it did."

Stephanie wrinkled her nose, trying to ignore the stab of irritation slicing through her. It was none of her business what John did when he was out of work, or with whom.

"Do you want to hear this or not?" John demanded, amusement in his voice.

"Do I have a choice?"

"She knew Rodrigo," John told her triumphantly and Stephanie was left speechless for a moment. "They hung out a few times for happy hour."

"How did you find this out?" Stephanie finally found her voice. "You didn't tell her..."

"Of course not!" John started his car and Stephanie heard the growl of the old Firebird's engine through the phone. "I have skills, partner, that you haven't seen."

"Ha!" Stephanie grinned. "I'll keep that in mind. Tell me what you found out."

"Hold on," John said, his voice becoming muffled. There was a short silence and then a click as he switched to his bluetooth. "You there?"

"Still here."

"So, the last time she saw Rodrigo was Monday night," John told her. "A bunch of them went to happy hour after work. She says he was quiet, but she didn't notice anything out of the ordinary. No one's seen him since and she was surprised when she heard the FBI was looking for him."

"Did you tell her you were one of the agents looking for him?" Stephanie asked.

"No. Marcy has no idea what I do, only that I'm a friend of Angela's."

"Hmm, somehow I don't think Angela would quite term it that way," Stephanie murmured. Angela harbored an obvious disdain for John that she made no attempt to hide from him. John chuckled.

"Angela is warming up to me," he retorted.

"If you say so," Stephanie said doubtfully.

"Do you want to hear the rest of this or what?" John asked.

"Yes."

"Rodrigo left their group at the bar when another friend of his showed up. They went off to a table together," John continued. "Marcy only noticed because the other man looked so familiar."

"She knew him?" Stephanie demanded.

"She did indeed." John's voice held a thread of excitement and Stephanie knew he had stumbled upon something good. "She met him at a banquet not long ago. Guess where he works?"

"Another bank."

"Bingo," John said. "He works in the IT department of New Federal Bank. His name is Phillip Chou."

"John, if you were here I would kiss you," Stephanie announced, her lips curving into a huge grin. "I take back everything I've ever said about your philandering."

"I told you it would come in handy someday," John said with a laugh. "I'm going to the office first thing in the morning to look up Mr. Chou. It looks like Rodrigo may have been part of that hacking ring after all."

"I never doubted it," Stephanie replied thoughtfully. "He was too scared to be lying, and what little information he gave us was right on. The question is, where is he now? And why did he change his mind about coming forward?"

"Maybe he decided he was more afraid of us than the North Koreans he works for," John said. "You can be intimidating, you know."

Stephanie rolled her eyes.

"Not as intimidating as...some others," she said, hesitating mid-sentence.

There was a sudden silence on the line and she knew John had caught the hesitation and knew exactly what she had stopped herself from saying. There was only one person they both knew who had the power to intimidate at will, and she was John's ex-fiancé. Alina had become the elephant in the room for both of them since Virginia, neither of them wanting to discuss what they had seen that night two months ago.

"Speaking of, have you heard from her?" he asked.

"Yes. She's back in town," she answered. "And so is he," she added after another hesitation.

"Oh great," John muttered. "Is your life insurance up-to-date?"

"Is yours?" Stephanie retorted.

"We should alert the local funeral homes and let them know they're about to get busy," John said.

Stephanie chuckled.

"It's not that bad," she said. "Alina didn't know he was coming, that much was obvious. She was surprised to see him. Angela seems to think..."

Stephanie stopped suddenly, remembering who she was speaking to.

"Angela seems to think what?" John asked.

"Nothing," Stephanie mumbled, closing the book in her lap and setting it on the side table.

"Steph..." John sounded amused again. "I'm a big boy. I think I can handle whatever Angela had to say."

"Angela seems to think there is something...unresolved...between Alina and Damon," Stephanie told him, trying to water down Angela's exact thoughts. While there was nothing between John and Alina anymore, and hadn't been for years, she knew John had big issues with Damon. The two didn't get along at all, and Stephanie was sure it was because of Alina. Watching John and Damon together was like watching two cocks in the same hen house. "I don't know if I agree with her, but Damon said he was here to see Alina, so who knows."

"Of course he's here to see her," John said. "Why else would he come to Jersey? It wouldn't surprise me if there *was* something more to their...relationship," he added thoughtfully. If he seemed to have trouble getting the word out of his mouth, Stephanie ignored it. "He's very protective of her."

"I'm protective of you," Stephanie pointed out. "It doesn't mean there's unresolved sexual tension between us."

John let out a bark of laughter.

"Is *that* what Angela said?" he demanded.

"Yes." Stephanie sighed and yawned. "She was rattling on about something to do with sandalwood candles and Chi...I don't know what she was going on about. I guess she's thought this ever since the Spring, when she saw them together at the house in Medford."

"You might want to warn Angela that they aren't what they seem," John said. "They're not normal people, like us."

"Are we normal?" Stephanie asked, her lips curving into a grin.

"As normal as we can hope to be," John retorted with a laugh. "I'm pulling into my parking lot. I'll see you at the office tomorrow, bright and early."

"I don't know what you're talking about," Stephanie said with another yawn. "I plan on sleeping in tomorrow. There will be no 'bright and early' going on."

"Then I'll come there and pull you out of bed," John informed her. "We have a lead. No time to waste sleeping in."

"Hmpf," Stephanie grunted. "If you show up here a second before nine, I'll put a bullet through your knee," she warned him.

John hung up with a laugh and Stephanie plugged her phone into its charger on the bedside table. She switched out the light and settled down under the covers. In the darkness, her lips curved into a smile.

They had a lead.

Chapter Three

Viper lowered the scope and pressed her lips together thoughtfully. The sun was just cresting on the horizon and the gray light of dawn was breaking overhead. She glanced behind her and disappeared into the shadows between a row of bushes and the brick building. Moving silently, she followed the side of the building to the end and peered around the corner. The grass courtyard was still cloaked in pre-dawn shadows, and Alina examined those shadows carefully before turning her attention to the back of the end unit. The patio was bare of furniture and the blinds were pulled tight across the sliding doors. She turned and quickly moved back to the front of the building, peering around the corner toward the parking lot. Lifting the scope to her eye again, she expertly zoomed in on the putrid green crossover parked at the back of the lot, partially hidden by a tree.

It had caught her attention because it was parked far down in the lot and away from the building, despite the fact that there were multiple parking spots available closer. It held her attention when she zoomed in and saw the man lounging in the driver's seat. He had been sitting there since she got here.

Lowering the scope again, Viper's eyes narrowed. Her gaze moved to the motorcycle parked a few yards away, in front of the end condo. It had taken no time at all to find out where Hawk had holed himself up. He was in a complex in Marlton, off route 70, about twenty minutes down the back roads from her. She found it easily.

So had someone else.

High-pitched barking erupted suddenly from the back of the building and a fluffy white miniature dog came bounding around the corner behind her. He yelped when his leash was jerked back, and then his owner came into view.

"Buffy, what's your problem?" the woman demanded of the yapping dog. "There's nothing there, you silly thing!"

And she was absolutely right. Viper had disappeared.

Next Exit, Dead Ahead

When Stephanie's cell phone started ringing at eight in the morning, she rolled over and pulled the pillow over her head with a groan. It stopped a minute later and she was just drifting back to sleep when her house line started to ring. She moaned and buried herself deeper under the covers, tightening the pillow over her ears, waiting for the incessant noise to stop. When it finally did, she loosened the pillow and determinedly willed herself back to sleep.

It was some time later when her cell began ringing again, but this time it was Led Zeppelin interrupting her dreams. Stephanie cursed, kicked her legs impatiently, and flopped over to her other side, facing away from the side table with her phone. The music stopped and silence ensued. She opened one eye, waiting to hear the voicemail alert. When there was no sound after a minute, Stephanie closed her eye again and settled back down to sleep.

Led Zeppelin sliced through the silence again.

She flipped over angrily and reached for the cell phone, knocking her book off the table in the process.

"I know I told you not a second before nine," she snapped into the phone.

"Sorry, Sunshine!" John's voice was gratingly cheerful. "Time to work! We have an arm."

"We have a...what?" Stephanie stared at the ceiling, trying to make sense of what he said. "Don't be cute, John. I haven't had coffee yet."

"Well, neither have I, since you mention it," he told her. "Feel free to get us some on your way."

"On my way *where?*" Stephanie growled, frowning at the ceiling ferociously.

"Mt. Holly Prison," John said. "The old one, on High Street. I have Rodrigo's arm here."

Stephanie sat up slowly, the mists of sleep evaporating as his words sunk in.

"Rodrigo's....arm?" she repeated.

"Yep."

"Where's the rest of him?"

"That, my dear, is the million-dollar question," John replied. "I just got here, but no one seems to know. Come on. Chop, chop! And don't forget my coffee!"

John disconnected and Stephanie dropped the phone onto her bed, speechless.

They had an arm? At the old Mt. Holly Prison? The prison she was just at the night before?

Stephanie threw the covers off and got out of bed, padding into the bathroom. Halloween was five days away. Of *course* they would find an arm in an old, unused prison!

So much for her relaxing Saturday morning at home.

Stephanie walked up the brick pathway to the front steps of the old prison, a large coffee in each hand. The immense gray brick building was set back from the road in the middle of the historical town of Mt. Holly. Nestled amidst huge, old Colonial and Victorian houses, it was a dark reminder of days past when people were incarcerated behind its walls and hung on its grounds. The bricks had turned smokey gray over the years, and the windows were dark, small rectangles placed high and far apart, covered with iron bars. Stephanie glanced up at the forbidding walls and shook her head slightly as a chill rolled over her. John spotted her from the top of the steps, where he was talking to a uniformed officer in front of the massive door. He waved and came jogging down the steps to meet her.

"You're a saint," he said, reaching out a hand for the coffee. "I'd just got to the office when they called me. I came straight here."

"Is it really his arm?" Stephanie asked, going up the steep steps to the old, solid wood door.

"According to the fingerprints," John answered. "Wait until you see where it is. I had them put it back so you could get the full effect. I know how you like that."

"Gee, thanks!" Stephanie shot him a look of disbelief as they stepped inside the massive, square building. "How badly is the crime scene messed up?"

"Not any more than it would be anywhere else," John told her, motioning to their right. "It's upstairs."

"I was just here last night for the haunted walk out back," she said, walking with him along the front corridor to a narrow flight of stone steps.

"Really?" John looked at her.

"Angela wanted to come," Stephanie told him, sipping her coffee and preceding him up the stairs. "Alina was with us. It was your typical haunted walk. Lots of fake blood, dry ice and strobe lights."

"Ironic, though." John followed her. "Did you see anything suspicious?" Stephanie shot him a look over her shoulder and he laughed. "Ok, dumb question."

They reached the top of the stairs and encountered two police officers. John waved them away as she flashed her FBI badge and led her down a narrow hallway. Windows were cut into the thick brick wall at regular intervals to their left and cells doors were to their right. Most of the cells had the original old wood doors secured to the wall next to the doorway, so visitors could enter the cells and look around. Stephanie glanced into the rooms they passed, noting the white-washed walls and painted stone floors.

"I held off on the pictures until you had a look," John said, motioning to the Bureau photographer at the far end of the hall. He was sitting on a radiator with his camera, talking to the medical examiner's assistant. Stephanie nodded to them as they looked down the hall. "They just got here, so they haven't been waiting long."

"Good," Stephanie said, stopping with him outside the center cell on the floor.

John nodded to the cell and Stephanie raised an eyebrow. Unlike the others, this one was closed off. The original door was affixed to the wall beside the opening, but entrance to the cell was blocked by a heavy, barred door. Stephanie sipped her coffee, running her eyes over the bars.

"Keys?"

"Downstairs."

She nodded and stepped up to the bars, looking through them. The cell was smaller than the others and a metal ring was sunk into the center of the floor. A white dummy, shaped like a man, was sitting on the floor with its back against the wall. A chain attached to its ankle connected it to the metal ring. A single, tiny window was cut into the thick back wall near the ceiling, allowing a trace of light from outside to filter into the cell.

"Solitary?"

"Yep." John stood next to her at the bars. "They call it the Dungeon. It's where prisoners were put in solitary confinement, and where they awaited their execution."

Stephanie nodded and lowered her eyes from the window to the cell floor. Propped up against the wall next to the dummy, for all the world like a forgotten broom, was a forearm. It had been disconnected from its body at the elbow and was resting on its severed end, the fingers pointed toward the ceiling. She looked at John.

"Door?"

"Locked."

"And the keys were downstairs," she murmured. She glanced around the hallway and shook her head. "This is a museum, right?"

"Yep."

"Complete with motion sensors?"

"Yep."

Stephanie looked at John. He was grinning like an idiot.

"Oh for God's Sake," she exclaimed. "You mean to tell me

Rodrigo's arm just appeared in a locked cell in a prison museum?!"

"I told you you'd want to see it for yourself," John said. "The guard who found it had to go downstairs and get the key to unlock the door."

"That's ridiculous," Stephanie muttered, looking back into the cell. "How the hell did they get it in there? And where's the rest of him?"

"We're still searching the grounds and the haunted maze out back," John said, motioning to one of the police officers. Stephanie moved out of the way as the officer came over and unlocked the cell. "As soon as the police pulled the name from the fingerprint, they called us."

Stephanie nodded her thanks to the officer as he opened the door and she stepped into the cell.

"Have they found anything yet?" she asked over her shoulder. John shook his head and she turned her attention into the cell. It was a small room, perfect for solitary confinement, and the air was cold and damp. "It smells in here."

"The whole place smells," John retorted from the doorway, making no move to enter the cell. "It's that musty, old building smell."

"Yeah, but this is different," Stephanie murmured, looking around with a frown. "This smells like...I don't know what."

She turned toward the forearm and crouched down, tilting her head to study it. It was a man's arm and the nails were manicured. She remembered that manicure. When she interviewed Rodrigo the week before, she noticed it immediately. The nails were still perfect. No struggle from the victim then, or the struggle had been extremely short-lived.

Stephanie turned her attention to the floor where the arm was resting. There was a smudge on the painted stone right next to where the arm rested and she glanced back at John.

"They moved it?"

"When they lifted the hand to put the finger on the machine for the identification, the arm fell over," John told her, trying to keep a straight face. Stephanie rolled her eyes and he gave up the struggle, a grin breaking over his handsome face. His pale blue eyes were dancing when they met hers. "They said they were careful to put it back exactly as they found it."

"God save me from well-intentioned uniforms," Stephanie muttered. "It would have been better if they just left it where it fell."

"Well, at least they didn't remove it altogether," John pointed out.

Stephanie nodded and rose to her feet. She was turning toward the door when a sudden pain shot through her gut and she gasped, her hand going to her side. The grin disappeared from John's face and he advanced swiftly.

"Are you ok?" he asked, noting the sudden gray pallor of her face.

Stephanie couldn't speak. Pain was ripping through her, robbing her of breath. Feeling as though a muscle cramp was tearing her apart from the inside out, she took a deep, calming breath, but the pain only seemed to intensify. John put an arm around her as she started to double-over, guiding her out of the cell quickly. He motioned for the medical examiners assistant as they exited the cell and the young man hurried over, his face creased in concern.

"Agent Walker?" he asked, unceremoniously pushing John out of the way as he grabbed Stephanie's arms. "It's ok. Let's just get you sitting down here."

The man moved her toward a radiator nearby and lowered her down onto it. Stephanie focused on his brown beard as she sank down, trying to breathe through the pain. Then, suddenly, it was gone! It dissipated as quickly as it had come upon her.

She lifted her eyes to the brown eyes of the assistant, crouching before her, then higher to John's blue ones.

"I'm fine," she said, shaking her head in confusion. "It's gone now. I don't know what happened."

"Maybe you stood up too fast," John suggested, looking down at her.

"Maybe," Stephanie murmured doubtfully, somewhat surprised to find she was still holding her coffee. She lifted it to her lips. "That was unsettling, to say the least."

"It's cold up here." The assistant stood up with a smile. "You probably just cramped up. Your color looks much better now."

"It must have been something like that," Stephanie agreed. She smiled at him. "Thank you."

The police officers at the end of the hall glanced at each other knowingly and shook their heads slightly.

"Spooky-ass place," one muttered and the other nodded in agreement.

"Between the chills, the pains, and the smells, the whole place needs to be exorcised," he said.

John perched next to Stephanie on the radiator and glanced at her.

"Can I send in the techs now?" he asked. Stephanie nodded, sipping her coffee again, and he raised his hand, motioning to the collection of techs at the other end of the hallway. The photographer stood up and led the procession down the hall and into the cell. Within minutes, his flash was going off inside the cell and the techs were taking turns rotating in and out of the small space. "You're sure you're ok?"

"Fine. I must have stood up too fast," Stephanie assured him, standing. "You start up here and I'll go downstairs and start with the night guard. What's his name?"

"Karl Didinger." John stood and looked down at her. "Watch out. He's a ladies' man."

"My favorite kind," Stephanie retorted with a grin and a wink, turning toward the stairs.

Alina glanced at the woman in front of her at the bakery, her ears perking up at a phrase she had only ever heard in Mexico: *Pan de Muertos.* Day of the Dead bread. She listened shamelessly to the conversation being held in Spanish between the customer in front of her and the woman behind the counter. The customer was ordering four loaves of the sweet, skull-shaped bread for the Day of the Dead Festival, the Mexican holiday that spanned several days, culminating on the Catholic All Souls' Day, November 2. In Mexico, that day would traditionally be celebrated with picnics at the cemetery, honoring the dead.

Viper studied the customer with interest from under her lashes. The woman was perhaps in her forties, and clearly an immigrant from Mexico. Her accent was still heavy and Alina thought she detected traces of a lilt common in the southern coastal regions of Mexico. Now what was a Mexican woman doing ordering pan de muertos in a little bakery in South Jersey? For that matter, what was a little bakery in Marlton doing selling pan de muertos? While the Day of the Dead was a huge celebration in Mexico, and had even migrated across the border into Arizona and Texas, it was practically unheard of in Jersey. As far as Jersey was concerned, the Day of the Dead was a movie, and a bad one at that.

Alina moved out of the way as the customer turned to leave the bakery, turning her head slightly out of habit so the woman would only see her profile. She passed without a glance and Alina's sharp gaze followed her out of the store as she moved up to the counter. The woman behind the case set aside her order pad and smiled at Alina.

"Can I help you?" she asked cheerfully in English.

"Six whole-grain bagels, please," Alina said, looking at the racks filled with fresh bread. She hesitated for a moment, then sighed imperceptibly. "And you'd better give me a loaf of white bread too. The country loaf is fine."

The woman nodded and turned to get the bread as Alina's cell phone started to vibrate against her thigh. She reached into her cargo pocket and pulled it out, glancing at the screen. She frowned slightly at the number she didn't recognize.

"Yes?"

Next Exit, Dead Ahead

"What are you buying me?" Hawk's voice was deep in her ear.

"Worthless white bread," Alina retorted, her lips twitching. "Where are you?"

"Across the street," he answered. "I'll meet you at your car."

Alina hung up, anticipation making her pulse skip. She paid the woman for the bread and bagels, and turned to leave, stepping out into the fall sun and dropping her sunglasses onto her nose with a sigh. Hawk was the only person who could make her pulse go from comatose to heart-attack with a few words. She rounded the corner of the building to find him leaning against the hood of her black Camaro, his arms crossed over his broad chest and sunglasses covering his eyes. He was dressed in jeans and a black tee-shirt and he smiled his slow smile when he saw her.

"Good morning," he murmured as she walked up. He uncrossed his arms and reached out to take the bag from her.

Alina looked around, her eyes scanning the side street, looking for the green crossover. It was nowhere in sight.

"Morning," she answered, bringing her eyes back to him. He was looking in the bag.

"You really did buy me worthless white bread!" Damon grinned at her. "You're too good to me."

"I know," Alina retorted, "but don't get too excited. It won't become a habit."

"Of course not," he murmured, leaning forward and pressing a kiss on her cheek. "But I'll take what I can get."

His voice was low and rolled over her like a caress. Alina swallowed and inhaled, drawing in the scent of musk and shower gel. Her pulse leapt in reaction and she moved back slightly.

"It was that, or have you eat all my bagels like you did at the cabin in August," she told him. "I opted for the least inconvenience to myself."

"Mmm." Hawk straightened up, a smile playing about his lips. "Trust me. It's not your bagels I'm interested in."

Alina couldn't stop the rush of warmth that shot through her and her lips curved into a grin.

"Then consider the bread a consolation prize," she retorted tartly.

Damon's grin was wicked.

"I won't need one."

His assurance made Alina's heart start pounding and her breath come quickly. She could feel a blush stealing into her cheeks and was thankful for the bright sun behind her making it difficult for him to see her face.

"We'll see," Alina murmured, reaching out to take the bakery bag back from him. "In the meantime, this will be at the house."

39

She beeped the car unlocked and Damon watched her open the passenger's door, depositing the bag on the seat. She slammed the door shut and turned to face him, once again in control of her breathing and her pulse rate.

"Why are you here, Hawk?" she asked softly.

"You know why I'm here," he answered just as softly, stepping close to her and removing her sunglasses gently. He set them on top of her head before pulling his own off. His dark blue eyes were glittering when they met hers. "We can't keep going on like this."

Alina stared at him with a curious mix of excitement and fear surging inside her. She knew he was right. They had been dancing around this attraction between them for months, years even, and they couldn't continue. It would start to affect their work, and that was something neither of them could afford. Even as she admitted this was something they had to deal with, something deep inside her shied away. Panic threatened and she frowned slightly in reaction.

"I know," she told him, her eyes locked onto his. She was being sucked into their sparkling depths, and Alina took a deep breath. "I'm not sure I'm ready for all this."

Damon's smile was slow and gentle. He cupped her face with his hands and lowered his head until his forehead was resting against hers.

"I know," he murmured simply.

Alina's heart thumped and she felt as if a weight had been lifted from her with those two words. He knew. Of course he knew. There were times she thought Hawk might know her better than she knew herself. She didn't have to explain herself to him. He was already aware of her hesitation.

She smiled into his eyes and his lips touched hers gently, undemanding. The kiss was over before it began and he was stepping back, putting his sunglasses back on. Alina dropped her own back onto her nose, her lips still tingling from the touch of his.

"I have to run up to New York," Damon told her. "I'll be back tonight."

"You know where you can find me," she said, smiling slightly.

Hawk grinned, turning to cross the street to where his motorcycle was parked facing the other way. Alina watched him get on and pull his black helmet over his head as she rounded the hood of her car to the driver's door. The motorcycle growled to life as she slid behind the wheel of her car, and they drove away in opposite directions.

Chapter Four

Stephanie rounded the corner of the Warden's House and walked toward the front of the prison. She had just finished going through the haunted walk again, this time looking for anything that would shed some light on the appearance of Rodrigo's arm inside the prison. Aside from discovering that Alina assaulted one of the actors last night, she had learned absolutely nothing. Stephanie decided against mentioning that she knew the mysterious woman who had repositioned the actor back into his cell with such efficiency. She got the distinct impression that he enjoyed the encounter a little too much.

John was just coming down the front steps with another agent, giving him instructions as they walked, and she smiled slightly. He dwarfed the other man by at least half a foot, and his demeanor was intimidating. Stephanie knew he enjoyed hazing the newer agents. She tolerated it because it amused her, and she couldn't deny that it got results. John had zero tolerance for mistakes, and the new agents learned quickly not to make them. He terrorized them, but they learned a lot under him.

Stephanie's mind wandered back to when she first found out that Alina's ex-fiancé was going to be her partner. She hadn't been thrilled, to say the least, but John turned out to be an excellent agent. He had grown on her over the year and a half they worked together, and they settled into a comfortable partnership. He looked over now, catching sight of her as he reached the brick pathway in front of the prison.

"Lunch?" he called. "You can drive."

"Yes!" Stephanie replied, joining him as the junior agent went on his way. "I'm starving."

"Any luck with the maze in the back?"

"Not a thing," she informed him. "There's no access to the prison from the haunt unless you're one of the actors, and even then there are only two doorways into the prison. Because of the way the walk is set up, no visitor could get access to the lower prison door. The other door is at the top of some steps and kept locked."

John sighed as they walked down the path toward the road. The entire front of the prison yard was taped off and news crews were loitering on the sidewalk, looking for an interview. John ignored them as they walked toward Stephanie's brand new Mustang. When her car was blown-up two months before in Washington DC, she cheerfully used the opportunity to upgrade from a charred six-year-old Maxima to a maroon red, Mustang GT. It was just over a month old, and Stephanie's pride and joy.

"The museum is closed and locked during the haunt, so there's no access from the front either," he muttered. "How the devil did they get in there?"

"Karl says the prison is haunted," Stephanie told him as they ducked under the caution tape. She beeped her car unlocked and they moved to it quickly as some of the press started toward them.

"Agent Walker, is it true..."

"There will be a press conference later," Stephanie cut off the press agent as she crossed the sidewalk. "Until then, we have no comment."

"Can you confirm that a human limb was found in..."

Stephanie and John got into the car, slamming the doors shut and cutting off the question. John glanced at her.

"Of course the prison's haunted," he said. "Aren't they all?"

"Yeah, but Karl swears this one really is," Stephanie replied, starting the engine. It came to life with a growl and she pulled away from the curb. "The motion detectors went off last night on the second floor."

"What?!" John exclaimed, looking at her. She nodded.

"Yep." Stephanie stopped at a red light on the next block and glanced at him. "Ask me what he did."

"Something tells me I'm not going to like it," John muttered.

"He turned off the alarm and looked at the surveillance monitor." Stephanie hit the gas as the light turned green. "When he didn't see anything on the monitor, he didn't go up to look."

"Some guard."

"He says those particular motion detectors go off all the time on their own." She looked at him. "It's common for them to get tripped and there's never anything there, so he didn't think anything of it last night."

"What time did it go off?" John asked.

"Once around two-thirty and again around four." Stephanie shook her head as she slowed for another red light. "Usually it doesn't happen twice in one night, so he went up and checked the second alarm, but nothing was there."

"Not even the arm?"

"He didn't look," she said disgustedly. "He said he checked the hallways and open cells, but didn't look in the Dungeon because it was locked."

John was silent for a long moment, absorbing the information. He stared out the window with a frown.

"So, the arm was put there either at two-thirty or four," he finally said slowly. "We don't know how they got in, how they got out, or how they unlocked the cell."

"Right."

Stephanie drove through downtown Mt. Holly and turned right at the end of High Street. They were both silent as she drove past the new prison and courthouse on the right, then past the run-down housing that characterized Mt. Holly. This town was comprised of a strange mix of historic elegance and depressed poverty. In an attempt to increase revenue, the town employed a lower sales tax rate than the rest of the state, but it didn't appear to help. It was a community struggling on the verge of collapse and, like most communities of that nature, the distinction between the Historical section and the rest of the town was startling. Where one block was well-kept and affluent, the next block was bordering on slums.

"What does Karl think happened?" John finally broke the silence as they headed out of the town and toward the bypass. Stephanie glanced at him, her lips twitching.

"Karl is a bit of a romantic, I think," she murmured.

"I told you he was a ladies' man," John said with a grin.

"Oh, he is!" Stephanie agreed with a laugh. "He's a heart-breaker alright, but that's not what I meant by romantic. He believes in things that are not quite...realistic."

"He thinks a ghost put the arm there?" John demanded incredulously.

"Let's just say that, according to Karl, it wouldn't be the first time physical items have appeared in places where they were never put."

"You've got to be kidding me," John muttered. "So a ghost got hold of Rodrigo's forearm and placed it in the Dungeon?"

"Halloween is in five days," Stephanie reminded him with a grin. "Did you really expect anything less?"

"Haunted prisons and disembodied limbs? You're right. I should have seen this coming," John answered, shaking his head. "Where are we going for lunch?"

"There's a Sonic on Rt. 38," Stephanie said, turning left onto the bypass. "This is turning into a corn-dog kind of day."

"Forget corn-dogs," John retorted. "If this keeps up, it's going to be a vodka kind of day!"

Alina stared at the search results on her laptop thoughtfully and her eyes narrowed as she sipped her water. She had run the license plate on the putrid green crossover when curiosity got the better of her. The man loitering in Hawk's parking lot this morning could have been anyone, but she felt instinctively that he had been watching Damon. While she knew Hawk could take care of himself, Viper's hunting instinct had taken over.

The search results, however, were not quite what she expected. The crossover was registered to a female. Her name was Jessica Nuñez, and a corresponding search pulled her alien registration photo.

Alina was staring at the pan de muertos customer from the bakery.

She frowned and set her water bottle down on the coffee table, picking up the laptop and sitting back on the couch. Her fingers moved swiftly over the keys as she pulled up several different databases and punched in Jessica's name. Within minutes, Viper had information coming in on Ms. Nuñez from several different sources. She had emigrated to the US eight years ago and settled in New Jersey after a short stint in Arizona. Her reason for moving to the Northeast was clear: her husband took a job with Rutgers University as a professor of Mexican History and Culture. They settled into a normal, quiet life and had no citations against them, not even for a parking ticket. The couple had a son aged seven, and a daughter aged four. Jessica worked with the Burlington County Board of Social Services and they volunteered at an animal shelter. The Nuñezes were the perfect residents.

So how had her vehicle ended up in Hawk's parking lot?

A loud beep sliced through the silence of the house and Viper's eyes shot up to the plasma above the mantle. Part of the front security quadrant, the entrance to the driveway out by the road, was flashing red. A black F150 turned into the trees from the road and Alina frowned, closing her laptop quickly. She pointed a remote to the plasma, turning it off, and stood up. Grabbing her laptop, she carried it into the front of the house and deposited it on the desk in the den. She glanced out the front window to the gravel driveway, waiting for the truck to come into view. A few moments later, it broke through the trees and rolled to a stop in front of the house. Alina watched as a tall, broad-shouldered man got out, looking around as he slammed the door closed. Shaking her head slightly, she went to the door.

"Are you lost?" Alina called, stepping out onto the front porch.

Michael O'Reilly looked every bit as handsome as he had two months ago in Washington, DC. His hair was a little darker, the red more pronounced, and his freckles were fading. His eyes, however, were just as sharp as they had been the last time she saw him, and his face creased into a grin when he saw her.

"Apparently not," he replied, walking toward her. "I thought I might be when the trees never seemed to end."

"You're not supposed to know where I am," Alina told him, holding her hand out to him in greeting. He grasped it firmly.

"It took some doing," Michael admitted, his hazel-green eyes glinting down into hers warmly, "but never underestimate a determined Marine."

Alina's lips twitched despite herself.

"I never do," she told him. "Do you have GPS in that truck?"

"Yes."

"You better pull it around back then," Alina said. "No offense, but I'll have to reprogram it before your location can be tracked. Oh, and I'll need your phone too."

"Is that really necessary?" Michael asked. The look he received made him grin. "Ok, ok! I'll pull around back. You don't have an interrogation hut back there, do you?"

"Getting worried?" Alina asked, her eyes laughing at him.

"With you? Always."

"Don't," she advised, as she turned to go back into the house. "I won't hurt you until you tell me how you found me."

"Well, that's comforting," Michael muttered as he went back to his truck. Her laughter followed him.

"You're the one that hunted *me* down," she retorted. "Welcome to the dark side."

Michael watched from his seat on the deck as Alina crossed the lawn from the driveway. She had settled him down with a Yuengling Lager before disappearing into his truck, armed with a small electronic notebook and a box-shaped device that looked suspiciously like a scrambler.

"Do I want to know what you did?" he asked her as she joined him on the deck.

Alina set the notebook and box down on the banister, sinking into the Adirondack chair next to him.

"Probably not," she answered. "Suffice it to say, there is now no evidence anywhere that you were ever here."

"So you could kill me..."

"And no one would ever find the body," Alina finished for him. Her brown eyes met his and she smiled. "It's good to see you again."

"You know, I'm not so sure how I feel about seeing you now,"

Michael retorted, his grin belying his words.

Alina laughed and stretched her legs out, leaning her head back against the chair.

"I've been trained to be invisible," she murmured, glancing at him from under her lashes. "By default, anyone who comes into my world must be as well."

"So everyone who comes here..."

"Has no satellite evidence that they were ever here," Alina told him. "Of course, they don't necessarily know that," she added and Michael laughed.

"I can't imagine Ms. Walker's partner would take kindly to that," he murmured. "He didn't strike me as having much of a sense of humor. How *is* Ms. Walker and company?"

"Doing well!" Alina answered. "They've been promoted and work mainly with anti-terrorism cases now."

"And you?" Michael looked at her. "How's the 'consulting' business?"

"It's fine," Alina said guardedly, glancing at him.

"That's a nasty cut you have on your face," Michael said softly.

Alina's dark eyes glinted briefly as they met his.

"Rock climbing," she lied smoothly. "My hand slipped and I hit a jagged piece of rock."

Michael's eyes narrowed and his lips twitched.

"Rock climbing?" he repeated doubtfully.

"Mmm."

"If that's what happens when your hand slips, I'm glad your foot didn't slip," Michael said, sipping his beer.

"How did you find me?" Alina asked after a moment of silence.

"Not easily," he answered. "The only reason I finally did is because I know something about your past."

Alina was silent again, gazing out over the backyard.

"Why?" she finally asked. "I was going to keep in touch. I believe I told you that when I said goodbye two months ago."

"I promised your brother I would look out for you," Michael retorted. "I believe I told *you* that when we said goodbye two months ago."

Alina looked at him and was forced to laugh. Michael had been in the Marines with her brother, and he had made a promise to him that he would keep an eye on Alina if anything ever happened. When Dave was killed in Iraq, that promise was put on hold for ten years when she disappeared into the military and Michael was unable to locate her. When their paths crossed again two months ago, Alina knew she was inviting a piece of her past back into her life permanently. She just hadn't expected it to be quite so persistent.

"If you're going to try to be a big brother, I think I'll have to re-evaluate our association," Alina decided.

"Hardly that," Michael said with a grin. "I'm just checking up on you to make sure you're not dodging any friendly fire this week."

"Well, I appreciate that."

"You know, I heard something from a friend in Mossad yesterday you might find interesting," he said, crossing his ankle over his knee and looking at her. His eyes were suddenly sharp and penetrating.

"I find it interesting that *you* have a friend in Mossad," Alina retorted.

"I'm Secret Service." Michael shrugged. "We have friends everywhere."

"Except the US."

"Keep it up, buttercup."

"Tell me what you heard from Mossad," Alina told him, grinning.

"Someone attacked a Taliban camp a few days ago," Michael said slowly, the laugh fading from his face. "Mossad thinks it was a US operative."

"Really?" Alina raised an eyebrow and suddenly wished Michael's eyes weren't quite so penetrating. "Why do they think that?"

"He wouldn't say. He did say whoever did it either had no fear, or was insane." Michael glanced at her and Alina was silent, a faint smile hovering around her lips. She was looking back at him with just a touch of interest on her face and Michael couldn't get any kind of read on her. "They allegedly went in alone at night and rescued a British prisoner from the center of the camp."

"How terribly heroic," Alina murmured. "Who was the prisoner?"

"*That* is all very hush-hush and I don't have a name," Michael answered. "All I know is what I heard from the rumor mill: that it was someone high up in the British SIS."

"In that case, I doubt it was a US operative," Alina said decidedly. "MI6 takes care of their own."

Michael shot her a sharp look and his lips curved reluctantly.

"You're right," he agreed. "Mossad must have bad information."

"I'm not saying that," Alina replied calmly. "All I'm saying is it's highly unlikely the British Secret Intelligence Service would call on the US for assistance with a rescue of one of their own."

"Unless, of course, the operative was one of a select few in the world capable of doing it, and was already in the region," Michael murmured silkily. Alina's eyes narrowed abruptly and she shot him a look from under her lashes. "But that would be too coincidental," he continued smoothly, "and SIS would had to have known the operative was there. What are the odds of that?"

Alina was uncomfortably aware of those sharp hazel-green eyes glancing at her again.

"Remote," she agreed.

Michael nodded and they were silent for a moment.

"Next time you go rock climbing, let me know," he said suddenly. "I haven't been in a while, but I still know a few good spots."

Alina met his gaze squarely.

"I'll keep it in mind."

Michael nodded and finished his beer.

"I'm headed up to see my folks in Brooklyn," he told her, setting the empty bottle down on the deck. "I'm on vacation for a week. Will you be here? Or are you traveling this week?"

"I should be here, unless something comes up," Alina answered with a smile.

"I'm assuming I'm free to come and go, now that you've worked your magic on my truck and cell phone?" Michael asked, raising an eyebrow questioningly.

Alina laughed.

"Yes, you're free to come and go," she told him. "Just do me a favor and don't get yourself followed."

"Yes, because my mother might follow me down from Brooklyn," he retorted. "You know how Irish mothers can get."

"Hey, I have to be careful." Alina shrugged. "I'm still in somewhat hostile territory."

"I guess I can understand that. I suppose I would feel the same way if our government had come after me," Michael said slowly. "I'll be careful."

"I appreciate that."

"Although, if my mother finds out about you, she just might follow me down after all." Michael winked. "She's a Giants fan."

"Give her my condolences," Alina replied dryly.

Michael laughed and was just standing when they heard the sound of tires on gravel from the front of the house. Alina sighed imperceptibly as she stood up.

"Sounds like you have more company," he commented. "You know, for someone who's trying to lay low, you seem to be having a busy day."

Alina glanced at him, her dark eyes dancing.

"I don't understand it," she said. "I try to be reclusive, and yet you people won't leave me alone!"

Michael grinned and they watched as a silver BMW pulled up behind his truck, effectively blocking him in.

"It looks like Brooklyn will have to wait a little longer," he murmured, watching as a honey brunette got out of the car.

"Looks like it," Alina agreed with a sigh. "And she can talk."

"Do you have any more beer?"

Angela slammed the door to her car closed, looking at the truck. She waved and started across the lawn toward the deck. She was dressed in jeans and a sweater with sheepskin boots on her feet. Her hair was pulled into the perfect ponytail and a Coach bag was thrown over her shoulder. Angela was Fall Casual today, with designer sunglasses on her face, and Alina bit back a grin.

"Am I interrupting?" Angela called as she came across the grass. "I was in the neighborhood and thought I'd drop by!"

Alina blinked. Angela hated coming here. She said it was the middle of nowhere with too many trees and bugs. There was no way she was just "in the neighborhood."

"Not at all." Alina waited for Angela to reach the deck before answering. "This is an old family friend of mine. Michael, this is Angela Bolan. Angela, this is Michael O'Reilly."

"Nice to meet you!" Angela held out a hand and Michael grasped it.

"A pleasure to meet you," he murmured.

"I was expecting to find Mr. Hunk O' Mysterious here," Angela said, propping her sunglasses on top her head and looking at Alina. "Did you scare him away already?"

"Do you really think it's possible to scare him?" Alina asked, uncomfortably aware of the curious glance from Michael out of the corner of her eye.

"I think you're fully capable of scaring Mike Myers *and* Freddie Kruger without breaking a sweat," Angela retorted cheerfully. "So 'fess up. What did you do?"

"I didn't do anything!" Alina exclaimed, feeling like she had been caught in a spotlight at night.

"Are you the Secret Service agent that helped clear up the misunderstanding down in Washington?" Angela dropped into a chair and turned her attention suddenly on Michael.

"Uh..." Michael glanced at Alina, looking like a deer in headlights and she felt some satisfaction in his discomfort. It was nice to be out of the hot seat. "Yes?"

"Wonderful!" Angela set her purse on the deck and smiled at him. "Stephanie told me all about you. She didn't mention you were so big,

49

though. You look like a Marine."

Alina bit back a laugh. Angela managed to make the word Marine sound like both a compliment and an accusation at the same time.

"That's because I am," Michael replied, leaning against the banister and crossing his arms over his chest. "I served with Dave, Lina's brother."

"Oh, this is *that* Michael!" Angela exclaimed, turning her bright green eyes back on Alina. "Didn't he get you plastered on Jameson after Dave died?"

"Ok." Alina turned to go into the house. "I think beers all around. Happy hour is coming early today."

"What did I say?" Angela asked innocently.

"I don't think plastered is an accurate description," Michael said thoughtfully as Alina disappeared into the house without a reply. "I think she went from sober to comatose in a few shots. She bypassed the plastered level altogether."

"That's entirely likely," Angela said with a laugh. "Lina never did handle whiskey well. I remember that episode. She was hungover for two days after that night."

"I think I was too," Michael admitted with a grin. "You must be one of the two friends she mentioned that night."

"Stephanie is the other," Angela told him. "Ironic, you being the agent to save Stephanie's life in Washington, don't you think?"

Michael glanced at the brunette settled comfortably in the chair, gazing up at him with a smile on her face. He wondered what, exactly, she had been told about Washington. Obviously, not the truth.

"Well..."

Michael paused in relief as Alina stepped back onto the deck, three bottles of Yuengling in her hands. She caught the look he sent in her direction and raised an eyebrow slightly.

"Angela, why does Michael look uncomfortable?" she asked, handing him one of the beers. He took it thankfully.

"I don't think he looks uncomfortable," Angela said, accepting a beer. "I was just saying how ironic it is that he ended up being the agent to save Stephanie's life down in Washington."

Alina glanced at Michael in sudden understanding.

"Ahh," she murmured, sinking into the other chair and sipping her beer gratefully. Angela was always good for keeping things interesting, she would give her that. She cleared her throat and looked at Michael. "Stephanie told us how you tracked down the person who killed her friend down there. What was her name again?"

"Gleason," Michael answered, having a hard time keeping a neutral expression on his face.

"That's it," Alina agreed smoothly.

"I think it's so funny how it turns out to be such a small world," Angela told them. "I mean, you working on that and then being in a position to help Stephanie and John, and all the time being an old friend of Lina's. Funny how things work out."

"That's the truth," Michael agreed, sipping his beer.

A cellphone started ringing and Angela sighed. She set her beer down and fished through her purse for her blackberry.

"Excuse me," she said, pulling it out and looking at the screen. "I have to take this."

She got up and went down the steps. As she strolled across the grass, Michael took the opportunity to look at Alina sharply.

"What was she told?" he demanded in a low voice.

"I was never in DC," Alina answered, her voice just as low. "We told Angela that Stephanie went down there to get some answers on her dead friend and you were already investigating. When attempts were made on Stephanie's life, you put her and John into a safe house and found the person trying to kill her."

"And Johann?"

"She doesn't know the two are related." Alina got up and joined him at the banister, watching as Angela spoke on her phone near the trees at the edge of the grass. "In the Spring, when Johann and the Engineer were here, Angela was shot. She took a bullet through her shoulder and it went out her chest. She doesn't know who the bullet was meant for or why, and she doesn't know I was anywhere near Washington, DC two months ago."

"Does she know what you do?" Michael turned to face Alina, leaning on the banister and watching her with his penetrating gaze. For the first time since he'd known her, Alina avoided making eye contact with him.

"She doesn't need to know what I do," she told him, her voice low and steady. "As far as she knows, I do security consulting and it involves a lot of traveling. That's all she needs to know."

Michael studied her thoughtfully for a moment before lifting his beer to his lips and turning his attention back to the woman on the phone near the trees.

"So I'm the hero in Angela's version of Washington," he said after a moment.

"Something like that." Alina glanced at him, a faint smile on her lips. "It was the least I could do."

"Oh, you still owe me," Michael informed her. "But at least now I know I'm not the only one you lie to."

"Ouch," Alina murmured. "Low blow, but fair."

"And Mr. Hunk O' Mysterious?" Michael asked as Angela turned back toward the deck. "Am I right in guessing the SEAL's a-shore?"

"You know, I'm starting to think maybe settling in New Jersey wasn't such a good idea, after all," Alina muttered with a sigh. "I don't think I like the scrutiny."

Michael burst out laughing and turned to her.

"Honey, there's nowhere you can go where you can hide from us now," he told her ruthlessly. "For better or worse, you're stuck with all of us." He glanced at Angela, watching as she tripped across the grass toward them in her designer clothes. "Is she always like that?"

Alina grinned. Her eyes shifted to Angela and a glint of something resembling fondness crossed her face. In an instant, the look was gone and, if Michael hadn't been watching her so closely, he would have missed the flash of emotion altogether.

"Oh, you haven't seen anything yet," she informed him.

Chapter Five

Alina slid the door to the deck closed with a sigh. Michael and Angela were both gone, leaving within minutes of each other. Angela had led a lively discussion ranging from Michael's marital status to Alina's fear of commitment. By the time she finished, Michael looked dazed and Alina felt like she had weathered a storm of bullets from the enemy. She wasn't sure who was more shell-shocked: her or Michael. When Angela finally finished her beer and got up to leave, she announced how thrilled she was that Alina and Michael had reconnected. She seemed to think it was something Alina desperately needed.

Turning from the back door, Alina crossed the living room to the hallway. She didn't think she needed to reconnect with her past, but if Angela kept this up, she *did* think she would be looking for a reason to get the hell out of Jersey!

Retrieving her laptop from the den, Alina carried it into the living room, sinking down onto the couch. The house was blessedly silent, with only the ticking of the clock coming from the front of the house and the refrigerator humming from the kitchen. She flipped the laptop open and reopened the databases, pulling up Jessica Nuñez again.

The silence was broken a few minutes later when her cell phone began ringing. Alina closed her eyes briefly and took a slow, deep breath. She reached into her cargo pocket and pulled out the phone.

"Yes?"

"It's me," Stephanie said. "You busy?"

"Would it matter if I said yes?"

"Not really," Stephanie answered. "Where's Damon?"

Alina's eyes narrowed and she closed her laptop.

"Not here," she said. "Why?"

"So he's roaming around loose?"

"You might want to rephrase that," Alina said softly, a dangerous edge to her voice.

There was a short silence on the phone.

"Remember how you said that, as far as you knew, his visit wasn't 'business-related?'" Stephanie finally asked, her voice a little less aggressive. "Do you still stand by that statement?"

"I do," Alina said with a frown. "What happened?"

"We're in Mt. Holly, at the old prison on High Street," Stephanie told her. "Why don't you come up? This is something you have to see to believe. Maybe you can help me figure it out. God knows I'm at a loss."

She disconnected and Alina lowered her phone slowly, her eyes resting on her laptop thoughtfully.

Jessica Nuñez would have to wait.

John handed the evidence bag to a tech and turned to jog up the steps from the basement. He nodded to Karl, the night guard who had taken up a position at the base of the stairway leading to the second floor of the prison.

"Agent Walker upstairs?" John asked him, one foot already on the first step.

"She just came down," Karl answered with a nod down the hallway. "She went into the welcome center."

"Thanks."

John turned and strode down the hall toward the room in the center of the first floor where Karl had indicated. The welcome center was the domain of the museum guide. It stood opposite the front door, and housed the register and small gift shop for the museum. He glanced in as he passed one of the two entry doors and found it empty. Frowning, he continued on down the hall. As he passed the front door to the prison, he looked outside and came to an abrupt stop. The door was set partially ajar so the agents could come and go easily without giving anyone from the sidewalk a clear view of the activity inside the prison. John watched through the opening as a woman dressed in black ducked under the caution tape at the sidewalk.

"Dreaming of freedom?" Stephanie came up behind him. "Or just getting some fresh air?"

"Neither," John retorted. "Did we know the Black Widow was coming?"

Stephanie looked past him to the woman striding up the brick pathway and grinned. John had nicknamed his ex-fiancé after the comic book femme fatale two months ago after seeing her in action. Stephanie had to admit that right now she looked the part. Alina was dressed all in black, with a lightweight jacket hanging open to reveal a fitted tank top underneath. She moved with a dangerous stride that made the uniformed officers watch her warily as she passed them.

"I called her," Stephanie told John, opening the door a little wider to push past him. "I want her opinion on the Dungeon."

"You think she'll know how they got in?" John asked skeptically.

Stephanie glanced back at him.

"Can you think of anyone else who might have a better idea?" she retorted.

"Good point." John grinned suddenly. "Maybe it was her."

"For God's Sake, don't say that to her!" Stephanie exclaimed with a laugh. "I already asked her where Damon was and she got decidedly frosty with me."

"Ah hell, is *he* running loose?" John's grin turned to a scowl.

"Yep." Stephanie stepped out onto the top of the steps. "She says he's not here on business."

"I'll believe *that* when I see it," John muttered. "I'm going to check on Mac out back. I'll meet you upstairs."

Stephanie nodded and watched as the woman approached the steps to the prison. Alina glanced up, her eyes concealed behind black sunglasses, and Stephanie smiled down at her old friend.

"Welcome to prison," she called down to her.

Alina started up the cement steps, casting her eyes over the gray brick front of the prison. It was a solid, imposing structure and her gaze paused on one of the old windows protected by iron bars. Even over 150 years later, the prison still had the power to intimidate and Alina shook her head slightly.

"It certainly still makes a statement," she murmured, joining Stephanie at the top of the steps. She took off her sunglasses and propped them on top of her head. "Should I be worried?"

"Not unless haunted prisons creep you out," Stephanie answered with a laugh.

Alina raised an eyebrow.

"Haunted?" she repeated. "Oh Steph, we need to get you out more."

"I'm just repeating what I was told," Stephanie retorted. "Come on. I want your professional opinion."

Alina crooked her eyebrow again and, after a last look around outside, she followed Stephanie through the massive doorway and into the prison. As soon as she stepped inside, the smell of history assaulted her and she sighed. Old buildings all smelled the same. It was an undefinable smell of age, must and something that Alina could only associate with history. It wasn't an unpleasant smell, but it was inevitably followed by the awareness of a presence that Alina usually tried to ignore. Her mind flashed back to the night before and the chill that had stayed with her until she was out from the shadow of this very prison's walls.

"Professional opinion doesn't sound good," Alina murmured as she glanced around the white-washed hall. "Don't tell me you found a body here." Stephanie looked at her sharply and Alina's eyebrows soared into her forehead. "Really?" she asked in surprise.

"Well, not a whole body," Stephanie qualified. "Just an arm."

"An arm?"

"Yes." Stephanie motioned for her to follow her down the narrow hall toward an open gate and a flight of narrow steps. "It gets better. I'll explain upstairs." They approached the steps and a museum guard nodded to Stephanie, his eyes sliding to Alina curiously. "This is Karl. He was the guard on-duty last night," Stephanie told her, motioning to Karl. "Karl, Ms.--"

Stephanie broke off suddenly, glancing at Alina in flustered confusion. Alina held out her hand to the guard and a faint, impersonal smile crossed her face.

"Ms. Woods," she introduced herself smoothly with one of her many aliases. Her dark eyes caught Karl's, commanding his attention and covering Stephanie's hesitation so flawlessly that Stephanie doubted he even noticed her stumbling stop. "Raven Woods."

"Ms. Woods." Karl grasped her hand and smiled into her eyes. "A pleasure."

"It looks like your shift turned into a triple," Alina commented. "You must be ready to go home."

"Not at all," Karl answered with a grin, releasing her hand after holding it a second longer than strictly necessary. "These old walls haven't seen this much excitement in years. I offered to stay on and help Ms. Walker out anyway I can."

"And I'm thankful you did," Stephanie said with a smile, starting up the steps.

"Careful on the steps, Ms. Woods." Karl moved out of the way so Alina could follow Stephanie. His eyes dropped to her feet. "They're not quite even. I wouldn't want you to trip in those boots."

"Oh, don't worry about me," Alina murmured over her shoulder with a wink.

She followed Stephanie up the steps, aware of Karl watching them. She didn't know about the walls of the prison, but she was pretty sure that Karl hadn't seen this much excitement in this old building in years.

"Flirt," Stephanie murmured in a low voice over her shoulder. Alina grinned unrepentantly.

The two women reached the top of the steps and were met by two uniformed police officers, both of whom looked at Alina curiously. She nodded to them as Stephanie ushered her into the hallway.

"This is the top floor of the prison," she told her, leading her along the narrow corridor. "It's where the serious offenders were held when the prison was in use. As you can see, the cells are open. The only one that's not is this one."

Stephanie came to a halt outside the Dungeon. Alina looked at the now-open door to the cell.

"They call this one the Dungeon," Stephanie told her, watching as Alina glanced at the bars before stepping up to the open doorway. "It was used for..."

"Solitary confinement," Alina finished for her, her eyes dropping to the metal ring in the center of the floor.

"Exactly." Stephanie nodded. "Inmates were also held here while they were awaiting execution."

"Charming," Alina murmured, her eyes scanning the small cell. "Not a very imaginative example of a tortured inmate," she added with a nod to the white dummy figure. Stephanie smiled briefly.

"Not really, no," she agreed.

Alina lifted her eyes to the small window near the the ceiling before looking at the walls thoughtfully.

"I saw a fireplace in one of the cells we passed. Do they all have fireplaces?" she asked, glancing at Stephanie.

"All but this one," Stephanie said. "It was part of the design for the prison. According to the museum guide, it was the first of its kind in this country. The architect designed it to be more humane, with windows and fireplaces in every cell."

"Interesting," Alina scanned the cell again slowly before turning to look at Stephanie, "but you didn't bring me here for a history lesson."

"No." Stephanie shook her head. "This cell is kept locked. As you can see, the door is made out of bars so visitors can see into the cell, but can't go in. Early this morning, at either two-thirty am or four, someone left an arm inside this locked cell."

"Who's arm?" Alina asked.

"Rodrigo Frietas," Stephanie answered, lowering her voice slightly. "He was an informant of mine."

Alina glanced at her quickly, her face unreadable.

"Was?" she asked softly.

"I don't think we'll find him alive, do you?" Stephanie replied.

"We've switched gears from looking for a missing person to searching for a body."

Alina nodded slightly and turned her attention back into the cell.

"Probably a good idea," she said. "How long has he been missing?"

"About a week." Stephanie glanced past her shoulder and Alina turned her head to watch as a tall, broad-shouldered man moved down the corridor towards them. His blond hair glinted in the light from the windows and his pale blue eyes rested on Alina assessingly. "We haven't been able to find a trace of him, until now."

"Not quite the trace I imagine you were hoping for," Alina remarked, turning to face John. She nodded to him. "John."

"Lina." He nodded back.

"When was the arm found?" Alina asked, returning her attention to the cell.

"This morning, when Karl made his rounds," Stephanie answered. "He had to go downstairs to get the key to unlock the door."

Alina shot her a look from under her lashes.

"Where was the arm?"

"Leaning against the wall, next to the dummy."

Alina looked at the dummy, then glanced at Stephanie again.

"May I?" she asked. Stephanie nodded and Alina stepped into the cell. As soon as she was two steps into the cell, a chill streaked down her spine and she frowned slightly. It was the same feeling she felt last night in the haunt behind the prison. "It was there?"

Pushing the feeling aside, Alina pointed to the evidence marker next to the dummy.

"Yes," Stephanie answered from the doorway.

She and John watched as Alina turned her attention to the high stone ceiling. She turned around slowly, scanning the walls and ceiling, before bringing her gaze to the metal ring in the floor. They watched as she crouched down and hooked a finger through the ring, pulling on it.

"Karl didn't hear anything? Where was he?" Alina asked, glancing up with a suddenly piercing gaze.

"Downstairs in the welcome center," John answered. "Aside from the motion detector alarms, he didn't hear a thing."

Alina's lips curved slightly and she lowered her gaze again, pulling her finger out of the ring and looking at the dummy thoughtfully. After a second, she stood up and turned to look up at the window again.

"Tell me about the alarms," she said without turning her head.

John glanced at Stephanie, who was watching Alina, and she nodded.

"The motion detector went off at two-thirty," John said, clearing his throat slightly. "It's a common occurrence, apparently, so Karl checked the monitors. When he didn't see anything in the corridors, he didn't come up to investigate."

"Of course not," Alina murmured. Her eyes rested on the glint of afternoon sun slicing through the gloom. The shaft of light fell in a triangle across the cell, resting on metal ring in the floor. The icy chill was spreading across her shoulders now, but she resolutely ignored it. "Let me guess." She turned to face them, her lips twisting. "Ghosts."

"I told you they said it was haunted," Stephanie replied with a grin. "Karl says this area is one of the two most active in the building."

"Where's the other one?" Alina asked sharply.

"In the basement," John answered.

"Hmm." Alina pursed her lips and looked at the evidence marker on the floor next to the dummy. "You said the motion detector went off twice? The second time was..."

"Around four." John slid his hands into his pockets and leaned on the edge of the cell door. "At that point, Karl *did* come and investigate."

"But he didn't see the arm until later?"

"He says he didn't look in this cell because the door was locked," John told her.

Alina glanced at him and met his pale blue gaze. The note of disgust in his voice was reflected in his eyes and she chuckled.

"Of course not," she murmured. "So you don't know *when* the arm appeared?"

"Not really."

Alina took one last look around and moved toward the door. The constant chill along her shoulders and back disappeared suddenly and she stopped short about a foot from the door. Stephanie and John both looked at her curiously as she turned swiftly to look behind her.

"What's wrong?" John asked.

Alina's eyes narrowed and she frowned, gazing about the empty cell slowly. She wasn't a fanciful woman, but there was no doubt in her mind about what she had just felt.

Something had grabbed her leg.

"Nothing," she said slowly as she turned back toward the door. "It's nothing."

"I'm assuming you've been all through this place with a fine-toothed comb?" Alina asked, glancing at Stephanie as they emerged from the prison the same way they entered.

"And then some," Stephanie agreed. "No sign of the rest of the body, and no signs of forced entry anywhere."

"What about the lock on the cell door?"

"Doesn't appear to be tampered with," she answered.

"Hm."

Alina jogged down the steps and dropped her sunglasses back onto her nose. She turned to look up at the structure for a minute before walking along the brick pathway running parallel with the front of the building.

"That's all you have to say?" Stephanie demanded, falling into step beside her. "Hm?"

"Well, it *is* Halloween in a week," Alina replied with a shrug. Stephanie grinned.

"That's what I told John," she said. "I swear, all the crazies come out this time of year."

"Don't forget the ghosts," Alina pointed out, a touch of sarcasm lacing her tone.

"Well, there must be something going on in there," Stephanie said thoughtfully after a moment. "That TV show about haunted places filmed an episode here, and Karl says several people have felt and seen things that are unexplainable."

"Like body parts appearing in locked cells?" Alina asked, raising her eyebrow and casting an amused look at Stephanie.

"Not body parts, no," Stephanie answered, unusually serious for once. "I've been told by several museum workers that objects are moved regularly and placed in other rooms throughout the museum when no one is there. Things happen that can't be explained away easily. Workers have heard banging and movement on empty floors. The Dungeon itself has its own weird things. People smell weird smells in there, and I got severe abdominal cramps in there myself earlier. Rachel, the museum guide, says it's common and has been attributed to the spirit of some prisoner who was hanged here. Something *must* be going on in there. That many people can't be delusional."

"Oh, there's something going on in there, all right," Alina told her. "I just don't think it has anything to do with ghosts."

"Let me ask you, just between us and off the record," Stephanie stopped walking and faced Alina, "do you think any of this is possible?"

"Any of what, exactly?"

"The arm in the locked cell," Stephanie clarified. "Do you think it's possible for a person, a *real* person, to have gotten the arm into that cell while it was locked?"

Alina stopped and looked up at the prison thoughtfully.

"Well, it's obviously possible," she said. "Someone did it."

"Could _you_ have done it?" Stephanie asked.

Alina's lips curved into a faint smile and she returned her gaze to Stephanie's face.

"Well, that's a different question," she said softly.

"And you won't answer it?"

Alina studied Stephanie quietly for a moment.

"You already know the answer," she answered quietly. "You wouldn't have asked me to come, otherwise."

She turned and followed the path around the corner of the Warden's House that was attached to the prison. Stephanie followed, a reluctant smile playing on her face. She had forgotten how slippery Alina could be when asked a direct question. She should have known she wouldn't get a straight answer.

"Have you sent anyone up on the wall yet?" Alina asked as they walked past the Warden's House and into the small parking lot behind it.

The car park was empty now, but the ropes cording off the lines where they waited last night to enter the haunted walk were still there.

"Are you volunteering?" Stephanie replied.

Alina laughed and stopped to look up at the massive stone wall enclosing the prison yard at the back. When she glanced at Stephanie, she was still smiling.

"Not this time," she answered. "It's all yours. Go up on the other side of the yard, though. This side is too exposed to the road."

"What am I looking for?" Stephanie asked.

Alina turned her gaze to the back of the prison, the second level of which was visible above the wall.

"A clear shot to the window of that cell."

Chapter Six

"Tell me again what I'm looking for?" John demanded, glaring down at Stephanie from the top of the wall.

"Any sign that someone else was up there recently, for starters," Stephanie retorted, sipping her coffee. She tossed a laser measurement gun up to him and he caught it deftly with one hand while he balanced himself on his knees with the other. "And I want to know if you can get a clear shot to the Dungeon window from anywhere along that wall."

"You'd have to be Spider-man," John told her, glancing behind himself. "I really need two hands to balance myself. It's not exactly like a walkway up here, you know."

Stephanie shaded her eyes with her free hand against the late afternoon sun and watched him as he examined the top of the wall. She honestly had no idea what to tell him to look for because she had no clue what Alina was thinking in that head of hers. However, if she had learned one thing in the past few months, it was that Viper's instincts were never wrong. If she thought the wall was significant, then it most likely was. End of story.

"Do you see anything?" she called.

"I see everything from up here, but nothing that can help us," John retorted as he moved carefully along the wall on his knees. He glanced into the haunted maze below, snaking around the prison yard. "You guys really went through there last night?"

"Yep," Stephanie answered. She followed John along the wall as he moved slowly, examining the top of the wall as he went. "It was fun!"

"It looks pretty lame." John's voice was muffled as he glanced down at something inside the wall. He paused, leaning forward to examine it, then shook his head and continued on slowly. "Are we letting them open it tonight?"

"We finished in there and came up with nothing, so I gave the green light," Stephanie answered. A brisk wind hit her in the face and she shivered, wishing she had her jacket. Now that the afternoon was moving on, the temperature was starting to drop. "No one will be allowed inside the prison, and I told them they couldn't use the front yard for the ticket stand. I also blocked off the Warden's House. There's a corridor that leads from the house to the prison. It's kept padlocked and rarely used, but I'm not taking any chances."

"You're a sucker." John glanced down at her with a grin. "Admit it. You like Halloween."

"I'll admit it freely," Stephanie retorted. "I love this time of year. It's fun, and I don't see why I should shut down the main attraction of the year for this museum unless I have a good reason for doing so."

"An arm isn't high on the good reason scale?" John asked. He paused in his progress to glance up at the Dungeon window. "I'm moving out of range of the window."

"What do you think?" Stephanie backed up a few feet and tried to see the Dungeon window from her position on the ground. "I can't even see it from here."

John held onto the side of the wall with one hand while he aimed the laser gun at the window and pulled the trigger. A red beam sliced across the prison yard and came to rest on the opening that was smaller than all the rest. He glanced at the measurement.

"Well, it's certainly within range of any decent shot," he said, glancing down at her. "It's a somewhat clear shot from here. I think it would be easier from further back, but only to an experienced shooter. Either way, it's a challenge. They would have had to balance themselves and make a moderately difficult shot at the same time."

"What about a pathway to the window itself?" Stephanie asked after a moment. "Can you see a way to climb to the window?"

"Again, not unless they were Spider-man." John lowered the gun and ran his eyes along the wall to the prison itself. "Unless..."

"Unless?" Stephanie prompted when he didn't continue.

"If they went up on the other side of the yard, they could have gone across the top of the Warden's House and crossed over to the prison roof." John glanced down to her. "Once on the prison roof, they could drop down to the window."

"You're really going along with this whole superhero thing, aren't you?" Stephanie asked dryly. John grinned.

"Hey, you asked," he retorted.

"Do you see any signs up there of someone else going along there recently?"

"Not on this section."

"Ok, Spidey, come on down."

Stephanie sighed and turned to walk back to the ladder they had rested against the wall. John cautiously turned himself around on the narrow ledge and started moving back toward the ladder. Stephanie's eyes rested on the upper branches of a tree visible over the wall near the back corner.

"Can you see the tree near the wall on the other side of the yard from where you're at?" she asked suddenly.

John paused in the act of stepping onto the ladder and glanced across the yard.

"Yes," he answered. "Why?"

"Does the maze block the tree in?"

"Not really." John stepped onto the top step of the ladder and looked across the yard at the tree in question. "The maze kind of skirts it, and there's a path running along the back wall. What are you thinking?"

"Could someone have come up this side of the wall, gone down this tree and gone over to the other tree?" Stephanie shaded her eyes and tilted her head to gaze up at John.

"Yeah, they could have gone around the back of the maze and along the back wall," he answered, looking to his left. John glanced down at her. "But if they were going to do that, why not just go over the wall on the other side to begin with?"

"It's more exposed than this side," Stephanie replied, echoing Alina's words. "With the police station right behind it, it would be too risky. It faces the road."

John backed down the ladder and dropped to the ground beside her.

"True. This side is more secluded, especially at night," he agreed. "I just think the whole thing is a little far-fetched, though. People scaling prison walls and going up and down trees with an arm in tow? Do you know how awkward that would be?"

"I know." Stephanie sighed again and turned to walk toward the front of the prison. "But they got it in there somehow, and our resident expert seems to think the wall and window are key components of the 'how.'"

"Our resident expert isn't normal," John muttered. He stopped and looked back along the high prison wall thoughtfully. "I guess I can see her point, though," he murmured. "If they didn't bring it in through the front door, and they didn't go in through the back door, that really *does* only leave the wall."

"Why here?" Stephanie wondered as they turned to continue toward the front of the prison again. "Why a prison?"

"Why just the arm?" John retorted. "And where's the rest of him?"

Next Exit, Dead Ahead

"This whole thing just doesn't make any sense," Stephanie complained as they rounded the front corner of the building. "Let's wrap it up here. I can't think anymore under the shadow of this place. Did you get the footage from the cameras inside the prison?"

"Yep."

"Ok. Let's go back to the office and take a look at it." Stephanie paused at the front steps to the prison. "And get someone up on a ladder inside that cell. I want some close-ups of the window. Have them measure it while they're up there."

"On it." John started up the steps to the front door, then paused and glanced down to her. "Are you heading to the office now?"

"Yes." Stephanie turned toward the road and her car. "I'll meet you there. Bring dinner back with you. It's going to be a long night."

The silence in the condo was broken by a quiet ding from the laptop on the dining room table. Damon swiped the touch screen and clicked on the button to close the connection to the external hard drive. Lifting his eyes from the laptop and stretching, he reached his arms far behind his head and yawned widely. His eyes fell on his empty plate and glass from a hasty dinner a few hours earlier and he sighed. He was hungry again.

Standing, he picked up the plate and carried it into the small kitchen. Now that his files were transferred, he could relax and make himself something more substantial to eat. He thought about the worthless white bread waiting for him at Alina's and smiled faintly. While he was on board with most of her healthy eating habits, the two indulgences he allowed himself were beer and white bread. Like Viper, Hawk firmly believed his body was his greatest weapon and he took care of it accordingly. He stayed away from preservatives, artificial coloring, any meat or produce that was not organic and GMO-free, and he avoided any and all soda like the plague. However, he also firmly believed that the only reason he was still sane was because he allowed himself beer at night, and white bread and real butter with his eggs in the morning. Alina had started to warm up to the beer in Washington, but she still called the white bread "refined cancer in a loaf."

Damon was putting his plate in the dishwasher, the smile playing around his lips, when something caught his attention. It wasn't a noise, exactly, but more of a sensation. It surrounded him, gripping his gut, and Hawk straightened up abruptly. The faint smile vanished from his face instantly. He closed the dishwasher and stood perfectly still, listening.

Silence surrounded him, but *something* had disturbed the peace in the small condo.

Hawk reached out and flipped off the kitchen light, reaching behind him to pull his constant companion out of its holster. Moving to the kitchen door, he glanced around the small dining room before silently crossing the room to flip the switch on the wall. The dining room was plunged into darkness and Hawk waited, listening. Silence still surrounded him, but something was wrong. All his instincts were humming. Setting his back flat against the wall, he moved along slowly until he was between the dining room and front room. The small living room was dimly illuminated by a single low-watt lamp, burning on an end table. Hawk glanced down the short, dark hallway that led to the bedroom, his eyes adjusting to the semi-darkness easily.

He stood perfectly still.

There! Something rustled outside and Damon cut his eyes to the front window. He flipped off the safety on his modified 9mm Beretta and watched the front windows, his ears straining for further sound. There was nothing. He frowned, glancing toward the sliding door at the other end of the dining room. All was silent again.

But he knew someone, or something, was outside.

Hawk moved swiftly and silently across the room, coming to rest with his back against the wall next to the living room window. All was silent as he stood perfectly still, his breathing even, waiting for something to happen. When there was no further movement outside the window after a few moments, Damon exhaled slowly. He turned his head and was about to peer behind the blinds when, suddenly, there was a loud rap on the glass. The sound was immediately followed by more rustling, and everything fell silent outside again.

Pressing his lips together grimly, Damon gently pulled on the blinds, glancing outside. There was no face peering back at him. His motorcycle was parked in its spot, unmolested, and the night was quiet. Frowning, he cast his eyes along the edge of the parking lot and watched as a crossover pulled out of the lot. The tires squealed as the driver hit the gas and sped off into the night.

Flipping the safety back on, Hawk tucked his Beretta back into his holster and stepped away from the window. He was turning away when he suddenly swung back and flipped up one of the blinds. Something was just outside the window.

Hawk dropped the blind and strode to the door. He glanced out the peephole before opening the door and going outside. It was late and the residents of the development were ensconced in their homes, their dogs walked, settled in for the night. He rounded the corner of the front alcove and stopped dead. His lips tightened and his eyes narrowed as he glanced around the darkness quickly, looking for any movement, but everything was dark and silent. Everything was as it should be.

Except for the head, impaled on a long pike, stuck into the ground next to his window.

Damon stared at it, his mind blank. Was it real? He moved up to the monstrosity, staring at it in disbelief. He judged the owner of the head to have been of Latin American descent and in his late twenties. Pressing his lips together again in a grim line, Damon stared at a pair of dark eyes, peering back at him lifelessly from a gruesome face.

It was real, and it was a grisly warning.

"You found a *what?*" Alina closed the refrigerator door, her phone pressed to her ear, and stared at the stainless steel in disbelief.

"A head," Damon repeated, amusement threading his voice. "If it sounds gruesome, that's because it is."

"First an arm, now a head," she muttered. "I'm seriously starting to rethink Jersey."

"An arm? What arm?" he asked sharply.

"They found an arm in the old prison in Mt. Holly this morning," Alina explained, turning away from the fridge and carrying a bottle of water over to the bar. She perched on a bar stool and sipped the water. "It belonged to one of Stephanie's informants."

"Where's the rest of him?"

"They don't know." Alina set the bottle down and pursed her lips thoughtfully. "I wonder if you have his head?"

"Who was he informing on?" Damon demanded. "Was he Latin American?"

"I don't know," Alina murmured. "His name was Frietas, so probably. Rodrigo Frietas, I believe."

"Brazilian?"

"Got me. You'd have to ask her." Alina's lips twitched. "But, honestly, I wouldn't suggest it. She already thinks you're trouble."

"Me?" Damon snorted. "You're the one who gets embroiled with terrorists and psychos."

"But you're never far behind these days," Alina pointed out.

"Someone has to keep you in check," he retorted, causing her to chuckle. "You have a knack for sniffing out trouble."

"Well, I certainly didn't sniff out a head," she shot back, a grin creasing her lips. "Where is it?"

"In front of my window, stuck on a pike of some kind."

"I hate to mention this, but in some cultures that would be considered a warning," Alina said thoughtfully. "What exactly were you doing in Mexico two months ago?"

"I already thought of that." Hawk sounded absurdly amused. "How the hell did they find me?"

"I don't know." Alina sipped her water, her eyes resting on the island in her kitchen. "Why don't you give me some data and I'll see what I can find out."

"I have to get rid of this head first," Damon retorted. "Any ideas?"

"Plenty, but none that would be appropriate," she murmured, her eyes dancing. "Have the neighbors seen it yet?"

"No, and I have to get rid of it before they do."

"You could tell them it's a Halloween decoration and throw some cobwebs on it," she suggested. "Then you don't have to move it at all!"

"Until the birds start eating its eyeballs," he replied. "You're not being very helpful."

"I'm sorry." Alina sounded anything but apologetic as she fought back a laugh. "My expertise is in severing the head, not disposing of it."

"Some partner in crime you're turning out to be. You're supposed to pull up with a shovel and a bag of lime in the trunk," Damon informed her with laughter in his voice. "You're from Jersey, for God's sake! This is what you people do!"

"I could call Frankie Solitto for you," Alina offered, grinning. "He probably has exclusive dumping rights to a few landfills."

"And owe the mob a favor? No thanks."

"I'm sure he would settle for a trade." Alina's shoulders were shaking with her laughter. "You whack someone for him, and he disposes of your stray head for you."

"I'll take my chances," Damon told her.

"Suit yourself." Alina capped her water and realized with a shock that she was having more fun now than she had in a long, long time. "Don't say I didn't try to help. We make contacts for a reason. What good is one in the Jersey mob if you won't use it?"

"I think I can handle this," he answered, his voice unsteady. "I just had an idea."

"Wonderful! Just make sure you put your spare helmet on it. You don't want to get a ticket for having a head riding unprotected on the bike."

"Thanks. I'll take that under advisement," Hawk said with a laugh.

Alina glanced up from her laptop as a loud beep echoed through the house. Frowning, she looked at the plasma above the fireplace. The perimeter at the back of the property, where the trees backed onto a wide creek, was flashing. She closed the laptop and got up, swiftly moving to the fireplace and reaching her arm up into the chimney until her fingers closed around metal. Alina extracted a shotgun from the rack attached inside the chimney, flipping it open and checking inside the barrel. Holding the shotgun with one hand, she opened a wooden box on the mantel and extracted a handful of shells. She quickly fed two shells into the gun and dropped the rest into one of her cargo pockets. A minute later, she was out the back door and on the deck, her eyes searching the darkness behind the house.

When Hawk emerged from the trees ten minutes later, spotlights flashed on and he stopped short, staring down the length of a double-barreled shotgun.

"For the love of God, Hawk, why are you sneaking through the trees?" Viper demanded, lowering the shotgun.

"Evasive action," he replied, his lips twitching. "A shotgun? Are you trying to harness Annie Oakley's spirit?"

Alina grinned.

"I think Annie O and I would have got along just fine," she said decidedly. "Who were you evading?"

"That's the big question."

Alina met his gaze, her smile fading, and nodded.

"You'd better come inside."

She turned toward the house with the shotgun tucked under her arm and Damon fell into step beside her. As they crossed the light-washed lawn, he looked down at her and grinned.

"Why do I feel like I'm on the frontier?"

"Because you brought up Annie Oakley," Alina replied immediately. "Come down into my command center and you'll forget all about shotguns."

"Is that a promise?" he asked.

Alina glanced at him, her eyes glinting.

"Absolutely," she answered.

"I think I like you, Annie Oakley," Damon told her with a wink.

"Get your mind out of where it shouldn't be," she told him. "You know that's not what I meant. Where's your bike?"

"Near the creek." Damon glanced at the roof of the house as they approached the deck and caught sight of a black shadow moving along the gutter. "I left it inside the perimeter."

"Good." Alina stepped onto the deck as Raven dropped down from the roof. He landed on the banister, gazing at Damon with his shiny black eyes. "If anyone followed you, we'll know."

"I won't stay here," Damon told her, following her through the sliding door and closing it behind them. Alina glanced at him as she headed over to the fireplace and set the shotgun on the mantle.

"Don't be ridiculous," she said. "Of course you will."

"Until I know who left a head in front of my window, I think it would be safer for you if I stayed away from you," he said, turning to face her. He encountered a laughing look.

"I think I can handle myself and anything that comes along," she murmured. "You'll stay here."

Damon watched as she grabbed her laptop and carried it over to the bar. She opened it and reset her security perimeter before turning to study him. His blue eyes met hers and she noted the tiredness in his gaze.

"What did you do with the head?" she asked softly.

"Relocated it."

"Do you have any ideas who might have put it there?"

"My gut tells me it's one of the Mexican Cartels," Damon answered and she nodded in agreement.

"Mine too."

Alina turned and went into the kitchen, reaching up to lift down a sauté pan from the pot rack above the island. She placed it in the center of the granite top and the island slid to the side silently, exposing an opening in the floor. Damon grinned.

"You were serious about the command center," he said as he came around the bar and into the kitchen. Alina nodded and turned toward the refrigerator.

"Of course!" She opened the fridge and pulled out two bottles of beer. "I'm one step ahead of you already."

Damon raised his eyebrow and accepted one of the bottles from her. He watched as she descended the stone steps, disappearing into the opening in the floor.

"Of course you are," he murmured, following her.

A moment later, the island slid back over the opening, leaving the kitchen empty.

Chapter Seven

Stephanie sat back in her chair and yawned, rubbing her eyes. She glanced at John. He was working on a digital mock-up of the Dungeon on his computer. They were the only two in the office on a Saturday night and the building was eerily silent. John had brought Five Guys back for dinner and Stephanie reached out to snag a cold fry from the leftover pile in the cup on her desk.

"I'm fading fast," she said with another yawn. Looking at her watch, she saw that it was almost ten. "How's that going?"

"Well, with the measurements of the window, I don't see how a person could possibly get in that way," John said, rotating the digital room on his monitor. "According to the prison records, someone *did* escape through the window in the past, so it can be done going out. I just don't see how anyone could possibly get in. Even if they managed to squeeze through the opening, which I know I couldn't do, it would take some wiggling and the window is too far away from any kind of ledge to make that possible."

"I agree." Stephanie got up and stood behind John, studying the digital cell on his screen. "I don't think an adult could get in there. So, if they didn't go in through the window, then we're back to the prison itself."

"The camera footage this morning showed Karl trying the cell door and then going downstairs to get the key." John sat back in his chair and picked up a pen from his desk, twirling it in his fingers. "So, we know he's not lying about the cell being locked this morning."

"Pull up the footage from yesterday." Stephanie leaned on his desk and crossed her arms. "Let's see what happened during the day."

John tossed the pen back onto the desk and leaned forward to type on his keyboard. The digital replica of the cell disappeared and, a moment later, the media player opened. John opened the file and let the surveillance tape play for a minute before he started fast-forwarding. The corridor outside the Dungeon was empty during the morning, but around lunchtime, a couple appeared. They made their way down the corridor, moving in and out of the cells while they looked around leisurely. John slowed the video as they approached the Dungeon. He and Stephanie watched in silence as the couple stopped. They peered into the cell, talking and pointing. The man tried to open the door and it was apparent that it was locked. Stephanie glanced at the time stamp in the corner of the video. 12:22pm.

Over the next three hours of tape, the Dungeon had four more groups of visitors. Each group tried to open the door, and each time it was still locked. Stephanie was somewhat surprised at the amount of visitors the museum received. For a building that she herself hadn't even known was open to the public until last night, the prison certainly got a fair amount of traffic. Rachel, the guide, appeared with one of the groups, talking and motioning animatedly. Stephanie spoke to Rachel after she interviewed Karl. She found the woman to be friendly, sensible and knowledgeable about the museum. Watching her on the surveillance footage now, it was also clear the woman enjoyed her job.

"They all try the cell door," John remarked after the fourth group had passed.

"It makes a good reference for us," Stephanie answered with a grin. "At least we know all this time, the cell was most definitely locked."

"True," John agreed.

He slowed the tape down again as another couple appeared in the corridor. The woman carried an over-sized tote bag over her shoulder and the man had a camera slung around his neck.

"Want to make a bet on how long before they try the door?" he asked, glancing back at Stephanie with a grin.

"Nope," Stephanie retorted as she watched the couple walked straight to the Dungeon. "Wait. They're not looking around. What are they doing?"

She sat forward and John snapped his head around to watch the monitor. The couple walked right past the open cells, not even glancing inside, and came to a stop outside the locked Dungeon. Stephanie's eyebrows soared into her forehead and John let out a low whistle as the woman produced a key and unlocked the cell, swinging the door wide open.

"Where's the camera footage in the cell?" Stephanie demanded sharply.

"There is none," John answered. "They only have footage of the corridors."

"What?" Stephanie looked at him in disbelief. "No cameras in the main attraction?"

"It's a small museum," John said with a shrug. "I got everything they had, and there are only cameras in the corridors."

"Great!" Stephanie glared at the footage on the monitor. "What are they doing in there?! I can't see anything!"

"I can enhance the shadows."

John hit some keys on the keyboard and the picture zoomed in on the door of the Dungeon. They couldn't see the couple in the cell, but they could see their shadows thrown onto the floor by the glint of afternoon sunlight shining through the window. The smaller shadow moved around the cell while the other stood to the side. John leaned forward with Stephanie as they studied the picture.

"I can't make out what she's doing," Stephanie murmured. "Is she near the dummy?"

"She's towards the back of the cell," John answered.

A minute later, the couple emerged and John and Stephanie watched as the woman locked the cell again. They walked away from the Dungeon and disappeared down the steps at the other end of the corridor, leaving the corridor empty again.

Stephanie looked at the time stamp in the corner of the screen. 3:49pm.

"You don't think..." John paused the video and glanced at her, his voice trailing off.

"That she put the arm in the cell just then?" Stephanie asked, meeting his pale blue gaze.

"She was carrying a large bag," he pointed out.

"Do you really think a woman would carry a severed arm around in a purse?" Stephanie demanded with a grimace.

"Well, they're the only ones who went in there," he said.

"Keep playing the footage," she told him. "The museum closes at 4, so there shouldn't be any more visitors."

John restarted the video. Sure enough, there were no more visitors in the next ten minutes of tape. About fifteen minutes after the museum closed, Rachel appeared in the corridor and walked through the cells. She stopped outside the Dungeon and tested the door, looking inside before continuing through the rest of the cells on the floor. After her quick walk-through, she disappeared down the steps toward the first floor again.

"Well, the arm obviously wasn't there then," John muttered. "She would have seen it."

"Yep," Stephanie agreed with a frown.

John sped up through the rest of the footage. The shadows lengthened as darkness fell. Around ten o'clock, Karl appeared in the corridor and strolled down, glancing into the cells as he passed. After that, the corridor fell empty again and remained so for the rest of the night.

"Well, at least we know the arm wasn't there at ten, either,"

Stephanie murmured. "Karl looked right into the cell."

"When you talked to the guide, did she say anything about letting a couple have the key to the Dungeon?" John asked.

"No," Stephanie answered grimly. "I'll be having another chat with her tomorrow."

"I'll run their pictures through our databases tonight and see if I can get their names for you before you talk to her," John said with a yawn.

"Do it tomorrow." Stephanie straightened up and headed back to her desk. "It's late. Let's wrap it up for today and start again with fresh heads tomorrow."

"I won't argue with that," John said as he rubbed his neck and yawned again. "I can't think straight anymore."

"Me either." Stephanie reached over, switched off her PC and pulled her purse out of her desk drawer. She gathered up her trash from their hasty dinner and dropped it into the can next to her desk. "I wonder if we'll have the report from the ME tomorrow?"

"He said he would have it for us in the morning. He's dedicated, our Larry, working on the weekend for us," John answered, switching off his computer. He stood up with a stretch. "I don't know what he can tell us from just an arm, though."

"At the very least, he can tell us if Rodrigo was alive when he lost his arm," Stephanie answered, turning to walk with him toward the elevators.

"You don't think he's still alive, do you?" John asked.

"No." Stephanie shook her head. "I don't."

"Why would they put his arm in a prison?" John asked for the hundredth time that evening.

Stephanie shrugged as they walked up to the elevators.

"I have a feeling that will end up being the biggest headache of this whole thing," she murmured.

Damon sipped his beer and leaned on the counter next to where Alina was seated in front of a laptop. Her command center was a long, narrow room lined with counters on one side and plasma screens on the other. He counted two servers spaced along the wall under the counter, and several desktop PCs in addition to the laptop she was currently accessing. Occasionally, a fan would kick on to cool one of the servers and the constant, quiet hum of technology filled the room. Two of the plasma screens displayed her security perimeter and the rest were dark. Damon knew from past experience that if she was in the middle of a job, all the plasmas would be lit up and running database searches. They would display remote views of relevant locations and maps, and hold information that she needed readily available.

One of the dark plasmas came alive while he was looking around and Damon found himself staring at the faces of three dead men he knew well.

"These are the three Cartel heads that were killed in August in Mexico," Alina announced, spinning around in her chair and glancing at him. "I'm sure you recognize them."

"Of course." Damon winked at her. "It was all over the news at the time."

Alina's dark eyes met his and she smiled slightly.

"I'm working on the assumption that the Cartels weren't happy when their leaders were shot in the head," she continued.

"I believe the news said it was a fire," Hawk murmured.

Alina's eyes danced and her lips twitched.

"My mistake," she answered. "Of course it did."

Damon nodded complacently and sipped his beer again. His eyes returned to the three faces on the plasma. He remembered the night, lit up with flames, and the shadows as they stumbled out of the burning buildings. He remembered watching through the scope, waiting for the three faces on the plasma to appear. He remembered every second of that night.

"How the hell could they have found out it was me?" he wondered out loud. Alina's lips compressed slightly.

"I don't think they found out on their own," she replied, picking up her beer and sipping it. "The Cartels don't have the resources to track people like us. They were given a tip."

"By Regina?" Damon asked, glancing at her. Regina Cummings was a woman who had caused a mess in Washington two months ago. Alina nodded and Damon looked back to the plasma with the pictures on it thoughtfully.

"She put a bounty on your head and sent it to every mercenary, assassin and covert agent she had access to," Alina pointed out. "It wouldn't surprise me at all for her to have also sent it to the Cartels."

"Actually, it wouldn't surprise me either," he agreed. "So which Cartel is it?"

"That's the question," she murmured. "Someone's been watching you. I spotted them this morning."

"Excuse me?" Damon looked at her and she shrugged.

"You knew I'd find out where you were staying," she answered unapologetically. "I wasn't the only one."

"Were they in a crossover?" he asked.

"Yes."

Alina swiveled back to the laptop and set the beer down.

"A crossover was leaving my lot tonight in a hurry right before I found the head," Damon said, turning away from the plasma to look down at her.

"Putrid, retro-green?" Alina asked, glancing up at him, and he shrugged.

"It was dark out," he replied. "I can tell you it was a medium color, but that's about it."

Alina nodded and pulled up a file on her laptop, motioning for him to take a look.

"Meet Jessica Nuñez," she said. "She's the registered owner of the crossover, but not the driver. It was a man camped outside your condo this morning, not a woman."

Damon leaned down and looked at the picture on the laptop screen. He reached over her and scrolled down, scanning the information she had gathered so far. Alina got a whiff of musk and her heart skipped a beat. His face was inches from hers, his eyes on the laptop screen, and she could feel the warmth of his body radiating from his closeness. Swallowing, she pushed her chair back to put some distance between them. Damon glanced at her, laughter leaping into his eyes.

"Just trying to give you more room," she muttered defensively.

"Mm-hmm."

"Mrs. Nuñez is as clean as they come," Alina said, ignoring him. "She and her husband don't even have a parking ticket between them."

"They're from Mexico," Damon said, scrolling down some more.

"Yep." Alina nodded. "They came to the States legally, spent a few months in Arizona, and then came here when Mr. Nuñez accepted a teaching position with Rutgers."

Damon finished scanning the information and straightened up. Turning to lean on the counter, he crossed his arms over his chest and looked down at her thoughtfully.

"Have you been able to find any connection between her and the cartels?" he asked.

"I haven't tried." Alina looked up at him with a grin. "You hadn't found a head in your yard yet. Was it really on a pike?"

"Yes."

"That's pretty intense," she murmured. "Can you pass me my beer?"

Damon glanced behind him on the counter and picked up her beer, handing it to her.

"How did they find me in Jersey?" he wondered. "Even Charlie doesn't know I'm here yet."

"That's something we need to find out quickly," Alina said, lifting the beer to her lips. "I don't like that you seem to have lost your invisibility. I was afraid something like this would happen when your face got sent out to hundreds of mercenaries."

"Charlie was able to get most of the images pulled, but there's no way of knowing how many times it had been reproduced and downloaded," Damon told her. "We knew there would still be a few lingering incidents of clean-up to be done. He's been monitoring everything, listening for chatter."

"It infuriates me all over again when I think about it," Viper said, her eyes darkening with anger. "When I think about all the damage that bitch did..."

"It's over. Forget it," he advised. "We knew we'd be cleaning it up for months. Let it go."

"It still makes me crazy." Viper looked up at him, her eyes glittering dangerously. "I would do it all over again, if I could," she said softly.

"I know."

Damon's dark blue eyes met hers and they stared at each other silently. He could feel the restless energy coming off her and he suddenly realized that Viper had kept moving for two months to help control the anger still simmering deep inside her. He smiled slowly. He could think of a few different ways to help her manage all that unresolved anger.

"I don't think I like that smile," Alina murmured. "You look like a cat that just saw a mouse."

"Do I?" he asked, raising his eyebrows. "Trust me, mice were *not* what was on my mind."

"I don't think I want to know what was," she said, pushing his legs out of the way and sliding her chair back over to the laptop.

Damon grinned.

"Chicken," he murmured.

"I have an associate in Mexico." Alina ignored him and opened a secure email. "I'll see what they can find out for us. Maybe they've heard something."

"Which of these can I use?" Damon finished his beer and set the empty bottle down, looking at the other PCs. Alina motioned to the one beside her without looking up from her laptop. Grabbing the only other chair in the room, he settled down beside her. "You check your source, and I'll check mine. Too bad we don't have anyone in the cartels."

"Mine is close enough," Alina murmured.

Damon glanced at her.

"You never cease to surprise me," he said, waiting for the secure portal to load on his machine. "After Solitto, I shouldn't be surprised. You managed to cultivate the head of the Jersey Mob easily enough. How many bad guys *do* you associate with?"

"As many as you," Viper returned promptly and looked up with a grin. "I learned from the best."

Hawk met her glance and smiled. It was true. She had never thought of using questionable people as assets until they met, by chance, in a Paris street a year after going into the field. They compared notes on their first year over dinner and she had learned from him how invaluable members of the criminal class were for information and supplies. In return, he had learned from her the value of having a storage unit in every city with back-up supplies. *That* was a tip that had saved his life more than once over the years.

He turned back to his monitor and opened his email. A comfortable silence fell between them and Hawk settled down to work. Someone had to have heard something somewhere. The cartels were never quiet about their intentions. If they were after Hawk, someone had to know about it.

And when Hawk found out which one was in Jersey, he would take them down, one by one.

Chapter Eight

Stephanie slammed the door to her Mustang and took in the scene before her. It was just past seven in the morning and the Mt. Holly Prison on High Street was teeming with activity. The local police were in the process of erecting a white screen on the brick sidewalk next to the steps leading to the prison door. A team from the FBI was preparing to descend upon the front yard to examine the ground for any forensic evidence, while another group of local LEO's kept the curious, early-morning spectators at bay on the sidewalks. John was supervising the whole thing, standing off to the side with his hands on his hips, looking none too happy. When he saw her, he turned and stalked towards her with a frown.

"It's too early for this shit," he informed her bluntly.

"They said it was a head," Stephanie said, handing him a large, hot Wawa coffee. John took it and his face brightened.

"You're the best," he murmured.

"I know. Is it Rodrigo's head?"

"Yep. Stuck on a post." John walked with her across the sidewalk and held the caution tape up so she could duck under it. "Appeared sometime last night. None of the uniforms saw it when they drove by the prison on their patrols. No one seems to know *when* it appeared."

Stephanie glanced at him and walked briskly along the brick pathway running parallel with the prison. A sergeant nodded to her and she nodded back, sipping her coffee as they walked up to the white screen. She rounded the corner of the screen briskly.

"For the love of...!" she gasped as she came nose-to-nose with Rodrigo's discolored and bloated face. She stepped back hastily and bumped into John. "It's definitely him."

"Yep."

John sounded grim as he steadied her with a hand on each arm. They both stared at Rodrigo's head. It was impaled on what looked like a bamboo rod about an inch thick. His face had a grayish pallor and one eye

79

was closed while the other was drooping.

"Why here?" Stephanie sipped her coffee and turned away from the grotesque sight. She glanced down at the ground. The stake had been driven into the grass next to the steps and not a blade was disturbed around the area. "What's their fascination with the prison? And who the hell has the balls to deposit a head on a pike just a block away from the police station?!"

"All good questions," John said, stepping back so she could exit from behind the screen. "I can't answer any of them. Here comes the ME."

Stephanie looked up and watched the man approaching from the road. He carried a duffel bag and was followed by the same assistant who had collected the arm the day before.

"Morning, Larry!" she called.

"Good morning, Ms. Walker," Larry answered cheerfully as he joined them outside the screen. He was in his mid-fifties, had an irrepressible twinkle in his eyes, and his hair was balding. He was Stephanie's favorite ME. "I hear we have a head to go with the arm."

"We do indeed." Stephanie motioned behind the screen. "Help yourself. If you can give me an approximate time of severance that would be wonderful."

Larry nodded and stepped behind the screen.

"Oh my!" he exclaimed, his voice slightly muffled.

"That seems to be everyone's reaction when they see it," John remarked.

"Well, it *is* disconcerting," Stephanie answered, looking around. "You don't expect it to be at eye-level, somehow. How did they get it here without someone seeing them?"

"I've got a uniform going door to door to see if anyone heard anything last night, but I don't think we'll have much luck," John said. "Kenny, the night guard on duty in the prison, didn't hear or see anything. He's in the Warden's House, waiting to speak to you."

"Karl had the night off?" Stephanie turned and began walking back down the path toward the Warden's House.

"Yes." John fell into step beside her. "At least we know, without a doubt, that Rodrigo is most definitely dead."

"That's the only thing we *do* know," Stephanie muttered. "I think we can call off the search on the river. I can't imagine they tossed a headless corpse into the water."

"Do you think we'll just keep finding parts of him?" John asked after a second of silence.

"Agent Walker!" Larry called from behind them before she could answer. Stephanie and John turned to see the medical examiner hurrying

80

towards them.

"What is it?" she asked as Larry closed the distance between them.

"It's the head," he said breathlessly.

"What about it?"

"It's missing its tongue!"

Stephanie and John stared at him speechlessly.

"What?!" Stephanie finally found her voice, and it was loud.

"I thought the jaw looked like it was sitting strangely," Larry explained. "I assumed it was because of how it had been...attached, so to speak...to the pole. It wasn't. It's because the tongue was cut out of the poor man's head."

"Before or after he was decapitated?" John asked, glancing at Stephanie's dumbfounded face.

"I can't be sure until I get it back to autopsy, but initial indications are that it was done before," Larry answered, shaking his head disgustedly.

"Thank you," Stephanie said. "Let me know as soon as you know for sure."

"Of course, my dear." Larry turned to go back and John looked at her.

"What the hell is going on?" he asked.

"I don't know," Stephanie answered, shaking her head. "I don't know what to think, to be honest."

"Well, that makes two of us," John muttered. "I'm hoping they'll find something when they comb the ground in the front yard. A footprint, a hair, a driver's license..."

"Wouldn't that be nice?" Stephanie asked with a short laugh. She glanced at the army of techs starting at one side of the prison yard. "I don't think we'll be that lucky, somehow. While they're doing that, do me a favor and go into the Dungeon again. I want some more pictures of the window."

"Oh?" John looked at her, his eyebrow raised.

She nodded.

"Yes. The ones we have from yesterday look like something was dragged through the window," Stephanie told him. "The middle of the window ledge was dust-free, but the edges weren't."

"On it," John said and turned to head toward the front of the prison.

"John?" Stephanie called. He turned back inquiringly. "When you're finished, call the Black Widow and get her up here."

"Are you sure about that?"

"Yes." Stephanie turned to go around the corner to the entrance of the Warden's House. "I want to know where her other half was last night."

Damon sipped his coffee and tilted his head sideways. A smile played about his full lips. Alina was in Crow Pose on the deck and he had an excellent view from where he stood in front of the bar. He had been up with the sun, expecting to have the house and command center to himself. Instead, he walked downstairs to find Alina getting ready to go out for a run. For the first time since boot camp, they went running together in the early dawn. Neither spoke much and halfway through the five miles, Hawk realized they were both speeding up. When he mentioned it, Viper laughed and sprinted ahead of him. They raced back to the house through the woods, splitting up and taking different routes through the trees, only to reach the back deck together. Old habits, apparently, never died. Their basic training competitive spirit was alive and well.

Damon went to shower and when he came down, Alina was on the deck, practicing her yoga. Sipping his coffee now, he watched as she extended into a hand-stand from Crow pose. Her body control really was amazing. No wonder she was such a weapon. He tilted his head more and watched as she held the pose for several breaths. He was still admiring the view when he realized her dark eyes were watching him upside down. Caught, Damon grinned and winked.

Finishing his coffee, he was turning to go into the kitchen to make another cup when Alina's cell phone started playing the Halloween theme song. He glanced at the phone laying on the bar and saw John Smithe's name displayed. Damon chuckled at the ballad of Mike Meyers and continued to the coffeemaker. Setting his mug under the spout of her state-of-the-art espresso maker, he hit the button to brew another cup of coffee. The grinder drowned out the sound of Halloween and he watched absently as the machine finished grinding beans and began brewing espresso into his coffee mug.

"Enjoy the show?"

Alina's voice made him turn with a grin. He watched as she silently slid the door to the deck closed behind her.

"I did, thank you," he answered. "You made my morning."

Alina shook her head and crossed the carpet to the bar, where her phone was flashing. She picked it up, saw the missed call, and set the phone down again. She looked past him to the coffee machine and Damon pulled out his mug, handing it to her.

"A peace offering," he said.

Alina laughed and took it, sipping it gratefully.

"Have you heard anything from your contacts yet?" she asked.

"Not yet." Damon turned to the cabinet over the coffeemaker and pulled out another mug. "I don't expect to hear anything much before tonight."

"Charlie called this morning." Alina leaned on the island and wrapped her hands around the mug. "Do you want him to know you're on US soil?"

"Knowing him, he probably already knows." Damon hit the button on the coffeemaker and turned to face her. "I don't mind if he finds out I'm here."

Alina studied him from under her eyelashes.

"So he would have no objection to you being here?" she asked, watching him. Damon shrugged.

"I can't imagine why he would," he said.

"Hmm..." Alina lifted the coffee to her lips, her eyes still watching him over the rim. Damon was uncomfortably aware that those brown eyes didn't miss much. "Why *are* you here, Hawk?"

His eyes locked with hers and they stared at each other for a long, charged moment.

"You know why I'm here," he murmured.

"I know why you say you're here," she replied calmly, her dark eyes unreadable. Damon's lips curved slightly. "I find it hard to believe you're here just for me."

"You severely underestimate yourself."

His voice was soft and rolled over her like warm caramel. The fine hairs on the back of her neck stood up as Alina's stomach lurched in reaction to the warmth in his voice. They stared at each other and Alina felt her pulse leap at the look in his eyes. There was something there that both excited and scared her, and Viper didn't scare easily. Damon held her gaze for a long moment, then turned and pulled his coffee out from under the spout, breaking the spell. Alina shook her head slightly, sighing as the silence in the kitchen was shattered by the Halloween Theme song.

"Yes?" she picked up the phone.

Damon leaned against the counter and sipped his coffee, watching as she listened in silence. She was staring at the floor, her lips compressed slightly. After a moment, her head lifted suddenly and her eyes locked in on Damon's. Her lips twitched and laughter made her eyes glow.

"Really?" she murmured, amusement dripping from her voice. "Have you called Ghostbusters yet?"

Damon lifted an eyebrow, drinking the espresso and watching as Alina listened some more. John was doing a lot of talking for such an early morning phone call.

"Fine." Alina glanced at her watch. "Give me an hour."

She pressed end and set the phone down on the counter, finishing her coffee. Her eyes were dancing when she looked at Damon.

"They found a head at the prison in Mt. Holly," she told him. A grin tugged at her lips.

"You don't say?"

"It appeared on a bamboo pike overnight." Alina moved forward and reached around him to rinse out the mug. Damon moved to the side, his face impassive.

"That's ironic," he said. "Who would think disembodied heads would be so common?"

"Ha!" Alina glanced at him and the grin won the fight with her lips. "You put it outside the prison?"

"I figured the arm could use the company," he replied with a wink and Alina burst out laughing.

"I shouldn't find it funny, but I do," she chortled. "Stephanie and John are beside themselves. They have a haunted prison, an arm, and now a head. Where the hell is the rest of him?"

"I think the chances are pretty good you'll have to ask one of the cartels," Damon answered before swallowing the rest of his coffee. "Are you being summoned to the scene of the crime?"

"Yes," Alina said, setting her mug upside down in the sink to drain. She looked at him, still grinning. "Stephanie wants to know where you were last night, too. I think we're both under the microscope."

"You know, your friends don't seem overly friendly, especially after I saved their lives," Hawk murmured. He changed places with her and turned on the water to rinse out his mug. "It's almost like they don't trust us."

"I know." Alina nodded and left the kitchen, heading down the hall toward the stairs. "I can't imagine why they think we're trouble," she threw over her shoulder with a grin. "I'm going to shower and then I'll go play their game for a while. The more information we get about the head, the better chance we have at identifying which cartel tracked you down."

"While you're doing that, I'll go back to the condo and get my things," Damon told her, heading toward the sliding doors.

"Try not to stumble across anymore body parts," Alina called, starting up the stairs.

Alina pulled up behind Stephanie's Mustang, put the Camaro in park, and watched the activity in front of the old prison. Spectators had gathered on the sidewalk as Feds swarmed around the front prison yard. A couple of local cops were keeping the curious at bay, and they glanced over to her car as she cut the engine. Alina got out of the car and beeped it locked as she walked around the front of the car to step onto the sidewalk. She approached the caution tape and an officer stopped her.

"I'm here to see Agent Walker," she told him.

"Your name?" the man asked, his face impassive.

"Just tell her Raven Woods is here."

The uniform turned away and spoke into the radio hooked onto his breast pocket. A moment later, he turned back to her and lifted the tape so she could duck under it.

Stephanie appeared from the Warden's House and came towards her. Her face was grim and dark rings were already starting to form under her eyes.

"Thanks for coming," she said, joining Alina on the brick walk in front of the prison. "Talk about a nightmare. First an arm, and now this. Did John fill you in?"

"He said you found a head outside the prison this morning," Alina answered. "Seems a little far-fetched to me, but he swears it's true."

"Oh, it's true enough, and it gets better," Stephanie muttered. "Now the prison guide is MIA. No one has seen her since the haunted walk closed last night. She never went home and her cell phone isn't registering a GPS location."

"That doesn't sound good," Alina murmured. She fell into step beside Stephanie as they moved along the walkway toward a white screen erected next to the steps. "Does the head belong to your informant?"

"Yes. John didn't tell you?" Stephanie asked, glancing at her.

"He talked a lot and didn't say much," Alina answered, her lips curving slightly. "All he really said was that you had a head on a stick and wanted to know where *we* were last night."

"Clearly, he hasn't improved in the public relations department," Stephanie murmured, having the grace to look sheepish. "I'll fill you in on everything once you've seen the head. The ME is ready to move it, but I want you to take a look before he does."

They came up to the white screen and Stephanie motioned for her to take a look. Alina rounded the screen and came to an abrupt stop. Stephanie watched as she stared at the head for a beat, her face impassive. Alina didn't show the slightest sign of discomposure at being eyeball-to-eyeball with a severed head. In fact, she looked amused. After considering the head for a moment, she looked down to examine the grass around the pike.

"It was placed here last night?" she finally asked, shooting

Stephanie a sharp glance.

"Yes. No one seems to be able to say when," Stephanie answered. "It wasn't here when the haunt closed last night, and the last actors left a little after midnight. Beyond that, no one seems sure. Right now, I'm working on a time frame of sometime between midnight and six am."

"Lovely." Alina crouched down to get a closer look at the grass. "Whoever put it here didn't leave any trace on the grass at all."

"I know." Stephanie nodded. "None of our people could find anything when they went over the ground this morning, either. It's like it just grew up out of the ground."

"What was his name again?" Alina asked. She straightened up and moved out from behind the screen.

"Rodrigo Frietas," Stephanie answered, motioning to a balding man hovering nearby with a large plastic sheet.

She led Alina toward the steps of the prison as the ME and his assistant moved behind the screen to remove the head. Alina glanced up at the door of the prison and sighed imperceptibly. As she placed her foot on the first step, an icy chill rolled over her and slid down her spine. She paused and Stephanie glanced at her. Her eyes narrowed at the pallor in Alina's face.

"You ok?" she asked.

"Fine," Alina replied, forcing herself to start up the steps. She tried to ignore the chill as she ascended the steps to the door.

"John should be finishing up in the Dungeon," Stephanie told her. "He's getting some additional pictures of the window for me."

"Did you find something interesting with the window?" she asked as they reached the top of the steps.

"The center of the sill was clear of dust," Stephanie said as they stepped into the prison. "I noticed it on the pictures taken yesterday. John is up there taking a look and getting some better pictures for me."

"Did you take a look at the wall outside?"

"I sent John up there," Stephanie said. She moved around her and led the way down the corridor to the stairs at the end. "There was a clear shot, but he thinks it would have taken a skilled shooter to make it. Frankly, we can't see anyway someone could have gotten into the window from the outside, and I'm still clueless on why you think a clear shot to the window is important."

Alina followed her down the corridor. A faint smile played around her lips as her eyes rested on the back of Stephanie's head thoughtfully.

"It may not be," she murmured. "Did you pull anything off the inside of the cell?"

"Several prints, all of which we're running, but we don't expect anything from them," Stephanie said as they mounted the stairs. "It's a public area. The biggest problem I have right now is the security cameras."

"No footage?" Alina asked.

"Oh, there's footage all right," Stephanie answered. "The problem is there are only cameras in the corridors and none in the cells."

"That's inconvenient," Alina agreed. "Do you have any leads from the corridor?"

"Yes." Stephanie glanced at her as she paused at the top of the stairs. "A couple unlocked the cell door and went in just before the museum closed yesterday. I have no idea what they did in there, but they came out a few minutes later, locked the door, and went on their merry way. The guide checked the cell about fifteen minutes after the museum closed and didn't seem to notice anything amiss."

"And now the guide is missing." Alina glanced into the empty cell to the right at the top of the stairs. "How convenient."

"Exactly," Stephanie agreed, walking toward the Dungeon.

Alina followed her, her eyes darting over the ceiling of the corridor as they went. Another chill shot down her spine and she looked ahead. Her eyes narrowed as they rested at the end of the corridor and she frowned slightly. The light coming through the windows was dim and the shadows were long, but even so, she could have sworn she saw something move in the shadows at the end of the corridor. Stephanie glanced at her, noting her intent gaze, and turned her head to follow her look.

"What's wrong?" she asked.

"Nothing," Alina murmured. She returned her dark gaze to Stephanie's face and forced a smile. "Overactive imagination, I think. You and your talk of ghosts have me looking for them."

"Ha!" Stephanie came to a stop outside the open Dungeon and Alina looked inside to find John on top of a wooden ladder, examining the small window. "John, Alina's starting to believe in ghosts."

"Well, this is the place to make you believe," John retorted, glancing over his shoulder at them. His blond hair glinted in the shadows in front of the window. "I could have sworn you were standing behind me a minute ago. I thought I heard you walk in, but when I looked, nothing was there."

"Good grief, not you too. We really have to get you guys out more," Alina muttered, stepping into the cell. She resolutely ignored the tingling taking over her senses and looked around. The dummy was still against the wall and the metal ring was still in the floor. Everything was just as it had been when she looked around yesterday, but now she felt strongly that something was different. Something had changed. "What's different in here?" she asked sharply, glancing at Stephanie.

Stephanie stared back at her blankly.

"Nothing," she answered. "We haven't touched anything since you were here yesterday, except to bring the ladder in so John can reach the window ledge."

"Something's changed," Alina said, looking around.

John backed down off the ladder and looked at her thoughtfully.

"Something like what?" he asked. "Has something moved?"

"No." Alina shook her head and turned around slowly, examining everything again. "Nothing's moved, but something is different. I can't explain it."

"And you say you have to get *us* out more," John murmured, his blue eyes dancing. "If you see a ghost languishing on the floor, do me a favor. Tell him to go somewhere else so we can get some work done in here."

Alina glanced at him, her lips twitching.

"I don't believe in ghosts," she retorted. "It's the smell. The smell is different."

"Yes!" Stephanie exclaimed. She stepped into the cell and looked at John. "Remember I said it smelled funny in here yesterday?"

"When there was an arm leaning against the wall? Yeah," John retorted.

"It wasn't the arm." Alina shook her head. "The arm wasn't here when I was here and I smelled something too. The smell is gone now. That's what's changed."

"So what?" John shrugged.

"Just making an observation," Alina replied. Her eyes fell to the metal ring in the floor again. Almost unconsciously, she crouched down and hooked a finger through the ring thoughtfully. "What's the story with the window?"

"You were right, Steph," John said. "There are streaks in the dust though the center of the window sill, almost like something went over it."

"Does it look like someone came through it?" Stephanie asked. John shrugged.

"Hard to tell," he answered. "Why don't you go up and look and see what you think?"

Stephanie shook her head and remained where she was, just inside the cell door.

"No, thank you," she muttered. "I'd rather not."

John looked at her and raised an eyebrow slightly, his lips twitching.

"Don't tell me you're afraid to come in here!" he exclaimed.

Alina glanced up from her study of the metal ring, her eyes resting on Stephanie's face. A slight flush infused her cheeks as she glared at John defiantly.

"Hey, last time I was in here, I got a God-awful, debilitating cramp in my stomach," Stephanie retorted. "Karl said it's common with people in here, and it's one of the reasons they started locking the door."

"It's damp in here," Alina said calmly, standing. "I can see it could make your muscles cramp up. I'll look at the window. I'm curious," she added with a slight grin and turned to go up the old wooden ladder.

Stephanie and John watched as she climbed the ladder and examined the window, careful not to touch anything but the top of the ladder. Alina glanced out the window and down into the back prison yard. The maze looked mundane and unexciting in the cold light of day, and Alina noted the high wall surrounding the yard. She looked at it thoughtfully for a moment, then dropped her eyes to the narrow stone sill. The window was cut into the thick outer wall and was barely large enough for her to fit her shoulders through. Alina tilted her head and studied the window briefly, then went back to the ledge. As John had pointed out, the outer edges of the ledge were covered in a fine film of dust and cobwebs, while the center of the ledge looked as though something had been dragged across it.

"Someone or something definitely came across here recently," Alina decided, glancing over her shoulder to Stephanie.

"Do you think it was a someone?" Stephanie asked from the door.

"There are no hand-prints," Alina answered slowly, returning her gaze out the window thoughtfully.

"So, we're back to square one," Stephanie muttered.

"Not necessarily," John said slowly. "We're making progress. We're eliminating possibilities. Any ideas on the head yet?"

"Not one," Stephanie replied, watching as Alina backed down off the ladder. "What do you think about the head, Lina?"

Alina turned to find both Stephanie and John watching her closely.

"I think you have a meat puzzle on your hands," she answered calmly. "And, whoever sliced up your informant has a twisted sense of humor."

"Well, that's helpful," John muttered and Alina shrugged.

"I could tell you a lot more, but then where would be the fun in that?" she asked blithely.

"Throw me a bone," Stephanie pleaded. "I've got nothing right now."

"I don't think you really want me to do that," Alina murmured, her eyes dancing. "You already have a head and an arm. Don't get greedy."

"Ugh." Stephanie rolled her eyes as John chuckled. "You know what I mean."

"I have a couple of theories, but they don't make any sense," Alina said, moving away from the ladder. Drawn by some invisible force, her eyes fell to the metal ring in the floor again. "I don't know how they got the arm into the cell, but I can tell you the head outside is some kind of warning. For who and for what, I don't know, but I would expect more pieces of your meat puzzle, if I were you."

"Warning?" Stephanie frowned thoughtfully. "I hadn't thought of that."

"Why would you?" John asked, watching as Alina stared at the ring on the floor again. "I thought heads on pikes went out with the Dark Ages."

"Only in some cultures," Alina murmured absently, raising her eyes to his. "In others, the practice is still very much alive."

Chapter Nine

When Alina pulled around the house, Michael's truck was parked in front of the garage next to Damon's motorcycle. The two men were standing near the trees at the back of the lawn with their backs to the driveway and Alina eyed them warily as she rolled to a stop. As she watched, Damon reached into his back holster and pulled out his weapon. Michael stepped to the side slightly to give him more room, watching as Damon steadied the handgun and fired off a round into the trees. Shaking her head slightly, Alina got out of the car and beeped it locked. Michael glanced over and waved.

"Do I want to even want know?" she called, strolling across the grass towards them.

"Probably not," Michael replied as she grew closer. "We're comparing range."

"Is that what you guys call it these days?" Alina retorted, raising one eyebrow slightly as she joined them in the trees.

"He modified his 9 mil," Damon told her, nodding to Michael. "We're comparing notes."

He moved out of the way and Michael pulled his weapon out of his side holster, aiming it through the trees. Alina looked in the distance and saw a can hanging from a tree branch about twenty-five yards away. Michael aimed and fired. The can flew up and around the branch.

"We both hit it," Damon said. "I'll move it back another five yards."

He headed off toward the can and Alina looked at Michael.

"Long time, no see," she said. "How was Brooklyn?"

"Fine." Michael looked at her. "Damon said you were sight-seeing."

"Mmm." Alina nodded. "An old prison museum."

"Is that so?" Michael's eyes glinted green in the speckled sunlight filtering through the trees. "See anything interesting?"

"Nothing to lose my head over," Alina murmured.

"I got a call from Blake this morning," Michael told her. "You remember him? You left a gun on his dining room table?"

"I remember," Alina said, amused. "How is he?"

"Fine. He still wants to know how you got past his pit bull," Michael answered with a grin.

"Buddy and I came to an understanding."

"How did you know his dog's name was Buddy?" Michael shook his head. "Never mind. I probably don't want to know."

Alina laughed and watched as Hawk finished tying the can to another tree and turned to head back towards them.

"I'm assuming Blake didn't call you to talk about Buddy," she prompted.

"No." Michael glanced at her. "He seems to think that a Mexican Cartel Lieutenant is wandering around New Jersey," he told her. "You wouldn't happen to know anything about that, would you?"

"A Mexican Cartel?" Alina asked. "In Jersey?"

"Well, its Lieutenant, at any rate." Michael nodded. "The guy popped up on Blake's radar after he evaded DEA agents in Arizona and disappeared."

"Interesting," Alina murmured. "Why do you think I would know anything about it?"

"Your SEAL had some pretty unsavory people after him the last time I saw you two," Michael said. "Now, here you are, here he is, and supposedly, here is a Cartel Lieutenant. It doesn't take much of an imagination to put it all together."

"I think your imagination is getting a little ahead of itself," Alina retorted dryly. "I'm not sure why Damon is here, but I'm fairly confident he's not chasing a cartel." *At least, not yet,* she added silently.

"Well, I won't lie. I'm relieved to hear that," Michael told her. "I don't need to tell you how dangerous those guys can be."

Viper shifted her dark gaze to his and Michael shivered involuntarily at the look in her eyes.

"They aren't the only ones," she said softly before turning to walk away. She went a few steps before pausing. She turned her head and Michael was relieved to see that the chilling look was gone from her eyes. "Just out of curiosity, did Blake give you a name?"

"Jenaro Gomez," Michael answered.

"Never heard of him," Alina murmured as Damon joined Michael again. "Happy shooting, boys."

Next Exit, Dead Ahead

Angela glanced at her watch and tossed her gym bag across to the passenger's seat before sliding behind the wheel. Sunday mornings were sacred time for her. It was the one morning of the week when she never let anything interfere with her routine. She went to the gym and then spent the rest of the morning focusing on herself. Sometimes she went to breakfast. Other times she went to get a manicure. Still others, she went shopping. This was her time. She could do what she wanted with a few precious hours before she had to start preparing for another week at work.

Another week in hell.

Angela was confident that no one had any idea just how much she despised the company that paid her. She was careful never to say or do anything that would reveal how much she hated it there. She started working for the bank straight out of college and had worked her way up the corporate ladder. The bank had been a smaller, local bank then. When it merged with the larger national One District Bank, Angela had weathered the storm of layoffs and come out even higher on the ladder. Now, after ten years, she held a comfortable title of Assistant Vice President and was on a solid course to make Vice President within the year. She would be the first female to advance to the title in the AML department in the history of the bank. After clawing her way through the male-dominated halls of a traditionally chauvinistic building, Angela wasn't about to let a little thing like her loathing for the parent company to get in her way now.

Each day was a struggle to get through, but Angela was too stubborn to pack it in. So many times she was tempted to quit and walk out. Yet, inevitably, she powered through the battle to come back and fight another day. The stress was taking its toll, however. Her body was starting to betray her. Her blood pressure was chronically high and the dosage of her anti-anxiety medicines were becoming larger and larger. Angela knew she couldn't keep this up much longer. Once she made VP, once she broke that last gender barrier, she would re-evaluate her position.

Until then, she had Sunday mornings.

Starting the engine, she put the car in reverse and backed out of her spot. Glancing at her nails, she decided a trip to the nail salon was in order. Angela was just pulling out of the parking lot when her blackberry started ringing in her purse. Stifling a sigh, she hit the hands-free button on her steering wheel.

"Hello?"

"Angela Bolan?" a male voice asked.

"Yes." Angela slowed to a stop at a red light.

"This is Lowell Kwan, from the IT Department at the bank," the voice told her.

"Yes?" Angela frowned.

"I'm afraid I have some disturbing news for you," Lowell told her. "I understand you were a friend of Rodrigo Frietas."

"Well, friend would be a bit of an overstatement," Angela murmured. "I know him through mutual friends. Wait. Did you say...were?"

"Yes." The voice on the phone paused for a moment. "You haven't heard yet?"

"Heard what?" Angela hit the gas as the light changed and headed toward the highway that would take her to her nail salon.

"I'm sorry to have to tell you, but Rodrigo Frietas is dead," Lowell said apologetically.

"What?!" Angela gasped, shocked despite herself. "But...I just saw him last Monday!"

"Yes, it's quite a shock," Lowell agreed. "It was a nasty business with his head. I'm afraid it gets even worse. I'm calling you because it appears that, before he died, Rodrigo accessed the bank mainframe with your credentials."

"WHAT?!?!" Angela swerved to the right, cutting across two lanes of traffic to get to the shoulder of the highway. Ignoring the indignant horns and hand gestures from the cars she cut off, she came to a stop at the side of the road and clicked on her hazards. Snatching the blackberry out of her purse, she hit the hands-free button again and put the phone against her ear. "What the hell do you mean he accessed the mainframe with my credentials? I barely knew him!"

"I understand." Lowell's voice was much clearer now that she was hearing it through the phone itself and Angela detected the trace of an accent in his voice. "I'm not sure how he did it, to be honest. I'm going through his desktop and I came across a file buried on the root drive. I'm looking at the logs now. Someone accessed the mainframe with your credentials from this PC the day before he disappeared last week."

"Wait a minute." Angela shook her head, trying to make sense of what she was being told. "Just...back up a minute. Obviously you think I know more than I actually do. What do you mean, before he disappeared? I didn't even know he *had* disappeared!"

"Oh dear," Lowell murmured. "Ok. Look. Maybe it would be better if you came into the office and I can explain everything to you."

"Come into the office on a Sunday?" Angela rolled her eyes. "Are you insane?"

"I think you'd better," Lowell said apologetically. "There's an awful lot to explain, and we need to figure out how he got your passwords. Not only that, but now you have to change them all."

"This can all wait until tomorrow."

"Miss Bolan, I don't think you understand the gravity of the situation. There's been a security breach, and he did it with *your* network credentials."

Angela felt cold all at once as she stared out the window and her mind drained of thought.

"I really think you need to come into the office this afternoon so I can get this sorted out and prevent any more damage."

"What kind of security breach?" Angela asked, her throat tight.

There was a short silence, then a sigh.

"That's just it," Lowell told her. "I have no idea."

Alina sipped her water and watched Hawk and Michael from inside the sliding door in the living room. They were still firing rounds into the trees and, as far as she could tell, they had moved the can three more times since she came inside. Clearly, they were evenly matched with their respective modified 9mm. She shook her head as Michael ejected his clip and pulled another one from the pocket of his jeans. The Marine and the Navy SEAL. They would be out there until kingdom come.

Turning away from the door, Alina capped her water bottle and moved to the laptop sitting on the bar. She settled down on a stool and opened it, setting her water down.

Jenaro Gomez.

What she told Michael was a bold-faced lie. Alina knew of Jenaro. He was notorious in Mexico, known to be one of the most ruthless and vicious men in the Casa Reino Cartel. Second in Command, he answered only to the head of the Cartel himself. When Hawk put a bullet in that head, Jenaro would have become the acting leader of the infamous Cartel.

Alina typed in a few commands, linking to her server in the basement. When the three heads were killed two months ago, the three largest cartels in Mexico were thrown into disarray. Power struggles erupted as the remaining leaders waged war on each other, trying to gain control of their cartels. The resulting disruption to the drug trafficking and regional control hurt them badly. The Mexican government was able to regain tenuous control over some of the regions previously controlled by the cartels, resulting in huge losses for the drug trade. The last she heard, the cartels were still in disarray and trying to regroup.

After a few moments of searching, Viper found herself staring at picture of Jenaro Gomez. His dark eyes were deep-set and his hair was thinning on top. A scar curved over his cheek from the corner of his eye and a tattoo covered half his neck. He looked like a sinister man who was capable of anything. Tilting her head slightly, Alina's lips curved.

He looked like a worthy opponent for Hawk.

She minimized the photo and pulled up a security portal into the government databases. After typing in her credentials, Alina stared into the kitchen thoughtfully while she waited for the security check to verify. If Jenaro was indeed in Jersey, then it was becoming more and more likely the Casa Reino Cartel was responsible for the head outside Damon's condo. Was *that* why Hawk had come back to Jersey? For Jenaro? If the cartel was responsible for the disappearance and dismemberment of Rodrigo Frietas, why him? Why would the Casa Reinos have any interest in Stephanie's informant?

Alina was still staring into space, lost in thought, when a text message alert went off on her phone. She frowned when she saw the incoming name. Her boss, Charlie, was sending her an image. He never sent images to her cell phone, preferring to use their secure email network for sensitive material. She touched the message file and raised an eyebrow when she found herself staring at another picture of Jenaro Gomez. There was no message or caption, just the photo.

Setting the phone down, Viper shook her head. She shouldn't be surprised Charlie somehow knew everything that happened around his agents, but she was surprised just the same. If Charlie was sending pictures of the cartel lieutenant to her phone, he had clearly not sent Hawk to Jersey after Jenaro. So why was Hawk here? And why was Charlie warning her that Jenaro was in Jersey? And what did any of this have to do with Stephanie's investigation anyway?

Shaking her head, Viper sent a secure email to Charlie. Once it was sent, she went back to the databases and started three searches: one on Jenaro Gomez, one on Rodrigo Frietas, and one on Jessica Nuñez. Somehow, all three of these people were connected and Alina had every intention of finding out how.

"I don't see what good it did having the Black Widow look at the head," John said, unwrapping his hoagie. "All she did was confirm what we already know."

Stephanie glanced up from her salad and watched as her partner bit into his Italian hoagie. Rodrigo's head had been taken away by Larry to join the arm, the Dungeon was locked up and under guard, and she had given the order to shut down the haunted walk. She had a BOLO out on the missing prison guide and the local police were already interviewing family and friends of the actors. When John suggested lunch, she jumped at the chance to take a break from the hellish day Sunday had become.

"I wouldn't say that," she said now as she picked up her fork and dug into her salad. "She pointed out the possibility that the head is a warning."

"Do you really think there's anything in that?" John asked. He wiped some oil off his lips and picked up a bag of chips. "Seems like a stretch. I mean, who leaves a human head on a stick as a warning?"

"Who leaves a human head on a stick, period?" Stephanie countered. "And yet, we have one."

John picked up his hoagie again and they fell into a morose silence. Stephanie speared a cucumber almost viciously, her gaze fixed on a point somewhere beyond John's right shoulder. The whole situation was ridiculous and she was thoroughly stumped. Why put Rodrigo's head on a stake and leave it outside the prison? John was right. It *was* a stretch to think the head was a warning, but what else could it be? A warning at least made some sense out of a seemingly vicious and senseless act.

"Maybe we're allowing ourselves to be distracted," Stephanie murmured.

John glanced up from his sandwich.

"You call an arm and a head a *distraction*?" he asked incredulously.

Stephanie's brown eyes moved to his and she nodded slowly. John stared at her and her lips started to curve.

"Yes!" she exclaimed suddenly, dropping her fork as the truth hit her. "Think about it! Rodrigo was going to give us information about a cyber-terrorist hacking ring working in the area, right?"

"Right," John agreed, setting his hoagie down and picking up the chips.

"And then he disappears before he can tell us anything," Stephanie continued, leaning forward. "What happens? We're looking for him, trying to discover what he was going to tell us, and we're covertly monitoring all the area banks for any signs of our mysterious hacking ring. Then, suddenly, his arm appears in a locked cell in an old prison museum."

"Right." John munched some chips, watching her. "And?"

"And we get so caught up trying to figure out how an arm got into a locked cell that we stop focusing on the investigation that brought us Rodrigo in the first place," Stephanie said softly, her eyes glittering.

John's eyes narrowed suddenly in shocked understanding.

"Oh my God..." he muttered.

"We've spent the majority of the weekend buzzing around Mt. Holly Prison Museum, instead of focusing on the hacking ring that Rodrigo claimed was at work in South Jersey," Stephanie murmured.

"And what about Rodrigo?"

"Whoever is behind the ring is behind his disappearance and murder." Stephanie picked up her fork again. "Given his untimely demise, I think it's clear someone found out he was going to talk and went through some extreme lengths to make sure that he didn't."

"Distracting us in the process," John added disgustedly. "They knew he came to us."

"Yes." Stephanie chewed thoughtfully for a moment. "And they knew we would be called in as soon as he was ID'd. Are they buying time?"

"Possibly." John dropped the chips and propped his elbows on the table. "They already bought themselves almost the whole weekend."

"I need the transcript of my interview with Rodrigo," Stephanie decided, pushing her chair back and standing up abruptly. "I'm going to the office. Why don't you follow up on the missing museum guide? She's the piece in all this that doesn't fit. We need to find her."

"Got it." John wrapped up the remainder of his sandwich and glanced up as Stephanie picked up her purse. "What?"

Stephanie was staring at him, her gaze suddenly arrested.

"When you had dinner with the blonde bimbo Friday night, you said she saw Rodrigo meet with someone else," she said. "Who?"

"Philip Chou." John stood up and shrugged into his jacket. "I was going to look him up yesterday, but got distracted with Rodrigo's arm."

"Indeed." Stephanie smiled grimly. "I think it's time I took care of that for you."

Chapter Ten

Damon's stomach growled as he went down the stairs and was assaulted with the sweet smell of garlic and tomatoes. Michael had left over an hour before to meet his friend Blake in the city for dinner, and Damon disappeared into the spare room with his laptop and phone. Alina was left to her own devices in the kitchen. By the smell of things, she had been busy.

"What smells so good?" he asked.

Alina was standing at the stove. A glass of wine sat on the counter next to her as she monitored a boiling pot of pasta on one burner and a large sauté pan filled with vegetables and what looked like chicken sausage on another. She glanced over her shoulder as Damon came into the kitchen.

"Dinner," she answered dryly.

"I can see that," he murmured, coming up behind her and peering over her shoulder at the vegetables and sausage in the pan. "It smells outstanding."

"I was going to make steak, but then thought better of it."

Alina sipped her wine and turned to face him, a rueful smile playing about her lips. Damon's blue eyes met hers and her pulse quickened at their closeness.

"Should I be worried?" he asked, his eyes glinting.

"Not tonight," she retorted. "I'm not tired of you yet."

"I'm not sure how I feel about you joking about that," Damon murmured. He turned away and went into the dining room to get another wine glass from the table. "It's still a pretty fresh memory."

Two months before, Alina had made him a delicious steak dinner over an open fire. He enjoyed it thoroughly, right up until she drugged him and ruthlessly relocated him to South America. When he woke up, their old mentor and friend, Harry, was with him and she was gone.

Alina chuckled now and picked up her wine.

"I promised you I would never do it again," she told him. "Trust me."

"Trust is earned, and so far, you haven't redeemed yourself," Damon retorted, returning with a glass. He picked up the open bottle from the kitchen island and poured himself some wine. "Say that again in about a year."

"A year!" Alina exclaimed. "It'll take you a year to get over it? Sheesh! I didn't even leave a bruise."

"No, you didn't," he agreed with a reluctant smile of approval. "In fact, I couldn't even find the injection mark. Where *did* you stick me?"

"In your ass." Alina set down her glass and turned back to the sauté pan on the stove while Damon struggled between laughter and outrage. "Can you move the salad into the dining room?"

Damon picked up a wooden bowl full of mixed greens and vegetables and carried it into the dining room. The table was already set with pasta plates and salad bowls. He placed the salad on the table, set his glass down next to one of the plates, and turned to go back into the kitchen.

"There's garlic bread in the oven, if you want to make yourself useful and grab it," Alina said over her shoulder as she poured the pot of pasta into a colander in the sink.

"You *have* been busy," Damon said, grabbing a potholder and opening the oven door. The smell of garlic poured out and his stomach growled in response. "If you keep this up, you'll never get rid of me."

He went through the cabinets until he found the plates and transferred the hot roll of garlic bread onto a large plate. He carried it into the dining room, then turned and watched as Alina tossed the contents of the sauté pan into the pasta. She reached behind her for some olive oil, drizzled it over the pasta and vegetables, and grabbed a block of fresh Parmesan. She started grating it over the pasta, glancing up when she sensed him watching her.

"What?"

"Nothing." Damon shook his head and smiled faintly. "It's...nothing."

Viper's eyes narrowed and she finished grating the cheese before picking up the bowl to carry it into the dining room. As she passed him, she glanced up into his rugged face.

"If you make one comment about women in the kitchen, I'll slice out your tongue," she told him.

Hawk grinned.

"I wouldn't dream of it," he murmured. He grabbed her wine glass from the counter and followed her into the dining room, setting it on the table near her plate. "You forget that I know the real you."

Alina shot him a look from under her lashes and sat down. Reaching for the salad bowl, her mind went back to boot camp. She didn't remember much from those long ago days when she first met Damon, but she was fairly certain they hadn't shared a lot with each other. They were too busy competing with each other to get to know each other very well. The 'real' Alina Damon knew was the Viper she had become.

"Stop thinking," Hawk said, watching her from his seat. Her gaze flew to his and he smiled. "I know you better than you think."

"You know what I've allowed you to know," Alina retorted as she filled her salad bowl. "Nothing more."

"Hmm." Damon's lips twitched and he accepted the salad from her. "I wouldn't lay bets on that, Ms. Maschik."

"I don't even know why we're having this conversation," she said impatiently. "It's all completely irrelevant. We work together, we respect each other, and we're close friends. That's all we really need to know."

"Tell me, does everything in your life always fit so neatly into your boxes for you?" Damon asked conversationally, setting the salad bowl aside and picking up his fork. He didn't miss the flash from the dark brown eyes next to him.

"Yes, as a matter of fact, everything does," Alina snapped, forking some salad and lifting it to her mouth.

"Outside of work, nothing in my life fits in boxes," he remarked, chewing thoughtfully. "I've always found boxes kind of boring."

"Do you have a life outside of work?" Alina asked, momentarily diverted.

Hawk looked at her, amused.

"Of course I do. The Organization isn't everything."

Alina was quiet for a moment, feeling a little sheepish for not knowing anything about Damon's private life. She supposed she should have asked at some point what he did for fun, or where he even lived, but they had lived by an unspoken agreement through the years. Don't ask and don't tell. The less they knew about each other, the better off they both would be.

"It seems a little ridiculous to be asking this now, but where do you live?" Alina finally asked after a few long moments of silence.

"Are you sure you want to know?" Damon asked softly.

Their eyes met and she sighed imperceptibly. They had been trained to live alone, in darkness and secret. They weren't supposed to know anything about each other, and they certainly were never meant to be sitting here together, having a cozy meal in her dining room. The Organization taught them to be ghosts, and ghosts did not have close friends. They were killers, trained to hunt and eliminate targets that were a threat to national security. They were not normal people, Hawk and Viper, and they shouldn't know anything about each other that could later become a liability.

Yet, somehow, the unspoken and unwritten rules had changed for them. Since day one in boot camp, an invisible bond had been forged between them. It was a bond neither of them had acknowledged until recently, and with it came a host of complications.

"Yes," she decided suddenly. "You know where I live, who my friends used to be, and even who I was going to marry. I think I can at least know where you call home."

"You already know where I live," Damon told her, his eyes glinting with amusement.

Alina stared at him, her salad forgotten for the moment. Her face was emotionless as her mind scanned back over the years, searching for some mention of his home. There was nothing in her memory. Unless...

"You grew up out west, didn't you?" she asked. "Out in the boondocks somewhere. Montana, wasn't it?"

"Oklahoma." Damon couldn't keep the laughter out of his voice.

"Same thing," Alina muttered, going back to her salad. The mystery was solved.

"Oklahoma is in a completely different part of the country!" Hawk exclaimed, startled despite himself at her complete disregard for her own country's geography.

"Anything west of the Mississippi is all the same," she retorted.

"Spoken like an East Coast city girl," he shot back.

Alina burst out laughing. Her eyes lit up with a laugh that came from deep within her and Damon grinned as his Jersey Girl made a sudden appearance. He missed the mystery girl who lurked deep inside Viper. The last time he glimpsed her was two months ago, on a tropical island.

"You still live out there, in Oklahoma?"

"Yes."

"Why?"

Damon finished his salad and reached for the pasta, glancing at Alina as he did so. She was sitting back in her seat, her wine glass in hand, studying him.

"I'm sorry?" he asked.

"Why?" Alina repeated. "You could live anywhere in the world. Why stay home in Oklahoma?"

"Why did you come back to New Jersey?" Damon countered swiftly. He instantly regretted it when her eyes narrowed and her mask slid swiftly back into place.

"Raven seems to like it here," Viper answered smoothly, setting her wine glass down and reaching for the garlic bread. "Besides, thanks to Regina, all my other houses were exposed. Until I finish establishing new living arrangements, this is the only location not compromised."

"I love it when you try to lie to me," Hawk told her, digging into his pasta.

Alina clamped her back teeth together briefly and took a deep breath, counting to ten before reaching for the pasta. She scooped it into her dish silently and set the dish down gently. Damon shot her a quick glance under his lashes. She appeared perfectly calm, but he hadn't missed the flash in those dark eyes of hers or the clamped jaw. He hit a nerve, and that amused him. He was getting to know his Viper well.

"My father passed away shortly after we met in Paris that first year," Damon spoke after a few moments of silence. Alina looked up, her face unreadable. "My mother decided to sell the ranch and move in with my sister. She got an outstanding offer from a group of developers, but I couldn't stomach the thought of the land I grew up on being turned into a shopping mall or cookie-cutter houses. I decided to buy the ranch through a middleman and outbid the developers. She has no idea who owns the property now."

Alina digested that for a moment, chewing thoughtfully. She didn't know Damon a sister. Somehow, the idea of him having family seemed absurd. He was too big for something as mundane as a family.

"Have you seen them recently?" she asked, glancing at him. Damon's face was unreadable, his jaw tight.

"Not since his funeral," he answered. "It's safer for them that way. Have you seen your parents?"

"No." Alina picked up her wineglass. "I decided when I joined the Organization it would be safer not to have any contact with them."

"What did you tell them?"

"Nothing." Alina sipped her wine. "They think I work for an international security corporation, running the European division. We exchange emails occasionally."

"Same here," Damon agreed.

"Have you been back to the ranch?" Alina asked, pushing her empty pasta dish away slightly and sitting back in her chair.

"Of course." Damon sipped his wine and grinned. "It's home, when I'm home."

Alina's eyebrow soared into her forehead.

"You actually live there?" she demanded. He nodded.

"It's perfect, really," he said. "It's a nice little spread, out of the way. No one knows when I come and go, except the twins."

"The twins?" Alina prodded, catching the thread of affection in his voice.

Damon nodded and got up from the table, going into the kitchen. He returned a moment later with the wine bottle.

"My dogs," he explained, refilling her empty glass.

"You have dogs?" she asked, surprised.

"Mmm. Two." Damon refilled his own glass and sat back down, setting the bottle on the table. He sat back with his glass, his eyes dancing. Alina looked stunned. "Bull mastiffs."

"Of course you have bull mastiffs," Alina muttered, sipping her wine. Her lips were twitching reluctantly.

"Meaning?"

"They fit you," she told him. "Who looks after them while you're gone?"

"I have a housekeeper and there are plenty of people in and out all day. I kept the family business going when I bought the property, so there are about fifteen people there during the week. The dogs are spoiled rotten." Damon sipped his wine and shrugged. "I got them as pups, with the intent for them to be guard dogs. That didn't work out quite as planned."

"They're not good guards?"

"Oh, they're wonderful guard dogs," Damon told her. "They were supposed to live outside. They took over my bedroom instead."

Alina laughed.

"I can't imagine you with pets," she said. "I wouldn't think you're home enough to give them the attention they need."

"You have Raven," Damon pointed out.

Alina shrugged.

"Raven's different," she murmured. "He takes care of himself. He hunts for his food and comes in to sleep when he's full. He doesn't need me."

"He guards you like it's his job," Hawk retorted. "That bird needs you, just as much as you need him."

"You're in a strange mood tonight," Alina said as she set her glass down. "What's the family business?"

"*I'm* in a strange mood?" Damon countered. "You're asking a line of questions I shouldn't be answering."

"Then stop answering them," Viper said with a faint smile, her eyes glinting.

Damon met her gaze and grinned.

"Horses," he told her, laughing when she rolled her eyes.

"Good Lord, you're a cowboy," she muttered. She stood up and gathered their empty dishes.

"Was there ever any doubt?" Damon demanded, laughing harder when she shook her head in disgust and headed into the kitchen with the dishes. He got up, picked up the salad and pasta bowls and followed her. "You knew I was a country boy when you met me. Do you remember the first thing you ever said to me?"

Alina set the dishes in the sink, her lips curving with the memory.

"'You look like a good, old-fashioned redneck,'" she said softly.

Damon set the bowls down on the island and turned toward her. Without thinking about it, he dropped his hands to her hips and rested his chin lightly on top of her head. Alina caught her breath. The back of her shoulders rested lightly against his chest and she was suddenly surrounded with the musky scent she loved.

"I knew you were going to be trouble for me from the very beginning," he murmured with a smile in his voice. "You and your feisty attitude reminded me of my favorite horse."

"No, you did *not* just compare me to a horse!" Alina exclaimed. She drove her elbow back and landed a hard, solid hit to his gut. Damon grunted in reaction, lifting his chin from the top of her head.

"She was a good horse!" he retorted, laughing. He pulled her hips back sharply, clamping her arms to her side. "She used to try to fight me too," he added with a grin.

"Oh, you're living dangerously," Alina murmured, leaning her head back and inhaling deeply. She didn't know what it was about Hawk, but the scent of his skin made her feel safe and powerful all at once. Turning her head, she pressed her lips to the side of his neck gently, his skin warm on hers. "I'm not a good horse," she added huskily as she twisted her right arm swiftly and closed her fingers around his wrist. She twisted it sharply as she turned in his arms, forcing him to move his arm with her or risk snapping his wrist. Once he did, she brought up both arms and pushed him away from her.

Alina started to turn back to the sink and the dishes, but Hawk had other ideas. He grabbed her arm to pull her back to him, and Viper gave in to the impulse to fight back. She stepped back and to the side swiftly, using the force of his own arm strength to throw him off balance. With one fluid movement, she twisted his arm up behind his back and forced him forward, against the counter.

"Maybe it was a poor choice of words," Hawk admitted, as she yanked his arm up behind him painfully with one hand and applied pressure on the back of his neck with the other.

"You think?" Viper asked sarcastically.

She just had time to hear his chuckle before he turned his head and shoulder, forcing her back with sheer strength. When her grasp on his arm loosened, he twisted quickly and was able to catch hold of her free hand. He leaned into it, forcing it down, and spun her around. A moment later, he had her pinned to the floor in a wrestling hold.

"Now that was just too easy," he murmured in her ear. "Are you slipping on me?"

Viper made a noise suspiciously like a hiss and Damon felt his hold slipping. A second later, he was flipped onto his back and found himself staring up at her with no clear idea of how she had done it.

"I wouldn't dream of it," she said breathlessly, straddling him and holding him down with a hand on his throat.

"Nice," Hawk commended her.

"Thank you." Viper smiled faintly.

Her dark eyes met his and her heart started thumping as she took a deep breath. Sparring with Hawk was always a challenge. He was so unpredictable and had no compunction about fighting dirty, even with her. It made him a good training opponent, but a formidable foe.

"I think I like this view," he murmured, his eyes darkening slightly.

He slid his hand softly up the arm that had his neck pinned to the floor, watching as goosebumps followed the light brush of his fingers. He smiled slightly and shifted his gaze back to hers. Alina's lips were parted slightly and her pulse was beating a rapid tempo at the base of her throat. At the brush of his fingers, her breathing increased and Damon felt desire shoot through him like a bolt of lightning.

Alina saw his eyes darken and her breathing grew shallow as her heart pounded in her chest. How she had ended up on top of him on her kitchen floor seemed irrelevant. All that seemed to matter was that she was drowning in a sea of blue glittering with passion and promise.

Catching her wrist with his fingers, Damon took advantage of her distraction. Swiftly pushing her hand off his neck, he threw her off balance and forced her down on top of him. When her lips touched his, he flipped her onto her back, one hand protecting the back of her head while his other arm supported some of his weight as he came down on top of her.

"I've been wanting to do this since I saw you walking toward me outside that old prison," he whispered as he lowered his lips to hers.

Alina caught her breath as his lips touched hers and a shock of desire shot through her. She had missed him. The past two months had been a blur of activity and work, but she had missed Hawk and this feeling of freedom mixed with passion he evoked every time he touched her. He made her feel emotions she never knew existed, passion she thought had died inside her over ten years ago. With Hawk, Viper let go of herself and rediscovered the woman she buried long ago. She lifted her arms and wrapped them around his neck, parting her lips beneath his and sighing into him.

Blinding passion rolled over her, causing her world to tilt precariously, and the only steady thing was his shoulders beneath her fingers and his heartbeat pounding against hers. Alina moved her hips instinctively, trying to get closer to him, and he groaned. The cold, hard floor faded in the face of raging desire and the only thing that existed was Damon. His body, his skin, his heat was all that filled Alina's senses. She couldn't get enough of him.

Damon lifted his head, his eyes dark with desire, and he smiled faintly.

"What's with us and kitchens?" he asked huskily.

Alina blinked and laughed breathlessly.

"I have no idea," she confessed.

Damon smiled slowly and was just lowering his lips to hers again when his cell phone started ringing. He groaned, closing his eyes and resting his forehead on hers.

"Ignore it."

Damon chuckled deep in his throat and kissed her swiftly.

"I can't. It's Harry," he told her. He pushed himself up and reached into his pocket to pull out his phone.

Alina closed her eyes and took a deep breath, willing her heart to slow down. Her senses were throbbing, her breathing uneven, and Viper wanted nothing more than to rip the phone out of Hawk's hand, throw it against the wall, and pull him back into her arms. She clenched her teeth and concentrated on taking deep, even breaths until her heartbeat slowed and her desire cooled.

"Hey."

Damon answered the phone, rolling off her and sitting up. He glanced down at Alina, breathing deeply with her eyes closed, and shook his head slightly. Harry couldn't have planned worse timing if he had tried.

"You're a never-ending source of heartburn," Harry greeted him. "What the hell are you doing in New Jersey?"

"Enjoying local attractions," Hawk murmured, sliding a finger along the edge of Alina's tank top. Her eyes opened and he found himself staring into their deep, chocolate depths.

"Hmm." Harry sounded amused. "Give her my love."

"I will," Hawk smiled faintly. "What do you have for me?"

"You're about to have a lot of company," Harry told him, growing serious. "Be careful. You have two other agencies with a presence there, and neither of them will take kindly to your interference."

"Do they know I'm here?"

"Of course not."

"Then what are you worried about?" Damon watched the pulse at the base of Alina's throat increase as he slid his finger under the edge of her shirt.

"I know you," Harry retorted. "You have a habit of taking things into your own hands."

Damon grinned as Alina smacked his hand away and sat up, shooting him a glare.

"That's what I'm paid to do," he answered, watching as she stood up fluidly and moved away toward the sink.

"You're paid to do it offshore," Harry replied. "Be careful up there. I'm sending you all the information I have, but there's one thing you should know now."

"What's that?"

"If you get compromised, so does the local attraction," Harry said bluntly.

Hawk's gaze rested on Viper as she turned on the water.

"That's not going to happen," he murmured.

Chapter Eleven

Stephanie glanced up as the elevator dinged loudly and the sound echoed through the deserted floor. She had been the only one in the building, besides security, all afternoon and evening and she had grown used to the absolute silence. Now, the sound of the elevator ascending seemed deafening. She stretched, yawning widely as there was another ding and the elevator doors slid open. A minute later, John appeared carrying a brown bag in one hand and carrier with two soda cups in the other.

"Please tell me you're having more luck than I did," he said as he set the soda carrier down on her desk and turned to his own desk across the aisle.

"No luck on the guide?"

"Nothing." John set the brown bag down on his desk and dropped his keys next to it. "She's just disappeared."

"I have a bad feeling about that," Stephanie said. "Rodrigo just disappeared too, and now look how he's showing up."

John nodded in agreement and opened the bag, pulling out containers of sushi.

"I stopped at your favorite sushi place," he said, handing her two containers of rolls. "I got you spicy salmon and a Boston roll."

"Thank you! I'm starving," Stephanie said, taking the containers. "I made some progress, though."

"Tell me."

John pulled his chair over and settled down with his own sushi. He ripped open a pack of chopsticks and glanced at her expectantly.

"Phillip Chou works in the IT Department at New Federal Bank," Stephanie said. She opened the spicy salmon roll and lifted a piece out with her chopsticks. "He's been there for two years and has a stellar employee record. Before that, he worked in Arizona for a small software company. Guess who else was on the payroll?"

"Rodrigo," John said, biting into his dinner.

109

"Yep." Stephanie reached for one of the sodas and turned to her computer screen. "They worked together in Arizona for four years before Phillip left the firm and came to New Jersey to take a position with New Federal."

"How did Rodrigo end up with a different bank in the same state?" John asked, his mouth full of sushi.

"That's where it gets interesting," Stephanie told him. "The software firm suddenly closed its doors and went out of business. The weird thing is that, on paper, the company was increasing profits and growing at a rapid rate. There was no reason for them to close up shop. They were doing well."

John glanced at her and raised one eyebrow in a motion eerily reminiscent of Alina.

"So why did they go out of business?" he demanded.

Stephanie shrugged and sipped her soda.

"That's just it," she replied. "I can't find any reason why they should have."

"What did they do?"

"Designed security software and firewalls for corporations," Stephanie said softly.

John whistled.

"Well now, isn't that interesting," he murmured.

Stephanie grinned.

"Oh, it gets better," she promised. "When the company closed down, the founding CEO, Jared Yang, disappeared. Rodrigo packed up and moved to New Jersey six months later to take a position with One District Bank. He was hired by their new Regional Vice President of TRMIS, the security operations branch of IT."

"Ok...." John poked a straw into the second soda and stared at her. "So what? We knew this already, didn't we?"

"Well, it took some digging, but I finally tracked down Jared Yang." Stephanie paused to eat another piece of sushi. "He changed his name. Well, to be more precise, he changed it back."

"Huh?"

"Jared Yang was born Lowell Mitchel Kwan," Stephanie explained. "His father was North Korean and his mother was an American Red Cross worker in Vietnam. They married, but it was not a happy marriage. According to court documents, the father was an abusive drunk who threatened to kill her and their son if she ever left. When Lowell was eight, his mother finally had enough. She took little Lowell and ran. She changed their names, got them to the United States, and hid from her husband in a little town in Arizona. Eventually, she remarried. Meanwhile, Lowell grew up and went to Stanford University on a full academic scholarship."

"You're right. This *is* interesting," John murmured. "So, we have a brilliant young IT genius who was taken away from his North Korean roots at a young age and brought up in the United States. He starts a successful security software firm and everything is going well. Then, one of his employees leaves the firm and goes to work for a national bank."

"Six months later, he closes his firm and disappears," Stephanie continued, her eyes glinting. "He changes his name back to his real one, and guess where he goes?"

John shrugged.

"A bank," he answered. "But which one?"

"Who do you think the brand new regional vice president was that hired Rodrigo?" Stephanie asked softly.

Angela strode up to the main door of the tech center in Mt. Laurel just as the sun was going down, her purse over her shoulder and her blackberry in hand. She finished sending an email as a tall man opened the door and held it open. His dark hair was cut unfashionably close to his head and he was dressed in jeans and an old faded sweatshirt. His sneakers were brand new and spotless, however, and Angela noted the G shock watch on his wrist as she stepped into the building.

"Miss Bolan, thanks for coming in," Lowell said, holding out his hand. "I'm Lowell Kwan."

"Nice to meet you. I'm sorry I got held up. I got here as soon as I could," Angela said, shaking his hand. Her freshly manicured nails glinted under the fluorescent lights and she admired the glittering dark red as she shook his hand. She glanced around the large foyer as she released his hand. "I've never been in this building before. Does IT have the whole building?"

"Yes." Lowell motioned for her to walk with him and started down a long hallway to the left of the entrance foyer. "It's not as fancy as your building, but it serves its purpose. Your badge wouldn't have worked on the door, so I'm glad you called to tell me you were coming." He smiled at her and his slanted brown eyes were warm and friendly. "Normally, I would have met you at your office to do this, but I'm in the middle of extracting data from three different PCs and really can't leave. Thank you for agreeing to come to me."

"No worries." Angela glanced into the rows of cubicles they were passing. "I want to get this sorted out as soon as possible. I'm still trying to wrap my brain around it all."

"I'm sorry to have sprung it on you like this." Lowell nodded to a side corridor and they turned right. "I thought you knew about Rodrigo's disappearance. I thought everyone in the bank knew."

"I didn't know him very well," Angela answered, following Lowell into a large department filled with half-cubicle walls. Piled on the floor in most of the cubicles were hard-drives, old monitors, and more keyboards than Angela had ever seen. "I saw him last week at happy hour with some friends, but that was about as well as I knew him."

"I think that's about as well as anyone knew him," Lowell admitted. "Rodrigo was on the quiet side. No one saw him again after Monday night. He went to happy hour and that was it."

"How surreal!" Angela followed Lowell into a larger cubicle and watched as he dropped into a chair at the desk. He seemed to have laptops and desktops everywhere, all wired into one box on his desk.

"Yes." Lowell motioned to a chair and Angela sat down. "Sorry for the mess. These are all his. I'm going through them and copying bank data onto a separate drive."

"You said he's dead. Something about his head? Did he hit his head?" Angela asked.

Lowell glanced at her and hesitated. For the first time since she entered the building, he seemed reluctant to look at her.

"The police found his head in Mt. Holly," he finally told her.

Angela stared at him, shocked. She felt the blood draining out of her face and a faint buzzing began in her ears.

"I'm sorry...what?"

"Unreal, isn't it?" Lowell asked, shaking his head. "The police found his head on a pole in Mt. Holly this morning."

"On...a...poll?"

"Yes." Lowell's gaze strayed to one of his flat-screen monitors and he leaned forward to type something on one of the many machines. When he was finished, he turned his attention back to her. "Outside a prison in Mt. Holly."

"A prison?" Angela gasped. "Not the old prison on High Street?!"

"Yes, I think so." Lowell nodded. "Do you know it?"

"I was just there Friday night for the haunted walk they do every year for Halloween," Angela murmured. She shivered. "How horrible! They just found his head?"

"That's what I heard," Lowell answered. "They called me this morning and told me to come in and gather all his equipment. The Feds want the computers, but I have to copy all the proprietary bank data from them first. He was working on some programming we need access to."

"The Feds?!" Angela tried to make sense out of what she was

hearing. "Why are the Feds interested in Rodrigo?"

"You got me." Lowell shrugged. "I'm just following orders. When I started going through his drives and saw he accessed the mainframe, I thought maybe he was up to something. When I saw your username in the logs, I knew something was wrong."

"I don't understand any of this," Angela complained, setting her purse on the desk and leaning forward. "How did he get my username and password? And why mine? And what was he doing?"

"All good questions, and ones I can't answer, unfortunately."

"Well, what did he do when he accessed the mainframe?" Angela demanded.

Lowell looked at her apologetically and shrugged.

"I don't know," he told her. "The logs will have to be analyzed and then maybe we can discover what he was doing. In the meantime, we need to get all your passwords changed to prevent any further security breach."

"Yes, of course."

Lowell nodded and spun around in his chair. He pulled another laptop out of a drawer and set it on the desk in front of her.

"I'll hook this into the network and then we can go through all the systems and get them all changed," he told her. "Hang on."

He ducked under the desk and emerged a second later with a network cable in his hand, which he plugged into the back of the laptop.

"You said you're copying all the bank data before the Feds take his hardware?" Angela asked as he powered up the laptop. Lowell glanced at her.

"Yes. I'm not allowed to remove anything, but I can make copies of the bank files we need," he said.

"So, the FBI is going to have access to whatever is on his hard-drives?"

"Yes."

Angela's mind was racing as the full implications of her situation became clear to her.

"So, they'll see my username and password accessing the mainframe from his hardware," she said slowly. "Just like you did."

Lowell paused.

"Well...yes, I suppose so," he said. "Why?"

"So, essentially, I'm about to be dragged into a Federal investigation as an accomplice!"

Angela felt her heart start to race and she could feel her blood pressure rising.

Lowell sat back and stared at her.

"I see what you're saying," he said slowly. "Yes, I suppose you are."

"This is ridiculous!" Angela exclaimed. "I barely even knew the man! Isn't there some way you can get rid of the logs?"

"Not without them knowing," he answered. "I'm sure they'll get to the bottom of it all and they'll find you had nothing to do with it. I wouldn't worry."

"Easy for you to say," Angela muttered. "You're not the one who's going to be suspected of hacking our bank's mainframe! I might as well kiss my promotion goodbye."

"I'm sure they'll sort it all out," Lowell said soothingly. "In the meantime, let's get your passwords changed. Here. We'll start with the main network password and go from there."

He turned the laptop to face her and Angela found herself looking at the initial portal into the bank network. She sighed and glanced at him.

"Just sign in?" she asked.

"Yep. Once you're in, we'll go to the password portal and change it," he answered.

Angela leaned forward and typed in her credentials, then waited while the network loaded her profile.

"It will take a moment for the laptop to build your profile because you've never logged into it before," Lowell explained apologetically.

Angela nodded, barely listening to him. Her mind was spinning. An FBI investigation would ruin her career. She worked in anti-money laundering, for God's Sake! This was a disaster! After working her butt off for this company and clawing her way up the ladder, she was going to lose it all over some IT geek she barely knew. It made no sense!

"Here we go," Lowell said, leaning forward. Angela looked up to see that the laptop had finished and she was in the network. "Let's get you to the password portal so you can change the network password first." Lowell was typing as he talked and a second later, she was looking at the change password screen. Angela sighed and thought for a moment, trying to think of a new password she would remember.

"I hate thinking up passwords," she muttered.

"Everyone does," Lowell chuckled.

"It's bad enough the system makes us change them every three months as it is," Angela said, leaning forward as she thought of one. "Now I have to do it off-cycle."

"I'm sure I don't have to tell you to make it something completely unique and different from what you had before," he said, watching as she started to type. The look she shot him made him grin. "Hey, just making sure! I've had people try to use the same word and change the number at the end. Not the brightest thing to do when someone knows your password already."

"Lowell, I didn't get to where I am in this company by being an idiot," Angela informed him, her smile taking the edge off her words. "I'm using something completely different."

"Good." Lowell sat back and picked up an old baseball, tossing it back and forth between his hands. He watched her for a moment, then cleared his throat. "Do you have any idea how Rodrigo got your password?"

"Not the faintest," Angela answered, sitting back as the network confirmed the password change. "I don't think I ever even had my laptop around him. As I said, I barely knew him."

"Strange," Lowell murmured. "Done? Ok. One down..."

"Fourteen to go," Angela finished for him. He grinned.

"Let's get moving, then," he said, leaning forward.

Damon sipped his water and stared at the picture on the plasma screen. Alina was typing away at the computer next to him in her command center and the sound faded into the background as Hawk stared at the deep-set, dark eyes of Jenaro Gomez. He had heard of the Lieutenant. Everyone had. The man was notorious. Ruthless and cunning, he had a reputation that instilled fear into the hearts of most men. His antiquated torture techniques were as legendary as his penchant for shocking, public executions. He had once disemboweled a man and hung him from a bridge in Mexico as a warning to others.

Hawk studied the face on the screen for a few more minutes before slowly raising his eyes to stare at an invisible point on the curved ceiling. Charlie and Harry had both warned him separately that Jenaro was in New Jersey. They suspected he was coming after Hawk as revenge for the cartel killings, but they could have saved their breath. Viper was one step ahead of them.

"What did Charlie have to say about it?" Viper broke the silence as she sat back in her chair. Damon glanced at her, his eyes automatically sliding to her monitor out of long habit. She hit a key and the screen went black. "Stop being nosy."

"Just habit," Hawk answered with a sheepish grin. "Charlie is concerned about how Gomez knew I was here."

"We knew he would be." Alina spun around in her chair and stared at Jenaro pensively. "You know I'm concerned about that myself."

"I think Charlie is more irritated that a Mexican Cartel Lieutenant knew where his agent was before he did," Hawk murmured. He sat back and laced his hands behind his head, staring up at the ceiling. "I'm more interested in why Gomez came himself. He has hundreds of soldiers he could have sent instead. The situation in Mexico is complicated enough. I would think his presence would be more beneficial there, rather than in New Jersey, chasing me."

"You underestimate yourself." Alina smiled faintly. "You're a formidable adversary. And you pissed them off."

"Hm." Damon was unconvinced, but he dropped it for the moment. "Charlie and Harry are both advising extreme caution. I think they would rather I got out of the States, but they know that's not going to happen."

"Oh, you won't run away?" Viper asked innocently.

Hawk glanced at her, laughter glinting in his eyes. Two months ago, he urged her to do just that. She had declined. Emphatically.

"Touché," he murmured, returning his gaze to the face on the plasma. "What have you found out about Jessica Nuñez?"

"Not much yet," Viper admitted and turned back to her computer. "Everything about her and the husband is squeaky clean. They don't even have an unpaid bill."

"No one is that clean," Hawk retorted, turning his chair around and glancing at her. Her eyes met his and she smiled.

"I know," she agreed. "I'll dig it out. There's a connection between her and Gomez. I'll find it."

"What about Rodrigo? Did Stephanie tell you anything?" he asked.

"No." Alina picked up her forgotten mug, took a sip, and grimaced at the cold coffee. "She's playing her cards close to her chest. She wants my input, but doesn't want to tell me anything. I think she's afraid of me."

Hawk turned and studied Alina. Her hands were steady and her face was calm. She didn't appear bothered by what she had just said.

"Because of what she saw in Virginia?" he asked softly.

"I think so," Alina said thoughtfully. "She's been different lately, more reserved. Almost cautious."

"That's to be expected," Damon murmured. "She saw a side of you she doesn't know and doesn't understand."

"Mmm," Alina agreed, swirling her cold coffee in the mug. "John started calling me the Black Widow."

Damon let out a bark of laughter.

"I like it!" he exclaimed, his eyes dancing.

Viper glanced at him, amused.

"I thought you would," she retorted. "He doesn't know I know, of course. Obviously, they were both discomposed with what they saw."

"How do you feel about that?" Damon asked after a moment of silence. He encountered a brief, unemotional glance from her.

"My feelings are irrelevant," Viper said shortly, standing. "They saw something they weren't meant to see. It's unfortunate, but now they know the truth. How they deal with it is up to them."

"As long as they don't compromise you in the process," Hawk murmured.

Viper met his measured gaze and nodded slightly.

"I'm keeping a close eye on them," she assured him. "I'm going to get fresh coffee. Do you want some?"

"Please." Hawk turned back to his computer as she moved down the long, narrow room toward the stone steps leading up to the kitchen. "Viper?"

She paused and glanced back at him questioningly.

"Yes?"

"We need to find out why Gomez cut Rodrigo into pieces," he told her. "The Fearless Feds are holding that particular card, whether they know it or not."

"I'll take care of it," she promised.

Hawk watched her disappear up the steps thoughtfully. He had no doubt she would get the information he needed one way or another. His only concern was whether the Jersey Girl he loved would interfere with the Viper he needed.

Chapter Twelve

Stephanie sipped her coffee and stared down at the blue Tiffany's box sitting on the bottom step of the prison steps. All in all, it looked cheerful, sitting there on the cold stone step in the early morning light, wrapped up with the signature white bow. It would have been fairly innocuous, if it weren't for the human tongue nestled inside.

"No one saw a thing," John said disgustedly as he came up beside her and looked down at the box. "We had two agents here overnight and neither of them saw anything."

"Of course they didn't," Stephanie muttered. "I'm starting to think we really *are* dealing with a ghost."

"Looks like Lina was right about the meat puzzle," John said.

"First his arm, then his head, and now his tongue." Stephanie stared at the box pensively. "What are they trying to say with all this?"

"Do you want me to call Stanton?" John asked, referring to the in-house psychologist.

"Not yet." Stephanie shook her head and sipped her coffee again. "I still feel like this is all a distraction to keep us away from the real issue." She glanced at him and smiled ruefully. "Besides, Stanton is creepy."

"I won't argue with that," John agreed. "What do you want to do now?"

"I'll get the tongue back to Larry so he can confirm it's Rodrigo's," Stephanie said. "Get a crew together and go through that damn maze at the back again. I want it torn apart. There has to be something somewhere to give some clue as to what the hell is going on."

"Got it." John nodded and motioned to one of the junior agents.

"Call me if you find anything." Stephanie turned to motion to a photographer. "I'm going to go visit Phillip Chou and see what kind of reaction I get from him."

"You don't think that will spook them?" John asked.

Stephanie raised her eyebrow and looked at him, amused.

"If having one of their hackers disappear and then start showing up in pieces hasn't spooked them already, I don't think I can do any worse, do you?" she asked.

John grinned.

"Good point," he said. "Do we have Rodrigo's hardware yet?"

"Tech is picking it up today," Stephanie said, moving out of the way so the photographer could get pictures of the Tiffany's box. "I'm also going to stop into the office and see if Matt had any luck with the surveillance video from that cell."

John looked at her.

"Matt?" he repeated.

Stephanie nodded.

"You didn't think I just forgot about our mystery couple who unlocked the cell and waltzed in there, did you?" she demanded.

John had the grace to look sheepish.

"With everything else, *I* did," he admitted. "Was Matt going to try to ID them?"

"Yes. I sent him the footage yesterday morning and he said he would work on it." Stephanie glanced at her watch. "It's almost seven. Why don't we meet for lunch to compare notes?"

"Sounds good," John said, turning to leave.

Stephanie lifted her coffee to her lips and returned her attention to the box on the steps. She never saw the flash of sun glinting off glass across the street as someone lowered a pair of binoculars thoughtfully. A few minutes later, a putrid green crossover eased out of a parking spot on a side street and turned to drive away from the prison.

Viper held the scope to her eye and watched as Jessica Nuñez got out of a black rental sedan and beeped it locked. She walked across the parking lot toward the large, square brick building that housed Burlington Social Services. Viper watched her go into the building and then turned her attention back to the black rental sedan. She made a note of the plate number and lowered the scope thoughtfully. So, Jessica had rented a replacement for her vehicle. Now why would she let someone else use her car while she was forced to rent one?

Alina was still mulling over the question when her cell phone beeped from the seat next to her. She frowned when she saw the incoming call.

"Yes?" she answered.

"Morning!" Angela greeted her. "What are you doing?"

"Working," Alina answered briefly. "Why aren't you?"

"I am," Angela said. "What are you doing for lunch?"

Alina's eyes narrowed at the slight change in Angie's voice. She gazed across the parking lot at the black sedan.

"I don't know yet," she answered. "Why?"

"Can you meet me?" Angela was doing her best to sound casual, but Alina caught the trace of anxiety in her voice.

"Where?" she asked simply.

"I can come to your house," Angie replied. "I'll bring salads."

"What time?" Alina glanced at her watch.

"Around noon?"

"I'll be there," Alina answered.

"Ok. See you then!"

Alina disconnected with a slight frown. Angela had definitely sounded anxious, and then relieved when she had agreed to lunch. Something was wrong there.

Before she had a chance to think any more about it, however, Jessica Nuñez emerged from the building again. Viper raised an eyebrow and lifted the scope to her eye. Jessica was hurrying down the steps looking distracted and flushed and, as Viper watched, she pulled a phone out of her purse. She swiped the screen and hit a speed dial button before holding the phone up to her ear as she hurried across the parking lot toward the rental sedan. Viper lowered the scope and watched her with a frown. Starting the engine to her Camaro, she watched as Jessica dropped her keys when she reached the car. Jessica ducked down to pick them up just as the crack of a rifle shot echoed across the parking lot. The passenger's window of the SUV parked next to the sedan shattered into pieces.

Viper turned her head swiftly. A black Chevy pick-up truck started its engine with a roar and she saw the glint of the morning sun on a rifle barrel as it was pulled from the driver's window.

"Shit."

She didn't hesitate. Throwing the car in gear, she hit the gas and shot out of her parking spot. Flying up the aisle toward Jessica's car, she watched in the rear view mirror as the pick-up reversed out of its spot and turned toward them. Her eyes dropped to the front license plate and she read it backwards, committing it to memory. As she approached the black sedan, Viper unlocked the passenger's door and slid the window down.

"Get in!" she called, screeching to a stop behind the sedan.

Jessica Nuñez was crouched on the pavement against the car, her face white. When Alina called out to her, she stared at her in shock.

"What?" she cried.

Next Exit, Dead Ahead

"You have about four and a half seconds to get in this car before the man who just tried to kill you comes up behind me," Viper informed her coldly. "The choice is yours."

Jessica hesitated only a second before grabbing her keys and scrambling towards the Camaro. Viper glanced in the rear view mirror and saw the truck accelerating towards her. Two men were in the cab, and the passenger had a gun in his hand. As Jessica reached the door, he fired. Because Viper had stopped the car at a slight angle, the bullet ricocheted off her back right bumper, missed Jessica and hit the back windshield of the sedan instead.

Jessica wrenched open the door and jumped into the car. Viper didn't wait for her to get the door closed. She hit the gas and Jessica was thrown back in her seat as the door slammed shut with the force of the acceleration.

"Hang on, Ms. Nuñez," she said calmly, reaching beneath her seat and pulling out her back-up 9mm. Lowering her window, she added, "You might want to keep your head down."

Jessica looked at the gun, her eyes as wide as dinner plates, and slid down in the seat as low as she could go.

"Who are you?" she cried.

Viper glanced at her speed, then slammed on the brakes and pulled the emergency brake. Spinning the wheel, she guided the sports car into a 180 degree spin until she was facing the pick-up truck.

"I'm the person saving your life," she answered shortly.

Viper leaned to the side and aimed out the window, steadying her firing arm with her other hand. Her eyes narrowed as she got a good look at the driver. It was the same man who had been watching Hawk Saturday morning. Exhaling, Viper fired off two rounds at the truck. The first one went through the windshield and hit the driver in the shoulder, while the second round buried itself in the front passenger tire. The truck swerved to the right violently and slammed into a parked car as the driver lost control.

Viper disengaged the emergency brake and hit the gas, accelerating past the truck as the passenger jumped out. He fired at the Camaro as she sped down the aisle, one of the bullets hitting the back quarter panel before she turned the corner and shot out of the lot.

"What just...how did you...who *are* you?" Jessica babbled from the passenger's seat.

Viper glanced in the rear view mirror before sliding her gun back under the seat into its holder. She looked at Jessica, still slouched down in her seat and staring back at her with wide, dark eyes. She still clutched her phone in one hand and her purse and keys were gripped in the other so tightly that her knuckles gleamed. Her hair, which had been in a neat chignon at the back of her head when she went into work, hung in heavy dark strands on either side of a flawless face.

"You can sit up now," Alina told her, turning her attention back to the road. "They can't follow us. I shot their tire."

"Did you...I mean, is he..."

"Dead?" Viper asked. "No. I just slowed him down. I couldn't risk killing him in daylight with possible witnesses."

"How do you know who I am?" Jessica asked, slowly sitting up in the seat. Her hands were shaking and she seemed to just realize that she was still clutching her phone. She dropped it into her purse absently. "How did you know my name?"

"Why did you leave work so quickly?" Viper countered with her own question.

"Were you watching me?" Jessica asked.

"Yes." Alina glanced at her. "Do you know who those men are?"

"Yes." Jessica pressed her hands to her cheeks and took a deep breath. "They're bad men. I left work because there was a message waiting on my desk. It said...it said..." Her voice caught on a sob and Jessica Nuñez suddenly sagged in her seat. After a moment, she seemed to pull herself together by some sheer force of will. "It said by the time I read it, my husband would be dead."

"Is that who you called when you left the building?" Alina asked.

"Yes." Jessica looked at her. "He answered the phone and said he was fine. He was about to go into class."

"Why does Jenaro Gomez want you dead?"

Jessica gasped and stared at her.

"How do you know about Jenaro?" she whispered.

"I recognized the driver as one of his men," Viper said, glancing at her. "I've seen him before, sitting in *your* car."

Jessica was silent for a long moment, twisting her hands together in her lap. Just when Alina decided she wasn't going to say anything, Jessica spoke in Spanish in a low voice.

"Dios mío, no sé en quién confiar."

"Yo puedo ayudarte," Viper replied.

Jessica looked at her, startled.

"You speak Spanish!" she exclaimed in Spanish.

"I speak several languages," Alina answered in kind.

"You say you can help me, but you don't know what that means," Jessica told her helplessly. "No one can help me."

"You don't know me yet," Viper murmured dryly.

"You don't understand. Jenaro Gomez is an evil man. No one can stop him," Jessica said earnestly. "The Mexican government cannot stop him. He does what he likes and gets away with it. Even here, even in the United States, he can come and do as he pleases. You don't want to get involved with this."

"I'm already involved," Viper retorted. "I just put a bullet in one of his soldiers."

"That's true," Jessica admitted. "You don't seem worried at all. Who are you?" she asked again.

"Someone who can help you," Alina said softly, glancing at her.

Jessica stared at her for a long moment.

"I believe you," she said finally. "I don't know why, but I do."

"Good." Viper turned onto the on-ramp for Rt. 295 south. "I'm going to take you somewhere safe. You'll need to stay there until I get this taken care of. They can't find out where you are, or they'll try again."

"I understand," Jessica said softly. "What about my family?"

Viper glanced at her as she merged into light traffic on the highway. She cut across the lanes until she was in the fast lane, then she dropped the gas pedal down.

"I'll see what I can do," Alina finally said a few moments later. "I can't guarantee anything."

"He has my son," Jessica told her, half-beseechingly.

Viper glanced at her sharply. She was silent for a moment before sighing imperceptibly.

"I'll see what I can do," she finally said.

"Why do you care about Jenaro Gomez?" Jessica asked as she stared out the window at the cars they were passing. "Why do you want to help me?"

"He's targeted a friend of mine," Viper answered coldly. "You have information that will help me find him."

"I thought it must be something like that," Jessica said ruefully. "People don't help strangers without reason." She glanced at Alina. "I'm grateful you did, though. You saved my life."

Alina was silent, her attention focused on the road. If she felt a slight pang of guilt, she pushed it aside. She had saved the woman's life. The reasons for it were immaterial.

"I hope you know what you're doing," Jessica continued, turning her gaze back out the window. "Jenaro is dangerous. He manipulates and uses people in ways you can't even imagine, and he has no conscience. He has no moral compass. Sometimes, I think he is the spawn of Satan himself. What you just did for me, that will make him angry. He won't stop until he finds you. I don't know who you are, but I hope you know what you're getting yourself into."

"Don't worry about me," Viper said grimly. "I'm rather good at getting to the untouchables."

"Jessica Nuñez."

Stephanie stepped into the forensics lab in the basement of the building and raised her eyebrow. Matt, the resident forensics guru, was standing with his back to her, watching as a complicated-looking machine analyzed the contents of a glass slide. He had spoken as she approached the door to his domain, tossing the name over his shoulder without turning around.

"How did you know it was me?" Stephanie asked as she glanced around the cluttered lab.

Each time she came down here, the large space seemed smaller and the mounds of equipment and clutter seemed larger. Matt was a genius with all things science, and the whole building knew it. Even though they had four other forensic techs, all the senior agents came exclusively to Matt. He was quick, accurate, and rarely made mistakes.

"I saw you in the elevator," Matt said, motioning to a TV monitor in the corner.

Stephanie rolled her eyes and grinned reluctantly. She should have known it was something simple like that.

"So Jessica Nuñez is my mystery woman?" she asked, picking up a magnifying glass from one of the long tables and twirling it in her hand absently.

Matt turned from his machine and looked at her. His sandy hair was askew and his white lab coat was wrinkled and looked as if it had seen better days. He was dressed respectably in navy slacks with a white button down shirt, but his shoes were faded Converses that looked as if they were original vintage. He pushed his glasses up on his nose and came forward to take the magnifying glass out of her hand.

"She's your mystery woman," he agreed. He set the glass back down and motioned for her to follow him. "The man was more of a challenge. I bet you'll never guess who he is!"

"I bet you're right," Stephanie agreed cheerfully. "Who is he?"

"His name is Lorenzo Porras," Matt told her, handing her a blown up glossy photo of the man who went into the Dungeon cell. "Get this. He's Mexican."

"With a name like that, I'm not surprised," Stephanie said, taking the photo and looking at it. He was medium height and built like a boxer. "What else did you find out?"

"He's a soldier for the Casa Reino Cartel," Matt said triumphantly.

"He's never set foot on US soil before, at least as far as immigration is concerned. In fact, according to his documents, he's not here now."

Stephanie looked at him, her forehead creased into a frown. "Mexican Cartel?" she demanded. "Are you sure?"

"Yep." Matt turned away again and fished a profile folder out from under a stack of papers and handed it to her. "Here's all the information I was able to pull from our databases. I'll give you the short version. A couple months ago, three top cartel heads were killed. Rumors at the time were that the CIA was involved, but of course it was never confirmed. One of the men killed was José Ramos, head of the Casa Reino Cartel. When he died, his cartel was thrown into war with the other two top cartels. Out of the ashes, Casa Reino is the only one that regrouped under a new head."

"And my mystery man is one of them," Stephanie said.

"Yep." Matt nodded. "And it gets more interesting. Lorenzo Porras has moved up the ranks with the restructuring. DEA suspects he's been working closely with the Cartel's Second-in-Command, Jenaro Gomez."

Stephanie looked up, her eyebrows soaring into her forehead. Matt nodded, catching her look of surprise.

"You've heard of him. Good. That saves me some breath," he said. "He was Ramos' Lieutenant and the acting head of the Casa Reinos until Martese Salcedo gained control. Most people think Gomez helped him take control in order to stabilize the Cartel quickly. The other two cartels are still in chaos, fighting among themselves, and losing money every day because of it. Salcedo's been able to stem the bleeding and start gathering his troops again. It's only a matter of time before he regains control of the drug routes that fund them."

"So, what's Lorenzo doing in Jersey?" Stephanie muttered.

"Well, according to the DEA, Jenaro Gomez came into Arizona a month ago," Matt told her, leaning against a table and crossing his arms over his chest. "They lost him almost immediately, but they believe he was heading east. If that's true, it explains why Lorenzo is here. We have a team out of Washington tracking Gomez."

Matt straightened up and turned to a laptop a few feet away.

"We do? The FBI is already looking for Gomez?" Stephanie asked, looking up.

Matt nodded.

"Yep. Give me a sec and I'll have the Agent-in-Charge for you," he murmured, typing away. "Hanover. Blake Hanover. He's the one tracking Gomez."

"I know that name," Stephanie murmured.

"Well, you might want to get in touch with him." Matt looked up.

125

"He might be able to shed some light on what your mystery man was doing in a museum cell in Mt. Holly."

"What about this Jessica Nuñez? Do we have anything on her?" Stephanie asked.

Matt shook his head.

"Nothing," he answered, shoving his glasses back up on his nose. "She's as clean as they come. The only connection I could see is she's originally from Mexico."

"Thanks, Matt." Stephanie turned to leave the lab.

"One more thing!" Matt stopped her. "Your head that Larry brought in yesterday?"

"Yes?" Stephanie stopped and looked back at him.

"Larry had me look at the pole it was stuck on," Matt told her, crossing the lab to another long table. He held up a long, heavy plastic bag with the pole inside. "He found some fragments inside the neck he thought might have come off the pole. They were minute fragments of bark and, as you can see, the pole is wood."

"Right." Stephanie nodded.

"Wrong." Matt grinned. "The pole is bamboo."

"And?"

"The fragments inside the neck were from a Red Mulberry tree," Matt told her. "I've gone over this pole twice. There are absolutely no fragments or residue from a mulberry tree anywhere on it."

"So I'm looking for a mulberry tree," Stephanie said.

"Yep." Matt nodded. "If you find one, bring me a piece of bark and I can tell you if it's the same tree."

"Good to know," Stephanie said with a smile. "Thanks, Matt. You're invaluable."

"Tell it to the boss," Matt retorted. "My review is coming up."

Stephanie had just reached her desk when her cell phone started ringing. She sighed and dropped the folders Matt gave her on the desk before pulling the cell phone out of its holster on her waistband.

"Hello?" she answered, glancing up as someone called her name across the department. Her boss, Rob Thornton, was waving from his office door. She held up her finger to indicate she would be there in a minute and he disappeared back into his office.

"We found Rodrigo," John told her.

Stephanie stilled.

"Where?"

"In the haunted walk at the back," he answered. "It's kind of a mess."

"Tell me." Stephanie sank into her chair and rubbed her forehead. It wasn't even nine o'clock yet and she was already getting a headache.

"He was in a section that was supposed to be an operating room. According to Karl, the actors portray a patient eating a doctor's head during the walk," John said.

Stephanie's mind flashed back to Friday night and the image of a young woman holding a severed head in her hands.

"I remember it," she said slowly. "The actress was dressed in a patient's gown and the doctor was on the table behind her. She was eating something out of a severed head."

"Appetizing," John muttered. "Well, what's left of Rodrigo is left on that table."

"What do you mean, 'what's left?'" Stephanie demanded.

"Aside from his missing arm and head, they sliced him open and disemboweled him," John informed her bluntly.

Stephanie swallowed and heard a faint buzzing in her ear.

"They...what?" she repeated faintly.

"It's a mess," John repeated. "It looks like they did it here. There's fake blood everywhere, so I've got a team going through it all to separate any real blood from the fake crap spread everywhere. Larry's on his way."

"Oh God!" Stephanie dropped her forehead into her hand and took a deep breath. "Rob just called me. I have to go see him, then I'll be on my way. Get as many pictures yourself as you can."

"Already done," John answered.

"Good. I'll be there as soon as I can." Stephanie stood up shakily. "I have IDs on our mystery couple. You're not going to like it."

"I think I'm beyond surprise at this point," John muttered. "Who are they?"

"Well, the man is Mexican Cartel," Stephanie told him.

John was silent for a long moment.

"I stand corrected," he finally said. "I'm apparently *not* beyond surprise. What the hell is a Mexican Cartel doing in Jersey?!?!"

"I don't know," Stephanie started walking across the floor toward Rob's office, "but I can tell you one thing. The Black Widow already knew."

"How do you figure that?"

"Remember what she said about the head being a warning?" Stephanie asked. "You said that practice went out with the Dark Ages. She didn't miss a beat when she said it was still prevalent in some cultures."

"And the cartels do crap like that all the time," John finished.

"I think we'll pay her a visit tonight," Stephanie told him. "It's time to find out what she knows."

Chapter Thirteen

Stephanie knocked briefly on Rob's open door and stepped inside, sliding her phone back into the holster at her waist. Her boss was seated at his desk, typing away on his laptop, surrounded by papers, folders and clutter. He looked up when she entered and nodded, standing.

"Stephanie!" he greeted her and motioned to a chair in front of his desk. Rob stood close to six feet tall and had friendly green eyes that usually held some sort of twinkle when they met hers. "I wanted to see where you're at with this Rodrigo Frietas thing."

"That's a good question, Rob," Stephanie murmured, sinking into a chair.

Rob raised an eyebrow and sat down, studying her over the desk.

"That doesn't sound encouraging," he said. "What's the latest?"

"John just called. He found Rodrigo's body in the maze behind the prison," Stephanie told him. "I'm on my way there now."

"Do we have his hardware yet?" Rob asked, sitting back and steepling his fingers under his chin.

"Tech picked it up half an hour ago." Stephanie rubbed the back of her neck and rolled her shoulders. "Matt says he might have something for me by the end of the day or tomorrow."

"I don't need to tell you the bank is nervous at the thought of any kind of breach into their network," Rob said slowly. "How confident are you that Rodrigo was one of the hackers?"

"I'm positive," Stephanie answered promptly. "I think I've got names on the other two as well."

Rob raised his eyebrows.

"That's good news!" he exclaimed. "Do you think we can wrap this up soon?"

"Hopefully," Stephanie answered. "But I've run into a hiccup."

"What's that?"

"It's starting to look like a Mexican Cartel may be involved,"

Stephanie said slowly and Rob's mouth dropped open.

"What?" he exclaimed. "I thought our intel says the hackers are working for North Korea!"

"It does." Stephanie crossed her legs and sat back in the chair, suddenly exhausted. "I don't know what to make of it. All our intel, including Rodrigo's initial statement, indicates the hacking ring is being funded by NicTel Corporation. It's an electronics firm that, among other things, is a major contributor to the North Korean regime. You know all about that already. However, now it appears that someone named Lorenzo Porras may have been the one to put Rodrigo's arm in the cell."

"And this Lorenzo Porras has ties to a cartel?" Rob asked, frowning.

"More than just ties. He's high up in the Casa Reino Cartel," Stephanie told him. "Matt just ID'd him from a surveillance photo from the museum."

"Fabulous," Rob muttered. "What the hell is a Mexican Cartel doing getting involved with the North Koreans?"

"I have no idea," Stephanie replied. "My gut tells me it's not just coincidence."

"No, no," Rob agreed, shaking his head. "If a cartel's in town, it's no coincidence."

"Apparently, we have an agent out of Washington who is already tracking one of the cartel members," Stephanie said slowly. "Matt says it's Blake Hanover."

"Blake?" Rob looked up. "I know Blake. He's a damn good agent. He's already tracking them, you say?"

"I don't say," Stephanie corrected with a tired smile. "Matt says. Supposedly DEA lost the cartel Lieutenant, a Jenaro Gomez, when he came across the border last month. Agent Hanover is looking for him."

"I'll call down to Blake's boss and see what I can find out," Rob told her. "He might be able to shed some light on your case. You'll like Blake. He's like you."

"Meaning?"

"He doesn't give up once he has his teeth into something," Rob answered with a grin. "I'll see what I can arrange."

"I appreciate that," Stephanie told him and stood up.

"Before you go," Rob stopped her. "I found something out this morning you'll find interesting."

"Oh?"

"Ever hear of a man named Jin Seung Moon?" Rob asked her.

Stephanie frowned and shook her head.

"No. Who is he?"

"He's a terrorist masquerading as a businessman, and as slick as they come," Rob told her. "He works for the North Koreans. No one can touch him. Interpol's been trying for years, but every time they come close, he slips away. He went to school at Oxford, apparently, and is smarter than your average radical."

"You think he's the one behind my hacking ring?" Stephanie asked, glancing at him sharply.

"I don't know," Rob shrugged, "but he was spotted in New York over the weekend. Seems a little suspicious, don't you think?"

"More than a little," Stephanie agreed.

"I'll send you what information I have," Rob told her and turned back to his laptop. Stephanie turned to leave the office, but his next words made her pause. "Tread carefully, Ms. Walker. If Moon *is* behind your hacking ring, what you do will have international consequences."

Lowell Kwan glanced at his phone when it beeped a warning at him. Picking it up, he swiped the screen and opened the tracking software blinking in his notifications bar. He frowned when he saw the purple tracker flashing and moving away from the Mt. Laurel Campus.

"Where are you going?" he murmured softly.

Opening up his laptop bag, he pulled out an electronic tablet. A minute later, he was looking at a larger version of the tracking software. The purple dot was moving across a map grid, out of Mt. Laurel and heading south.

Lowell watched it thoughtfully for a moment. He had hacked into the GPS systems in Angela Bolan's car and phone, inserting a tracking virus while she was sitting at his desk changing all her passwords the night before. He let her go yesterday after he captured her network credentials, but he had her on a short leash. Angela Bolan was a liability he couldn't let get too far away from him. Really, if the truth were told, he should have taken care of her last night after he got what he needed from her. However, at the last minute, he decided she still might prove useful. After making sure he would be able to keep an eye on her, he let her go.

When the tracking dot kept moving out of Mt. Laurel, he got up and picked up his keys. She was venturing a little too far for just a lunch run. Grabbing the tablet and phone, he turned to leave his cubicle.

Alina glanced at her watch and disappeared into her walk-in closet. Raven watched from his perch in the corner of her bedroom as she emerged a minute later, pulling a black V-neck sweater over her head. Glancing up, she found him watching her with his shiny black eyes and she smiled.

"We're going to have company in a minute," she told him. "Angela is worried about something. I would appreciate it if you wouldn't scare her when she gets here."

Raven tilted his head slightly to the side and blinked.

Alina sat on the edge of the bed to pull on her boots. She had left Jessica in a hotel suite in Delaware with strict instructions not to make any phone calls or leave the room. Jessica had handed over her cell phone and electronic tablet reluctantly after Viper ruthlessly informed her both could be tracked by the Cartel. After assuring her that she would contact her husband for her, Viper left with the promise that she would return that evening to move her to a more secure location.

A loud beep echoed through the house, pulling Alina out of her thoughts. She glanced at the plasma screen on the wall and saw the front driveway quadrant flashing on the security monitor. Angela was pulling into the driveway. Alina looked at Raven.

"Remember," she murmured, "behave."

Raven turned his head toward the skylight and stretched. A moment later, he disappeared out the opening and onto the roof. Alina grinned. Standing, she headed out of the bedroom and down the stairs.

Striding down the hallway toward the back of the house, Alina picked up the remote from the bar and clicked the plasma above the fireplace off. She opened her laptop, turned off the security perimeter and closed it, going to the sliding back door just as Angela pulled her BMW around the house and stopped in front of the garage. She parked and got out of the car, turning toward the house. Sliding the door open, Alina stepped out onto the deck and Angela waved. She was carrying a large white take-out bag in one hand and her purse was slung over her shoulder.

"I hope you have water," she called. "I forgot to get soda."

"Of course." Alina waited until Angela had reached the deck to answer. "Come on in."

Alina turned to lead the way into the house. As she did, Raven dropped off the roof at the other end of the deck and landed softly on the banister. His black eyes seemed to study Angela.

"Is he getting used to me?" Angela demanded, looking down the length of the deck to the hawk. "He usually tries to buzz my head."

"I think he's just behaving himself today," Alina murmured, glancing at her pet. She winked at him and he bobbed his head.

"Well, I'll take it," Angela said and followed her into the house. "I heard he won't even let John up on the deck anymore."

"No." Alina grinned suddenly. "The last time John tried to come to the back door, he almost lost an eye."

"I can't say I blame Raven," Angela muttered. "John's an ass."

"That I won't deny," Alina said with a laugh.

She went into the kitchen and pulled two bottles of water out of the fridge while Angela set the large bag on the bar. She pulled out two containers filled with salad.

"I got grilled chicken Caesar," Angela announced, setting them on the bar.

"That's fine," Alina said, handing her a bottle of water. She opened a drawer and pulled out two forks, handing one to Angela as she rounded the bar. "Thanks for bringing lunch."

"Thanks for having me," Angela replied, sitting on a bar stool and lifting the clear plastic lid off her salad. "I need to talk to someone."

Alina sat next to her and took the lid off her salad.

"About?" she prompted when Angela didn't continue. She glanced at her friend to find her picking through her salad absently.

"I think I'm in trouble," Angela finally said slowly.

Alina's eyes narrowed slightly and she shot her friend a look from under her lashes.

"You think?" she repeated. "Or you know?"

"I know," Angela said positively.

Alina ate her salad, patiently waiting for Angie to elaborate. Angela's hands were trembling slightly as she picked at her lunch. What on earth had she been up to now? With Angela, it was always something.

"How's the physical therapy going?" Alina finally asked when Angela made no attempt to continue talking.

"Ok," Angela said. "I only go once a month now. The scar isn't as bad as I thought it would be."

"I'm telling you, get a tattoo around it." Alina set down her fork and opened her water. "It'll look hot."

"Like what?" Angela demanded with a laugh.

"A bullseye," Alina answered promptly, causing Angela to choke on a piece of lettuce.

"Do you have any new tattoos?" Angela asked her.

Alina hesitated. She had a tattoo once, but Angela knew that. They had all gone together about a year before she joined the Navy. When she

133

went into training for the Organization, it had been removed. All identifying marks were removed from operatives. It was standard operating procedure.

"No," Lina said, setting her water down. "No, I never got another one."

"I thought all sailors got tattooed," Angie said.

Alina grinned.

"Not this one," she retorted.

Her distraction worked. Angela's hands were steady again and some of the tension had gone out of her shoulders.

"Maybe I *will* get a tattoo around the scar," Angie said with a grin. "If nothing else, it would be a conversation starter."

"See? There's a bright side to everything."

"I'm going to be investigated by the FBI," Angela blurted out.

Alina glanced at her and raised an eyebrow.

"Excuse me?"

"Something happened at work," Angela told her, setting down her fork and shifting in her seat so that she could face her. "Somehow, some guy I barely even knew used my network credentials to access the bank's mainframe. Now, he's dead and the FBI took all his computers. They're going to see that my network credentials logged into the mainframe from his hardware and they're going to think I did it!"

Alina blinked and stared at Angela impassively.

"That's inconvenient," she murmured.

Angela huffed and threw her hands up in the air.

"That's all you have to say?" she exclaimed.

"Ok." Alina pushed her salad away and looked at her old friend. "Run it by me again, with a little more detail this time."

"Some guy I barely even knew..."

"Name?"

"What? Oh...Rodrigo. Rodrigo Frietas," Angela told her.

Alina's eyes narrowed sharply and Angela got her undivided attention.

"Go on," Viper said shortly.

"Well, I barely knew the man. I knew him in passing, and he went out with a couple of us for happy hour once or twice. He was a friend of a friend of a friend, if you know what I mean."

"Yes. I get it. You barely knew him," Alina said dryly, picking up her water. She sipped it, her dark eyes watching Angela's face. "How do you know he accessed the mainframe with your credentials?"

"I got a call from a guy in IT yesterday," Angela explained. "He said he was going through Rodrigo's hardware, getting it ready for the FBI to pick up, when he saw some logs. He said my username and password were used to access the mainframe, causing a security breach."

"Did he say what Rodrigo did on the mainframe?" Alina asked.

"No. He said that would take a lot of digging and the FBI would do that." Angela realized she was clutching her fingers together tightly and forced herself to let go. "He had me go into the office last night and reset all my passwords to prevent any further damage."

"Why are the FBI taking the computers?" Alina asked, playing dumb.

"Apparently, Rodrigo turned up dead yesterday," Angela said. "Well, his head turned up, anyway."

"I'd say chances are good that he's dead, then," Alina agreed, her lips twitching despite herself. "And you think the FBI is going to question you?"

"Of course!" Angela exclaimed. "Lowell said they would be able to see the same logs he saw, showing them my credentials accessing the mainframe from Rodrigo's computers. He said there was no way he could erase them."

Alina was quiet for a moment, her mind working rapidly. Angela picked up her fork again and picked through her salad, glancing at Alina's face.

"What are you thinking?" she finally asked.

"You should tell Stephanie," Alina answered absently, swirling the water in her bottle.

"I can't tell Stephanie!" Angela exclaimed. "She's *with* the FBI! She'll feel obligated to tell the agents with Rodrigo's computers that she knows me."

"I don't think you should let that worry you," Alina murmured.

"Oh, you just don't get it," Angela said disgustedly. "If I go to Stephanie, she'll be put in a bad position between her job and her friend. I don't want to do that to her, but I need someone to help me. I'm in a hell of a mess here, and I didn't even do anything! I've worked my ass off at that stupid bank for ten years and now I'm going to lose my promotion, and probably lose my job, because some geek got a hold of my network credentials and used them to hack the mainframe!"

"Oh, I get it," Alina assured her. "But you need to tell Stephanie. I'm not sure what you think I can do to help you."

"Well, that's not everything," Angela admitted after a slight hesitation. "I think I'm being followed."

Angela waited for Alina to start laughing at her, but there was no sound. She glanced at her to find Alina watching her seriously with a detached and unemotional look on her face.

"Why?" she asked simply.

"Last night, when I got home, I forgot something in my car," Angela said slowly. "I went back out after about ten minutes and there was a car sitting at the end of the road. People park along the road all the time, so I wouldn't have noticed it at all except when I stepped outside, I saw the interior light switch off. It was dark and they were parked away from the street lights, so I saw the light clearly. I guess I really didn't think anything of it. I mean, it could have been anyone doing anything."

"But..." Alina prompted when Angela paused.

"I saw the same car this morning when I stopped for coffee on my way to work from the gym," Angela said. "I know it could be a coincidence, but something just feels funny to me."

"If it feels funny, it probably is," Alina told her. "Did you notice anything before you went to see this IT guy last night?"

"No." Angela shook her head.

Alina was quiet, staring at the top of the bar thoughtfully.

"Did you see the car when you left work just now?" she asked. Angela shook her head. "Where did you go when you left work?"

"Just to Angelo's to pick up the salads, and then I came straight here," Angela said.

Alina looked at her steadily for a moment, debating with herself. Finally, she got up and went over to the counter where her laptop sat. Opening the lid, she typed in a few commands and armed the security perimeter again. Within a few seconds, she had all the perimeter cameras scanning slowly. Hitting a button, she pulled up all the camera views on the screen.

"What are you doing?" Angela asked, watching from her spot at the bar.

Alina ignored her, watching the twelve cameras intently. After a minute, she clicked on the front quadrant and smiled coldly. A navy sedan was parked in the trees near the front of the driveway.

"Gotcha," she whispered.

Viper picked up the remote and turned on the plasma screen above the TV. Redirecting the front quadrant onto the screen, she motioned for Angela to look.

"Is that your mystery car?" she asked.

Angela spun around on her seat and gasped at the security footage on the plasma screen.

"Yes!" she exclaimed, getting off the stool and walking across the living room to stand in front of the screen. "What is this? You have cameras?"

"I have a whole security system," Alina told her as she joined her in

136

front of the plasma screen. She smiled faintly when Angela stared at her. "I'm in security consulting. What do you expect?"

"I didn't...I guess I never thought...." Angela looked away from the faintly amused glint in her old friend's eyes. "That's definitely the same car. I *am* being followed!"

"Want to go find out what they want?" Alina asked her cheerfully. Angela looked horrified.

"No!" she exclaimed. "What if it's the same person that cut off Rodrigo's head?! What do we do?"

"Find out who it is," Viper answered. She turned and went back to the laptop.

"How?" Angela followed her.

Alina zoomed in on the dark blue sedan and got a good shot of the license plate before she turned her attention to the interior. A man was sitting in the car with a sweatshirt hood pulled over his head. He held what looked like a tablet in his hand and he was watching the driveway.

"I'll take care of it," Viper said coldly. "Looks like you weren't being paranoid."

"What should I do?" Angela asked, her face pale. Viper glanced at her.

"Let me handle it," she said shortly. "I wouldn't advise going back to work today. Can you take the rest of the day off?"

"Yes." Angela nodded. "I had a meeting this morning, but I don't have anything for the rest of the day. I can call and tell them I'm working from home this afternoon."

"Good." Alina closed the laptop and turned to go down the hallway toward the front door. "Do it."

"What are you going to do?"

"I'm going to get a closer look at our visitor," Viper said calmly. "Stay here."

"Are you insane?!" Angela cried. "You can't go out there. He could have a gun!"

Alina glanced at her and the look on her face sent a cold chill down Angela's spine.

"One can only hope," Viper murmured before she disappeared out the door.

Chapter Fourteen

Lowell stared at the tablet in front of him with a frown. According to the tracking dot on Ms. Bolan's GPS software, he was supposed to be sitting in the parking lot of a mall. He raised his eyes to the dirt road that emerged out of a forest of trees. Instead, he was in the middle of the Pine Barrens somewhere. It didn't make any sense.

He caught up with Angela when she stopped to pick up lunch at an Italian pizza place just outside Mt. Laurel. Expecting her to turn around and head back to work, he had been surprised when she pulled out of the parking lot and continued heading south. Now, he was just confused. He checked both the GPS tracking on her car and her phone, and they both thought they were in a mall parking lot.

Pulling his hood over his head, Lowell settled down in the seat and started updating the tracking software on the tablet. Something must have gotten hung up somewhere. He would update the software and then he would be able to see where the hell they were. Not for the first time, he wished he hadn't given his own GPS system to Philip.

While he waited for the scan on the tablet to complete, Lowell leaned his head back and stared at the roof of the car. The Feds had come to the building this morning and picked up Rodrigo's laptop and two hard drives. By the end of the day, Angela Bolan would be implicated in the security breach and everything would be back on track. It was unfortunate that Rodrigo got cold feet in the end. They could have been on their way already, mission accomplished and no one the wiser. Instead, Rodrigo seemed to have been attacked with something resembling a conscience.

Lowell shook his head slightly.

It had taken two years to get to this point. Rodrigo had been willing to throw away all that work and careful planning. While it was shocking he lost his head, Rodrigo really couldn't have expected to just walk away from this without any consequences. He really couldn't have been that naïve. Life didn't work that way. They all knew going into this that they were in it for the long haul, and there was no going back. The only question now was, who had gotten to Rodrigo? Lowell had been waiting for him to resurface so that he could take care of himself, but someone beat him to it. Who?

Lowell lifted his head and glanced at the tablet. The scan was finishing and then the software would begin pulling down the updates. He looked at his watch. It should take about ten minutes or so, then he could confirm that the tracking viruses on Angela's car and phone were working properly. Until he killed her, he needed to know where she was at all times. She was their scapegoat. Without her, the Feds would start looking more closely at Rodrigo's associates, past and present, and that would never do.

Lowell looked up as a black F-150 appeared on the road, heading towards him. He slid down in his seat as the truck slowed down and turned into the dirt road right near the front of his car. The driver glanced at the car, but continued into the trees without slowing down. Lowell breathed a short sigh of relief and sat back up. What was down the dirt road? He wanted to get out and walk through the trees and see what was back there, but he needed to finish the software update first. There was no point in seeing what was down the road if he didn't even know *where* the road was.

Lowell was still staring at the tablet in his lap a few minutes later when there was a tap on the glass of the passenger's window. He started violently and raised his eyes to see the man from the pick-up truck peering into the car. Swallowing, Lowell slid one hand into his sweatshirt pocket to close around the gun there. With the other, he pressed the button to lower the window slightly.

"Yes?" he asked.

"You're parked on private property," Michael told him, his eyes narrowed. He pulled out his badge and flashed it through the window. Lowell stilled at the sight of the badge. "I'm a Federal Officer. Are you lost?"

"Actually, I am," Lowell said, releasing the gun in his pocket and doing his best to look confused. "My GPS on this tablet doesn't seem to know where I am, and I pulled off the road to try to update it."

Michael studied the stranger through the glass.

"If you follow this road, it'll take you back into town," he told him, motioning to the road behind them. "You're a fair way out, though, so just stay on this road until you hit civilization again."

"Where would that be?" Lowell asked, starting his engine.

"Medford," Michael answered and stepped back. He watched as the man pulled his hand out of his sweatshirt pocket and set the tablet on the seat next to him. Michael glanced at it and saw an upload just finishing up on the tablet. "Once you hit the center of town, your GPS should be able to get you where you're going."

"Thanks, man!" Lowell waved and backed out of the trees.

Michael nodded and watched as the sedan switched gears and drove away down the road. He shook his head slightly and turned to head back into the trees. Rounding a tree, he came face to face with Alina, looking decidedly annoyed.

"What do you think you're doing?" she demanded.

Michael raised an eyebrow and glanced down at the gun in her hands.

"Getting rid of someone who looked suspicious," he answered easily. "What are *you* doing?"

"I was trying to find out who he was," Viper retorted, tucking the gun into her back holster. "I saw him on the security camera."

"So you came out armed? What am I missing?" Michael asked. His green eyes glinted in the afternoon sun trickling through the trees.

Alina sighed and turned to walk through the trees beside him.

"Nothing good," she replied. "And I'm always armed. You know that."

"And here I just spent last night convincing Blake there was nothing to be worried about here," he sighed, falling into step beside her. "Am I going to regret that?"

"That depends," Alina answered, her lips twitching.

"Are you going to tell me what's going on, or do I have to figure it out myself?" Michael demanded. "I will, you know, so you might as well tell me what's going on now and save us both some time."

"I don't doubt you," Alina murmured. "Angela is at the house. She came for lunch and it seems like she's got herself into a situation."

"Did Coach go out of business?" Michael asked dryly.

Alina bit back a laugh and shook her head as his truck came into view, stopped in the middle of the long dirt road that snaked through the trees to the house. She glanced at him, debating how much to tell him.

"Hardly. Angela is being followed," Alina told him.

Michael raised an eyebrow in surprise as he opened the passenger's door to his truck for her.

"Angela?" he repeated. "By whom?"

"That's what I was trying to find out," Alina retorted, climbing into the truck.

Michael slammed the door closed and went around to get behind the wheel.

"That guy was waiting for her, not you?" he asked, starting the engine and putting the truck in gear.

"Unexpected, right?" Alina looked out the window as they

bounced through the trees. "I'm so used to it being the other way around."

"What did she get herself mixed up with?" Michael asked after a moment of silence.

"Stephanie and John's investigation, as far as I can make out." Alina glanced at him. "They have a dead informant on their hands. Angela knew him at work and somehow he got hold of her network credentials and used them to hack into the bank mainframe before he turned up dead."

Michael whistled softly.

"And now she's being followed," he said slowly.

"Yep." Alina turned her attention back to the trees. "It started last night, or at least, that's when she first noticed it."

"Does Stephanie know?"

"Not yet." Alina shrugged. "Angela says she doesn't want to put Stephanie in a bad spot, but she doesn't know yet Stephanie is the one heading the investigation."

"Wait, back up," Michael shook his head. "If she doesn't know Stephanie's in charge, how does she know she's gotten mixed up in their investigation?"

Alina sighed and leaned her head back on the head rest.

"The FBI went to get the dead man's equipment today," she explained. "It's a long story, but the basics are the dead man hacked into the bank's mainframe from his computer with Angela's credentials. Someone in the IT department caught it when he was copying data from the computers to get them ready for the Feds. He told Angela. Now the Feds have the computers and they'll see the logs for themselves."

"Angela has no idea how this happened?"

"None." Alina shook her head. "She really does have rotten luck sometimes. She doesn't know Stephanie and John are the agents working on the case. She just knows she's about to be implicated in something she had no part of." Alina raised her head as the dirt driveway gave way to gravel. They approached a clearing in the trees and the house came into view ahead. "She went to work last night to change all her passwords and when she got home, she spotted her tail."

"That certainly doesn't sound good," Michael murmured. He followed the drive past the front of the house and turned left to follow it to the back. "She'll have to tell Stephanie."

"I know," Alina agreed. "In the meantime, I want to find out who's following her."

"You think she's in danger?" Michael asked, stopping the truck in front of the garage and turning the engine off. He glanced at Alina to find her frowning slightly.

"I do," she answered quietly. "Stephanie's informant is showing up in pieces. Whatever is going on, it's not good."

"What can I do to help?" Michael asked simply.

Alina glanced at him as she reached for the door handle.

"Help me keep an eye on Angela."

Stephanie stared at the scene before her. John was right. It *was* a mess. The makeshift operating room in the maze had been decorated to look like a massacre had taken place there, and fake blood was splattered everywhere. The fake corpse of the headless surgeon had been tossed aside into the corner and in its place on the gurney lay Rodrigo Frietas.

Or what was left of him.

Stephanie swallowed heavily as her stomach rolled over slowly in protest of the gruesome sight. Rodrigo had been cut from the base of his breast bone to his abdomen and splayed wide open. As if that wasn't enough, whoever did it had pulled half of his intestines out.

"I told you it was a mess," John said, watching Stephanie's face drain of color. "You look like you need to sit down."

"I'm...I'll be..." Stephanie started to speak, then turned abruptly and left the area.

John nodded to Larry, who waiting a few feet away, and followed Stephanie around a corner in the maze. She dropped down onto a prop chair, lowered her head between her knees, and waited for the wave of nausea to pass.

"Two of the techs so far have lost their breakfast," John told her, watching as she kept her head down and took some deep breaths. "You're in good company. It's not a pretty sight."

"Who does that?!" Stephanie exclaimed, lifting a white face and looking at him. "Who the hell *does* something like that!?"

"A sick bastard," John answered promptly.

Stephanie shook her head and lowered it down again, taking deep breaths and trying to forget the sight. The nausea was starting to pass now that she was away from the sight and smell of Rodrigo's mutilated remains.

"How did they get in here?" she demanded. "We had this locked down and agents posted over-night. How the hell did they bring a body in here?"

"The outer door to the parking lot behind the Warden's House was found unlocked," John answered. "One of the techs found traces of bodily fluid and a footprint just inside the door. It looks like they brought him in that way."

"And neither of our agents saw anything?" Stephanie raised her head, staring at John in disbelief. "How incompetent can we get here?"

"Trust me, I asked them that very same question," John answered grimly. "It's almost like we *are* working with a ghost. They walk through walls, unlock doors, no one ever sees them, and no one ever hears anything."

Stephanie took a final deep breath and sat up.

"Ghosts don't slice people up like that," she muttered. "Did Larry have any initial observations?"

"Only that he was already dead when he was cut open, but we knew that already," John said, crossing his arms over his chest and leaning against a metal support beam. "He estimates that Rodrigo was killed sometime between two and nine on Saturday. He did say that according to his examination of his head, Rodrigo's tongue was cut out before the head was severed."

"Was he still alive at that point?" Stephanie asked.

"Larry thinks so," John answered quietly.

"So they cut off his arm and cut out his tongue while he was still alive, then beheaded him." Stephanie shook her head and took another deep breath. "Lovely."

"It's consistent with cartel antics," John said slowly. "They're barbarians, most of them. Do we have a name yet?"

"I have three," Stephanie said, getting to her feet shakily. "Show me the footprint and fluid inside the door to the maze and then I'll tell you what Matt found out."

"We already got a cast of the print," John told her, leading her back through the maze. When they passed the operating room, she glanced in to see Larry and his assistant bending over the gurney. "The fluid could be from Rodrigo, or it could be from the people who brought him in here. Matt should be able to tell us once he gets it tested."

"Who was the museum guard on duty inside last night?" Stephanie asked.

"Karl."

"Interesting," Stephanie murmured.

John glanced at her.

"What are you thinking?"

"Bad things seem to happen when Karl's here," she answered quietly. "First, the arm shows up when he's on duty, and now a tongue and body appear."

"He wasn't on the night the head showed up," John pointed out.

"I still don't like it," Stephanie said. "Let's do a more thorough background check on Karl."

John nodded.

"Ok."

They approached the beginning of the maze and he motioned to a corner just inside the door leading to the parking lot. A couple of techs were just packing up their bags and they nodded to Stephanie as they approached.

"We just finished," one of them told her. "We got a cast of the footprint, samples of the fluid, and we also found this."

He held out a sealed evidence bag and Stephanie raised an eyebrow. Inside was a cigarette butt.

"Where was that?" she asked.

"Marker 3," the tech answered, motioning to the little plastic evidence markers. "It was near the footprint."

"That was careless of them," Stephanie murmured. She crouched down and examined the footprint in the soft earth. "Are they getting sloppy on us already?"

"Maybe they were in a hurry to get inside the door," John said, looking out the open door to the parking lot. "If a patrol car was pulling into the side street to get to the station, they may have been caught and had to get out of sight quickly."

"Perhaps." Stephanie glanced up and looked out the door. "Kind of ballsy to be smoking a cigarette while you're moving a headless corpse around, don't you think?"

"If you think that's the riskiest part of this whole mess, then I'm going to have to rethink our partnership," John told her. "The whole thing is ballsy, starting with the arm in the cell."

Stephanie grinned sheepishly.

"You're right," she agreed, standing. "A cigarette is the least of their worries right now. Still, it's a lucky break for us. At least we can confirm our suspect now."

John nodded and they walked through the door and outside the wall of the prison yard. Stephanie glanced around the parking lot and the bevy of activity as techs and agents bustled around together, processing everything from the maze. It was a daunting task, going through every inch of the haunted walk, but John seemed to have organized everyone quickly and the process appeared to be going smoothly.

"Tell me about the Cartel," John said quietly as they moved away from the commotion and walked toward the Warden's House.

"The man is named Lorenzo Porras," Stephanie told him. "He's a soldier in the Casa Reino Cartel. Three months ago, the head of the Cartel was shot and killed. Matt says there were rumors at the time the CIA was behind it, but that was never confirmed. When he was shot, the second-in-command, a man named Jenaro Gomez, took over temporarily and helped to get a new leader in place quickly. Lorenzo Porras is known to have been working closely with Jenaro the past few months."

"And he's the one who went into the Dungeon on Friday," John said slowly.

"Yes. Matt ID'd him from the surveillance video." Stephanie stopped walking and turned to face John. "That's not all. Jenaro Gomez entered the country through Arizona about a month ago. DEA lost him, but they think he was heading east. An FBI team out of Washington is looking for him."

"So we have a confirmed cartel soldier in Jersey, and probably the second-in-command of the cartel as well," John muttered. "Fabulous. What the hell are they doing here?"

"That's the million-dollar question," Stephanie replied.

"What about the woman?"

"Her name's Jessica Nuñez. She doesn't seem to have any connection at all with either Rodrigo or the Cartel," she told him. "She's a legal resident and works for Social Services. She doesn't even have a parking ticket. That's all I had time to find out about her so far."

"Why would a Mexican Cartel be interested in a hacking ring working for North Korea?" John asked with a frown. "It makes no sense."

"I know." Stephanie shook her head.

"Could we be wrong about NicTel?" he wondered. "Could our information be wrong?"

"I don't think so," Stephanie said slowly. "Over the weekend, a terrorist was spotted in New York City. His name is Jin Seung Moon. Ever hear of him?"

"No." John shook his head. "Who is he?"

"Apparently, he's one of North Korea's top terrorists," Stephanie told him. "Interpol hasn't been able to catch him. He's virtually untouchable."

"And he happens to be less than two hours away from here," John said.

Stephanie nodded and they looked at each other grimly.

"There seem to be a lot of coincidences here," John said after a moment.

"I don't believe in coincidence," Stephanie retorted. "It's getting crowded, and they're all here for a reason."

"You think our hackers are the magnet?"

Stephanie nodded.

"I think Rodrigo was in the middle of it all," she said.

"If that's the case, then Phillip Chou is next," John said slowly.

145

"I've already sent an agent to keep an eye on him," Stephanie replied. "I'm one step ahead of you, partner."

Damon lifted the military binoculars to his eyes and his lips curved into a cold, satisfied smile. He studied the green crossover, parked in the narrow alley between two sets of row homes. Jessica Nuñez's car was backed into the alley and parked, for all the world like it was a driveway. Hawk lowered the binoculars and sipped his water thoughtfully. The row homes were deteriorating with age and neglect, and the narrow street they fronted was strewn with debris. A convenience store on the corner sported thick iron bars in the windows and the ground floor windows of all the row homes had smaller iron railings fixed onto them. Even the sun declined to shine on this depressed neighborhood, disappearing behind thick clouds and casting gray shadows over the buildings.

Hawk had been settled on the roof of an equally dilapidated structure across the street since early morning, watching the corner house. He scored a lead on the car in the early hours of the morning when the registration popped up in the police databases. Jessica's car received its first parking ticket the night before in Riverside, near the Delaware River. Once it was on the grid, finding it was easy.

Damon set down his water bottle and turned to his laptop while he was waiting for signs of life to emerge from the house across the road. A few minutes later, a black pick-up truck pulled up in front of the house and parked half on the sidewalk. Damon picked up the binoculars, watching as the driver jumped out and ran around to the passenger's side. He opened the door and leaned in, helping the passenger out of the truck.

Hawk raised an eyebrow as he watched the passenger emerge. His shoulder was wrapped up in gauze and blood was seeping through the bandage. Zooming in on the faces of the two men, Hawk clicked a button on the side of the binoculars and snapped a series of pictures of both men. He frowned as he watched the injured man impatiently wave the other away. They went up the cement steps to the door and disappeared inside, leaving the truck angled out front of the house.

Damon turned his attention to the truck. The windshield had a bullet hole in the driver's side and the front passenger tire was a spare. Damon lowered the binoculars slowly.

Something had certainly gone very wrong for the two cartel soldiers this morning. A bullet hole at that angle meant the shooter was a better-than-average shot. Hawk considered the truck thoughtfully for a moment, then raised the binoculars again, searching the windows for signs of movement. A few moments later, he was rewarded when the driver ripped open the curtains on a second floor window. He turned away from the window and Hawk watched as he spoke to someone out of sight in the large room. The injured passenger was sitting on a folding chair, his right arm laying on a folding card table. As he watched, a large man came into view, his back to the window. He leaned over the man and started unwrapping the bandage from his shoulder. He turned his head to say something to the driver and Hawk snapped a picture of his profile. His smile was arctic as he lowered the binoculars.

He had found Jenaro Gomez.

Chapter Fifteen

Alina watched as Michael drove away with Angela in the truck next to him. She shook her head slightly, not envious of that drive. When she and Michael returned to the house, Angela pounced on them. Alina was pretty sure that Angela would still be talking now if Michael hadn't finally told her to be quiet. Alina grinned now and turned away from the plasma screen above the mantel when the truck pulled out of the trees and onto the road. Michael had no idea what he had let himself in for by offering to drive Angela home to pick up some things.

For that matter, Viper wasn't quite sure what she had got *herself* into by telling Angela to stay with her until they found out who was following her and why.

The grin on her face faded as Alina went into the kitchen and pulled a mug out of the cabinet. She was already regretting the necessity of having Angela stay here, but there was nowhere else she could go where Viper knew she would be safe. Setting the mug under the coffee spout, she hit the brew button on her coffeemaker and leaned on the counter. At least if Angela was here, she could keep an eye on her.

Viper glanced at her watch as coffee began pouring into her mug. She was glad Michael had agreed to help. She still had Jessica Nuñez to deal with, and that would take up most of the evening. With Michael babysitting Angela, Alina could focus on getting Jessica somewhere safe.

"Good Lord, why is nothing ever simple in this state?" she muttered, pulling out the mug and sipping the hot coffee.

Alina turned and carried her mug over to the bar, setting it on the shiny black marble before grabbing her laptop. She settled down on a stool and opened the computer, sipping her coffee gratefully and taking a moment to enjoy the silence. Viper had a feeling it would be a while before she had the house to herself again. She savored her coffee for a moment, then turned her attention to the laptop. It was time to get to work.

She was still sitting there an hour later when Damon slid open the door to the deck and stepped into the living room.

"Whose car is that?" he asked, sliding the door closed behind him.

Alina glanced over her shoulder.

"Angela's," she murmured. "She's staying here for a few days."

Damon raised an eyebrow and moved into the kitchen. He opened the fridge and pulled out a bottle of water, holding it up questioningly. Alina nodded and he pulled a second bottle out. Closing the fridge, he walked over to hand her the water.

"What's going on?" he asked.

Alina stretched and took the bottle.

"Someone's following her," she told him. "She's managed to get herself involved with the Rodrigo mess. He used her network passwords to hack into the bank mainframe, and now someone's been following her for the past twenty-four hours."

"That's not good," Damon murmured. "How did she know Rodrigo?"

"To hear her tell it, she didn't." Alina sipped her water. "She says she barely knew him and she has no idea how he got her credentials."

"And now someone's following her? How do we know?"

"I saw them," Alina told him grimly. "Blue sedan. He was parked inside my perimeter, in the trees. I went to find out who he was, but Michael beat me to him and scared him away."

Damon drank some water, watching her with his sharp eyes.

"Is Michael still alive?" he asked dryly and Alina grinned despite herself.

"Yes. He's paying for it by babysitting Angela," she said.

Damon laughed.

"Ouch," he murmured. "You play hardball. Where are they?"

"He took her to pick up some things from home that she'll need." Alina turned her attention back to the laptop and Damon and moved around the bar. He glanced over her shoulder at the monitor. A shining black Audi A7 was on the screen. He raised an eyebrow.

"Shopping?" he asked in surprise.

"Browsing," Alina answered evasively.

"I saw the Camaro was missing." Damon sat down on the stool next to her and looked at her. "Did I miss anything fun?"

"Not especially." Alina yawned and stretched her arms high over her head. "Let's just say it was compromised."

"I don't think the Audi is really your style," Hawk said thoughtfully, accepting her cryptic explanation without question.

"Do I have a style?" Viper asked, smiling faintly.

"Oh, you have a certain flair, yes," he murmured. "What else are you looking at?"

"Nothing in particular." Alina shrugged. "I have the Jeep for now. It's not pressing."

"Hmm..." Hawk reached over and minimized the Audi window. Behind it was another window with the Aston Martin Vanquish. "Now, *that's* more your style," he said approvingly.

"A little conspicuous for Jersey, though," Alina said, smacking his hand away from the laptop. "It would be nice in Europe."

"That's true." Damon nodded, smacked her back, and swiftly minimized the Aston Martin. "Wow! Now, that's a surprise!" he exclaimed, staring at the next car. He just caught Alina's soft sigh.

"You really can be a nuisance, you know that?" she asked, trying to minimize the car.

Hawk grinned and pushed her hand away.

"So *this* is the one you're really looking at," he stated, rather than asked. When she was silent, he glanced at her just in time to catch the slight flush on her cheeks. "Interesting."

"It's just a car," Viper muttered, not meeting his bright blue gaze. She didn't know why she suddenly felt so exposed. It was just a car.

A car she had loved since she was a teenager.

"This is not just a car." Hawk shook his head. "It's a piece of American history. This is the Shelby GT 500."

"Yes, I'm aware of that," Alina retorted dryly.

"I would never have pegged you as a Mustang girl," Damon told her. He was looking at her with a faint smile, and something in his eyes made her cheeks heat up again.

Alina cleared her throat. Her heart skipped a beat, and she tried once again to minimize the screen. He ruthlessly smacked her hand away with a grin.

"See that? You learn something new every day," she said tartly.

"With you, yes." Hawk sat back and they both stared at the car on the screen. It was the latest model, fully loaded, and cobalt blue with white racing stripes. He glanced at her. "How long have you wanted one of these?"

"Since high school," Alina admitted with a faint smile.

She raised her eyes from the car and met his bright blue ones. That strange look was back on his face, the one that made her feel like he knew something about her that she didn't. Her heart started beating faster and her mouth went dry.

"Then I think it's about time you gave in," he murmured softly.

Alina stared at him, feeling completely exposed for a moment. He wasn't supposed to know about the Mustang. The Shelby was a little piece of her from long ago, a part of her that she wasn't sure she wanted Damon to know. It was a silly thing, but it was representative of a younger, more carefree girl. A girl she had buried deep inside her years ago.

"We'll see," Viper said, reaching out and closing the browser window. "It's not high on my list of priorities right now."

"What is?" Damon asked, dropping the subject of the car as her mask slid into place, closing her off from him. He had rattled her somehow, and he wasn't quite sure how.

"Jessica Nuñez," Alina answered promptly.

"Talk to me."

"I have her."

Hawk stared at her for a beat.

"I'm sorry. Care to run that by me again?" he asked softly.

Viper smiled slowly.

"I have Jessica Nuñez," she repeated.

Damon was speechless for a moment, then his lips twitched and he shook his head.

"Ok. You win," he told her. "Tell me what happened."

Alina grinned and picked up her water again, turning to face him. Her eyes were sparkling and Damon couldn't stop the reluctant grin pulling at his lips.

"I was watching her this morning, to see where she went, etc., etc. Nothing serious, just doing some research," Alina explained. "She went into work and then came running out again a few minutes later. She headed to her car and one of Gomez's men took a shot at her."

Damon's eyes narrowed and he stared at her, his attention arrested. "What?"

"Right in the parking lot, with no silencer, right in broad daylight," Viper said disgustedly. "You should have seen the rifle they used. These guys really are ridiculous. They have no sense of discretion whatsoever."

"Not everyone can be as skilled as we are," Damon murmured, his eyes dancing. "I'm assuming he missed?"

"She dropped her keys and bent down to get them as he fired," Alina answered. "I had a split second to make a decision."

"So, of course, you decided to take the witness," Hawk said dryly.

"Well, it seemed a shame to just let our only solid lead get shot in the head," Viper retorted.

"What happened to the shooter?" Damon asked, sipping his water innocently.

"I slowed him down," Alina said with a shrug.

Hawk nodded, a slow smile lighting his face.

"Of course you did," he murmured, picturing the bullet hole in a black truck's windshield. "Where is Ms. Nuñez now?"

"Safe." Viper capped her water bottle and glanced at her watch. "I have to move her to another location."

"What have you found out from her so far?" Damon asked.

"Gomez is threatening her family."

Alina closed her laptop and stood up.

"What does she have that he needs?" Hawk wondered with a frown.

"I'm going to find out when I move her tonight," Alina said grimly. "If everything goes the way I want it to, she'll lead me right to Gomez."

"If she does, hands off," Hawk said sharply. His eyes were suddenly arctic. "Gomez is mine."

Viper met his gaze and smiled slightly.

"Understood."

Angela unlocked the front door to her townhouse and glanced at Michael. His hazel eyes were scanning the street, looking for any sign of surveillance. She had to admit she felt much safer with him standing next to her.

"Come on in and make yourself at home," she told him, stepping into the house. "It will only take me a few minutes to get everything together."

"Take your time," Michael said as he followed her in and closed the door behind them.

He glanced around the living room, taking in the wood floors and white walls. The house was spotless, and he was somewhat surprised at the classic elegance of the furniture. Angela had decorated with dark, classical wood furniture contrasting with pristine white walls and light sage-colored sheers at the windows. There was no clutter anywhere and the gleaming wood side tables and coffee table were void of knick-knacks. Aside from a vase here and a framed photograph there, there was nothing to take away from the instant feeling of having stepped into a model room in a furniture store. He didn't know what he had been expecting, but this was not it.

"I'll just run up and get some things together," Angela answered, dropping her keys on a hall stand just inside the door. "Finding the carrier will take a few minutes."

"Carrier?" Michael repeated, his eyes meeting hers in question.

"For Annabelle," Angela explained, "my cat."

Michael's eyebrows raised into his forehead and he turned his head at the sound of a bell tingling down the stairs. An orange tabby cat came trotting into view as if on cue.

"Does Alina know you're bringing your cat?" Michael asked, watching as the cat strutted up to Angela and rubbed its head on her leg. Catching sight of Michael, it stopped and pinned him with a curious look from green cat eyes.

"I may have failed to mention it," Angela admitted with a grin. "Annabelle will be fine there. She's a good cat, and she loves Alina."

Annabelle stared at Michael, unblinking, and he bent down to rub his fingers together. Responding to the invitation, Annabelle cautiously moved toward him, watching him warily.

"I get the feeling all animals love Alina," Michael murmured, watching as Annabelle lifted her face to sniff his hand. After a few seconds of sniffing, she tentatively nudged his hand with her nose. "You do realize she has a wild hawk living in her house, right?"

"It'll be fine," Angela said, unconcerned. "Raven only goes into her bedroom, and Annabelle won't be in there."

Michael stroked the cat and smiled slightly as it started to purr.

"Well, don't say I didn't warn you," he said, glancing at Angela.

"I'll be down in a few," Angela said, waving away the warning with a smile. "There's soda in the fridge if you're thirsty."

She turned to jog up the stairs and Annabelle turned away from Michael abruptly, trotting after her mistress. Michael straightened back up and wandered through the living room into the kitchen. The kitchen was small, but bright and cheerful. The counters were spotless, and the only thing showing signs of heavy use was the coffeemaker in the corner. Opening the fridge, Michael pulled out a Diet Pepsi and closed the door, noting that the fridge was half-empty. Clearly, Angela was not a cook. In fact, Michael got the impression she didn't spend much time at home at all.

Carrying his soda into the living room, he sat down on the couch and pulled out his phone. He was scrolling through his email a few minutes later when his text message alert went off and a message icon appeared on his phone. Touching it, Michael opened the text from Blake.

Are you sure your girl isn't up to something?

Michael grinned and typed a reply.

She's not my girl, and I can't be sure of anything. Why?

He closed his email and waited for Blake to reply. It took a few minutes before his alert went off again.

I just got off a conference call with Stephanie Walker's boss. Looks like her investigation is running into mine. Last time I ran into Ms. Walker, your girl was neck deep in it.

Michael frowned and raised his eyes to stare unseeingly at the white wall on the other side of the room, lost in thought. Was Alina involved again? It was a bit of coincidence that the SEAL was back and Angela had been dragged into Stephanie's investigation, albeit through no fault of her own.

I don't know about her, but one of her friends is neck deep in it.

Michael finally typed back reluctantly. If Blake was going to be working alongside Stephanie, he was going to find out about Angela's involvement eventually.

Great. What am I looking forward to?

A bell jingled as Annabelle came trotting down the stairs and Michael glanced up as Angela followed. She had a large, leopard print overnight bag thrown over her shoulder and a rolling suitcase in either hand. She looked like she packed half her wardrobe. Michaels lips twitched and he lowered his eyes to his phone again.

I can tell you this much, you won't be bored!

Stephanie glanced up as John motioned to her from the door of the make-shift operating room in the maze. Larry had removed Rodrigo's remains and the techs had finished analyzing the real bodily fluid from the fake. She was listening as one of them explained how Rodrigo's torso had to have been positioned when he was cut open, trying not to show her repulsion on her face, when John appeared in the doorway.

"Excuse me a moment," Stephanie murmured, interrupting the tech. "Hold that thought."

She moved out of the area and joined John in the walkway.

"What?"

"You're gonna love this," John told her. "Jessica Nuñez is gone."

Stephanie stared at him.

"What do you mean, gone?" she demanded.

"There was a shooting at her place of work this morning," John answered. "She got to work on time, as usual, and then went flying out again. Her boss said she had a message waiting for her and when she read it, she became visibly upset. As she ran out the door, she said there was an emergency with her husband. Obviously, her boss didn't press her for details. A few minutes later, gunshots were fired in the parking lot. Witnesses say a black sports car, most likely a Camaro, was seen speeding out of the parking lot."

"Did anyone get plates?" Stephanie asked.

"Of course not," John replied. "But it gets better. A black pick-up truck was crashed into another car, right near Jessica's, and witnesses say a man who appeared to be of Latin American descent got out of the truck and fired off rounds at the Camaro as it was leaving."

Stephanie's mouth dropped open.

"We have witnesses to this?"

"Yep. Local police already have the statements and photos." John tucked his hands into his pockets and leaned back on his heels. "Jessica Nuñez hasn't been seen since. Her husband says she called him around the time of the shooting, probably just before, as he was heading into class. He hasn't heard from her since."

"Holy crap," Stephanie breathed, running a hand through her hair. "Get over there and get the statements and photos. Get everything. Interview the husband and the boss. See if anyone saw the driver of the Camaro, or how many people were in it. Whoever it was must have taken Jessica."

"On it," John said, turning to head out of the maze. He paused, then turned to look back at Stephanie. "Sounds like whoever was in the car may have saved Jessica's life."

"Let's find out who it was before we make assumptions," Stephanie said grimly. "Get a BOLO out on Jessica, the pickup truck and the Camaro. Let's find her before the Cartel does."

Viper pulled into the underground parking garage and swiped a badge through the access box. The iron gate blocking the entrance ponderously began to open and she glanced at Jessica.

"No one can get into the parking garage without a resident access card," she told her. "The same card is used to access the elevators. Once you're inside, it's as safe as it can get."

Jessica nodded.

"Thank you," she said.

Alina eased the Jeep forward through the gate and drove onto the ramp leading to the upper levels of the parking garage. She acquired the safe house a month before when she was replacing those that had been compromised two months ago. The building was in the heart of Old City Philadelphia, where the residents paid for a certain level of exclusive elegance and security. She had been impressed with the high level of security provided, and as she pulled around to the assigned parking spot for the condo, Viper took note of the bright lights illuminating the parking level and the abundance of security cameras.

"Once I get you inside, there's no coming out again until I come get you," Alina said, switching off the engine and looking at Jessica. "You understand?"

"I understand," Jessica answered. "I won't do anything stupid. My family's lives depend on it."

"*Your* life depends on it," Alina retorted.

Jessica nodded.

"I know."

Alina nodded and got out of the Jeep, her eyes scanning the parking level. They were the only people there and when she slammed the door shut, the sound echoed through the garage. Jessica climbed out and joined her, looking around.

"There are a lot of cameras," she commented.

"That's a good thing for you," Alina answered, turning toward the alcove a few feet away that led to the elevators. "Come on. Let's get you inside."

Jessica followed her to the elevators and watched as Alina swiped the badge through a scanner at the elevator doors. The doors opened silently and they stepped into the elevator. Once the doors closed, Alina pressed a button and the elevator started moving up.

"How will I know when it's safe?" Jessica asked.

"I'll contact you," Alina told her. "There's a phone in the condo. You can use it to contact me, but not for anything else. You can have no contact with your family, friends, work, not even pizza delivery. You have to assume Gomez has an ear on everyone and everything you've ever known."

"Knowing him, he probably does," Jessica said bitterly.

The elevator stopped with just the slightest of bumps and the doors slid open silently. They stepped into a long hallway, thickly carpeted with deep burgundy pile, and Alina led the way down the hall to a door halfway down and on the left. She pulled out a key and unlocked it, stepping inside.

"It's beautiful!" Jessica exclaimed, following her.

The condo was richly furnished with cream furniture and dove gray carpet. The small entryway was pale gray marble and opened directly into the living room. A large bay window with burgundy drapes over-looked the city, and a wood-burning fireplace took up part of the wall to the left. On the right was a large, eat-in kitchen, and on the left was a hallway leading to the master bedroom.

"There's food in the freezer and I've arranged for more to be delivered if you're still here in a few days," Alina told her, dropping the keys on a side table. "I'm afraid I didn't know what you ate, so I had it stocked with meat. If you're vegetarian, we'll have to arrange something."

"Oh, meat's fine," Jessica assured her with a smile.

Alina nodded and went over to the windows, pulling the drapes across to seal out the night.

"You have cable and a game system, but you can't access the internet from the game system, so don't bother trying," she said, turning to face Jessica. "Do you read?"

"Yes."

"There's a Kindle in the bedroom. You can download whatever books you want to keep yourself occupied."

Alina crossed over to the small dining room and drew the curtains there.

"Why are you doing this for me?" Jessica asked.

Viper glanced at her.

"Because there's no one else who can," she answered simply.

Jessica stared at her for a beat before dropping onto the overstuffed cream sofa.

"Well, thank you," she murmured.

"Tell me why Gomez came after your family," Viper said, crossing back over into the living room and perching on the arm of a matching armchair. "Why you?"

"When I lived in Mexico, before my husband and I were married, Jenaro Gomez was already coming up in the ranks of the Casa Reino Cartel," Jessica began quietly. She raised her dark eyes to Alina's and slipped into Spanish unconsciously. "Even then, he was a ruthless, evil man. I was home from university, visiting my parents, when he came for them. The Cartel was demanding what they called a protection fee from the villagers. They wanted two hundred and fifty dollars a month from them, ostensibly to protect them from other cartels. In reality, it was just extortion. My father refused to pay them. I was not home when Jenaro came. He did unspeakable things to my mother, forcing my father to watch, and then he cut off his head. When I got home, my father's head was hanging from a tree out front by its own ponytail, and my mother was unconscious, laying in a pool of her own blood. They left her to die. I was able to get her to a hospital and she regained consciousness long enough to tell us what happened. She died later that night."

Jessica paused and Alina stood up. She went into the kitchen and returned a moment later with a bottle of water, which she handed to the woman. Jessica nodded thankfully.

"I went back to university with the single goal of getting my degree and getting out of Mexico," she continued after a long drink. "My fiancé

157

was already a professor at that point and he agreed that we would move. He did not want us to raise a family there. Even then, the cartels were starting to take over the local governments and we knew it was only a matter of time before they took over completely. I got my degree and we were married. A few months later, he received a job offer from a college in Arizona. It was the best thing to happen to us. We moved to Arizona and immediately applied for US citizenship. I thought we were safe."

"You weren't?" Viper prompted softly when Jessica didn't continue.

She shook her head slowly.

"No," she said. "What I didn't know was that after the murder of my parents, my cousin went after the Cartel. He managed to kill four soldiers before Jenaro got a hold of him. That's when Jenaro found out about me. He didn't know, until then, that I had been home from school when he massacred my family. He followed us to Arizona. He told me they held me responsible for my cousin's actions and he demanded payment for the four soldiers he killed. It took all our savings, but my husband paid him the money. Jenaro left and went back to Mexico, but we knew he would be back. A man like that, he never lets go once he has you. My husband started talking to head hunters for universities on the east coast, trying to get us as far away as he could. When the offer came from Rutgers, he took it."

"And now Jenaro's back," Viper murmured. "Why? What brought him here?"

Jessica shook her head and sipped the water.

"I don't know," she said. "He's in the middle of something, but I don't know what. He took Marcus, my son, and said if I wanted him back I had to do exactly when he wanted."

"What did he want?"

"All kinds of things," Jessica told her. "He needed identifications and transportation. He made me give him my car for them to use, and made me order breads for the Day of the Dead festival in a week. Then he found out about Rachel."

"Rachel?"

"A good friend of mine. She works at the Mt. Holly Prison Museum. She's a guide there." Jessica drank some more water. "He made me ask for the key to the Dungeon upstairs. I told her I wanted to show someone the cell. He sent one of his soldiers to me and I took him there. He made me carry this heavy bag. When we got inside the cell, he opened it and pulled out...he pulled out an arm."

Jessica shuddered at the memory and Alina raised an eyebrow slightly.

"An arm?" she repeated.

158

"Yes." Jessica looked at her. "It was wrapped up in a white plastic bag."

"What did he do with it?"

"He made me put it behind the dummy in the cell," Jessica told her tiredly.

Chapter Sixteen

"Did you tell her we were coming?" John asked as Stephanie pulled off the road and into the trees. The sun had set long ago and Stephanie switched on her high beams as she navigated down the winding dirt road that led to Alina's house.

"No," Stephanie answered shortly. "I thought it might be better if we caught her off guard."

"Do you really think it's possible to catch the Black Widow off guard?" John demanded, stifling a yawn.

Stephanie glanced at him.

"Possibly not," she admitted with a slight grin.

John turned his attention out the window to the trees. He caught sight of a pair of glowing eyes and watched as a deer backed away into the trees.

"Have you heard anything about Rodrigo's computers yet?" he asked, glancing at his watch.

"Nothing," Stephanie replied. "I'll follow up with tech in the morning, after I meet with Blake Hanover."

The Mustang's tires rolled onto gravel and the trees fell away as they pulled into the clearing where Alina's house was nestled. Stephanie followed the drive past the front of the house and turned left to go around to the detached garage in the back. She and John both raised their eyebrows when they saw a black F-150 and a silver BMW already parked in front of the garage.

"Looks like she has a full house," John murmured. "Is that Angela's car?"

"Yes."

Stephanie pulled behind it with a frown and cut the engine.

"Whose truck?"

"I don't know." Stephanie killed the engine and glanced at John. "It might be Damon's."

John made a face and undid his seat belt.

"I guess you're going to tell me I have to play nice," he muttered and Stephanie chuckled.

"I would, if I thought it would make any difference," she retorted. "Come on. Let's see what the hell they're up to this time."

They got out of the car and turned toward the house. Light poured out from the living room and, as they started across the grass toward the deck, the outside lights switched on. John glanced up to the roof, looking for Raven.

"Where's that damn bird?" he said under his breath.

Stephanie looked at him, amused.

"I'm sure he'll make an appearance," she replied. "There's Angie."

Angela slid open the door on the deck and stepped outside, followed by a tall redhead with broad shoulders. Stephanie's eyebrows soared into her forehead.

"Hi!" Angela called, glancing up at the roof. "I don't know where the hawk is, so you better keep your eyes peeled."

"He's probably off eating some kid for dinner," John retorted as he and Stephanie reached the deck. "You're keeping some shady company here," he added with a grin and a nod to Michael.

Michael held out his hand and grasped John's firmly.

"How's it going, John?" he greeted him with a grin.

"No one's trying to kill me, so it's a good day," John answered, shaking his hand.

"When did you get into town?" Stephanie asked, smiling as Michael turned to her and held out his hand.

"Just yesterday. I was up visiting my folks in Brooklyn," Michael answered easily.

Stephanie nodded and went up the shallow steps to join them on the deck.

"It's good to see you again," she told him.

John placed his foot on the bottom step of the deck and cast his eyes over the roof again. When he didn't see any shadows moving, he continued onto the deck.

WHOOOSH!!!

Raven let out a screech as he swooped down from a tree near the house. Diving in an arc across the deck, he extended his claws in front of him, his eyes fixed on John.

"Holy Mother of Christ!" Michael exclaimed. He ducked out of the way as Raven rushed past his head, the tip of his wing just missing his face.

"For love of God!" John cried at the same time, ducking and jumping off the deck.

161

The large black hawk followed him and John cursed as he covered his head with his arms and dove down into a crouch on the grass. Raven's claws brushed the top of his head before the hawk turned and flew back to the deck, landing on the banister. He hunkered down, staring at John menacingly.

"You better go get Alina," Stephanie told Angela. "She's the only one who can call him off."

Angela stared at her.

"She's not here," she said.

"What?" Stephanie stared back at her. "Where is she?"

"I don't know. She said she was going out." Angela shrugged. "That was a couple of hours ago."

"Does he always do that?" Michael demanded, looking from Raven to John, who was slowly straightening up.

"Only with John," Stephanie replied, her lips twitching despite herself. "He's not a big fan."

"I can see that!" Michael shook his head. "That was crazy!"

"Did I just hear that Lina's not even here?" John called from a safe distance.

"Apparently not," Stephanie replied.

John shook his head and muttered something about insane women and rabid birds. Michael glanced at the hawk, standing guard near the steps, and pulled out his phone.

"I'll text her and see where she is," he said, his lips twitching.

"What are you doing here if Lina's not even here?" Stephanie asked Angela. Her eyes narrowed suspiciously when Angela wouldn't quite meet her gaze.

"I'm just visiting with Michael," Angela answered evasively. "I opened a bottle of wine. I'll get you a glass."

Angela turned to go back into the house, avoiding Stephanie's searching look. Stephanie glanced at Michael, then at John before turning to follow Angela inside.

"I could use a glass of wine," she admitted as she stepped off the deck and into the living room. "It's been a hell of a day."

She looked around as she stepped into the house, noting the case of Diet Pepsi sitting on the island in the kitchen. Stephanie raised an eyebrow and glanced into the dining room. The table had an open white Macbook Pro sitting at one end with a blackberry and an empty soda can. At the other end was a black, widescreen Dell laptop with an external hard-drive plugged into it and a half-empty bottle of beer. The space in between was cluttered with various phone and tablet chargers plugged into an extension cord running from the wall.

"Working late?" Stephanie asked, looking at the mess.

Angela looked over her shoulder from the sidebar cabinet where she was getting a wine glass.

"I had some things I had to take care of, and Michael was checking emails, I think," she murmured, her cheeks flushing a pale pink. Stephanie's eyes narrowed again.

"Interesting," she murmured.

Angela turned around with the wine glass and went over to the bar and an open bottle of Pinot Noir.

"Not really," she said breezily. "I have a project due for a meeting at the end of the week and one of my colleagues emailed me some data for one of the graphs. I figured I would get it taken care of while I was waiting for Lina to get back."

"You don't know where she went?" Stephanie asked, setting her purse and keys down on the bar.

"No. You know Lina. She doesn't say much," Angela answered. She handed her the glass of wine and summoned up a carefree smile. "Cheers!"

"Cheers," Stephanie murmured, raising the glass to her lips. She sipped the wine and studied Angela over the rim of the glass. "Have you seen Mr. Hunk O' Mysterious?"

"No. I think she scared him off again," Angela said, shaking her head. "You know, if I had a man that looked like that coming after me, I wouldn't be running in the other direction. I'd have him locked up at home. I just don't understand Alina at all."

"I don't think God himself understands Alina," Stephanie answered with a grin. "Has he left again?"

"I don't know. Michael said he was here yesterday, but I haven't seen him today." Angela shrugged. "He seems to just come and go. They're strange, those two. It's like they never sit still for more than a day and then one of them is off again!"

Stephanie sipped her wine and was silent. While she knew why that was, Angela did not. When Alina decided to keep Angela in the dark about her identity, Stephanie had agreed readily. Not only did she think Angela wouldn't be able to handle just what, exactly, her old friend did for a living, but Stephanie knew first-hand just how dangerous it was to be part of Viper's world. Angela wouldn't last a day.

The door to the deck slid open and Michael stepped inside, tucking his phone away into his pocket.

"Alina will be here in a few minutes," he announced, sliding the door closed behind him. "John and the bird seem to have come to an understanding."

"What's that?" Stephanie asked, raising her eyebrows.

Michael grinned.

"John is sitting on the grass and the bird is settled down on the banister," he replied.

Stephanie burst out laughing.

"Poor John," she said.

"I've never seen anything like it," Michael said, crossing into the dining room and picking up the half-empty beer bottle. "As soon as John starts toward the steps, that bird stands up and gives every indication he'll claw his eyes out. If it was a dog, he'd be growling."

"Raven really doesn't like John," Angela said with a grin. "Can't say I blame him. He's an ass."

"He's gotten better," Stephanie protested. Angela snorted and sipped her wine.

"I'll take your word for it," she retorted. "Did she say where she was?" she asked Michael.

"No. Just that she was a few minutes out," Michael answered before he drained what was left of the beer and headed into the kitchen. "I'm going to take a beer out to John to make his exile more comfortable."

"I'm kind of surprised Raven lets you come and go," Stephanie remarked. "He still buzzes my head occasionally."

"Oh, I give him wide berth," Michael assured her with a laugh. He opened the fridge and pulled out two more bottles of beer. "I have nothing but respect for anything with claws and a beak that large."

"Wise man," Angela said with a laugh.

"Or extremely foolish," Michael retorted, turning to head back outside with the beer. "These days, I'm starting to wonder."

Alina stopped at a red light on route 70 and stifled a yawn, glancing at the clock on the dashboard. It was after nine and she was on her way home. Her mind was still processing all that Jessica told her. She had been extremely forthcoming with information, answering every question Alina asked with a straight-forward, no nonsense attitude Viper appreciated. The hell on earth that Jenaro Gomez had created for the woman was staggering, but Viper knew Jessica was just one of many. The cartels were turning Mexico into an apocalyptic state.

Her phone beeped from her pocket, pulling her thoughts away from Jenaro, and Alina pulled it out. She glanced at the text alert and swiped the screen, reading the text from Michael quickly.

Might have a little problem here.

Alina raised her eyebrow and hit her hands-free button to call him. He picked up after one ring.

"Define little problem," she said, dispensing with greetings. The light turned green and she hit the gas.

"Stephanie and John showed up," Michael answered.

"So?"

"So did your bird," he said simply.

Alina paused as understanding hit and her lips twitched.

"Does John still have eyes?" she asked after a short silence.

"For now," Michael answered.

"I'm about ten minutes out," Alina told him, turning off the highway and switching on her brights.

"See you soon," Michael said and Alina disconnected.

She dropped the phone on the seat beside her and lowered the gas pedal. What did Stephanie want now? Had she found out about Angela's credentials being used by Rodrigo? Alina sighed. She didn't like it when Stephanie showed up unannounced. It usually meant she wanted information from her, information Viper usually wasn't willing to give.

Perhaps settling in New Jersey wasn't the smartest move, Alina admitted to herself as she sped through the darkness of the Pine Barrens, keeping a wary eye out for deer. It was turning out to be more complicated than she anticipated. She had thought she would be able to keep her old friends at a distance, and to a certain extent she had. But then Michael showed up, and Rodrigo started leaving his body parts laying around, and now Angela was mixed up in some kind of hacking scam. Jenaro Gomez was looking for Hawk, and Hawk was pursuing her. Really, it was getting to be ridiculous. These things just didn't happen anywhere else. If she had an ounce of sense, she would get the hell out of Jersey and stay out.

Inexplicably, Alina's mind flashed back to the memory of Angela lying face down in her arms, blood seeping through a ridiculous brown trench coat. She sighed imperceptibly. If she left Jersey, Angela would be on her own when she needed Viper the most. She didn't know it, but she was in more danger now than she had been last Spring when a bullet tore through her shoulder and out her chest. Then, she had simply been in the wrong place at the wrong time. Now, someone had deliberately pulled Angela into their spider web of intrigue.

Viper's eyes narrowed coldly.

They were about to find out what a mistake that was.

"So, tell me what's going on," Stephanie said as she sunk onto the chocolate brown sofa and sipped her wine.

Angela sat down on the other end of the sofa.

"What do you mean?" she asked innocently.

Stephanie looked at her, amused.

"There's a case of soda on the bar, your laptop on the table, and all your chargers plugged in and charging, including your phone," she replied calmly. "Lina never touches soda, but you live on it. Your purse and keys are nowhere in sight and, if you were just hanging out with Michael waiting for Alina to come back, your purse and keys would be with your laptop. You wouldn't be charging your phone unless you knew you weren't going home to charge it, and the same goes for your tablet. So, I say again, tell me what's going on."

Angela wrinkled her nose and sipped her wine.

"Sometimes I really hate it that you're a detective," she muttered.

"But I am, so you might as well come clean," Stephanie retorted. "Obviously, you're staying with Alina. Why?"

"I...something happened and she thought it would be better if I stayed here for a few days," Angela said evasively.

Stephanie raised an eyebrow.

"What happened?" she asked.

Before Angela could answer, tires crunched on gravel and the spotlights outside flashed on.

"Alina must be back," Angela announced in relief and jumped up.

Stephanie sighed and got up to follow Angie out the sliding door. They watched as a black Jeep Rubicon pulled up behind Michael's truck. Raven straightened to attention and his shiny eyes watched as Alina got out of the Jeep. She was dressed in black SWAT-style cargo pants and a black tank top, layered under a lightweight black nylon jacket. Her hair was pulled back into a braid at the back of her head, and she looked as menacing as her hawk as she closed the door and turned toward the deck.

"It's about time you showed up," John called from his seat in the grass next to Michael. "Your guard dog won't let me near the house."

Alina flicked him a brief glance before turning her gaze back to her pet. Michael stood up and watched as she moved toward the deck, her eyes locked on Raven's.

"What's she doing?" he asked John.

"Talking to it," John muttered, getting to his feet and brushing some dead leaves off his jeans. "Don't ask."

Alina ignored them as she passed, her attention focused on the hawk perched on the banister of the deck. Michael watched, transfixed, as she walked up to the deck and held out her arm. Raven hopped from the banister onto her arm, his black eyes locked on hers. As the hawk settled onto her arm, the two black figures appeared to join as one in the shadows. Michael blinked. The razor sharp claws didn't appear to make any impression on Alina as she murmured something in a low voice he couldn't understand. The hawk made a sound low in its throat in response and Alina turned her head toward Michael and John.

"Go on inside," she told them.

John started toward the deck, taking a wide path around the two. Michael waited until John had made it safely onto the deck without a murmur of protest from the hawk before he moved forward.

"You're just a never-ending barrel of fascination," he murmured as he passed Alina and Raven.

Her eyes met his and she smiled faintly.

"Don't worry. I'm not a witch," she murmured. "I won't put a spell on you."

"Too late for that," he retorted.

He went up onto the deck and turned to watch as Alina murmured something more to Raven. The hawk bobbed its head and launched off her arm, disappearing into the dark trees. Alina watched him go, then turned and strode onto the deck. She looked at them all standing there, collected outside the door, and raised an eyebrow.

"Am I having a party I didn't know about?" she asked dryly.

"Yep! You have wine and beer," Angela answered promptly with a grin. "Come on in!"

Alina glanced at Michael and caught the laughter in his eyes. She shook her head slightly.

"I told you that you couldn't hide from us anymore," he murmured as she passed him.

"I hope you don't mind us dropping by," Stephanie said, following her inside. "I didn't know you had a full house."

"Neither did I," Alina murmured humorously. She waited until everyone was inside before she slid the door shut after a brief, searching glance outside. "Is everything ok?" she asked, her gaze cutting to Stephanie.

"Depends on what you consider ok," Stephanie replied with a grimace. "It's been a long day."

"I'll second that," Alina said. "Is there any wine left?"

"Enough for a glass," Angela answered, heading back to the couch.

Alina nodded and turned toward the bar. Her eyes fell on the case of soda and she raised an eyebrow. Without a word, she picked up the case and continued into the kitchen, opening the fridge and sliding it onto the bottom shelf.

"Where's Damon?" Stephanie asked, leaning on the bar with her glass of wine as John and Michael joined Angela in the living room.

"I'm not sure," Alina replied, turning from the fridge. She opened a cabinet and took out a red wine glass. "He stopped by this afternoon for a few minutes, then left again."

"That doesn't raise any questions for you?" John asked from the living room.

Alina picked up the wine and poured what was left into her glass, her dark eyes glinting as they glanced at John.

"Not especially," she answered. "I'm not his keeper."

"I don't understand you guys at all," Angela announced from the sofa. "He says he came to see you, but as far as I can see, he's not seeing you. So, what's he doing?"

"I don't think you need to be worried about what Damon is doing," Alina said, moving into the living room with her wine. She perched on the arm of the recliner where Michael had settled himself.

"Well, that depends on what he's doing," John muttered.

Alina's eyes glinted dangerously and Stephanie hastened to intercede before John prodded Viper too far.

"I'm still waiting on an answer from Angela as to what *she's* doing," she said, joining Angela and John on the sofa. "Why is she staying with you?"

Alina glanced at Angela.

"You didn't tell her?" she asked her, sipping her wine. Angela shook her head.

"Not yet."

"You need to," Alina told her calmly.

"Tell me what?" Stephanie asked. She looked from Angela to Alina and back again.

"I told you something happened," Angela said slowly, twirling her wine glass absently in her hand. "I've gotten into a....situation."

"That's one way of putting it," Michael murmured.

Alina's lips twitched and she shot him a glance, her eyes dancing.

"Oh, spit it out, Angie," John said impatiently. "What happened?"

Alina watched as Angela's cheeks flushed and she hesitated. Alina sighed.

"Rodrigo Frietas stole Angela's network credentials at the bank and used them to hack into the mainframe before he started turning up in pieces," Alina told Stephanie and John matter-of-factly. Angela shot her a look of relief mixed with thanks. "Now, she's being followed by a man in a

168

navy sedan. I suggested she stay here for a few days where she's protected by my security system."

Stephanie's mouth dropped open and John stared at Alina, stunned.

"What?!" Stephanie found her voice first and swung around to stare at Angela. "When did you find this out?"

"Yesterday," Angela told her. "I got called into work by the IT department. They saw the logs on Rodrigo's computer when they were getting it ready for the FBI to pick up today."

"Hold on." John leaned forward and set his empty beer bottle on the coffee table. "The IT department called you? Why would they do that?"

"Because of the security breach, I had to change all my network credentials," Angela explained. "Obviously, they had to tell me why."

"How did Rodrigo get your credentials?" Stephanie demanded. "Did you know him?"

"Barely." Angela finished her wine and set the glass down. "I met him a few months ago when a bunch of us went out for happy hour. I only knew him in passing. He was a friend of a friend of a friend."

"You could have told me!" Stephanie exclaimed. Angela looked surprised.

"Why would I?" she asked.

"Because he was my informant!" Stephanie told her.

Angela gasped.

"You mean, *you're* the FBI agent investigating his death?" she asked.

"I told you she should know," Alina murmured. She got up and picked up Angela's empty wine glass.

"You knew she was the agent in charge?" Angela demanded, looking at Alina. "Why didn't you tell me?!"

"It wasn't my place to," Alina replied with a shrug and turned to go into the dining room. "I think we're going to need another bottle of wine," she added as Angela sputtered incoherently on the sofa.

"Ok. Let's start at the beginning," John suggested calmly. "When did your IT department contact you?"

"Yesterday."

"When yesterday?"

"Oh, uh, in the morning." Angela thought for a minute. "It was just after I left the gym, so it must have been around eleven."

"They called your personal cell?" Stephanie asked.

"No. They called my work blackberry. They said my credentials had been compromised and I would need to come in and change all my passwords."

"Did they say what happened?"

"Well, he told me that Rodrigo's head had been found and that my network credentials had been used on his PC to access the bank mainframe," Angela told them. "Because of the severity of the situation, he suggested I come into the office and change all my passwords as soon as possible. I went in last night and met him at the IT building."

"You just up and went into an empty building at night because someone told you to?" John demanded incredulously. "Are you an idiot?!"

Angela glared at him and pressed her lips together. Her eyes narrowed.

"The building wasn't empty," she snapped. "This is how things are done at a bank. You can't just change your password over VPN if it's been compromised. At my level, I have to be physically hardwired into the network. Normally, he would have come to my desk, but he said he was in the middle of something and I had no reason to doubt him. I called him at his desk phone on my way and he was already inside a secure building. Short of asking for ID and a background check, I did everything I could to make sure it was safe."

Alina's lips twitched as she twisted the corkscrew into the cork. She could hear the contempt dripping from Angela's voice and knew John had hit a nerve.

"When did he tell you about Rodrigo's head?" Stephanie asked suddenly.

Alina glanced up from the bottle of wine at the cutting edge to Stephanie's voice. Her eyes narrowed slightly and she paused in the act of withdrawing the cork. Michael glanced at her, his eyes mirroring her sudden attention.

"When he called me, I think," Angela answered.

"Are you sure?"

"I don't know. I think so." Angela frowned, flustered. "Let me think. Yes. It was when he called me. He said it was a nasty business with his head. I didn't know what he meant until I saw him later. I thought he meant Rodrigo had hit his head." Angela looked back and forth between Stephanie and John as a heavy silence fell in the room. "Why?"

Alina's lips tightened and her hands stilled. Viper waited for Stephanie to confirm what she already guessed.

"Whoever you spoke to couldn't have known we found Rodrigo's head yesterday morning," Stephanie told her grimly. "That wasn't made public until last night."

Viper released her breath and pulled the cork out of the wine bottle, meeting Michael's glance across the room. He looked grim.

"Who did you speak to?" John asked suddenly.

Next Exit, Dead Ahead

"What?"

"The name!" John said impatiently. "What's the name of your IT guy who called you?"

"Kwan," Angela answered. "Lowell Kwan."

Chapter Seventeen

"For the love of God, Angie, what the hell did you get yourself into?" Stephanie muttered, finishing her wine in one gulp.

"Me?" Angela exclaimed. "You think I'm happy some geek hacked the mainframe with my credentials and then went and got his head cut off?!" She twisted around on the sofa and glared over the back at Alina. "See? I told you I shouldn't tell her. She's thinks it's my fault!"

"No one thinks it's your fault," Alina said calmly, walking over and handing her a full wine glass.

Without a word, Stephanie passed Alina her empty glass. Alina suppressed a grin and went to refill it.

"I'm assuming the name Lowell Kwan means something to you two?" Michael asked, breaking his silence and reminding them of his presence.

Stephanie glanced at him.

"Yes," she said. "We think he's the head of the hacking ring we're investigating."

"You mean...you mean *he's* one of them?" Angela asked. Her mouth dropped open.

"I believe so," Stephanie said tiredly. "I have no proof, yet. You said someone was following you? When did that start?"

"Last night. I saw them after I got home, and then again this morning," Angela told her. "That's when I called Lina. I wanted to know if I was crazy."

Stephanie and John looked at Alina as she came into the living room and handed Stephanie her full glass back. She smiled slightly.

"She's crazy, but not because of that," Alina answered the unspoken question in both their faces. "A navy sedan followed her. I have it on my security footage. I would have a name for you, but this one was over-enthusiastic and scared him away," she added and motioned to Michael.

He made a face at her.

172

"I didn't know what you were doing," he retorted. "I saw someone acting shady and took care of it."

"Do we have anything to go on?" John asked. "Anything at all?"

"Of course!" Alina went back to her seat on the arm of Michael's chair. "I have the car and tag number on camera. Give me five minutes and I'll have a name for you."

"How about you give *me* the video and let me handle it?" Stephanie asked dryly.

"I think Ms. Walker is asserting her jurisdictional superiority," Michael murmured, drawing a faint smile from Alina.

"Sorry," Stephanie said with a sheepish grin. "It's habit. I'm used to doing everything."

"Well, this is something I can do for you," Alina said easily. "Use me while you have me."

"If Lowell is part of this whole thing, then why did he have me change my passwords?" Angela asked suddenly. "Why didn't he stay quiet and leave it to the FBI to hang me? Why the show?"

Alina glanced at Angela, her eyes glinting in appreciation. Angela was quicker than any of them gave her credit for, and Alina was amused at the sudden look of comprehension that crossed Stephanie's face.

"Oh my God," she breathed, her eyes widening. She looked at Alina. "That's why you want her here where you can keep an eye on her!"

Alina nodded.

"He got what he needed from her," she said quietly. "She's a liability now."

"Hello? I'm sure this all makes perfect sense to you, but I'm in the dark over here," John interrupted. "What did he get? Why is she a liability now?"

"Rodrigo used Angela's credentials to get into the mainframe and presumably plant some kind of a virus," Stephanie explained, "but then he disappeared. Lowell would have been able to see whose credentials Rodrigo used, but not the password. With Rodrigo dead, the only other person who would know the password used is Angela."

John stared at Stephanie.

"So, he called her in and had her change her passwords," he said slowly. Understanding burst upon him suddenly. "She had to type the old password in to change them!"

"Giving Lowell the password Rodrigo used to access the mainframe," Stephanie finished.

"But...if Rodrigo already planted a virus, why does Lowell need to get back in there?" Angela asked, frowning.

"It depends on what the virus is doing," Michael answered her. "If

173

it's gathering information, it could be linked to a harvesting program that only responds to the credentials used to set it up."

"Or, if he's being thorough, he could be going back into the mainframe to remove it before it's detected," Stephanie added. "I'm leaning towards what you said, though, Michael. They're too smart to run the risk of getting caught going in to take the virus out. Unfortunately, we won't know until we find out what they did on the mainframe."

"So he used me?" Angela demanded. "And now what? Now he's just going to kill me?"

"Something like that," Alina said cheerfully. "Aren't you glad you came over for lunch now?"

"I think I should have her moved to one of our safe houses." Stephanie ignored Angela's indignant sputter. "I can't let you take on responsibility for her."

Alina met Stephanie's gaze, amused.

"Do you really think your agency can do a better job of protecting her?" Viper asked softly.

Stephanie flushed slightly.

"That's not the point," she muttered. "It puts you in danger, too."

John started to laugh, but covered it up with a cough when Angela looked at him.

"Steph's right, Lina," Angela said. "If all this is true and I stay here, I'm putting you at risk."

"Don't be ridiculous," Alina said shortly, standing up.

"Well, if Michael stays too, then at least we have a Federal agent in the house," Angela mused slowly.

Stephanie glared at John as he started coughing again.

"I'd feel better if I knew Michael was here," she agreed, resisting the urge to laugh by biting the inside of her lip. Hard.

"I can postpone going back to Brooklyn for a day or two," Michael announced, his eyes dancing. Alina's dark eyes met his and he almost burst out laughing at the look of exasperation in their depths. "Do you have enough spare rooms?"

"I'm sure we can work something out," Viper replied, her face impassive.

She picked up her empty wine glass and went into the dining room. She felt like she was in the middle of a Vaudevillian farce. What the hell was she doing? Alina picked up the wine bottle and refilled her glass. If Harry ever got wind of this, he would never let her live it down. A Secret Service agent was supposed to protect *her*?

"That's settled, then," Angela said cheerfully. "I won't be any trouble, Lina. I promise."

174

Next Exit, Dead Ahead

Alina sipped her wine and turned around. Before she could open her mouth to answer, there was a sudden crash upstairs. Her gaze flew to the hallway as something banged at the top of the stairs. Alina set down the wine glass and was reaching behind her back for her gun when a high-pitched screech echoed down the stairs, pausing her hand.

Yeeooow!

A bell jingled frantically as something galloped down the stairs and a flash of orange streaked down the hallway and through the living room. Viper raised an eyebrow as Raven dropped over the banister and landed on the floor in the hallway, his black eyes darting into the living room. A loud, guttural growl was followed by an even louder hiss from behind the recliner and Alina moved into the living room, tilting her head to look behind the chair. A pair of panic-stricken green eyes stared back at her from an enormous poof of orange and white fur.

Viper blinked.

"Why does there appear to be a cat in my living room?" she asked softly.

The silence in the room was deafening.

Alina turned around slowly, pinning Angela with an astounded look.

"Did you really bring your cat into a house with a wild hawk?" she asked incredulously.

"I didn't think Raven would know she was here," Angela stammered. "I thought he only went into your bedroom. I didn't think Annabelle would go in there."

Alina stared at her speechlessly. Out of the corner of her eye, she saw Raven hop up onto the bar and start moving toward the end that was more in line with the recliner. Annabelle made her protest known by hissing again and letting out a loud spit.

"Stop!"

Viper spoke sharply and Annabelle abruptly stopped hissing. She hunkered down behind the chair and stared up at Alina with huge eyes. Turning her head to Raven, Alina stared at him silently. He stopped walking along the bar and settled down, glowering at her with his black eyes. When they were both quiet and still, Alina turned her attention back to Angela.

"You do realize that Raven eats small animals?" she asked softly.

Angela just stared back at her.

"I couldn't leave Annabelle alone in the house," she said defensively. "What was I supposed to do?"

"I warned her," Michael said. A grin tugged at his lips. "I tried."

"You should have tried harder," John remarked and glanced over the couch at Raven. "My bet's on the bird. I'll put twenty dollars on it."

175

"Oh John, for God's Sake," Stephanie said disgustedly.

"What?" he asked innocently.

"Angie, come here," Alina said, shaking her head. "You take Annabelle and I'll take Raven."

"What are you going to do?" Angela asked, coming over and reaching behind the chair to pick up the hyper-extended ball of fur that was her cat.

"Try to defuse the situation," Alina retorted shortly and moved toward Raven.

When Angela picked up the cat, Raven straightened up, watching them with his beady black eyes. With his mistress advancing upon him, he shifted from one foot to another, bobbing his head. Alina held out her arm and he stepped onto it, his eyes darting between hers and the cat. Alina began to murmur something in a low voice and the hawk shook his head sharply, fluffing out his feathers and shifting his weight between his feet. Ignoring his obvious displeasure, Alina continued to murmur quietly, holding her arm up so the hawk was at eye level with her.

Stephanie shook her head, watching as Alina mesmerized the hawk effortlessly. She had seen her old friend do this before through the years, but each time it was still just as bizarre. She would never understand this knack Alina had of communicating with animals.

"You're lucky Lina can control that thing," John told Angela quietly.

"So are you," Angela retorted. "You would have lost twenty bucks."

They all watched as Alina turned, moving out of the living room and down the hallway with Raven still perched on her arm.

"Did you even close her bedroom door?" Stephanie asked as Alina disappeared up the stairs with the hawk. "How did Annabelle get in there?"

"I thought I did," Angela answered, carrying the cat over to the couch and sinking down. She stroked Annabelle's back absently. "I guess it wasn't completely latched."

"Poor Annabelle," Stephanie crooned and reached out to rub her head. "Did the big bird scare you?"

Annabelle started purring and her fur began to settle back down as she was fussed over by Stephanie and Angela. Michael looked at John and grinned as John rolled his eyes.

"I think I would have bet on the bird, too," he told him.

Next Exit, Dead Ahead

The comfortable blackness of nothing disappeared as Viper came awake with a start. Her heart surged into her throat and her eyes popped open, awareness streaking through her like lightning. Something had shifted in the dead of night, unceremoniously pulling her from the darkness of her dreams. Her bedroom was dark and the house was silent, but something had disturbed the peace.

Alina didn't move. She concentrated on the silence, detecting where the movement that had awakened her originated. After a second, she exhaled silently. Someone was in the room with her. She could hear their heartbeat and feel their presence.

Viper's fingers closed around the handle of her Ruger, tucked between the mattress and box spring. She rolled over swiftly, withdrawing the gun in the same movement and aiming it at the shadow standing near the window. Her finger stilled on the trigger when she saw a familiar outline of broad shoulders highlighted by the moonlight filtering through the sheer curtains.

"Sweet Lord, you're living dangerously, Hawk," she hissed, sliding her finger off the trigger and lowering the pistol.

"I was starting to wonder if you were going to wake up," Hawk retorted. "I've been here for almost a minute."

"I woke up the second you came in," Viper muttered. She set the gun on the nightstand and sat up with a yawn.

"You have a full house," Hawk said, crossing the room silently toward the bed. He was dressed in black and moved with that jungle-cat grace she knew so well. "What's going on?"

"You don't want to know," Alina muttered, running a hand through her hair. She leaned back on the headboard and watched as he sat on the edge of the bed. "Where were you?"

"Taking care of some business," Hawk answered vaguely. "Where's Raven?"

Alina glanced at the empty perch in the corner of the bedroom and grimaced slightly.

"Out sulking," she said. "There was an incident earlier and he wasn't happy with the results."

Damon raised an eyebrow.

"What happened?"

"Angela brought her cat into the house and I stopped him from ripping it apart," Alina answered bluntly.

Damon stared at her for a beat before his lips curved into a grin.

"I keep missing all the fun," he murmured. "What's the gunny doing here?"

"Angela thought it would be a good idea to have a Federal agent in the house. She seems to think she's putting me in danger by being here," Viper told him, her lips twitching humorously.

"Excuse me?"

"You heard me."

Damon stared at her for a beat before his shoulders started to shake silently with laughter.

"Harry would love this," he said chuckled.

Alina smiled reluctantly and shook her head slightly.

"Harry can never hear about this. I would never hear the end of it. I don't know how much longer I can play the normal life card with Angela," she admitted. "This is more complicated than I thought it would be. Charlie would be appalled if he knew."

"You know, I don't have these problems on my ranch," Damon murmured with an unholy grin on his face. "No one bothers me and no one questions what I do. I think it must be Jersey. Y'all are a breed onto yourselves here."

"Did you just 'y'all' me?" Viper demanded, her eyes dancing.

Damon winked.

"Tell me about Jessica," he said, changing the subject abruptly.

Pulling his Beretta from his back holster, he set it on the nightstand next to her Ruger before stretching out on the bed next to her. He propped his shoulders against the headboard and turned his head to look at her, his face inches from hers. Alina raised an eyebrow.

"Comfortable?" she asked politely.

He smiled slowly.

"Very."

"Jessica is somewhere safe," Viper told him, ignoring the wicked grin on his face. "Jenaro has her son."

"What?" The amusement disappeared from Hawk's face at her words. "Where?"

"I don't know. He took him last week to ensure her cooperation. He's had her running errands for him and has been using her address for IDs, etc. She's done everything he asked for fear of what he will do to her son."

"Hell." Damon frowned ferociously and stared across the dark bedroom, crossing his arms over his chest. "How old is he?"

"Seven." Viper leaned her head back. "If he's still alive, he could be anywhere. You know the cartels are human-traffickers. He could be halfway around the world by now."

"Do you think that's what he did?" Hawk asked, shooting her a sharp look.

Viper hesitated for a second, then slowly shook her head.

"No," she answered. "I think he's using him here somehow. If Jenaro wanted to sell a child, Jessica has a four-year-old daughter who would make him more money. I have the feeling the boy's still close by."

"If he is, then Jenaro has him stashed away somewhere, out of sight." Damon rubbed his jaw tiredly. "I've been watching them and there's no sign of a child there."

Viper glanced at him sharply.

"You found him?" she asked.

Hawk's smile was cold and deadly.

"Of course," he said softly.

"And you haven't seen the boy?" Viper pursed her lips thoughtfully. "I wonder what he's up to."

"The child makes things more complicated," Hawk murmured. He stacked his hands behind his head and stared at the ceiling. "I'm assuming you told Jessica you would find him?"

"I didn't tell her anything," Viper retorted, "but I *will* find him. I'm not going to let someone like Gomez get away with her son."

"Just remember, Jenaro's mine," Hawk told her, his voice like ice.

"I'll do my best," she said, unfazed by the harshness in his voice.

"Anything new with the Fearless Feds?" Damon asked, changing the subject again.

"Yes, but I don't know what it is. They came here tonight for a reason, but never got around to addressing it. They weren't expecting Angela and Michael. They did drop a name tonight. Lowell Kwan. I'll run it in the morning."

"Lowell Kwan?" Damon glanced at her.

"Mmm." Alina yawned. "They think he's the one who was running Rodrigo."

There was a scraping noise on the roof and they both looked up as the skylight swung open. Raven dropped into the room and onto his perch, shook out his feathers, and looked at them curiously.

"The prodigal bird returns," Damon murmured. "Should I be worried?"

Alina smiled faintly as Raven bobbed his head and settled down on his perch to clean under his feathers.

"I've told you already. He likes you," she replied. "Michael had to call me earlier because Raven wouldn't let John up on the deck. When I got here, John was sitting in the grass and Raven was standing guard on the banister."

"Good bird," Damon said to the hawk.

Raven lifted his head to nod at Damon, then went back to cleaning his feathers.

179

Alina chuckled and settled back down under the covers. "He has his moments," she murmured contentedly.

Chapter Eighteen

The sun was just starting to rise, lighting the sky with a pale gray tinge, when birds started chirping outside. Alina let go of the wispy tendrils of sleep still clinging to her consciousness and rolled over.

"Ooof."

Her eyes popped open as she rolled into a warm, solid wall of skin. Damon was laying with his back to her, fast asleep under the covers. She frowned at the strange feeling of contentment that washed over her as she inhaled the warm, comfortable smell of his skin. Had she gone to sleep with him there? And why did it feel so right to have him sleeping next to her?

Alina stared at the back of his shoulders, resisting the sudden urge to trace the long scar that ran down his back. It was an old scar, and even though she had seen it before, it still served to remind her of their inescapable mortality. They survived only through the will of fate and luck, she and Hawk, and one day they would face a wound that would leave no scar, only their memory. It was a statistical probability she had known before she walked through the doors of the training facility five years ago. She willingly accepted it, deciding then the risk was well worth the opportunity to fight for those who could not fight for themselves. She and Hawk were two of a few, a select, who would do the impossible to eliminate the untouchable, even if it meant giving their lives. They did what others could not do, knowing the price they would pay would be greater than what most were willing to contemplate. It was who they were. It was what they did. And it had never bothered her.

Until now.

Alina lifted her eyes from the faded scar on Hawk's back with a slight frown. Absurdly, she thought of two bull mastiffs on a ranch somewhere out in the middle of Boondocks, Nowhere, USA. Who would take care of them if Hawk didn't come home? A shaft of something painful sliced through the contentment and Alina scowled.

What was it about Jersey that made her forget who she was? There was no place in her life for thoughts like these. Viper had a job to do, and so did Hawk.

Alina poked him in the back sharply with her finger.

"What?" he murmured, his voice husky with sleep.

"You're in my bed," she told him crossly.

Damon rolled onto his back and turned his head to look at her. Too late, Alina realized she had been better off staring at his back. His dark hair fell over his forehead in disarray and his eyes were startlingly blue in a face still flushed from sleep. His jaw was lined with dark stubble and he scratched it absently, yawning widely.

"You say that like it's a bad thing," he said, his full lips curving into a grin as she glowered at him.

Ignoring the sudden jump in her heart rate, Viper sat up, putting some distance between them.

"I don't remember inviting you," she said. Any menacing effect that statement may have had was lost when she slipped into a jaw-cracking yawn.

Damon watched her lazily, his gaze unreadable.

"I don't remember asking," he retorted. Viper glanced at him, her eyes flashing, and he grinned unabashedly. "In fact, I don't even remember falling asleep," he added.

Viper's flash of annoyance evaporated and she chuckled reluctantly.

"Neither do I," she admitted, tossing the down comforter aside and swinging her legs out of bed. "You'd better get moving before the natives start stirring. The last thing I need is Angela seeing you slink out of my bedroom."

"Angela?" Damon propped himself up with pillows and watched as she headed toward the master bathroom. His eyes slipped to her long legs appreciatively. "I thought you'd be more worried about your Marine."

Alina glanced over her shoulder, laughter lighting her dark eyes and making them glow.

"I can handle Michael," she replied. "Angela, however, is a whole other matter."

"Don't tell me Viper is afraid of a banker!" Hawk murmured, his eyes dancing.

Her response was to hold up the finger as she disappeared into the bathroom. Damon chuckled and glanced up to the perch in the corner of the bedroom.

"Is she always this moody in the morning?" he asked the hawk conversationally. Raven lifted his beak from where it was buried in his feathers and blinked at him. "That's what I thought."

Damon glanced at his watch and yawned again, shaking the

lingering remnants of sleep from his head. He swung his legs out of the bed and reached over to pick up his Beretta, tucking it into the back of his jeans. He smiled faintly as his glance fell on Viper's Ruger. It seemed completely natural to have the two guns sitting side by side on the bedside table. Too natural.

Damon shook his head slightly and stood up. Things were getting more and more complicated with Viper daily. While he was perfectly willing to explore this attraction between them and see where it led, he was also acutely aware of the dangers of engaging in a serious relationship with her. Not only would a relationship increase both their risks of exposure, but it would inevitably become a distraction neither of them could afford. Right now, when he left her, he was able to set Viper completely out of his mind and focus on his job. Damon knew that would become more and more difficult if they continued down this road. It was only a matter of time before one, or both, of them allowed themselves to become distracted.

"What a mess," he muttered and pulled his shirt over his head.

Two months ago, he was on an old goat trail in the mountains above Lima, Peru when he was blind-sided with the sudden realization that he was in love with Viper. Damon knew it would be complicated when he boarded the private jet that carried him back to the United States and into her orbit. He had been as powerless to stop that driving force then as he was now.

The feeling of contentment that had engulfed him since he opened his eyes next to her evaporated as the sun rose on a new day. Of all the women in the world for him to fall for, it had to be *her*. The one woman in the world he couldn't intimidate, couldn't deceive and, worst of all, couldn't ignore. He had never been able to ignore her. She had always been there, poking and prodding deep in his subconscious, surfacing just long enough to remind him that he wasn't alone, that there was someone else who was fighting just as fiercely and losing just as much of herself. Viper had become his mirror over the years. Each time he saw her, she reflected his own shadows back to him. If there was one other person on this God-forsaken earth who knew what monsters really lurked in the darkness, that person was Viper. She fought them too.

She was Hawk's only hope that he could withstand the shadows and hold on to what was left of the Damon Miles he used to know.

"Lina, are you awake? I thought I heard voices."

Angela poked her head into the bedroom and looked around. The bed was a mess, but empty, and Raven was sitting on the perch in the corner of the ceiling. At the sound of her voice, he turned his head and considered her with his shiny black eyes. Angela wrinkled her nose and stepped into the room.

"Lina?" she called.

A crisp breeze blew through the open window and rustled the red sheers. Angela shivered, glancing at the hawk.

"Doesn't she know it's fall?" she asked him, striding over to the window and closing it. "It's freezing out there!"

"Who are you talking to?" Alina asked, emerging from the walk-in closet. She cast a sharp look around the room and breathed a silent sigh of relief at only seeing Angela.

"Raven," Angela replied. "I closed your window. It's freezing in here!"

Alina's eyes rested briefly on the window and a faint smile touched her lips before she turned her attention to the bed. Her eyes fell on her Ruger and she glanced at Angela, who had picked up a book from the dresser and was looking at it cursorily. Alina slid the gun off the bedside table and into her back holster silently.

"You're up early," she said, dropping her shirt over the holster and pulling the comforter and sheet back to the foot of the bed.

"I didn't sleep well," Angela answered with a shrug. "I kept thinking about how I sat in an empty building across from a criminal who wants to kill me. No one knew I was there. He could have killed me and hid my body and no one would have known!"

"Well, he didn't." Alina shook out the fitted sheet and tucked it back under the corner of the mattress. "No point in thinking about it."

"Easy for you to say," Angela muttered. She put the book down and went to the other side of the bed, helping Alina pull the top sheet up and fold it back. "Why do you think he let me go?"

"He's making sure he doesn't need you again," Alina answered bluntly.

"Oh, very nice." Angela glanced at her. "Are you even human?"

Alina laughed and reached for the comforter.

"Well, you asked!" she exclaimed. Angela helped her pull up the comforter and Alina straightened it, glancing at her. There was a strange, hard glint in her eyes that made Angela shiver involuntarily. "Don't worry. He lost his one chance. He won't get another."

"Are you ever afraid of anything?" Angela asked her, straightening up and looking across the bed at her old friend. "Nothing seems to faze you."

"Fear is counter-productive," Alina said shortly. "I don't have time for it."

"Wow! Ok then. How's the weather on your planet?"

"Apparently not as freezing as it is on yours," Alina retorted with a grin.

Angela shook her head and turned toward the door.

"I heard Michael moving around in the other spare room," she said over her shoulder. "Looks like we're all early risers. I think I'll make pancakes. I need something to cheer me up."

Alina glanced at the closed bedroom window before turning to follow her out.

"You'd better make extra," she said. "There might be another one for breakfast."

Stephanie stifled a yawn and opened the door to the small conference room. She was a few minutes early for her meeting with Blake Hanover, the agent from Washington, and Rob. She expected to find the room empty. Instead, there was a man sitting at the oval conference table with a large Wawa coffee next to his laptop. He looked up when the door opened and Stephanie was caught in a sharp gaze from warm brown eyes.

"Oh!" she exclaimed, closing the door behind herself. "I wasn't expecting anyone to be here yet."

"You must be Agent Walker." The man stood up and came around the table, holding out his hand. He was tall, topping six feet, with rich brown hair that fell over his forehead in thick curls. "It's a pleasure to finally meet you. We never got a chance to connect two months ago in Washington."

Stephanie set her coffee down on the table and reached out to shake his hand. His fingers closed around hers firmly and she smiled.

"No, we didn't," she agreed. "It was a little hectic down there. It's nice to finally meet you, Mr. Hanover."

"Call me Blake," he said, releasing her hand with a grin. "When people say Mr. Hanover, I still look around for my father."

"Fair enough," Stephanie said with a laugh. She set her laptop down next to her coffee and watched as Blake went back to his seat. "I thought I would get here early and knock out some email."

Blake glanced at her as he settled down in front of his laptop.

"Great minds think alike," he murmured, picking up his coffee.

Stephanie smiled and sat down, opening her laptop. A comfortable silence fell between the two as they sipped their coffee and typed on their respective machines. Every once in a while, Stephanie found herself glancing across the table at him. He was a rugged man, who looked as if he would have no problem flattening anyone who got in his way. His ruthless charm was tempered, however, by the warm glint in those brown eyes of his. Something about him made Stephanie want to get to know him and have a conversation with him. Blake Hanover was nothing like what she expected.

The door behind her opened suddenly and Rob swept into the room, coffee in hand.

"Good morning!" he greeted them both cheerfully as he closed the door. "Glad to see you both here, bright and early."

Rob was a funnel of energy in the mornings, fueled by caffeine and sugar, and Stephanie grinned as he dropped a battered notebook and pen on the table. Rob was also old-school, eschewing technology in favor of his own, unique shorthand.

"Good morning, Rob." Blake stood again and held out his hand to Rob. His face was creased into an amused grin. "Still carrying around that same, ratty old notebook? We really need to work on that."

"Ha!" Rob laughed, grasping his hand. "My ratty old notebook can't be hacked, deleted or infected with worms."

"True enough," Blake admitted and sat back down.

"You two didn't start without me, did you?" Rob asked, seating himself and glancing at them.

"Of course not," Stephanie answered easily.

"Good." Rob rubbed his hands together and sat back in his seat. "I wanted you to meet face to face. I know you never got the chance down in Washington."

"Small world, really," Blake said with a smile. "What are the odds of running into each other on different cases?"

"Slim," Stephanie agreed with an answering smile.

"Well, I know you're both short on time, so let's get down to business," Rob said. "Since your cases *do* seem to have coincided, it makes it easier to share information. What do you have for us, Blake?"

"Jenaro Gomez is the Lieutenant and second-in-command for the Casa Reino Cartel, answerable only to the head himself," Blake said, closing his laptop and sitting back. He picked up his coffee and sipped it. "They call the new head La Cabeza."

"Not very original," Stephanie murmured.

Blake grinned.

"Not very, no," he agreed. "His real name is Martese Salcedo. Jenaro helped place him in his position after the former leader was found dead a few months ago. He was killed in a fire, along with two other cartel heads. We don't know what they were doing together or why, but there was an explosion and all three were killed. Jenaro was the acting head for a time before he managed to install Salcedo as the successor. Now, the Casa Reino Cartel is regrouping and starting to regain some of its lost footing."

"And Jenaro picked now to come to New Jersey," Stephanie murmured. "Why?"

Blake set his coffee down and opened his laptop again. He pulled up a file and turned the laptop around so Stephanie and Rob could see the picture.

"I think it has something to do with this man," he said.

Stephanie's eyes narrowed on the grainy photo. It was taken in a crowd and the man had his face half-turned toward the camera. Even though the image was clearly taken at a distance, there was no mistaking the identity of the man.

"Philip Chou?" Stephanie asked, looking at Blake sharply. He was watching her closely.

"You know him. Good. That means we're on the right track." Blake turned the laptop around again and sat back in his seat.

"He's one of my suspects," Stephanie said. "I've got an agent watching him and I'm going to see him today. What do you know of him?"

"He ran into Jenaro a few years back," Blake replied. "From what I've been able to piece together, he was a student at Stanford at the time, doing an internship at an import company. He crossed paths with the Casa Reinos then, and the rumor is he ended up stealing a shipment from them."

Stephanie raised an eyebrow and Rob whistled.

"What kind of shipment?" Stephanie asked.

"We think it was probably heroine." Blake shrugged. "Jenaro found out it was Chou that altered the electronic records, but by then, he had already disappeared. I'm working on the theory that Jenaro finally tracked him down here, in New Jersey, and came to settle the debt."

"After, what, four years?" Stephanie asked doubtfully.

"Clearly, you haven't worked with the cartels much," Blake murmured. "They have long memories, and even deeper roots in revenge. You don't just steal a shipment from them and expect them to forget about it."

"And you think that's what brought Jenaro to Jersey." Rob rubbed his jaw thoughtfully. "What's your interest in him?"

"Jenaro Gomez has been directly involved in the murders of no less than six DEA and two FBI agents," Blake said calmly. "He's been on our radar for years. Until now, he's avoided coming anywhere near us."

"Wonderful," Stephanie sighed. "And you think Philip Chou is what brought him out now?"

"Right now, it's my best lead," Blake answered. "Something not only pulled him away from home during a crucial time in the rebuilding process, but it also pulled him out to where we can reach him. Either he's getting over-confident and sloppy, or he's after something much larger than revenge."

"Money," Stephanie said. She raised her eyes to Blake's. "He's after the money."

"What money?"

"Last year, we got some intel indicating that a radical communist cell was hacking into mainframes and siphoning off billions of dollars from various companies," Stephanie explained, glancing at Rob. At his nod, she continued, "We were able to track them down to NicTel, an electronics firm that DHS believes is directly funding North Korea. The trail ran cold there, until a few weeks ago. I was approached by Rodrigo Frietas, a man who claimed to be one of the hackers involved. He wanted to exchange information for protection. According to him, they had expanded from public companies to banks, and were working on two of the main banks on the East Coast."

"Which banks?" Blake asked.

"He was killed before he could tell us, but we believe we've identified them. Philip Chou works at New Federal, and Rodrigo worked at One District."

"What makes you link Chou to this Rodrigo?"

"They worked together at a software firm in Arizona run by a man named Lowell Kwan, who currently holds the title of Regional VP in the IT department of One District Bank," Stephanie told him. "The software firm was doing well when Kwan suddenly up and closed the company. Six months later, all three men turned up in New Jersey, working in the banks IT departments."

"That seems like a solid link to me," Blake muttered. "What happened to Rodrigo?"

"He started showing up in pieces," Stephanie answered grimly.

"I'm sorry?" Blake blinked.

"First his arm, then his head, then his tongue." Stephanie picked up her coffee. "We finally found what was left of him yesterday."

"That's a classic Cartel calling card," Blake said, "especially for Jenaro. He likes to send messages with other people's body parts."

"That's why I called you," Rob said. "We ID'd the person we believe left the arm to start the ball rolling. His name is Lorenzo Porras."

"Lorenzo?" Blake looked up sharply. "Lorenzo's here too?"

"What do you know about him?" Stephanie set aside her cold coffee with a grimace.

"He's Jenaro's cousin by marriage, and he's been rising fast in the Cartel," Blake replied. "If he's here too, it means Jenaro only brought his most trusted soldiers with him."

"Meaning?"

"Meaning whatever these hackers of yours are doing, it's big enough for the Casa Reinos to want in on it," Blake answered. "Jenaro coming here alone was suspicious enough, especially with the unrest among the cartels at home, but if he brought his entourage, it's even bigger than I thought."

"Of course it is," Stephanie muttered. "Why is nothing I get involved in easy anymore?"

Blake grinned and his brown eyes met hers, a glint of pure excitement making them glow.

"What on earth would you want with easy?" he demanded.

Stephanie met his gaze and a reluctant smile curved her lips.

"You're about to find out just how complicated my cases tend to be these days," she told him bluntly. "Ask me that question again when we're all through here."

Chapter Nineteen

Lowell frowned fiercely as he pressed the disconnect button on his phone. Philip still wasn't picking up his phone. He glanced at his watch and his lips tightened. It was almost ten o'clock in the morning and so far, his day was not going remotely as planned. He had lost track of Angela altogether sometime during the night. When he went to bed, the software still had her car sitting in the mall parking lot that didn't exist, but when he got up this morning, it was gone. Somehow, someone had disabled the software on Angela's end, effectively concealing her from him. The only thing he knew for sure was she hadn't come to work today and her voicemail had a message saying she would be out of the office for the rest of the week. His only recourse was to go back to the dirt road in the woods and see if she was still there.

Lowell set down his cell phone and glanced up as a co-worker walked by, nodding to him distractedly. Philip was supposed to have emailed him confirmation when the virus was extracted on his end this morning. So far, he hadn't received any such confirmation. Where *was* he?

Lowell's eyes shifted involuntarily to his email, still open on his laptop. Then, there was *that*. The mystery email. It arrived yesterday, sent from a secured, untraceable IP. Glancing around to make sure no one was within view of his cubicle, Lowell clicked on the email again. There was no message, just a screenshot, pasted into the email. It was a picture of a tongue, laying in a blue Tiffany's box.

He had no doubt whose tongue it was. He was being warned not to talk, as if he would. He spent hours last night trying to back-trace the email, only to come up empty. Whoever sent it was well-versed in the art of concealing their cyber-trail.

Everything was unraveling, all the careful planning and years of preparation. Rodrigo was dead, his tongue in a box, and now Philip was missing. What the hell was going on?

Lowell glanced at his watch again and closed his email. They were on a strict time schedule and he had to start the harvesting program no later than four today. That meant he had until three to find out if Philip had extracted his end. If he hadn't, Lowell would have to override the failsafe.

Standing, he picked up his phone and his keys and turned to leave the cubicle.

They were running out of time.

Blake exited the prison from the main door at the front, a frown creasing his face. Stephanie brought him here after their meeting with Rob to show him the infamous Dungeon and maze. She was still inside speaking to one of the uniforms on duty, and Blake shook his head slightly to himself as he descended the steep prison steps. It took some balls to place an arm in plain view in the middle of the day. Only Jenaro would come up with something so flamboyantly gruesome. What the hell was he driving at? Who was he sending a warning to? Lowell? Philip? Someone else?

Blake paused at the bottom of the steps and turned left to stroll along the brick path. The fact that the prison guide was missing bothered him. He knew Jenaro too well to question where the guide had gone. The only question he had was where they would find her body. Running a hand through his hair absently, Blake paused and turned to look at the busy road in front of the prison. The building sat on a major thoroughfare in the middle of what appeared to be a busy little town. There was rarely a break in the traffic driving by, and pedestrians were milling up and down the street at regular intervals. Behind the prison was the police station, and a few blocks over from *that* was the new county prison. It was hardly a secluded setting. He turned and looked up at the prison. So, why here? What about this place had captured Jenaro's interest?

He turned to continue walking along the pathway, still mulling over the questions in his head, when he sensed he was being watched. Glancing at the busy road again, he paused. His eyes narrowed and he stopped, looking across the busy street.

A woman was on the other side, leaning against a street light. She was dressed all in black and sunglasses concealed most of her face. She had her arms crossed and appeared relaxed as she leaned against the pole watching him. Even from this distance, Blake could sense the dangerous energy surrounding her. They stared at each other for a moment and Blake knew, without a doubt, that he was staring at Michael's mysterious Viper.

The traffic streaming between them seemed to disappear as Blake studied the assassin his friend had risked so much to save two months ago.

She was every bit as intimidating as he would have expected and his lips twitched slightly. Intimidating to everyone except his pit bull, Buddy.

After studying him for a long moment, Viper raised her hand and touched her forehead briefly in a salute. Blake nodded in acknowledgement just before a public transportation bus rumbled by, blocking his view as it pulled to a stop in front of the prison. The doors opened and a young man ambled off. The bus rumbled forward again and Blake blinked.

There was no sign of the woman in black anywhere.

Viper had disappeared.

"Let me get this straight," Stephanie said, holding her phone to her ear and pausing in the act of opening her car door. "Jessica Nuñez has disappeared, you can't find any trace of this Lorenzo Porras, we still have no leads on the guide, and now Karl is missing?!"

"That about sums it up, yeah," John answered through the phone.

"What the hell, John!" Stephanie exclaimed, wrenching open the driver's door and getting behind the wheel. "Do you have *any* good news for me?"

"Matt found the logs on Rodrigo's PC," John replied.

"And?"

"Rodrigo definitely used Angela's credentials to access the mainframe."

"Oh, well, that's a relief," Stephanie muttered sarcastically. She started the engine and switched to her Bluetooth. "I was waiting for you to say the logs had disappeared too!"

Hitting the gas, she pulled into traffic and headed away from the prison.

"Blake thinks he can find Porras and Jenaro," John said after a few seconds of silence. "If he concentrates on them, we can focus on Philip and Lowell. Have you heard from the agent you have tailing Philip?"

"Yes." Stephanie slowed down as she approached a red light. "He left his house this morning and went straight to work. He hasn't left the building since. I'm on my way there now to pay him a surprise visit."

"You're going alone?"

"I don't want to scare him," Stephanie answered. "I just want to see what we're dealing with there. I want you to find at least one of our missing persons. Do you think you can handle that?"

"No need to be nasty," John retorted without heat. "It's not my fault everyone is disappearing on us."

Next Exit, Dead Ahead

"I just don't understand how we're losing all our witnesses!" Stephanie exclaimed, frustration making her voice sharper than she intended. "What's going on?!"

"A Cartel is in town, that's what's going on," John muttered. "If I thought there was a chance my head would end up on a bamboo spike, I'd run too."

"According to Blake, that chance is pretty high for both of us," Stephanie told him. "Jenaro doesn't care for law enforcement of any kind, and apparently he has a particular hatred for Federal law enforcement."

"He won't try it on US soil," John scoffed. "Even he can't be that ballsy."

"I wouldn't take bets on it, if I were you." Stephanie pulled onto the highway and accelerated. "He walked into a disused prison in the cops' backyard and deposited multiple body parts. Something tells me he's not worried about playing it safe."

"You think he's behind our missing persons?"

"I wouldn't be surprised. Without them, we have nothing, and he knows that," Stephanie said. "We need to find them. You concentrate on that and I'll see where I can get with Philip Chou."

"You got it. What about Angela?" John asked.

"Lina is taking care of her," Stephanie answered. "She ran the plates on the mystery car this morning and texted me. It belongs to Kwan, but we already suspected that. Frankly, Angie is the least of my worries right now. Out of everyone, she's the safest."

"Are you going to talk to the Black Widow about the Cartel? Or are we just going to ignore the fact that she knew they were in town?"

"Oh, I'll get to her, don't worry," Stephanie said grimly.

"Do you think she's somehow involved with the search for Jenaro?" John asked.

"I don't know," Stephanie replied, shaking her head slightly. "It's possible, but I don't think Jenaro is her typical mark. I think it's probably more likely that she knows more about this Moon character."

John whistled softly.

"I hadn't thought of that," he admitted. "If Jin Seung Moon is a terrorist for North Korea, then he'd be right up her alley of...expertise."

"Exactly. Rob's already warned me to go carefully where Moon is concerned," Stephanie told him. "If we come across any evidence Moon is behind our hacking ring, we have to notify him immediately. He's afraid of the international ramifications if we mishandle him."

"If Alina is after Moon, I don't think we'll have much of a chance to mishandle anything," John retorted.

"Trust me, I already thought of that," Stephanie replied. "If she's after Moon, we've got an even bigger problem on our hands."

Michael picked up his phone when it started ringing and glanced into the dining room where Angela was busy on her laptop. She had her Bluetooth hooked into her ear, listening to a conference call as she worked on a spreadsheet. He had to admit that she was a hard worker. She had been at the laptop for three hours now, on and off the phone, working constantly.

"Hello?"

"How's Brooklyn?" Blake asked.

Michael turned his attention back to his own laptop.

"I don't know. I haven't made it back up yet," he answered. "How do you like Jersey?"

"There's quite a mix of interesting characters here," Blake replied dryly. "I even saw your girlfriend."

Michael lifted his eyes from his laptop sharply, a frown creasing his face.

"Where?"

"Across the road. She was watching me. Any ideas why?"

"None come to mind." Michael closed his laptop and got up off the couch, heading over to the sliding doors. He stepped out onto the deck and slid the door closed behind him. "How do you know it was her?"

"Call it a hunch." Blake's voice got muffled for a moment and then Michael heard the sound of a car door slamming. "She was across the road from an old prison. It's a museum now. She kind of looked like..."

"What?" Michael prompted when Blake didn't continue.

"Well, don't laugh...but she kind of looked like The Black Widow," Blake told him.

Michael burst out laughing.

"Now that you mention it, there *is* a resemblance," he admitted. " And she was wearing black when she left the house today."

"Oh really?" Blake drawled. "How do we know what she was wearing today?"

"I'm staying with her temporarily," Michael answered, suppressing a sigh.

"Is that so?" Blake demanded. "I thought you said it wasn't like that? In fact, I distinctly remember you biting my head off when I suggested..."

"Yes, yes, I know," Michael cut him off crossly, causing Blake to start laughing. "It's not what you think. One of her friends got herself into a jam. I'm babysitting."

There was a moment of complete silence on the phone and Michael waited, resigned. He didn't have long to wait.

"You don't say?" Blake's voice was shaking slightly. "I didn't know you took up moonlighting in your off-hours. How much do you charge for that?"

"Shut it, Twinkle-Toes," Michael growled. At the mention of his old nickname from their military days, Blake guffawed into the phone. "It's only until Viper can take over."

"Oh, this is priceless," Blake chortled. "You mean, you're doing it for *her*? What's the matter? Is she busy saving the world again?"

"Stop being an ass."

"I can't help it. I was born this way," Blake retorted cheerfully. "This friend who got in a jam? Anything I should know about there?"

"Why do you ask?" Michael leaned on the banister around the deck and gazed out over the back lawn.

"Oh, I don't know." Blake resorted to sarcasm. "Maybe because you're spending your vacation babysitting the friend of one of our government's top assassins, while I suddenly find myself working with her *other* friend. I don't know about you, Mike, but I'm starting to think Viper's just bad luck to her friends."

"I wouldn't go that far yet," Michael murmured. "As far as I can tell, Viper has no involvement."

"Yet," Blake retorted. The word hung heavily between them for a moment, then Blake moved on. "Well, if anything comes up that I should know about, let me know."

"Will do." Michael frowned slightly at the undercurrent in Blake's voice. "Everything ok?"

"Jenaro Gomez is here," Blake told him somberly, "and he's making statements with other people's body parts. I don't like the fact that Ms. Walker's investigation appears to be linked in with him. I don't know what the story is with your babysitting gig, but watch your back, gunny. I have a bad feeling about all of this."

Michael watched as Damon materialized out of the trees next to the garage and started to move silently across the grass.

"I hear you," he murmured, watching Damon. "I'll take care of this end. You just make sure you take care of yours."

"Is she inside?" Damon asked, stepping onto the deck silently as Michael tucked his cell phone into his jeans pocket.

"Which one?" Michael asked dryly.

Damon's blue eyes rested on Michael thoughtfully.

"Mine," he answered softly.

Michael's eyes met his steadily, flashing briefly at the subtle warning in Damon's voice before his lips tightened imperceptibly.

"No. She went out a few hours ago." He watched as Damon leaned against the banister next to him. "The other one is in there working."

"I hear you got assigned babysitting duty," Hawk said, crossing his arms over his chest. His blue eyes glinted with amusement as he glanced at him. "How's that working out for you?"

"So far, uneventful," Michael answered with a grin.

"Nice of you to give up some of your vacation to help out." Damon's lips were twitching.

"I couldn't really refuse," Michael retorted. "Besides, the look on her face was worth it."

Damon chuckled.

"God, I wish I could have seen it," he admitted. "Did Raven really go after the cat?"

"Yes." Michael started laughing. "I'll give Jersey this: it's not dull."

"You're from Brooklyn? Were you going to see your parents?"

Michael glanced at Damon. He wasn't sure he wanted to know how Hawk knew about his family.

"Yes, but it's ok," he answered. "They didn't expect me to stay the whole week. Bingo and All-You-Can-Eat buffets aren't really my thing."

Damon couldn't stop the grimace crossing his face.

"I can't imagine they would be," he murmured.

"Where are you coming from?" Michael asked, glancing at him. "Lina thought you would show up for breakfast."

"I had some things to take care of," Damon answered.

"On foot?"

Damon grinned at the incredulous look on Michael's face.

"I have my bike. It's in the woods inside her security perimeter," he told him. "It's easier to get in and out unseen through the back of the property."

Michael considered him thoughtfully, but was silent.

"Tell her I'll be back tonight if you see her," Damon said after a moment, straightening up and turning toward the steps.

"Come in and wait if you like," Michael said. "It's a full house."

Damon glanced at him with a faint smile.

"No thanks," he murmured. "I'm not in the mood to be treated to a seminar on the beneficial effects of sandalwood and incense."

Michael raised an eyebrow.

"Eh?"

"Ask Angela." Damon started down the steps. "She'll be more than happy to explain." Hawk got to the bottom step and paused. He turned and looked at Michael. "Move Angela's car into the garage so it can't be seen," he told him.

"Is that necessary out here?" Michael asked.

"He knows where he last saw her," Hawk answered. "He can find his way back."

"Do you really think he'll come back?" Michael asked him, his gaze serious. "Why would he think she's still here?"

"When he can't find her, he'll go back to the last place he knows she was," Hawk replied. He turned to leave again, but hesitated.

"What is it?" Michael asked.

Hawk raised cold, blue eyes to his.

"Viper trusts you," he said softly. "Don't disappoint her."

Michael nodded slowly, studying him.

"It's not just Kwan I should be worrying about, is it?" he asked.

Hawk smiled slightly.

"You're a quick learner, gunny," he said, turning and striding across the lawn. A few seconds later, he disappeared into the trees.

197

Chapter Twenty

Viper lowered the binoculars thoughtfully, her eyes resting on the large gray structure in the distance. The police still had the front yard to the prison taped off and two uniforms were making sure no one got curious. It hadn't taken two seconds to spot the plain-clothed, FBI agents stationed at the prison, one in front and one in back. She really should talk to Stephanie about the art of blending in for her agents. The FBI could be so much more productive if they weren't so glaringly obvious.

Setting the military binoculars down, Alina pulled a small tablet from one of her cargo pockets. She pulled up the latest newspaper articles on the events at the prison and scanned through them, stopping when she got to a picture of Karl, the friendly night guard. Alina studied the picture thoughtfully before highlighting his face and copying the image. Opening a customized database, she pasted the picture and tapped to run a search. Lifting her eyes, she turned her attention back to the prison while her tablet searched the database for information on Karl.

Allowing Blake Hanover to see her had been a risk. Only a handful of people in the world had seen her and recognized her, and those people were all known liabilities in her mind. She added another today, but she wanted Blake to know she was here, and that she was watching. He took a chance on her two months ago in Washington. Viper wanted him to know that she was willing to return the favor.

An alert flashed on her tablet and Viper glanced down as information on Karl Didinger poured in from various government and private databases. She raised an eyebrow slightly. Karl certainly had a checkered past, and his financial situation was a mess. She noted his home address before sending the information to her private server at the house. A moment later, she turned off the tablet and slipped it back into her pocket. After taking one last look at the prison, she got up and turned to leave the roof. Dropping over the side and onto a fire escape ladder, Viper silently disappeared into the afternoon.

Stephanie sat on the uncomfortable couch in the entryway and watched as the woman behind the desk picked up the phone. She had been asked to wait over five minutes ago after showing her badge and requesting to speak with Philip Chou. Crossing her legs, Stephanie suppressed an impatient sigh and pulled out her phone. Swiping the screen, she opened her email and scrolled through it while she waited. Still nothing from Matt on Rodrigo's PCs and still nothing from the BOLOs they had out on the missing guide, Jessica Nuñez, Karl, or Lorenzo Porras.

Closing her email in frustration, Stephanie glanced up as a man emerged from a hallway on the other side of the entryway and approached the desk. Her eyes narrowed as she watched him adjust his tie nervously while he spoke to the woman at the desk, glancing in her direction. A feeling of foreboding stole over Stephanie when he turned toward her.

"Agent Walker?" the man asked, moving toward her. She stood up and he held out a shaking hand. "I'm sorry to keep you waiting. I'm Scott Reynolds, the head of Program Development here. I'm Philip Chou's boss."

"Hello." Stephanie shook his hand. She frowned at the damp palm grasping hers. "Is everything alright, Mr. Reynolds?"

"Yes, yes." Scott pulled his hand away and smiled nervously. "Well, in a manner of speaking, anyway. Is Philip in any trouble?"

"Not at all," Stephanie assured him, resisting the urge to cross her fingers behind her back. "I just have a few questions for him regarding an ongoing investigation. Nothing to be concerned about."

"Good, good! I guess I don't have to tell you that we don't get visits from the FBI very often."

"Of course not," Stephanie murmured. She looked at him expectantly and Scott seemed to hesitate, looking slightly embarrassed. "What's the matter, Mr. Reynolds?" she asked bluntly.

"Well, the thing is, Agent Walker," Scott said, taking a deep breath, "I can't seem to find Philip."

Stephanie stared at him.

"I'm sorry?"

"It's really the strangest thing," Scott said, shaking his head and running a hand through his dark hair. The unruly curls, already a mess, seemed to stand up on end when he pulled his hand away. "He was here not more than an hour ago. We had a conference call and he was at my desk with me. When the meeting was over, he went to the bathroom. No one seems to have seen him since."

"Mr. Reynolds, are you telling me you lost your employee?" Stephanie asked after a moment of incredulous silence.

"Well, in a word, yes." Scott shook his head again and turned to the front desk. He motioned for her to join him. "We've been calling his cell phone and paging him, but...well...nothing."

"Could he be in the lunch room? Visiting a friend in another department?" Stephanie suggested. "I'm sure he didn't just disappear."

"I've got security checking the entire building," Scott told her. He looked at the woman behind the desk. "Anything yet?"

"I'm sorry, sir, nothing," she answered apologetically.

Stephanie pressed her lips together and pulled out her phone again. While Scott leaned over the desk and picked up a phone, presumably to check with someone else, she turned away and hit speed dial. It was picked up after one ring.

"Connor? Are you still outside?" Stephanie asked, her voice low.

"Yep. I saw you go in," Connor answered. "What's up?"

"They've lost Philip Chou," Stephanie told him grimly.

There was a short silence on the line.

"His car's still here. I'm staring at it," Connor answered. "He hasn't come out of the building since he went in five hours ago."

"Did you see anything suspicious? Anything at all?" Stephanie asked.

"Nothing." Connor paused for a moment and it sounded like he was sucking soda through a straw. "There were a lot of people coming and going over the lunch hour, but he wasn't one of them. In fact, he hasn't gone out for lunch for the past two days. He never leaves the building until it's time to go home."

"Ok. I'll be out soon," Stephanie said and disconnected. She turned back to the front desk as Scott was hanging up the phone.

"I just spoke to security," he said. "They haven't found him. They're still looking, but the only places left to check, Philip doesn't have access to. They're checking anyway. This is really quite embarrassing."

"Do you mind if I take a look at his desk?" Stephanie asked, slipping her phone back into her purse.

Scott looked startled, but nodded quickly.

"Of course not," he said. He turned to the desk again and grabbed a sign-in log and a visitor's badge. "Sorry. You have to sign in and wear this," he said apologetically, flashing her a twisted smile. "I feel stupid asking a federal agent to do this, but it's company security policy."

"Not a problem," Stephanie assured him, signing the log quickly and dropping the lanyard with the visitor's badge over her head. "I understand."

Scott nodded and turned to lead the way into the hallway he emerged from earlier.

"I'm sure he'll show up," he said as they walked past cubicles filled with people staring at computer screens. "This is very unusual. Philip is kind of a loner, you know. He's a cool guy, but he doesn't socialize much. He usually comes to work, eats at his desk, and doesn't stray far from the department."

"What does he do, exactly?" Stephanie asked.

"Oh, he's one of my top programmers," Scott answered readily. "He's been working on a security program for the mainframe for the past few months."

Stephanie glanced at him sharply under her lashes.

"Is that so?"

"Yes. After all the banks were hacked last year, Philip came up with a program that would make the mainframe virtually impenetrable. I'm sure you remember the incidents last year. It was all over the news. Most of the banks in the US were hacked and mainframes shut down. The hackers didn't take anything, but the disruption in business was catastrophic. We had clients unable to access their accounts for days. It was a mess."

"I remember that," Stephanie murmured. "They hit all the banks over a few months, didn't they?" she asked, pretending ignorance of the incident that jump-started her whole investigation.

"Yes." Scott motioned for her to precede him around a corner into another short hallway. "Well, after that incident, we were given the impossible task of trying to ensure it would never happen again. I didn't see how we could do it when we didn't even know how they got in to begin with. I mean, how do you plug a hole you don't know is there, right? But Philip figured it out. He figured out how they got in, and has been working on a firewall program for the mainframe ever since."

"So, he's kind of a smart guy, then," Stephanie remarked with a smile.

"Scary smart," Scott agreed.

"Just one question." Stephanie stopped walking at the end of the hallway and turned to look at Scott. "If the bank wanted to install a security layer on the mainframe, why are they doing it through this building? Isn't your main office in New York?"

Scott chuckled.

"The main office is, yes, but this is the main IT hub," he explained.

"Ah. So, you guys are the big guns of New Federal's IT," Stephanie said with a grin.

Scott grinned back.

"I've been called worse," he told her with a laugh, "but that's about the size of it. Here we are."

Stephanie looked around as they emerged into a huge space divided into sections with half-cubicle walls. A dozen programmers were at their desks, engrossed in their work. The level of privacy was minimal, resulting in an impression of openness and team-oriented work.

"Philip's desk is over here," Scott said, leading the way around the perimeter to a desk on the other side of the large room.

Stephanie stepped into the cubicle that housed Philip Chou's desk and glanced around. The desk was littered with notepads and pens, a stress ball shaped like a baseball, and an assortment of network cables and flash drives. Philip had two, twenty-two-inch flat screen monitors, both dark, and a desktop PC on the floor under the desk. There was also a docking station on the desk and Stephanie glanced at Scott.

"Does he have a laptop?" she asked, pointing to the empty docking station.

Scott nodded and his frown deepened.

"Yes, he does. He had it earlier at my desk," he said, looking around the cubicle. "It doesn't seem to be here, does it? I wonder if he went home. It would be odd for him to leave and not tell anyone, but I don't know where else he would have taken his laptop."

"He didn't go home," Stephanie said grimly.

She pointed to a set of car keys sitting on the corner of the desk, alongside a blackberry silently lit up with several missed calls.

"How many does this make? Five?" Rob demanded. The edge in his voice made Stephanie wince as she strode toward the Mustang, her phone pressed to her ear. "How do you lose five witnesses?!"

"With respect, sir, *I* didn't lose them. They seem to have lost themselves," Stephanie retorted.

"What are we doing to find them?"

"We have BOLOs out on Nuñez, Porras and the guide," Stephanie answered as she reached for her door handle. "John put one out this morning on Karl, and we'll get one out on Philip now."

"I'll take care of that," Rob said. "I'll do it as soon as I hang up with you. You worry about finding at least one of them."

"I'm working on it," Stephanie answered, sliding behind the wheel. "I have a lead on Philip. Connor, the agent I put on him, said a white catering van pulled around the building at lunch time, unloading food for one of the conference rooms. It was the only vehicle that went in or out of the parking lot that wasn't an employee."

"What was the name of the catering company?" Rob asked.

"Los Azteca Mexican Restaurant," Stephanie replied.

There was a short silence before a heavy sigh.

"Too much of a coincidence," Rob muttered. "Follow it up. I'll get the BOLO out on Philip and put one out on the catering van. What's the tag?"

Stephanie pulled out the piece of paper where Connor had scrawled the license plate number and read it off to Rob.

"Got it," Rob said. "I'll call this in now."

"Thanks." Stephanie started the engine and the Mustang came to life with a growl.

"And Stephanie?"

"Yes?"

"Be careful."

Michael glanced over to the dining room table where Angela was still working away. He shook his head slightly and turned his attention back to his laptop. After a moment's hesitation, he opened up his work VPN portal and logged in, his curiosity getting the better of him. He had never been one to sit by and let everyone else have all the fun.

He sipped a bottle of water while he waited for the network to load. Alina still hadn't reappeared and he didn't expect to see her anytime soon. She hadn't said where she was going, and he knew better than to ask. Angela hadn't seemed to notice Alina's attire, but Michael had noted the multi-pocketed cargo pants and loose-fitting jacket with interest. He hadn't seen much of Alina's alter-ego two months ago, but he saw enough to know that cargo pants seemed to go hand-in-hand with work. Wherever she had gone, Viper was prepared for any eventuality.

That made Michael nervous.

He set the water bottle down on the coffee table and sat back as the network finished loading. He typed in Lowell Kwan's name and waited. He didn't know if he would pull up any information on the software expert, but Michael figured it was as good a place to start as any. The Secret Service databases were the best in the country, but you had to have a reason to be included in them. As far as he could tell, Lowell Kwan had flown under the radar until now. Therefore, Michael was surprised when he got an immediate hit.

Raising his eyebrows, he clicked on the file and scanned the information quickly. Born Lowell Kwan, he was raised in Arizona by his mother under the name Jared Yang. Lowell was an early bloomer, brilliant and quick from a young age. He got a full academic ride to college and when he got to Stanford, he was on track to becoming the next Bill Gates. Then, midway through college, he developed relationships with some of the more radical political groups on campus. By graduation, Jared Yang had made it onto two government watch lists, both for radical political affiliations.

Michael frowned and stared at the screen thoughtfully. Jared Yang made quite a name for himself, and the Department of Homeland Security added him to *their* watch list just before he closed down his software company and changed his name back to Lowell Kwan. The name change didn't fool DHS, and upon moving to New Jersey, Lowell Kwan was being watched by the government very closely.

Michael clicked to move on to the next file, only to find that there weren't any. He scowled, glancing at the date on the last report. It was 18 months old, and the last record available.

"What the..."

Michael spent the next half hour trying to discover why the trail on Lowell Kwan suddenly ended before finally giving up and pulling out his phone. He hit speed dial and waited. It was picked up before the first ring had even completed.

"Mike! I was just about to call you," Chris Harbour, his direct boss, answered the phone.

"Oh yeah?" Michael asked. "Good timing, then."

"What are you doing working while you're on vacation?" Chris demanded. "I thought I told you to relax."

"I *am* relaxing, I'm just...wait, how did you know?" Michael asked with a frown.

"Because I just got a not-so-nice call from the CIA," Chris answered bluntly. "Why are you interested in Lowell Kwan?"

"Why is the CIA interested in why I'm interested?" Michael retorted.

Chris chuckled.

"That's what I said," he admitted. "They never actually answered that particular question."

"They never do," Michael muttered. He closed his laptop and glanced into the dining room where Angela was still talking on her bluetooth. "What are they doing monitoring Kwan's file?" he asked, lowering his voice.

"I don't know, Mike, but they aren't happy with you poking around," Chris answered. "They wanted to know what you're working on that led you to Kwan. I stalled them for now, but they won't go away for good. What *are* you doing?"

"It's a long story, Chris," Michael sighed. "A friend of a friend got herself into a jam and this Kwan character is making life uncomfortable for her."

"How uncomfortable?"

"Very."

Chris sighed.

"I know it's pointless to tell you to go back to Brooklyn and play pinochle, or whatever your folks do up there, but I'm going to try anyway," he said.

"Bingo," Michael interjected with a grin.

"Whatever this Lowell Kwan character is all about, you don't want to be involved." Chris ignored him as if he hadn't spoken. "Leave your lady friend to the proper authorities, whoever they may be in that area, and go back to vacation. Have a beer. See a show. It's Halloween in a few days. Go to a haunted house."

"The haunted attractions around here seem to make people lose their heads," Michael murmured dryly.

"Mike, do my acid reflux a favor. Drop it," Chris said. "The last time you got involved in the CIA's backyard, your kitchen was set on fire."

"Since I'm not home, that's not a concern this time," Michael retorted cheerfully.

"This doesn't have anything to do with that rogue agent, does it?" Chris demanded after a moment's silence.

"She wasn't a rogue agent," Michael snapped. "She was cleared."

"Oh God." Chris groaned in resignation.

Michael chuckled.

"What can you find out for me?" he asked.

"Not much," Chris replied. "They have it all locked up. I'll see what I can do, but don't hold your breath."

Michael pursed his lips.

"How bad do you think it is?" he asked after a moment.

"They knew what you were doing three minutes after you ran the search," Chris told him. "Whatever it is, Kwan is a priority for them. Hell, they probably already have a lock on your location."

Michael glanced at his laptop, then at the dark plasma screen above the mantel. He thought of Alina and her paranoid, GPS-altering security measures and smiled.

"I wouldn't lay bets on that," he murmured.

Chapter Twenty-One

Stephanie hadn't even made it out of the parking lot before her phone started ringing again. She glanced at the caller ID and pulled off to the side of the lot, putting the Mustang in park.

"Matt, tell me you have something good!" she answered.

"I have something good," Matt obliged.

"Thank God!" Stephanie exclaimed. "What is it?"

"I've got a few things for you," Matt said. Stephanie could almost picture him pushing his glasses up on his nose. "Let's start with the cigarette butt."

"Cigarette butt?"

"From the maze where you found your informant's remains," Matt reminded her. "You didn't forget about it, did you?"

"Matt, if you had any idea what's going on, you'd understand how a cigarette butt slipped my mind," Stephanie told him. "But now that you've brought it back to my attention, did you get anything off it?"

"Of course I did," Matt answered cheerfully. "I'll spare you the fun, forensic details and skip right to the important points. The cigarette was a regular, full-tar Marlboro, *but* it was a Mexican-produced Marlboro."

"Is there such a thing?" Stephanie asked, surprised.

"Oh yes. Marlboro produces cigarettes in several other countries, and Mexico is one of them. They have their own factories there," Matt explained.

"I'm not going to ask how you can tell the difference between cigarettes produced in the States and ones produced in other countries, but someday, you'll have to explain that further," Stephanie said, momentarily diverted.

"Anytime you want a lesson, you know where to find me," Matt replied. "Now, not only was the cigarette Mexican, but so was the smoker. It's a shock, I know, but try to contain yourself."

"Ha! You're being funny today. Did you get a DNA match off it?"

Stephanie asked, her pulse quickening.

"I did," Matt told her. "I ran it against our databases and got a perfect match. Ramiero Losa. His DNA was collected from a crime scene in Puerto Vallarta last year. He was arrested, but never convicted. He's an enforcer for your new friend, Jenaro Gomez."

"Matt, if you were here, I would kiss you," Stephanie said with a grin.

"Now, now, I'm not finished amazing you yet," Matt retorted. "That's just the cigarette butt. I haven't gotten to Rodrigo's computers yet."

"You finally have something from them?" Stephanie asked. "It's about time!"

"I beg your pardon!" Matt exclaimed. "Do you have any idea the level of encryption built into those machines? I'm talking government-level encryption here. He had two booby traps built into the layers, not to mention the unique coding he...oh, never mind. You're just lucky I had two of the encryption analysts down here with me, or you'd still be waiting."

"I'm sorry," Stephanie apologized. "You've spoiled me, Matt. When you're on the job, I'm used to fast results."

"I should hope so," Matt retorted, mollified.

"Tell me what you found on the computers," Stephanie said.

"Rodrigo planted a virus on the bank's mainframe by injecting it into the back-end coding," Matt told her. "The crazy part is, the virus was actually injected six months ago. When he went in again just before he disappeared, he didn't do anything with the actual virus. I'll put all the details in my report, but the essential point you need to know now is that the virus is still there. At least, it was when we got the computers. It's been built to work undetected for any amount of time. When you're finished, you go into the mainframe and extract the coding, erasing the evidence. It's like it was never there."

"What does it do?" Stephanie asked.

"I can't know exactly what it's doing without seeing the extraction logs, but it appears to have been designed to withdraw a designated amount of money at regular intervals from multiple accounts," Matt said. "My guess would be that it pulls a small amount from all accounts. The genius of it, however, is when it pulls the money, it doesn't transfer it anywhere. So no alarms go off within the system at money being moved around from millions of accounts. Instead, the virus takes it from the accounts and holds it in a file within the system. The system fail safes don't catch it because, even though the money is gone from the accounts, it's still technically in the system."

"I don't understand. The money doesn't go anywhere?"

"Not until the virus is extracted," Matt said triumphantly. "It's

207

really quite brilliant. Once the virus is extracted, the money disappears. All evidence of the virus is gone, and so is the money. The system alarms go crazy, the system locks down, but it's too late. Anything able to show what happened has been erased."

"So the banks would have no idea until it's all over," Stephanie exclaimed.

"Exactly. Brilliant, isn't it?" Matt sounded almost reverential. "Do you have any idea what they can do with this? They could crash the global economy and no one would know what happened."

Stephanie was silent, her mind spinning.

"What do you need to find out exactly what this virus is doing?" she finally asked.

"Well, I would need access to the bank's mainframe," Matt said matter-of-factly. "That's the only way to know for sure I'm right, even though we both know I'm never wrong."

"Get your report to Rob ASAP," Stephanie said grimly. "Let's see if we can get you that access."

"Are you kidding?" Matt demanded, half-laughing. "It's a bank! They're not going to just hand over the keys to the vault."

"They will if we can stop them from getting robbed," Stephanie replied. Her phone beeped in her ear and she glanced at the screen. "I have to go, Matt. I have a call coming in. Get that report to Rob!"

Stephanie hung up on him before Matt could argue and switched over to the incoming call.

"Tell me good news, John," she said without preamble.

"I found Lorenzo Porras," John told her.

"Fabulous!" Stephanie exclaimed and put the Mustang in gear. "Where is he? Have you talked to him yet?"

"Not exactly," John replied. "We're at the marina in Riverside. I don't think he's going to be very chatty, though. He's been shot in the head."

Back in its heyday, the old abandoned building used to be a bustling factory. The factory floor was a huge open space that occupied the majority of the ground level, with a small front room separating the entryway from the rest of the building. The cement floor was crumbling now, and the upstairs offices and foreman areas had long since collapsed, weakened by the elements that poured through gaping holes in what was left of the roof. Located in an isolated section along the River Line train tracks that ran from Camden to Trenton, the old building was almost part of the landscape. People passed by it every day and never gave it a second glance. It was just another decrepit, deteriorating shell from the past that had been abandoned and forgotten.

Late afternoon sunlight filtered through the holes in the roof, making its way through the dank atmosphere in a half-hearted attempt to shed light on the deep shadows of the factory floor. In the far corner were a couple of folding chairs and a camping table. Aside from that corner, the old factory was bare of furniture or debris. It had been swept out and emptied, leaving a wide, desolate expanse of space that was cold and dark. If one looked closely and took the time to notice the details, they would note that the corner still had metal support beams running overhead. Looped over one of the beams were two two-inch thick, stainless steel chains, hanging about seven feet from the cement floor. The walls were discolored and there was a strange odor lingering there, at once both sour and sickening.

The smell didn't appear to bother the men lounging on two of the chairs, playing cards on the camping table. They were using an empty bottle as an ashtray, and the heavy fumes of cigarette smoke hung around them.

Jenaro Gomez walked onto the factory floor from the direction of the front of the building, glancing past them into the corner where a figure lay slumped on the floor.

"Turi, is this his?" he asked, motioning to a laptop sitting at the end of the table.

"Yes," one of the men answered, stubbing out his cigarette. "He had it with him."

"Did you have any trouble?" Jenaro asked, stopping at the table and opening the laptop. He hit a key and frowned when a password prompt came up on the screen.

"No."

Jenaro nodded and closed the laptop, glancing at the two men.

"Where's Lorenzo?" he asked.

"Went to see someone last night," the other man answered. A cigarette hung between his lips as he selected a card from his hand and laid it on the table. "Not back yet."

Jenaro watched him, his eyes narrowing.

"Go find him," he ordered.

The man glanced up at him, startled, and nodded. A line of ash fell off his cigarette and he pulled it out of his mouth, dropping it into the bottle. He stood, pushing the chair back as he did so, and threw his cards on the table.

"You're lucky this time," he told Turi as he pulled his jacket off the

209

back of the chair. "I had two pair."

He turned to leave, grabbing his pack of cigarettes off the table, and nodded to Jenaro. He was halfway across the floor when Jenaro stopped him.

"Ramiero!" he called.

Ramiero Losa turned to look at him questioningly.

"Don't come back without him," Jenaro told him, the scar on his face twitching.

Ramiero nodded and turned to disappear into the front of the building.

"You think he found a drug house?" Turi asked, gathering up the cards and glancing at Jenaro.

"If he did, he won't find it again," Jenaro retorted. "How long's he been out?" he asked, nodding to the slumped figure on the floor.

"Couple hours."

"Wake him up. Use the salts."

Jenaro took off his jacket, draped it over the back of Ramiero's chair, and picked up a steel case from the floor. Setting it on the table, he unsnapped the locks and opened it up. Inside, neatly arranged in padded sections, were a variety of blades, pliers and screws. Glancing up, Jenaro watched as Turi went over to the slumped figure in the corner and bent over him. A few moments later, Turi straightened up and nodded to Jenaro.

"He's coming around," he said as he stepped back.

"Good." Jenaro nodded and motioned to a tall metal stand nearby. "Turn on the light."

Turi switched on a blinding spotlight, lighting up the corner like a beacon. The figure on the floor groaned and raised his bound hands to shield his eyes from the glare as he lifted his head. His dark hair was on the longer side, brushing his ear lobes and flopping over his forehead in disarray. A swelling lump on his temple showed just how Turi and Ramiero had convinced him to come with them.

"You missed our appointment, little Philip." Jenaro stood outside the circle of light and watched coldly as the man tried to peer past the white light. "I had to send Turi after you. That was an inconvenience."

"The files weren't ready. I told you. I can't rush it," Philip replied, struggling into a sitting position.

"According to Rodrigo Frietas, you can," Jenaro answered calmly. "He was very informative. It only took...a little persuasion."

"Rodrigo wouldn't understand," Philip muttered. "We all have our own roles in the project. His was planting the virus. He didn't design it."

"No." Jenaro pulled a chair over to the edge of the bright circle and sat down. He crossed his arms over his chest and studied the man leaning against the crumbling wall. "Neither did you. So tell me, how do you trigger the transfer?"

"It takes two of us," Philip said. "Killing me won't help you. Lowell can't do it alone."

"Who said anything about killing you?" Jenaro asked smoothly. "No, no, no. I'm not going to kill you. Not yet."

Philip swallowed with difficulty and Jenaro watched as a fine sheen of perspiration appeared on his forehead. Shifting in his chair, Jenaro crossed his legs and made himself comfortable.

"When you stole two and a half million dollars of heroin from me, you *did* design that virus, didn't you?" he asked almost pleasantly. Philip was silent. "That *is* how you altered the manifests, isn't it? Did you and your Korean friend really think I wouldn't know exactly what was supposed to be on those trucks? Did you really think we wouldn't miss it?"

Jenaro watched as Philip stared at the floor silently. He didn't fidget or shift positions. He showed no sign of response. Jenaro studied him thoughtfully.

"I told you two weeks ago, we want our money back," he said softly.

"You'll get your money," Philip said, lifting his head, "when we harvest the virus."

"No, Philip. We'll get it now. All of it," Jenaro said softly. "I gave you enough warnings. Now, we will take everything."

Philip's eyes flared wide and Jenaro's thin lips curved into a terrible smile.

"You were kind enough to show us the benefits of technology, you and your friend Lowell," Jenaro said, standing up and setting the chair out of the way. "People think the cartels are primitive and uneducated, especially here in the States. It's true we prefer more basic forms of human manipulation, but that doesn't mean we're not open to growth and progress."

Jenaro motioned to Turi and together they advanced on Philip. Grabbing each of his arms, they hauled him to his feet.

"When you exploited our limited software capabilities, you made us realize just what could be accomplished with that kind of technology," Jenaro continued, dragging him forward. Turi grabbed his tied hands and inserted a long, steel hook into the thick rope. Once it was secured, Jenaro reached up and grabbed one of the steel chains hanging from the cross-beam and tossed it to him. Turi hooked it onto the other end of the hook and Jenaro looked into Philip's alarmed face. "Really, you did us a favor. Once we have the virus, we'll be able to manipulate whatever government we choose."

"You'll never get it," Philip announced.

The sweat was pouring down his face now and he watched with wide eyes as Jenaro reached for the other chain. Jenaro smiled at him and pulled. Philip cried out as his arms were wrenched up above his head painfully. Jenaro pulled with both hands again and the make-shift pulley system started to lift Philip up off the ground. Turi grinned as Philip began to kick out with his legs, trying to land a kick on one of them. He circled the thrashing man and joined Jenaro at the chain. Together, they pulled Philip up off the ground until he was hanging with his feet a good twenty-four inches above the cement.

"Of course I will," Jenaro replied, reaching up and wiping moisture off his thick brow. He turned away to the case on the table and returned with a long, curved blade in his hand. "You're going to give it to me."

Viper dropped silently into the apartment from the skylight above and glanced around. Karl's third-floor walk-up was small, but unexpectedly tidy. Located in an apartment complex off Route 38 in Lumberton, it boasted hardwood floors and a washer and dryer in the unit. The skylight was a bonus, probably installed to add incentive for walking up three flights of wooden, exterior stairs.

The small dining room she landed in was separated from the kitchen by an open counter with bar stools along one side. On the other side of the dining room, the living room housed a couch, a coffee table, and a flat screen TV sitting on a low entertainment table. Karl kept a neat house, and the table was clear of any clutter, save three remotes and an X-box controller, all neatly lined up in a row. Alina turned her attention to the kitchen, noting the spotless counters and floor. She moved into the kitchen, glancing into the stainless steel sink. A rinsed out coffee mug was inside, along with a single spoon. Viper turned to the fridge and opened it. Aside from a case of Yuengling Lager taking up the bottom shelf, the refrigerator revealed nothing out of the ordinary and she let the door swing closed again silently. Karl clearly lived alone, and did not entertain. A quick look into the cabinets revealed only a four-setting dish set, and the glassware consisted mainly of pint glasses with faded beer logos on them.

Viper moved out of the kitchen and turned to go down the hall to the bedroom and bath. She poked her head into the bathroom. Shaving cream and razor were still sitting on the vanity, but there was a glaring absence of toothbrush and toothpaste. Alina raised an eyebrow and silently pulled the shower curtain back. Shampoo and Axe Body Wash were balanced on the edge of the tub, but the inside of the shower curtain and tub were bone dry. Reaching out a gloved hand, Viper lifted the body wash bottle and glanced beneath at the tub surface. The water mark was clear, but also dry. She replaced the bottle thoughtfully and turned to leave the bathroom.

Crossing the hall, Alina went into the bedroom and glanced around. The bed was made neatly and nothing was out of place. A quick inspection of the closet and dresser revealed the absence of a museum uniform and a half-empty bottom drawer.

No sign of struggle, so he left voluntarily, Alina thought, turning around in the middle of the bedroom. *No signs of anyone else staying with him. More importantly, no sign of a little person.*

As she was turning to leave the bedroom, something sticking out from under the bed caught her eye. She bent down and gently pulled out the shoebox protruding at an angle. There was no lid on the box, and Viper raised an eyebrow. Stacked neatly inside in rows were piles of money. They were all used bills and each stack was its own denomination. Alina stared at the box of money thoughtfully before pushing it back under the bed, replacing it exactly as she had found it.

Standing swiftly, she turned to leave the bedroom.

Wherever Karl had gone, he definitely expected to return. And that was all she needed to know.

Lowell watched from his car as another van pulled up outside Philip's building. The FBI had arrived at the apartment complex twenty minutes before, swarming to Philip's door like a bunch of black jacket clad bees. He frowned and shook his head, glancing at his phone again. A call to Philip's boss earlier had elicited the information that Philip and his laptop were missing, and the FBI were looking for him. Scott seemed more worried about the FBI than Philip, and Lowell hung up with the promise to call him if he heard anything from Philip.

Now the FBI were searching his apartment.

Lowell started the engine and pulled out from his parking spot across the street, easing into traffic. He had already been through Philip's apartment and was crossing the street, returning to his car, when the first FBI van pulled into the parking lot. He knew they wouldn't find anything in the apartment to incriminate either Philip or himself. Lowell had made sure of that.

But where was his laptop?

Lowell shook his head and turned a corner, heading away from the development. He wasn't worried the laptop would be compromised. They all had the same security layer built into their hardware, and he had designed it himself. There was no way anyone was getting into that laptop except Philip. Lowell scowled and glanced at his watch. They had an hour left. Wherever Philip had gone, and whatever he was doing, he had an hour to extract the virus and notify Lowell. If it wasn't done in time, three years of planning would go down the drain, and Lowell would have to answer for the failure.

Lowell tried to ignore the nagging sense of unease trying to creep into his mind. First Rodrigo, now Philip. Philip had been acting jumpy ever since Rodrigo disappeared. When his head showed up, Philip had been almost beside himself. Lowell had never seen him so scared. He stopped going out and wouldn't even leave his work to go to lunch. Philip had been convinced that someone was going to come after him.

And now he was missing.

Lowell slowed down for a light and stared absently at the car stopped in front of him. What if Philip knew something he hadn't been telling him? Lowell just assumed Philip's unease stemmed from the fear that Rodrigo would talk and reveal what they were doing. What if it had stemmed from something completely different? What if he *knew* who had killed Rodrigo?

A chill streaked down Lowell's spine and his lips tightened. What if the head had been a warning? And the tongue? What if they had been warnings for Philip, not just macabre tokens of a psychotic mind? What if Philip was right and the killer had come after him?

His phone chimed loudly in the silent car, making Lowell start. The light ahead turned green and the traffic started to move again. Glancing at the phone on the passenger's seat, Lowell sighed as relief washed over him. Philip's unique and encoded alert was flashing on the phone.

The virus had been extracted.

Lowell smiled and reached for his phone, opening the text message alert. It was sent automatically from the system as soon as the virus was extracted from the mainframe. Glancing down at the code on the screen, Lowell frowned. He pulled off the road, flipped on his hazards, and stared down at the code on the screen in confusion.

His first thought was that there was some kind of mistake. The code he was looking at, streaming in from the system, was *not* the extraction code. Lowell reached into the backseat and hauled his laptop forward. The code looked vaguely familiar, but he couldn't place it. Opening his laptop, he pulled a USB cable from his console and plugged one end into his phone and the other end into his laptop. Within seconds, the code was streaming into his laptop.

Lowell stared at it with a frown. Where had he seen it before? What was it? What was Philip doing?

He was still frowning in concentration, watching as the code started to repeat itself, when the realization hit Lowell like a truck. It was Philip's old code that he had come up with back at Stanford, the one he used to steal...

Lowell's head snapped up and his mouth dropped open.

Philip wasn't extracting the virus. He was warning him!

Lowell threw the car in gear and hit the gas, pulling out in front of a truck without a second glance. The truck slammed on his brakes and laid on his horn, but Lowell never heard it. He pressed the gas and flew down the road, heading back to the office.

Chapter Twenty-Two

Stephanie slammed her car door and glanced around the marina parking lot. The Riverside police had blocked off the lot and the only people inside were FBI and local LEOs. Larry was just opening the back doors to the medical examiners van while his assistant climbed out of the passenger's side. He was carrying a toolbox in one hand and half a burger in the other. Her stomach started to growl at the sight of the burger and Stephanie realized she hadn't eaten at all today. She was running on coffee with a side of more coffee.

Sighing, she turned to look across the grassy median toward the docks. A small group of workers was clustered off to one side of the main walkway, watching as John directed a group of techs at the end of one of the piers. Stephanie started toward the pier tiredly, glancing at her watch. It was almost three, but she felt like it was closer to ten. John looked up and waved as she came across the grass.

"Welcome to the party!" he called.

Stephanie shook her head slightly. A vehicle honked behind her and she turned her head, pausing to watch as Blake pulled through the barricade and into the lot. He pulled his black SUV up next to her Mustang and got out.

"You certainly don't waste any time, do you?" she asked as he joined her.

Blake glanced down at her, sunglasses concealing his eyes, and grinned.

"Nope," he replied. "Rob called me on my cell. Have you seen him yet?"

"I just got here myself," Stephanie answered, turning to walk with him toward where John was waiting at the end of the pier. "I've got another missing witness. This is the last thing I need."

They stepped onto the pier and John nodded to Blake as they walked up.

"Blake."

"John."

Stephanie looked at the body stretched out on a black tarp at the edge of the pier. Lorenzo Porras had dark hair, now matted and stuck to his head. His gaunt face was discolored from being in the water, and he was missing a shoe. Stephanie pulled a pair of latex gloves out of her pocket and put them on as she crouched down beside the body. The hole in his temple left no mystery about the cause of death.

"When was he found?" she asked, glancing up at John.

"The workers say he floated up to the pier a little after lunch, around one," he answered.

"Nice watch." Stephanie nodded to the Rolex on the body's left wrist. It was a submariner and the last time she saw it, it was strapped to Rodrigo Frietas' arm.

John nodded.

"I was wondering if you'd recognize it," he murmured. "More proof the Cartel is behind Rodrigo's death."

"Care to fill me in?" Blake asked, glancing from John to Stephanie.

"Rodrigo Frietas was wearing that watch when we interviewed him," John told him, "but it wasn't on his body when we found him."

"Did you see this?" Stephanie asked, carefully turning the corpse's arm with the tip of a pen. On the inside of the forearm was a small, discolored circle.

"Yeah. Looks like a bruise of some sort," John replied.

"That might be consistent with his medical history," Blake said.

John glanced at him.

"How so?"

"Porras is, or was, a diabetic and a chronic drug user," Blake told them. "I'm sure your ME can shed more light on it, but it could be from a needle."

"Hmm..." Stephanie looked up and across the water. "Isn't there a drug area not far from here, John?"

"There's a few. You think that's where he was?"

"Could be," Stephanie said, standing. "Check with the local cops over there in the parking lot. See where the closest hot spot is."

"On it," John said. He turned away and headed down the pier as Larry and his assistant ambled onto the planks.

"Does this one have all his parts?" Larry asked as he approached.

Stephanie's lips twitched.

"All present and accounted for, at least all the visible ones," she told him, stepping to the side so he could join her. "I don't think there's much debate over the cause of death."

"Certainly wouldn't appear to be," Larry agreed, looking down at the body. "However, we don't want to jump to conclusions before I've had a good look. The dead have a habit of talking just when you think you've got it all figured out."

"I'll leave you to it, then," Stephanie said, turning away and stripping off her gloves. "Let me know when you're ready for me."

"Of course," Larry murmured, already crouched down and leaning over the body. Stephanie and Blake hadn't gone two steps before Larry called her back. "Ms. Walker!"

Stephanie turned back and raised an eyebrow. Larry motioned her over.

"This man had a recent injury, aside from the one on his head," he told her. Stephanie and Blake peered over his shoulder as he motioned to the left shoulder of the body. "It looks like any bandage was pulled off in the water, but here..." Larry reached over and carefully eased the edge of the wet tee-shirt away from the shoulder, revealing a gunshot wound.

"Was it done at the same time as the one on his head?" Blake asked.

Larry shook his head.

"No bullet hole in the shirt," he answered, "and it appears as if the wound was already starting to heal before he ended up in the water. I'll know more once I get him back and on the table, but at a rough guess, I'd say this wound is at least twenty-four hours old."

"Two gunshots in two days. He wasn't very popular, was he?" Stephanie murmured, straightening up again.

"I'll let you know what else I find," Larry said and waved them away.

"Is it possible Jenaro could have killed him?" Stephanie asked Blake as they moved away to give Larry and his assistant more room.

"Doubtful," Blake answered, scratching his jaw. "He's aware of Lorenzo's drug habits, but he keeps them in check. If there's a problem, he traditionally handles it a little differently."

"I suppose it's possible Lorenzo got himself shot by a dealer," Stephanie mused.

Blake glanced at her, smiling faintly.

"You really think it will be that easy?" he asked.

Stephanie looked at him and chuckled reluctantly.

"No," she admitted. "But I can dream. I'm going to go talk to the marina workers. You're welcome to come, if you'd like."

"Actually, if you don't mind, I'd like to join John with the cops," Blake told her. "I have some questions for them about the neighborhoods around here."

Next Exit, Dead Ahead

"Knock yourself out." Stephanie waved her hand and started in the direction of the workers still huddled in a group, watching the proceedings avidly. "John might be able to help you out as well. He grew up not far from here."

Blake nodded and turned toward where John was talking to two of the uniformed officers near the barricade into the parking lot. He glanced at the road as a black Jeep drove by the parking lot entrance. The driver was cast in shadows, but the Jeep slowed slightly as it passed. He sighed and glanced back toward the pier. The activity at the marina was clearly visible from the road and Blake shook his head slightly. It wouldn't be long before the press and local residents were gathering near the parking lot. Hopefully, he would be long gone before the circus arrived.

Chris Harbour stepped out into the sunlight and took a deep breath. The air was crisp and the scent of fall blew through the streets of Washington DC, sweeping away the last remnants of a hot and humid summer. Glancing up at the cloudless blue sky, Chris smiled to himself. It was the perfect weather for football. The best time of year was upon them. The air was cool. The leaves were changing, and all was right with the world. He stepped out from under the shadow of the tall building he worked in every day and turned to walk down the busy city street. People were leaving work, hurrying to get home or to Happy Hour, and Chris joined the throng, briefcase in hand.

Glancing at his watch, he sighed. He was leaving later than he wanted, thanks to Michael O'Reilly and his sudden interest in Lowell Kwan. Chris pulled out his cell phone and hit speed dial. He would have to warn his wife he was going to be a few minutes late for their son's football game. She got nervous when he wasn't on time to family events. He supposed he couldn't blame her. The last time he had been late, he was in the hospital with a bullet in his chest. That was over twenty years ago now, but she wouldn't let him forget it. Karina had a memory like an elephant, bless her, and Chris knew she would be checking her watch soon. He waited while the phone rang, coming to a stop with a group of people at a corner, waiting for the light to change. After a few rings, it went to her voicemail.

"Hi, it's me. I'm on my way," Chris spoke into the phone after the tone. "I got out of work later than expected, but I should be there soon."

He disconnected and tucked the phone back into his pocket as the light changed and the crowd moved forward. He was just stepping onto the curb on the other side of the road when someone grasped his elbow lightly.

"Good afternoon, Chris!"

Chris turned his head swiftly and encountered an assessing look from dark brown eyes. He frowned slightly. The man looked familiar. He was dressed in a tailored charcoal suit and his salt and pepper hair fell neatly across his forehead. His chin was square, his shoulders broad, and the man exuded enough power to light up the city. Chris knew he had seen him before, but for the life of him, he couldn't place a name to the face. That, in itself, was unusual enough to give him pause. Chris was famous for remembering every name and face of everyone he had ever met.

"I'm sorry, do I know you?" he asked.

The man smiled faintly and Chris realized he was being gently guided out of the flow of human traffic and into a small corner bar.

"You do, but you may not realize it," the man murmured as they stepped out of the late afternoon sunlight and into the dark interior of a swanky martini bar. "We've passed each other on the Hill many times."

Chris frowned and glanced at his watch.

"Look, I'm running late as it is..."

"Don't worry. Matt's game is being delayed due to some referee trouble," the man informed him. "You'll be there in plenty of time for kick-off."

Chris looked at him, startled.

"How do you know..."

"I know everything, Chris," the man replied. He held out his hand. "I don't believe we've ever been formerly introduced. You can call me Charlie."

Chris grasped his hand automatically, his mind scrambling for an elusive memory. Charlie...the name was familiar...but how?

"I'm sorry," Chris said apologetically. "It's very embarrassing. I'm usually quite good with names."

"I know you are," Charlie assured him. "I won't take it personally. Only a handful of people in Washington know me, though almost everyone in government sees me on a regular basis. Come. There's a table in the corner where we can talk comfortably."

Bemused, Chris followed Charlie to a secluded pub table in the back corner, partially hidden by a huge, potted fan palm. Once they were seated, a waitress materialized with two glasses of water with lemon slices. She set them down before them and disappeared again with a smile.

"I believe you spoke with one of my colleagues earlier," Charlie said once she had gone. He unbuttoned his suit jacket and picked up the glass of water, sipping it while he studied Chris over the rim.

"Of course!" Chris breathed as the light bulb turned on. "You're..."

"Yes." Charlie cut him off before he could get out the initials. "I

220

was quite impressed with your handling of the situation in August involving one of your agents. Many others would have allowed Art Cosgrove to run their investigation for them. You showed considerable backbone in allowing your agent to follow his nose instead of bowing to Art. Congratulations on your promotion, by the way."

"Thank you." Chris smiled and shook his head. "So, I have you to thank for that, do I?"

"I merely made an observation to someone who listened," Charlie replied. "I believe you did the rest."

Chris chuckled and glanced up as two pints of beer were set before them. He didn't have to taste it to know that it was his preferred micro-brew. Shaking his head, he looked across the table at his companion, partially hidden in the shadows.

"Is there anything you don't know?" he asked, picking up the glass.

Charlie's white teeth flashed in the shadows.

"No."

Chris sipped the beer appreciatively and set the pint down on the table.

"So, Michael strayed into something serious, did he?" Chris asked, his voice low.

"Let's just say I would rather he left this particular situation alone," Charlie answered softly, picking up his pint glass and tasting the beer. "Hmm. Not bad."

"I'm glad you approve," Chris replied with a quick grin. "Are you a beer drinker?"

"When the occasion calls for it," Charlie answered cryptically.

"I tried to get Michael to drop it after your colleague called me." Chris returned to the main topic and reached for his glass. "He's like a dog with a bone when he gets his mind set on something, though. He's not likely to let it go until he finds what he's looking for."

"And what's he looking for?"

"God alone knows," Chris answered. "I certainly don't."

"It was my understanding he was on vacation," Charlie said, glancing at him with those sharp eyes.

"He is." Chris set down his glass and studied Charlie across the table. "Apparently, a friend of a friend got herself mixed up in something. Michael seems to think she may be in danger."

"Of course." Charlie seemed amused again. "Marines are so predictable sometimes, always wanting to protect and serve. Would you say Michael was prone to over-reaction?"

"Absolutely not. In fact, I'd lean toward the opposite. He tends to be cautious about jumping to conclusions," Chris said slowly. "That being said, once he decides something is not as it should be, it would take a nuclear bomb to stop him."

"Quite." Charlie sipped his beer again and considered Chris thoughtfully.

Chris stared back at the man in the shadows, uncomfortably aware that Charlie was seeing and hearing much more than Chris was saying. What on earth had Michael gotten himself into this time?

"This 'friend of a friend' he thinks is in danger," Charlie finally spoke softly, "is in New Jersey?"

"He didn't say," Chris replied.

Another long silence followed this and Chris finished his beer while he waited for Charlie to speak again. When he finally did, his voice was soft and Chris had to lean forward to hear.

"I can't stop Michael from trying to protect this person, but I must insist he doesn't touch Lowell Kwan. I need you to make sure he understands this, and complies. The situation is complicated. If he does something to upset the tenuous balance that exists there, I cannot vouch for his safety, or the safety of this 'friend of a friend.'"

Chris studied Charlie thoughtfully for a long moment.

"You're really concerned for Michael, aren't you?" he asked, unable to conceal his surprise.

Charlie met his gaze with a faint smile.

"We're not all heartless ogres," he murmured. "Some of us even have some semblance of a soul left."

Chris chuckled and nodded.

"Understood," he said. "I'll do what I can."

"If you value your agent, you'll do whatever you have to," Charlie told him, his soft voice threaded with steel. In an instant, the steel was gone and Charlie was smiling faintly again. He stood up and re-buttoned his jacket. "Next time he takes a vacation, tell him to consider a cruise. They tend to be safer than New Jersey these days."

The sun was beginning to set as Stephanie and John watched Larry slam the doors on the van closed, locking Lorenzo Porras's remains inside. His assistant was already in the passenger's seat, clipboard in hand, making notes and Larry gave them a final wave as he disappeared around the side of the van. A moment later, the engine started up.

"I'm starving," John announced, watching as the van backed out of its spot. "What do you think of a dinner break?"

"I think it sounds like heaven," Stephanie agreed.

John nodded and glanced at the small crowd gathered outside the police line at the parking lot entrance. They were moving the barricades to allow the ME van to pass and he raised an eyebrow as he glimpsed a familiar face.

"You've got company," he told Stephanie.

She frowned at him.

"What are you talking about?"

"Well, she's not here to see me," John replied, nodding toward the road.

Stephanie followed his gaze. Alina was leaning against her black Jeep across the road, her arms folded across her chest. Stephanie glanced at her watch.

"I wonder what she wants," she said. "Where do you want to have dinner?"

"I'm thinking somewhere with beer and burgers," John answered with a grin. "There's that new place down on 38. They have micro-brews and gourmet burgers."

"Sounds like a good idea," Stephanie agreed with a laugh. "Let me see what's going on and I'll meet you there."

John nodded and turned toward his car. He paused and glanced across the road at the motionless figure.

"How the hell did she know where we were?" he wondered.

Stephanie couldn't stop her reluctant grin.

"I don't think we really want to know," she retorted.

"Probably not," John admitted, beeping his car unlocked. "Keep it short. I'll give you ten minutes, then I'm ordering for you."

"Make it fifteen," Stephanie shot back and started across the lot.

She nodded to the police officer as she passed through the barricade, ignoring the blatantly curious looks from the local residents. Glancing up, she saw Alina watching her with an unreadable expression on her face.

"What are you doing here?" Stephanie asked, crossing the road to join her.

Alina straightened up and uncrossed her arms.

"I have some information you might find useful," she answered calmly.

Stephanie raised her eyebrows.

"That should surprise me, but it doesn't," she murmured. "What do you know?"

"I stopped by Kwan's work this morning and found his car," Alina told her. "It now has a tracking device on it."

"I shouldn't be hearing this," Stephanie said, grinning despite herself. "Where is he now?"

"Back at work. He's been there now for a few hours." Alina glanced at her watch. "What I thought you'd find interesting is where he was earlier."

"Amaze me," Stephanie invited her.

"He was at your missing Philip Chou's apartment," Alina said softly.

Stephanie gasped.

"How do you know about Philip?" she demanded.

Alina smiled slightly.

"His name popped up when I was running Lowell's," she said shortly. "Then, I saw your BOLO. Lowell was at his apartment before your people got there. In fact, he was still outside when your agents showed up."

"What?!" Stephanie exclaimed. "Then he knows Philip's missing!"

Alina nodded.

"He left and went straight back to work," she said. "I'm monitoring him closely to make sure I have a heads-up if he starts heading towards the house."

"Is Michael still there with Angela?"

"Yes. He's keeping her in the house for now. So far, everything has been quiet there." Alina stretched with a yawn. "There's one other thing."

"What's that?"

"I have Jessica Nuñez," Alina told her.

Stephanie's jaw dropped.

"What?!" she exclaimed.

"You heard me." Alina reached into her jacket pocket and pulled out a flash drive. "Here. This is her testimony."

"What do you mean, *you* have her?" Stephanie demanded, reaching out and taking the flash drive automatically. "We've been looking for her since yesterday morning!"

"I know," Alina said, amused. "You've got quite a few BOLOs out. Are you losing all your witnesses?"

"For the love of God, don't you start too," Stephanie snapped. "How do you know about them, anyway? You know what, nevermind. I don't want to know. What I *do* want to know is what you're doing with Jessica!"

"She seemed to be in need of assistance," Alina murmured dryly.

"Oh God!" Stephanie stared at her. "The Camaro. It was you!"

"Everything you need for your investigation is on that drive," Alina said, ignoring the accusation. "Jessica is safe for now. You can have access to her once I decide Jenaro Gomez is no longer a threat. In the meantime, that should help you out."

"What do you know about Jenaro Gomez?" Stephanie asked sharply.

"A lot more than I want to," Alina answered obscurely and turned toward the door of the Jeep.

"Clearly." Stephanie reached out and grabbed her arm. "You knew about the Cartel before we did. How?"

Viper looked at the hand on her arm, then raised her eyes slowly to Stephanie's face. Stephanie released her quickly at the look in those dark eyes.

"Go get something to eat, Stephanie," Alina told her, opening the door to her Jeep. "You look like you need it."

Chapter Twenty-Three

Michael yawned as the email alert on his laptop dinged. He glanced at his watch and frowned when he saw that it was already after six. Sitting up in the recliner, he looked into the dining room where Angela was still at the table with her laptop and blackberry. They had both been silent all day, each working on their laptops and not bothering one another. Michael was actually somewhat surprised. He had almost forgotten she was there.

"Are you hungry?" Angela asked now as she stretched and glanced at him.

"Nope."

"Thirsty?"

"Nope."

"Ok then."

Angela made a face at him as he turned his attention back to his laptop and got up to go into the kitchen. She glanced at the clock, surprised to see that it was already past six. She had been on conference call after conference call all day and was starting to feel cross-eyed from staring at the laptop screen for hours. Opening the refrigerator, she pulled out a can of Diet Pepsi and popped it open, running her eye over the contents of Alina's fridge with a grimace.

"Want to order pizza for dinner?" she called out to Michael.

"Hmmm."

Angela rolled her eyes and let the refrigerator door swing closed. She had no idea if the noise he made was a yes or a no. Looking across the bar and into the living room, she watched as he typed, his attention focused on the screen.

"I thought you were on vacation," she said, moving out of the kitchen and wandering into the living room. Annabelle was curled up in the corner of the couch and Angela reached a hand down to rub the top of her sleeping cat's head. Annabelle started briefly, then settled back down, purring as her eyes slid closed again.

226

"I am," Michael replied, still typing.

"Then why have you been working all day?" Angela asked.

Michael glanced at her.

"I'm trying to find out everything I can about this Lowell Kwan character," he said. "I like to know what I'm up against."

"Do you really think he's going to try to kill me?" Angela asked, straightening up and sipping her soda.

"I think you're in a bad situation," Michael answered evasively.

"That's a yes," she murmured.

Michael smiled reluctantly.

"It's an 'I don't know,'" he told her. "Better to be safe than sorry."

"I'm starving," Angela said, changing the subject and turning back toward the kitchen. "You're really not hungry?"

"No."

"I think I'll order pizza," Angela decided after another look in the refrigerator. "All she has in here is healthy stuff that needs cooking."

"Ordering pizza isn't a good idea," Michael muttered. "Make yourself a sandwich."

"I don't want a sandwich," Angela retorted. "I want pizza."

"Well, you're not ordering it," Michael informed her bluntly.

Angela's eyes narrowed and she glared at him from the kitchen, "Why not?"

"It's not safe," Michael said, ignoring the mutinous tone in her voice. "You're hiding, remember? We don't want Kwan to know where you are."

"And ordering pizza is going to alert him?" Angela demanded. "Don't be paranoid."

"You're not ordering pizza," Michael repeated. "If you have to have it, call Lina and tell her to pick it up on her way home."

"I can do that," Angela agreed, brightening considerably. "She can bring beer too."

"*That* I'll agree with," Michael murmured, relieved to have won the argument fairly quickly. He hadn't liked the martial look that had appeared in Angela's eyes.

Angela set her soda down and crossed into the dining room to pick up her phone. She hit speed dial and waited impatiently, watching as Michael went back to his laptop. It rang a few times before going to voicemail.

"Voicemail," she announced, disconnecting and dropping her phone back onto the table. "I wish I had Damon's number."

Michael glanced at her.

"Why?"

"Because then I could call and ask him," Angela replied, looking at him as if he should have known that.

Michael blinked and went back to his email, wondering if Angela would be so quick to call Lina and Damon for pizza delivery if she knew what they did for a living. Somehow, he didn't think it would make a difference. Angela seemed to live by her own rules.

"This is going to be a long couple days," Angela muttered, turning to head down the hallway. "I'm going to have a shower. If you happen to hear from her, tell her I want the usual."

"The usual what?"

"Pizza!" Angela exclaimed, throwing her hands up in the air.

Michael watched her flounce off down the hallway, a grin tugging at his lips as she muttered to herself all the way. He caught the words 'men' and 'oblivious' before she disappeared up the stairs. Looking over at her cat, still curled up on the couch, Michael allowed himself to chuckle. Annabelle opened one eye and looked at him questioningly.

"God help the man who gets stuck with her," he murmured.

Annabelle flicked her tail once, closed her eye again, and went back to sleep.

Damon rode his motorcycle through the shallow creek separating Viper's property from state-protected game land. He had to admit that her little spread was perfect. She was surrounded by forest, and flanked on two sides by state-protected land prohibited from being developed. Her closest neighbor was not close at all, and she had her own private trail through the back to her house. Really, she could have done much worse and, coming from a country boy like himself, that was high praise indeed.

He throttled back the engine and guided the bike carefully through thick trees and past her security perimeter before cutting the engine and getting off. Hawk glanced around and pulled a black cover out from under a huge pile of leaves mounded up between two pine trees. Shaking it out, he threw it over the bike and secured it before turning to start the mini-hike back to Alina's house. He stopped short, coming face to face with Viper.

She was leaning against a tree, dressed in black, her hair hanging down the back of her shoulders in a braid. She had her arms crossed over her chest, a knife strapped to her ankle, and Hawk knew her .45 was nestled in the holster in the small of her back. Her dark eyes watched him silently, and her lips were pursed into a grim line.

"We need to talk," she told him shortly, making no move to

straighten up from the tree.

"About?" Hawk raised an eyebrow, taking a step toward her. Her next words made him stop.

"Jin Seung Moon."

Hawk studied her for a moment, his blue eyes hooded.

"The North Korean?" he finally asked.

"That's the only Jin Seung Moon *I* know."

"Ok. What about him?"

"I came across his name this morning when I was pulling information on Lowell Kwan," she told him, still not moving from her position against the tree. "Kwan's an avid admirer of his."

"From what I understand, Moon has a lot of them," Damon murmured, sliding his hands into his pockets and leaning back against his bike. "He's rich, fanatical, and heads an elite terrorist network for the North Koreans. What's there not to love for young, misguided activists? I'm not surprised to find out Lowell Kwan is one of them."

"It looks like he's more than just an admirer," Viper told him. "Kwan has been in contact with Moon's network since he was at Stanford. When he left the University and started his own software company, guess where a lot of the profits ended up?"

"How did you find this out?" Damon asked, raising an eyebrow.

Viper smiled slightly.

"If you don't ask, I won't have to lie," she replied.

Damon grinned.

"Fair enough. So, Kwan was financing Moon. What does that have to do with us now?" he asked.

"Kwan is hacking into two of the main banks on the East Coast," Alina said. "If he was financing Moon in the past, I wouldn't be surprised to find this whole operation he has going here is for Moon."

"Even if it is, it's none of our business," Hawk pointed out. "Let the Fearless Feds handle it."

Viper considered him silently for a moment, her face unreadable. Hawk had no idea what was going on behind that mask and he frowned slightly.

"If Moon's behind it, they're way out of their league," Alina finally said. "You know that as well as I do."

"Don't go borrowing trouble, Viper. I think they have enough to handle with the Cartel, don't you?" Damon straightened up and moved toward her. "If it turns out Moon is behind Kwan, he's too smart to do anything stupid and risk getting caught. He'll feed Kwan to the Feds, Stephanie will get her man and Moon will continue on his merry way, just as he always does."

Alina watched as Damon moved toward her, his blue eyes dark in the shadows of twilight. She uncrossed her arms and straightened up as he stopped in front of her.

"I'm going to ask you this once," Viper said softly, her dark eyes probing his, "and only once. Did you know Moon is in Manhattan?"

"If he is, it's none of our business," Hawk replied, reaching out and brushing a stray strand of dark hair out of her eyes. "You know the rules. Charlie won't take kindly to you getting involved in unsanctioned hits on international targets. Find Jessica Nuñez's son, protect Angela, and keep your Fearless Feds safe if you think it's necessary, but stay away from Jin Seung Moon. He's not your target."

Alina stared into Hawk's blue eyes thoughtfully. He was right, of course. Moon wasn't her target. Just because he was close by didn't mean he was fair game. If he *was* behind Kwan's hacking scheme, he wouldn't do anything too rash. If Stephanie and John got to Kwan, Moon would most likely cut him loose, as Hawk said, and disappear, taking the loss. He certainly wouldn't try to take revenge on two FBI agents on US soil. Moon was too smart to jeopardize his tenuous standing with the US. He knew each time he crossed onto US soil, he was being watched.

"People like him are the reason we do what we do," she said quietly.

Damon nodded slowly.

"We still have to work within the boundaries we're given," he answered just as quietly. "If we don't, we're no different from him. His time will come."

"As will ours," Viper murmured.

Hawk paused, his eyes boring into hers. The stark reality was that they would meet their end sooner rather than later, and Damon was uncomfortably aware of just how long their run had been so far. They made it this far by being the best at what they do, but they both knew it couldn't last. Even the risks he took just last week in Spain could have ended differently, and regardless of how much she wanted to play dumb, Hawk knew damn well Viper had been the one to court death in that Taliban raid that had the whole Middle East buzzing.

The sudden verbalization of the reality they lived in made Damon feel something he hadn't felt in years. A feeling akin to panic was trying to take hold, rolling over him like a massive wave, intent on crushing anything in its path. Without thinking, Hawk lowered his lips to hers, pulling her close. He needed to feel her warmth and know that, at least for now, they were here and they were alive.

Alina was caught by surprise when Damon suddenly pulled her into his arms. In the split second before his lips touched hers, she caught a fleeting glimpse of raw emotion in his eyes. Its intenseness made her catch her breath, and her heart jumped into her throat. It wasn't passion that had her heart pounding out of her chest, but something much, much worse. Somehow, Hawk's flash of panic had communicated itself to her and the sharp edge of fear sliced through her, fear of losing him.

As his lips touched hers, Alina wrapped her arms around him, holding him close. She felt his heartbeat pressed against hers, his shoulders strong and firm under her fingers. He was alive, holding her close and kissing her deeply as if he wouldn't get the chance again. Alina felt a tremble go through her as she pulled him closer. She felt as if he was trying to steal her soul. Another tremble went through her as Alina realized that she was willing to give it. With that simple acceptance, Viper suddenly felt stronger than she had in weeks. This was where she wanted to be, nowhere else.

The trees around them disappeared, and Jin Seung Moon and Jenaro Gomez faded out of consciousness as Hawk exchanged breaths with the one woman in the world who meant more to him than anything. Tomorrow wasn't guaranteed, but right now, he could feel her pulse and taste her skin and know they were alive. He knew he had taken her by surprise. He had surprised himself with this sudden need to hold her and taste her. The panic driving him was so consuming that Hawk didn't think he could have stopped himself from touching her if a bomb had gone off right beside them. It wasn't desire coursing through him, but something stronger and more compelling. It was the need to have *her*, if only for a few seconds. He needed to feel her soul, and be comforted by her strength.

Damon didn't need to know why he suddenly felt this unfamiliar shaft of panic. He simply gathered Alina close and kissed her for all he was worth, trying to pour an infinite amount of emotion into one minute of contact. He felt her pull him closer, her fingers digging into the backs of his shoulders, and she seemed to sigh into him. In that instant, Hawk felt as if he could live forever. In a flash, the panic and fear disappeared, leaving an all-consuming love in their wake.

Realizing he was all but crushing her, Damon loosened his hold slightly and lifted his head, looking down into her face. She was slow to open her eyes, and when she finally did, Alina seemed dazed. He smiled slowly and brushed his nose against hers softly.

"Sorry," he whispered huskily. "I couldn't help myself."

Alina loosened her grip on his shoulders and watched him from under her lashes, her eyes dark.

"Are you okay?" she asked softly.

"I am now," Damon answered, pressing his lips against hers softly. He pulled her close again and rested his chin on the top of her head. "I am now."

Michael glanced at his watch when his phone started ringing. Angela was still upstairs, her cat had wandered up looking for her, and he had just closed his laptop with a loud yawn. Reaching into his pocket, he pulled out his phone, frowning when he saw Chris's number on the caller ID.

"Hey," he answered.

"Are you alone?" Chris asked, his voice low.

"I can be," Michael said. He swung himself out of the recliner and headed for the sliding doors to the deck. "What's up?"

"I have something for you," Chris answered. "I got a surprise visit this afternoon as I was leaving the office."

"Oh yeah? Who from?"

Michael stepped out onto the deck and slid the door closed. The sunlight was gone now and the yard was cast in long, dark shadows. Raven glided across the yard, coming to rest on the roof of the garage. He gazed watchfully with his black eyes as a bat fluttered past the deck and disappeared into the trees to the side of the house. Michael took a deep breath of fresh, crisp air and leaned on the banister to the deck, cradling the phone against his ear.

"Someone from the CIA," Chris told him. "You really ruffled some feathers today."

"What did they say?"

"You need to back off Kwan," Chris said bluntly. "They're concerned you may end up in the middle of something where they can't protect you."

Michael's eyebrows came together in a scowl and he stared out into the trees absently.

"Since when is the CIA concerned with protecting me?" he asked.

"Since you wandered into what seems to be the middle of a bad situation on US soil," Chris retorted. "Let me put it this way. I was told, in no uncertain terms, to make sure you stay away from Kwan. Reading between the lines, I think they're monitoring him because he's either working for them, or they want him to lead them to someone."

"And they don't want me messing it up," Michael finished.

"I don't think it's just that." Chris lowered his voice again. "Before I left the office, I put a call into an old friend over in Homeland Security. I didn't expect to hear back from him until tomorrow, but he called me as I was leaving Matt's game. According to him, Lowell Kwan is on their radar for ties to a North Korean regime. Guess who heads the regime?"

"I don't have to guess," Michael retorted, a grin breaking across his face. "You called to tell me."

"Jin Seung Moon," Chris told him triumphantly.

Michael froze and his blood ran cold.

"Are you sure?" he demanded, all humor gone.

"Yes. Mike, Moon is in New York," Chris said seriously. "Now look, I don't know what's going on up there, and I don't want to know, but you know as well as I do that Moon is bad news."

"Well, that explains why the CIA has all the files blacked out," Michael murmured. "Do you think they're running Kwan?"

"I don't know," Chris answered, "and frankly, I don't want to know. I'm telling you because I thought you should know what kind of deep shit you managed to get yourself into up there."

"I appreciate that."

"You want my advice, go back to Brooklyn and play Bingo with mom and pops, and stay out of Jersey until this is all over," Chris said.

Michael shook his head slightly.

"You know I can't do that," he replied. "But don't worry. If Kwan is involved with Moon, I know I can't touch him. All I can do is make sure he doesn't come after..."

Michael's voice trailed off as a black Jeep came around the house and pulled up outside the garage. He watched Alina open the door and climb out with two large pizza boxes. All at once, he inhaled sharply.

Jin Seung Moon was a notorious terrorist for the North Koreans, and Interpol had spent over five years trying to prove it. He was on every list of every Western government security agency. Everyone knew he was a terrorist, but no one could do anything about it. The death toll attributed to him was staggering, yet he was so influential in the financial market that time and again, he evaded prosecution. Michael's eyes narrowed as he watched Alina lean back in and pull something out of the back of the Jeep. Moon was just the sort of person Viper hunted.

And someone in her agency wanted him to stay out of it.

"Mike? You still there?"

"What? Yeah, I'm here," Michael said. "Look, thanks for the heads-up. I have to go. I'll talk to you later."

"Ok. Be careful up there," Chris said.

"I will," Michael assured him grimly, watching as Alina turned toward the deck with a six-pack in her other hand.

He disconnected and slid the phone back into his pocket, moving toward the steps of the deck.

"I guess Angela got a hold of you?" he called, going down the steps

233

and meeting her on the grass.

"She didn't need to," Alina answered dryly. "As soon as I saw she called, I knew what she wanted."

"Wow, you know her well," Michael said. He reached out and took the pizza boxes from her.

"I know she doesn't cook," Alina retorted with a laugh. "I don't buy prepared food. She probably had a heart-attack when she looked in the fridge."

"Something like that," he agreed, turning to walk with her. "You've been gone all day. Do anything fun?"

"Just taking care of some errands," Alina answered vaguely, moving up the steps of the deck. Michael followed her, his eyes narrowed. "They took longer than I expected."

"I thought maybe we scared you away from your house," he murmured, forcing a smile.

Alina glanced at him thoughtfully as she slid open the door to the living room.

"It takes more than a Marine to scare me," she informed him with a slight smile.

Michael grinned and went into the living room. Viper watched him go, her eyes narrowing behind his back. She hadn't missed the sharp, searching look he gave her as he took the pizzas from her. He was getting suspicious, and Alina wondered what had happened to make him so.

Before she could give it any more thought, a shiver of awareness shot down her spine. Viper turned her head and cast a searching glance across the back lawn. Her hand moved instinctively to her side, ready to reach for her weapon if needed. When the tall shadow emerged from the trees, her shoulders relaxed and the tension disappeared as her heart thumped in her chest. No matter how many times Hawk appeared out of the shadows, Alina didn't think she would ever get over the little rush of excitement that shot through her at the sight of him.

Michael looked over his shoulder to see why she wasn't following him, only to find Alina standing at the door with her head turned toward the yard. The look on her face made him pause, and he glanced out the door into the darkness, searching for what had arrested her attention. When Damon crossed into the light, moving toward the deck, Michael glanced at Alina again. The look that caught his attention was gone, and she was smiling faintly, appearing slightly bored as she waited for Damon to cross to the deck.

Chapter Twenty-Four

"I smell sausage!" Angela sang, tripping down the hallway and into the bar area.

Michael and Damon already had the pizza boxes open on the bar, investigating the two large pies, and Angela joined them, trying to peer between their broad shoulders. Alina glanced over her shoulder as she pulled plates out of the cabinet next to the sink, watching in amusement as Michael nudged Damon over so he could reach the beer sitting on the other side of the pizza. Damon nudged back harder, causing Michael to bump into Angela.

"Really?" Alina demanded, going over to the bar and setting the plates down. "You guys are acting like kids. The pizza isn't going to disappear, and neither is the beer."

Michael grinned at her and grabbed a plate.

"You never saw Dave and I at the mess hall," he retorted, scooping up a slice of sausage and pepperoni and plopping it onto his plate. "We used to tackle guys out of line."

"Somehow, that doesn't surprise me," Alina murmured, caught off guard at the casual mention of her brother. "Dave never could stand to miss a meal."

She bit her lip, suddenly remembering her brother when they were much younger, making peanut butter and jelly sandwiches. He would make three of them after school and eat them standing up in the kitchen while she worked on her homework at the table. The unexpected memory blindsided her and Alina quickly turned away to go over to the cabinet as a suspicious lump formed in her throat.

"I don't think any man can," Angela was saying behind her as she pushed Michael out of the way. "Whatever happened to ladies first? Move over!"

"Wait your turn," Michael retorted, eliciting a gasp from Angela.

"Hey! If it weren't for me, you'd be eating lettuce!" she retorted.

235

Reaching around him, she grabbed a plate. "So, move it!"

Alina took a deep breath and reached up to open the cabinet with the wineglasses. It had been a long time since she thought of Dave. They were inseparable, right up until he joined the Marines and went off to fight the good fight. He was killed in Iraq when an insurgent put a bullet through his head. Devastated, Alina joined the Navy less than a year later. Over the years, Viper learned to keep Dave in a little box somewhere deep inside her, opening the box only rarely, and only when she was alone.

A strong hand reached over her shoulder and pulled out a wine glass, handing it to her. Alina turned her head and met bright blue eyes.

"You ok?" Damon asked softly, those eyes probing hers gently.

"Fine," Alina replied.

Damon studied her lazily with his sharp blue eyes. A faint smile played about his lips and Alina had the uneasy feeling she wasn't fooling him for a minute.

"Someday, you'll have to show me a picture of this mysterious brother of yours," he murmured, grabbing two pint glasses and another wine glass from the cabinet.

"He's not mysterious. He's dead," Alina retorted shortly. "And you're going to miss out on the sausage and pepperoni if you don't get over there. I think Angie just took half the pie."

Damon didn't even bother to look, his eyes locked with hers.

"You're going to have to let me in eventually, Viper," he told her, his voice so low she had to strain to hear it.

Alina's lips tightened as she struggled to take a breath. She felt as if she was suffocating and she didn't like the feeling one bit. Before she could respond with a biting retort, however, Damon turned away. He carried the glasses over to the bar, leaving her to suck in a deep breath and collect herself.

"What wine do we want?" Angela called from the dining room, where she had the wine cabinet open and was surveying their choices. "Pinot Noir?"

"Fine!" Alina called back, her voice sharper than she intended. "I'll bring the corkscrew."

She turned to open a drawer and scowled when she saw her hand shaking. Damn Hawk! Who did he think he was, trying to get inside her head? Her brother was part of her life before she joined the military, before she met Damon in basic training, and before she learned to forget who she was, focusing instead on what she had to become. Damon didn't need to know that person. He didn't need to know anything about her. All that should concern him was who she was now and the life she lived here. Her past had no place with them, just as his had no place with her.

Alina grabbed the corkscrew and shut the drawer impatiently. And damn Michael for mentioning Dave and stirring this all up in the first place!

Michael was in the middle of amusing the table with a funny anecdote involving Blake and a monkey in the streets of Delhi when Alina's phone started vibrating against her thigh. Both pizza boxes were empty and they were all still sitting at the table, two empty beer bottles and half a bottle of wine in the center. Setting her wine glass down, Alina reached into her cargo pocket and pulled out her phone as Damon set a fresh beer on the table in front of Michael. He glanced over curiously as she swiped her screen before reaching behind him for another beer for himself.

Alina glanced at the alert flashing on the phone. Touching the screen, she opened the software for the tracker she had attached to Lowell Kwan's car. Hawk's eyes narrowed as the faint smile was wiped from her face and he paused in the act of lifting his beer to his lips.

"What is it?" he asked, cutting Michael off mid-sentence, his eyes on her face.

Viper raised dark, emotionless eyes to his.

"We've got company."

Damon set the beer down, untouched, and glanced at Angela. She was sipping her wine, looking from one to another curiously.

"What do you mean, we have company?" she asked. "Is Stephanie coming over? Should we open another bottle of wine?"

Michael watched as Alina pushed her chair back and Damon turned to cross over to the windows along the back of the house. He set down his beer as Damon started pulling the heavy drapes closed.

"How do you know?" he asked simply.

"I tagged his car," Alina said over her shoulder as she moved into the kitchen swiftly. She opened a lower cabinet and pulled out her laptop, setting it on the counter and flipping it open. "He's less than a mile away."

"Who?" Angela asked. "What's going on?"

"Kwan's on his way here," Michael told her, standing.

"What?!" she exclaimed, startled. "How do we know? How does he know I'm here?"

"He doesn't." Damon finished drawing the drapes across the sliding doors and turned to head down the hallway toward the front of the house. "He's going back to the last place he saw you."

"Then let's turn off all the lights and stay away from the windows,"

Angela said, setting her glass down. "Then he'll go away."

"I wish it was that simple," Michael murmured, smiling despite himself.

"Well, then what do we do?" Angela demanded, getting up and setting her hands on her hips. "What's the plan?"

"9 minutes!" Viper called down the hallway to Hawk, closing the laptop with a snap. "I armed the perimeter so we know where he is, but it won't stop him."

"9 minutes till what?" Angela cried. "Lina, what the hell are you talking about?!"

"Until he breaches the perimeter," Alina said shortly over her shoulder. "Michael, take her upstairs."

"Like hell I will," Michael retorted. "You stay with her. I'll take care of Kwan. Just tell me where he is."

"Spoken like a true Jarhead," Damon muttered, emerging from the hallway. "All the lights are out in the front of the house. If he wants to see inside, he'll need night-vision goggles."

"He won't get close enough to need them," Viper said grimly, spinning around and heading for the back door. "Michael, last warning. Take her upstairs."

"STOP!!!" Angela screamed as her hand touched the sliding door handle.

Viper swung around, her hand reaching for her gun even as she realized there was no threat. Michael's eyebrows soared into his forehead with the shriek and Damon rolled his eyes, grimacing at the sound.

"What?" Alina demanded impatiently.

"You're not going out there! Are you crazy?!" Angela cried. "He could be armed!"

"I hope he is," Alina said under her breath.

"No!" Angela stalked over to her and stomped her foot. "You're *not* going out there!"

Damon's lips twitched. He crossed his arms and leaned against the wall in the living room, watching silently.

"Angie, I'll be fine," Alina said, trying to be rational. "Michael is here to protect you, so he has to stay here with you. If it'll make you feel better, I'll take Damon."

"No. Michael can go," Angela said obstinately.

"Well, thanks," Michael murmured, his eyes dancing. "I'm glad I made such a good impression on you."

"Well, you're used to this sort of thing," Angela explained, spinning around to face him. With her back to Alina, she missed the incredulous look that crossed her face. "You're a Federal Agent."

238

Michael nodded gravely, not trusting himself to speak just yet as Alina almost rolled her eyes out of her head.

"Ang..."

"No. Michael goes, or no one goes." Angela spun around again and crossed her arms over her chest. "He knows how to handle stuff like this. I don't want you to get hurt because of me."

"For the love of God, I'm not..."

"She's right," Damon spoke up, cutting Alina off. Her eyes flew to his and he winked behind Angela's back. "You stay here with Angela and I'll go with Michael. Between the two of us, we should be able to...persuade Kwan to leave her alone."

Viper met Hawk's gaze and read the subtle warning deep in his eyes. She glanced at Angela and suddenly understood what he was doing. Angela looked at her, waiting, and Alina allowed herself to sigh and nod reluctantly.

"Fine," she said ungraciously and released the door handle. "I have ear pieces. Put them in and I'll direct you from here," she added, crossing the living room to the hallway. "They're in the den. I'll get them."

"Time's wasting," Damon murmured as she passed him. The look she shot him made him grin. "Just sayin'."

Viper muttered something in German under her breath that surprised a bark of laughter from him and disappeared down the hallway.

"What did she say?" Michael asked, standing close enough to have heard the muttered remark. "It sounded like German."

"Nothing fit for the tender ears of a Marine," Hawk told him, his eyes still dancing. "I don't think she cares for the arrangement."

Michael chuckled.

"I'm enjoying it, myself," he admitted.

"How can you be enjoying this?" Angela muttered, sinking down onto the couch. "This is a nightmare. What if he's armed? What if he shoots you?"

"He'll have to be pretty quick to get the chance," Michael replied. "Trust me."

"Well, I do feel better that Damon's going with you," Angela admitted. "He's in the Department of Homeland Security, you know, so he carries a gun too."

Michael shot Damon a startled look and Damon smiled blandly.

"Here. Take these." Alina came back before Michael could think of an appropriate remark. "I'll monitor the perimeter from here and guide you to him."

"Oh my God!" Angela suddenly cried from the couch. The three turned to look at her. "What if he has people with him?"

"Don't worry." Michael turned toward the back door. "Just stay with Alina and stay out of sight. We'll take care of you."

Viper couldn't stop her eyes from narrowing at Michael's taunting words as he judiciously moved out of her reach. Damon grinned and tucked the ear piece into his ear.

"See what happens when you live in Jersey? I don't have these problems on my ranch," he murmured softly, laughing at the murderous look she shot him. "Take her upstairs," he called over his shoulder as he followed Michael.

"Yes, thank you," Alina snapped.

"Don't forget to lock this behind us!" Michael called, only the slightest tremor in his voice betraying how much he was enjoying her discomfiture.

The door slid shut behind the two men and Alina stalked over to flip the lock. She glanced at her watch, then turned to Angela.

"Turn off the lights," she told her, heading over to her laptop on the counter. "It's safer upstairs."

"Why?" Angela asked, getting up and walking over to the light switch on the wall. She flipped off the lights in the living room, then moved into the dining room. "And why are we turning off the lights?"

"It makes it harder for an intruder to navigate without giving away his position," Alina said shortly, flipping off the kitchen lights. The back of the house plunged into darkness. "And it's safer upstairs because I have a good view from the windows. If he somehow makes it past H—Damon and Michael, I'll see him before he gets to the house."

Alina turned down the dark hallway, shaking her head slightly at her near slip. This whole situation was ridiculous. She should be the one out there, not Michael. She understood why Damon sent her the silent warning, though. It was a miracle Angela didn't suspect something already. As it was, too many people around here were aware of her true identity.

"How are they going to convince Lowell to leave me alone?" Angela asked as she followed her up the stairs.

"I think we'd rather not know," Alina muttered truthfully. While Angela would be horrified if she knew just how Hawk 'persuaded' people to do what he wanted, *she* would be horrified if Michael didn't use equivalent pressure. "It's best to just let them handle it." *And if they don't, I'll blow his head off,* she added silently.

"Do you want me to get the lights up here?" Angela asked as they reached the second floor.

"Please," Alina answered, glancing at her watch. "We'll go into the room you're sleeping in. It has the best view of the front."

She disappeared into the spare room as she spoke, switching the light off as she entered. Angela went into the next room to turn off the lights and Alina waited a moment for her eyes to readjust to the darkness. When they had, she moved over to the window and glanced out over the dark trees.

"Not to be a pest, but which way are we going?" Hawk's voice murmured low in her ear.

"Give me a second," she murmured, opening her laptop and setting it on the floor next to her. She opened the security perimeter cameras and started scanning them. "Ok. The car is parked in the trees near the road, just about where it was last time he showed up."

"What about him?" Michael asked.

"Still looking," Alina replied, scanning the camera angles. "Hold on."

"All the lights are off," Angela said as she came into the room behind her. "Now what?"

"Sit down out of sight," Alina said over her shoulder.

Angela sank down onto the floor beside the door with her back against the wall, watching as Alina moved from one quadrant to another on her laptop. She stayed quiet, watching the black and white images from across the room. Alina examined each one before swiping over to the next one on the touchscreen monitor. She examined one, swiped to the next, then quickly went back again, leaning in to examine it more closely.

"Found him," she breathed, a smile curving her lips. "He's using a maglite. Looks like he's alone."

"Great. Where is he?" Michael asked.

"About fifty yards from you, to the south," she answered, glancing at the camera Michael and Damon had just passed.

"Thanks," Michael said.

Alina watched on the cameras as Damon and Michael turned, moving through the trees to the south. She smiled slightly at Hawk's lethal, jungle-cat stride, caught by surprise at the rush of affection rolling through her.

"Can you see them?" Angela asked, breaking the silence in the room.

Alina glanced at her.

"Yes."

Angela got up and came over, sinking down beside her and looking at the widescreen monitor.

"Where are they?"

Alina pointed to the screen.

"They're about to come into this quadrant....there," she said.

"And where's Kwan?" Angela asked.

"There." Again, Alina pointed to another box.

Angela watched silently as Lowell swung the thin flashlight over the ground, moving through the trees.

"What happens if he gets to the house?" Angela asked after a moment.

Alina glanced at her and Angela shivered involuntarily at the look in her eyes.

"He won't."

Stephanie stared at the ceiling above her sofa, her mind and body numb. It was close to ten and she was too exhausted to get up off the couch and go to bed. Her mind kept spinning, going over every fact and every coincidence they had come across in the past four days. Somewhere, there had to be a common thread. Somewhere, it all had to come together and make sense. But where?

The flash drive Alina gave her with Jessica's testimony on it helped clear up some points. Now, at least, they knew why Jessica had been willing to assist with placing the arm inside the Dungeon. Because of her testimony, they also had more proof the Cartel killed Rodrigo. What it *didn't* tell them was what brought Jenaro Gomez to Jersey in the first place.

Stephanie sighed and rubbed her eyes. She was almost positive Jenaro had come here after Philip Chou, but how to prove it? So far, there had been no contact that they knew of between Chou and Gomez. There was no word yet on the BOLO they put out on the mysterious Mexican Catering van, the only thing they had that could possibly link Chou to the Cartel. Essentially, she had absolutely nothing.

Kwan was another story altogether. Alina said he was at Chou's apartment moments before her agents got there, but how to prove it? An illegal tracking device couldn't be admitted as evidence. Philip's laptop hadn't turned up, and there was no way to link Kwan to the hacking ring without either Philip's laptop or Kwan's own hardware. It didn't matter that she had all kinds of circumstantial evidence burying him neck deep in the events of the past four days. Without proof, she had nothing. Even if Angela could be convinced to testify to Lowell's knowledge of Rodrigo's head before it was made public, a good lawyer would shred it in minutes. As far as Lowell Kwan was concerned, Stephanie still had nothing.

A knock on her front door pulled Stephanie out of her reverie and she frowned, glancing at her watch. She swung her legs off the sofa and went over to the door, peering through the peephole. Blake stood outside, his head elongated and distorted, staring at the peephole.

"Hey!" Stephanie opened the door. "What's up?"

Blake smiled at her.

"Sorry it's so late," he apologized. "I wanted to stop by on my way back to the hotel to tell you we found the catering van."

Stephanie raised her eyebrows and stepped aside, motioning him inside.

"When?" she asked, closing the door behind him as he stepped into her living room.

"About an hour ago," Blake answered, glancing around. "It was abandoned at an old empty building down in Riverside."

"Anything useful in it?" Stephanie asked, crossing back over to the couch.

"Not really." Blake shook his head. "I sent it over to have the forensics team go through it. Maybe they'll find something." He crossed over to sit on the edge of an armchair, looking at her thoughtfully. "You look exhausted."

"I am," Stephanie admitted, rubbing the back of her neck. "I can't seem to settle down."

"You've got one hell of a mess on your hands," Blake said. "Your best bet to figure it out, though, is to get some sleep. You won't be much good without it."

Stephanie looked at him.

"How are you making out with Jenaro?" she asked. "Any luck?"

"I think I've narrowed down the neighborhoods he can be in, but it's slow. I know how he works and he's like an eel. Just when you think you have him, he slips away." Blake shrugged. "But I think we're getting close."

"I got some information today about Jessica Nuñez," Stephanie told him. "It's her testimony, on a flash drive. I'll get you a copy. Apparently, her parents were murdered in Mexico by Gomez. He followed her to the States and was bought off by her husband. He left them alone after that, until now."

"Sounds about right for him," Blake murmured. "What does he want from her?"

"He used her to run errands for him, one of which was placing Rodrigo's arm inside the cell where we found it," Stephanie said tiredly. "He has her son. That's how he guaranteed her cooperation."

Blake whistled softly.

"There's a complication," he murmured. "Any ideas where?"

"Nope." Stephanie shook her head and yawned widely. "We've put out an amber alert, but we have nothing to go on."

"Where *is* Ms. Nuñez?"

"In protective custody, of sorts," Stephanie muttered. "I don't have access to her yet."

Blake stared at her and she waved her hand, her face showing her frustration.

"Don't ask," she told him. "I can't tell you. Suffice it to say she's in good hands until Jenaro is no longer a threat."

Blake stared at her thoughtfully for a long, silent moment.

"So, Ms. Nuñez is in hiding and her son is being held by Gomez," he finally said slowly. "And the husband?"

"He and the daughter have two agents with them," Stephanie answered. Her brown eyes met Blake's. "Not for nothing, I'm confident the boy will be found sooner, rather than later."

Blake raised an eyebrow.

"That's optimistic of you," he commented. "Any particular reason why?"

Stephanie smiled faintly.

"He's got a couple aces on his side," she murmured, "and I'm starting to learn they never lose."

Chapter Twenty-Five

Hawk shook his head and grimaced as Michael stepped on a dead branch. The resulting crack echoed through the trees, causing both men to freeze, listening to the night. An owl hooted nearby and the night air was cool and crisp. Hawk took a deep breath of the fresh air, enjoying the fall bite. His ears strained for noise outside the normal creaking and popping of scavenging animals, and he motioned to Michael when he detected the sound of movement a few yards away in the trees. Michael nodded and slipped behind a thick tree trunk, watching the darkness as Hawk moved silently around to the other side. Between them, they had Lowell flanked.

Michael waited patiently, watching for the tell-tale beam of light to show him Kwan's location. He didn't have long to wait. A thin slice of light cut through the darkness a moment later, a few feet away. He glanced over to where Hawk had moved, but his companion seemed to have disappeared into the darkness. Michael frowned slightly, then shrugged to himself. Pulling out his 9mm, he silently slid the safety off and waited in the shadows for Lowell to come closer.

The beam of light grew brighter, and Kwan emerged from between two trees, his attention focused on the ground. He never glanced up as he passed the tree concealing Michael, and was caught completely by surprise when Michael stepped out behind him.

In one fluid motion, Michael had his arm wrapped around his throat and the barrel of his gun pressed against his neck.

"I seem to remember telling you this is private property," Michael growled.

Lowell froze for a split second before twisting swiftly and bringing his hand up in a quick jab. Without quite knowing how, Michael found himself pushed backwards, his gun skidding across the ground into a drift of dead leaves. He caught the white flash of teeth as Kwan grinned briefly in the dark before swinging his foot in a high arc, aiming it at his head. Michael's military training came back to him in an instant. Swiftly blocking

245

the kick with his forearm, he twisted his wrist and latched onto Lowell's ankle. Where Lowell was small and wiry, Michael had sheer strength on his side. He pulled, throwing Lowell off balance. Lowell flew backwards, tried unsuccessfully to catch himself with his other leg, and ended up on his back. Releasing his ankle, Michael raised his foot to bring it down on his other knee, but Lowell twisted out of the way hurriedly. He kicked one of Michael's ankles and Michael stumbled heavily with a curse.

"You people and your Kung Fu," he muttered, reaching down and picking Lowell up by the neck of his shirt. His fist connected solidly with his jaw and Lowell's head snapped back painfully, his body going limp. "All your fancy moves, and still no match for an old-fashioned, hard punch," Michael said disgustedly, dropping Lowell's unconscious form onto the ground.

"There's nothing wrong with martial arts when used effectively," Hawk remarked, materializing from the shadows. Michael glanced at him as Damon looked down at Kwan. "*That* was not effective."

"Where the hell were you?" Michael demanded, leaning down and scooping up his gun from the pile of leaves. He flipped the safety back on and blew debris off the gun. "Way to be a wingman."

"I figured I'd let you show me what you've got," Hawk answered with a grin. "I know how you Marines like to show off."

"If you want lessons, you just have to ask. We're always glad to help a squid out," Michael retorted, drawing a laugh from Damon.

They stood and looked down at Lowell together. He lay unconscious, across a dead tree branch, his head tilted at an odd angle.

"What are you going to do with him?" Hawk finally asked.

"Damned if I know," Michael admitted.

Damon glanced at him, his lips twitching.

"You've really thought this through, haven't you?" he asked.

"Give me a break," Michael said. "Your agency has expressly forbidden me from touching him. All I can do is keep him away from Angela. This is new territory for me."

"My agency?" Hawk raised an eyebrow. "How did they find out?"

"I accessed his file in the system. They had it flagged and came down hard on my boss." Michael scratched his chin. "Technically, I suppose I shouldn't have even touched him."

Damon grinned at the unrepentant look Michael's face.

"You knew that when you came out here?"

"Yep."

"And you still came?"

"What was I supposed to do? Let Viper come and show Angela that she clearly isn't who Angela thinks she is?" Michael asked with a shrug.

He glanced at Damon thoughtfully. "You know, *I* can't touch him..."

Hawk grinned as Michael's voice trailed off.

"You're gonna owe me another beer," he told him, referring to a bet they made two months ago on the trails in Peru.

"Bullshit. You still owe *me* beer," Michael retorted with a grin, reviving the old argument.

Hawk chuckled and bent down to grab Lowell's wrist. He was in the process of hauling him up to toss him over his shoulder when Lowell started to come around. Without missing a beat, Hawk slammed his fist into Lowell's jaw, sending him back to never-never land.

"Tell Angie to rest easy," he said, hefting Kwan over his shoulder. "I'll make sure he gets the message."

"I know you will," Michael murmured.

Alina and Angela were waiting for him on the deck, settled in the Adirondack chairs with glasses of wine, when Michael stepped through the trees into the back yard. The back spotlights were on and Raven perched on the banister, watching him as he emerged onto the lawn. As soon as he appeared, Angela jumped up and ran down the steps to cross the lawn.

"I watched the whole thing on Lina's security camera thingy," she told him, running up to him and throwing her arms around him. "Thank you, thank you, thank you!"

Michael blinked, taken aback when she launched herself into his arms. His arms closed around her automatically and he sent a startled look over her head to Alina. She just sipped her wine and shook her head.

"Uh, you're welcome," he mumbled.

Angela pulled away, not seeming to notice his surprise at her impulsiveness.

"Where did Damon take him?"

"I've no idea," Michael answered truthfully, walking up the steps of the deck.

"Lina doesn't know either. I wanted to say thank you." Angela sounded disappointed. "Does this mean I can go back to my house now?"

"No."

Michael and Alina spoke in unison and Michael grinned. Angela seated herself on her chair again and looked from one to the other.

"Why not?" she asked. "He's going to leave me alone now, right?"

"After Damon's finished with him? Most likely," Alina said, a trace of amusement in her voice. "But it's better to be safe and make sure."

She reached down beside her chair and picked up a cold bottle of beer, passing it to Michael.

"How long do I have to wait?" Angela demanded.

"As long as it takes to be sure," Michael said, taking the beer with a smile. "Thanks. You're a woman after my own heart."

"I thought you deserved something," Alina replied, her eyes glinting in the dark. "It wasn't quite the show I hoped for, but it was beer-worthy."

"I appreciate that," Michael murmured.

"I thought it was wonderful," Angela announced. "Really, Lina, sometimes I think you're just blood-thirsty. What did you want him to do? Blow his head off?"

"That would have been one option," Alina murmured with a faint smile, "but he *is* a federal agent. I guess I shouldn't expect too much."

"Keep it up, buttercup," Michael retorted without heat.

"Lina, he was a Marine," Angela pointed out, coming to his defense.

"My point exactly," Alina said swiftly, winking at Michael.

He chuckled and Angela looked confused.

"But....I don't get it. Your brother was a Marine," she said, looking at Alina.

Alina laughed.

"I know. I'm being a smart-ass," she told her. "It's a Navy thing."

"There's an oxymoron," Michael murmured, drawing another laugh from Alina.

"Touché," she murmured.

Angela shook her head and glanced at her watch.

"Well, I'll leave you two to insult each other as you see fit," she said, standing up with her glass of wine. "I have to feed Annabelle and I want to catch The Voice on TV. Thanks again, Michael."

"You don't have to thank me," Michael said, watching as she went to the sliding door.

Angela disappeared into the house and Michael took her place in the Adirondack chair. He and Alina were silent, looking out over the dark lawn and darker trees. The breeze ruffled her hair and Alina sighed, sipping her wine contentedly. She leaned her head back against the chair and listened to an owl hoot in the trees while the raccoons chattered back and forth to each other. The sky was overcast, but some moonlight shone through the clouds and a crisp, cool breeze ruffled her hair. It was a perfect fall evening.

"What will he do with him?" Michael broke the comfortable silence.

"Persuade him that Angela isn't a loose-end that needs tying," Alina answered.

"Your agency tied my hands with him, you know," he told her.

Alina glanced at him sharply.

"How so?"

"Someone from the CIA came down on my boss pretty hard today. Essentially, I was told I can't touch Kwan," Michael said, looking at her. "Any idea why they're protecting him?"

Alina's dark eyes were hooded and her face gave nothing away.

"I'm not privy to the Director's files," she said. "If I had to venture a guess, I'd say they want him for themselves, but I really have no idea."

"That's my thought," Michael agreed, lifting his beer to his lips. "That or they're running him."

Alina turned her attention back to the dark trees silently. She couldn't tell Michael about Moon, but she suspected he already knew about him anyway. If the CIA had taken the trouble to warn Michael off Kwan, his boss would have wanted to know why. What concerned her was why they had approached Chris Harbour at all. Why were they so worried about keeping Kwan safe?

"So, have we scared you away from Jersey yet?" Michael asked after another lengthy silence.

Alina chuckled and shook her head.

"You're getting close," she admitted, "but not yet. With any luck, Stephanie will wrap her case up and take Kwan off our hands for good. Then, at least I'll get Angela out of the house."

"She really has no idea, does she?" Michael asked, leaning his head back. "About you?"

"I don't know," Alina said, pursing her lips thoughtfully. "Angie sees more than she lets on. I don't know how much she's figured out, if anything."

Michael glanced at her.

"It really bothers you, doesn't it?" he asked quietly. "Having so many people know what you do."

Alina's glance was swift, her mask firmly in place.

"The more people who know, the more dangerous it is for them," she said shortly. "I've made a lot of enemies who would have no compunction about taking out innocents to get to me."

"Would it make you feel better to know all the files pertaining to Washington DC two months ago were sealed?" Michael asked.

Viper laughed shortly and humorlessly.

"Not really," she replied. "I know how easy it is to get into sealed files."

Michael remained silent, knowing nothing he said would convince her that her identity was fairly safe. It wasn't the sealed files or the fact that they were all federal agents that made it so, but the fact that they all loved and respected her. They had an emotional investment in the woman at his side, and Michael knew it was stronger than any oath or sealed file. He also knew only time would prove it to Viper. She had forgotten what true friendship meant, and it was going to take a long time to remind her.

"What about Damon?" Michael changed the subject. "He was compromised as well."

"He's still cleaning it up," Alina said, finishing her wine. She got up restlessly and moved over to lean against the banister, setting her empty wine glass on the edge. "Regina left a trail of pictures with every mercenary, assassin, and government agent out there. We were able to seal off the digital path, but there's no way of knowing how many times it was saved or reproduced. The one thing working in his favor is the habit most of us have of permanently deleting pictures and files of a hit once we've read them."

"She really did a number on you two, didn't she?" Michael asked softly. He didn't miss the flash of anger in her eyes as she glanced at him. "I'm surprised they still have him in the field."

"As I said, he's still cleaning it up," Alina answered, tamping down the sudden flash of anger ripping through her at the thought of Regina. "For now, he's considered uncompromised."

Michael nodded and watched her thoughtfully. Her restlessness grew and she turned to look over the dark expanse of grass, tension in every fiber of her body. She was still furious, he realized. Killing Regina hadn't appeased the fury still simmering below the surface, fury he suspected was due more to what Regina did to Damon, rather than to her.

"What's done is done," he said quietly. Alina turned her head slightly, her only acknowledgement of his words. "You can't change what she did. All you can do is help repair the damage and hope for the best."

"I never was much good at just hoping for the best," she muttered, turning to face him again. She had reigned in her anger, he noted, and her face was back in the neutral expression she habitually wore. "If Hawk becomes compromised because of her, it will be my fault. I can't just brush that away with happy thoughts of butterflies and daisies."

Michael couldn't help the chuckle that escaped at that.

"If he was going to be compromised, it would have already happened," he said, standing and joining her at the banister. "It's been two months, plenty of time for any enemies he's made to get hold of the picture. They would have moved by now."

Alina thought of Jenaro Gomez and her lips tightened.

"Perhaps," she murmured.

Next Exit, Dead Ahead

"You two are pretty close. You met in basic, didn't you?" Michael asked, lifting his beer to his lips.

"Mmm." Alina turned to look out into the darkness again. "We haven't seen much of each other over the years. It's only the past few months we've had the chance to reconnect."

"So what's the story there? I always got the impression you secret agent people were loners."

Alina smiled faintly at his weak jab at her agency.

"We are," she answered. "Unfortunately, some people like to ignore that."

Michael grinned at her not-to-subtle jab back.

"And Damon's one of us?" he asked. "I got the impression in Peru he was used to being alone, and so were you."

"We are," Alina replied quietly. "When he was sent to be my backup last Spring, neither of us knew how to work as a team. We still don't. I think we make it up as we go along." She glanced at him and Michael glimpsed the Lina he met years ago deep in her dark eyes. "What we do is a lonely job. Not many people can understand it."

"I guess it's like going to war every day," Michael said thoughtfully. "When I got back from my last tour in the Middle East, I felt like no one could possibly understand the things I had seen. Blake felt the same way. We helped each other in that regard."

"Something like that, yes."

"It's good you were able to reconnect with him, then," Michael told her gently. "You probably need each other more than you realize."

Alina fell silent for a moment, tamping down the abrupt feeling of melancholy threatening to overcome her. The crisp night air suddenly seemed cold and the sounds of the night owls were starting to grate on her nerves.

"Damon and I....it's complicated," she finally said, her face shuttered.

"I can see that," Michael answered. He considered her thoughtfully. "How complicated?"

"Why are you asking?"

Michael met her gaze unflinchingly.

"I need to know," he answered softly.

Alina stared into his green-hazel eyes and felt something tug deep inside her, something akin to longing, but not as sharp and insistent as the haunting feeling that hovered just below the surface with Hawk. If things were different, if *she* was different, Michael would have been perfect for her. As it was, he was out of reach to her now, and somewhere deep inside her, Alina knew she regretted that.

"There's nothing you need to know, Michael," she replied, her voice just as soft. "Only what you *want* to know."

Michael smiled faintly and raised his hand to cup her cheek gently. "There's a lot I want, but most of it's not in the cards, is it?"

"No." Alina smiled slightly, bringing her hand up to cover his. "And you don't really want what my reality is. You've seen what I do, what I become, who I am. That's not for you."

"You really need to stop thinking you know what's best for everyone else," Michael murmured. "Maybe it's time you start thinking about what's best for you."

"And that's you?" Alina couldn't help the grin that curved her lips, taking the edge off her next words. "You Marines really do suffer from a bloated sense of self-confidence."

"It comes with the uniform," he retorted with an answering grin. He moved his hand from under hers and closed his fingers around it, letting their joined hands drop from her face. "I'm sure Dave didn't anticipate any of this when he asked me to look out for you, but like it or not, you're stuck with me. It may not be in the role I would like, but I'm in your life to stay. You might want to warn your SEAL of that."

"He knows," Alina murmured.

Michael nodded and looked down at their joined hands. The light from above the deck glanced across them and he traced a soft line across the back of her knuckles. He glanced up at her and the light caught the green glint in his eyes, making them glow like cats' eyes.

"I'll be here if you need me," he said softly. "You don't scare me, Viper."

Alina flinched at the sound of her codename on his lips, but she couldn't seem to make herself tear her gaze away from those sparkling green eyes.

"You're a good man, Michael O'Reilly," she whispered, her voice catching.

"And you're a good woman, Alina Maschik," he replied, "even if you don't realize it."

Alina smiled faintly and released his hand, turning to go into the house. Michael stopped her as she reached for the door.

"And you're wrong, you know," he said, leaning against the banister and crossing his arms over his chest. He looked at her steadily.

"About what?" she asked, turning her head to glance back at him.

"I've seen what you do and I saw who you become in order to do your job," Michael told her, "but I haven't seen who you *are*. Not yet. There's more to you than Viper."

Alina felt as if she had been hit in the chest and had all the air knocked out of her. She stared at Michael, the blood pounding in her ears, as she tried to ignore the rush of emotions suddenly crashing over her. Michael watched her mask slide seamlessly into place, effectively blocking her thoughts from him.

"I wish I could believe that," Viper answered shortly.

"You don't have to believe it," Michael retorted. "It's the truth and always will be, whether you believe it or not."

Alina stared at him wordlessly for a moment, her eyes shuttered and emotionless, before she turned and went inside. Once she had closed the door, Michael turned to look out over the darkness. A slow smile pulled at his lips. For a minute, before the shield came down, he had glimpsed her surprise...and fear. For a moment, he had seen Lina Maschik, the young woman he had drunk Jameson with years ago. She still lurked there, buried beneath all the armor and all the years of fighting.

Dave, I'm trying, Michael thought, glancing up at the sky, *but she's not making it easy.*

Chapter Twenty-Six

Awareness came to her slowly. It was the silent hour just before dawn, when the birds were starting to stir in their nests and the night was getting lighter, but the sky hadn't started to change from midnight blue to gray just yet. Viper didn't question what had awakened her. She simply opened her eyes and listened. The house was silent, neither Angela nor Michael were stirring, and Raven was settled on his perch, his beak buried in his shoulder, fast asleep. Rolling over in bed, she glanced at the window. It was closed, the sheer curtains hanging still before it.

Alina yawned and stretched before tossing off the down comforter and getting up. Raven lifted his beak and blinked, gazing at her sleepily as she headed into the bathroom. A few minutes later, she emerged and disappeared into the walk-in closet. When she reappeared, Viper was dressed in gray yoga pants, a tank top, and running shoes. Raven stood up and stretched, ruffling his feathers and shaking his head. As she went silently out the bedroom door, he moved to the end of the perch and flew up to the skylight, disappearing through the trap door.

Hawk watched from the trees as Raven hopped out onto the roof and looked around. His black eyes latched on Damon unwaveringly and Hawk smiled faintly. He swore that bird had radar. He shifted his gaze to the deck as a light came on in the living room and Viper appeared at the sliding door, dressed in yoga pants. He *knew* she had radar.

Damon waited for her to come onto the deck before moving out of the trees and onto the grass. She looked at him and stretched, coming down the steps toward him.

"Morning," she murmured, joining him near the trees.

"Morning." Hawk looked down at her and smiled faintly. "You're up early."

"So are you," she muttered. "How'd it go last night?"

"Kwan decided Angela wasn't much of a threat after all," Damon told her.

Alina nodded.

"No surprise there," she said with a quick grin. "Can he still walk?"

"Of course," Damon answered, turning to walk with her into the trees. "He may have some trouble typing for a while. His right hand may or may not have some broken bones, but he'll live."

"Good. Anything new on Jenaro?" Viper asked, glancing at him.

"I'm getting closer," Hawk told her. "Have you found the boy yet?"

"I'm getting closer," Alina retorted, drawing an appreciative grin from him. "I have a pretty good idea who has him. I just have to find out where he's keeping him."

"I haven't seen any sign of a little one with Gomez," Hawk told her, stopping and leaning against a pine tree. "Are you sure he's still in New Jersey?"

"Positive." Alina stood in front of him and looked up into his face. "Let me find him before you take out Gomez. I don't want to risk losing the boy if you eliminate the only person who definitely knows where he is."

"Then hurry," Hawk said, his blue eyes hard. "I'm not waiting much longer."

"I'll find him soon," Viper assured him. She looked at him, noting the rings under his eyes. "You look exhausted. Did you sleep?"

"For a couple of hours," Damon replied. "I checked into a hotel. You have a full house and I thought it was best not to climb in through your window again."

Alina tilted her head and considered him.

"That's probably true," she agreed softly. "Have you eaten?"

"Is that an offer for breakfast?" Damon asked with a smile.

Alina chuckled and turned back toward the house.

"Yes, and coffee," she said over shoulder. "You look like you need it."

"Throw in access to your command center for an hour and I'm all yours," Hawk replied.

"Oh, I know you are," Alina murmured.

Damon grinned and reached out to grab her wrist, jerking her up against him swiftly. Lowering his lips to hers, he kissed her until she had no breath left inside her. When he finally lifted his head, his own breathing came in ragged gasps and his eyes pulsed a dark, mesmerizing cobalt blue.

"Just making sure we're on the same page," he murmured, his lips curving slightly.

Alina shook her head slightly and pulled away.

"Come on. Let's get you fed and into the command center before the natives start stirring," she said, pushing away the rush of desire threatening to send her back into his arms. "They don't know it's there, and I'd rather keep it that way. I want to keep *some* secrets from Michael."

"For a Marine, he's a good guy," Damon remarked, falling into step beside her as they emerged from the trees.

"I'm glad you like him." Alina glanced at him. "He said to tell you he's not going anywhere."

"Oh, I'm aware of that." Hawk glanced up to the roof where Raven watched them protectively. "As long as he doesn't get in my way, I have no problems with him."

"What happened in Peru, exactly?" Viper asked, stopping at the foot of the deck steps and looking at him. "You two came back buddies."

Hawk grinned at her.

"It's a guy thing," he told her with a wink. "We bonded on a goat trail."

Alina's eyebrow soared into her forehead and she turned to go up the steps.

"Oh Hawk, there are so many things I could say to that," she murmured, "but I'll keep them to myself."

Stephanie stood silently, staring at the body hanging from the tree in front of the prison. The rope creaked eerily as a brisk wind caused the body to sway in a slow, grotesque movement that made the corpse appear almost alive. A white screen had been hastily erected around the tree, concealing it from the busy road and curious onlookers, and Stephanie was glad of the semi-privacy it provided as she stared mutely at the sight.

Philip Chou was missing one shoe and his right hand. His dark hair hung limply over his eyes like a veil and his head was twisted at an odd angle, suggesting he really had been hanged to death. He wore the clothes he was wearing when he disappeared out of the office, according to Scott's statement, and his shirt was liberally splattered with blood. Stephanie knew she should feel ill at the thought that the blood spatters were undoubtedly from his own severed hand, but she couldn't seem to feel anything but numb. After an arm, a head, and a tongue, she supposed she should be grateful that, with the exception of the missing hand, Philip seemed to be all in one piece.

John rounded the corner of the screen with a large Wawa coffee in each hand and his eyes went straight to the corpse suspended from the tree.

"Holy Mother of God! You weren't lying," he exclaimed, staring at the body.

Stephanie glanced at him and reached out to take one of the cups.

"Did you really think I would make this up?" she demanded, sipping the hot coffee thankfully.

"No. And, it *is* the day before Halloween," John replied, examining the body from where he stood. "How the hell did they get him up there? It must be at least fourteen feet up to that branch."

"How did they do any of it?" Stephanie retorted. "Of course, no one saw anything. He's hanging from a tree, right on a main road, in the middle of the front yard of a prison *and no one saw a thing!*"

John raised an eyebrow at the uncharacteristic sharpness in her voice.

"Who found him?" he asked, sipping his coffee.

"One of the uniforms over there." Stephanie jerked her head back toward the group of policemen standing near the side of the prison. "He drove by about five and saw him hanging here."

"Why are they standing all the way over there?" John asked.

Stephanie shrugged defensively.

"I may have told them to keep their incompetence contained elsewhere so it wouldn't contaminate my crime scene," she said.

John choked on his coffee.

"And you say *I* need to work on my inter-agency diplomacy," he exclaimed, laughter leaping into his pale blue eyes.

"Well, they *are* incompetent," Stephanie retorted. "How do you patrol a neighborhood every night and not see someone get hanged from a tree? Or not see someone put a tongue on the steps? Or leave a head on a spike? I mean, seriously? These people aren't ghosts. There's no excuse for this!"

"Maybe the Cartel has an ear on the scanners and knows when the patrols go by," John suggested, turning his attention back to the hanging body of Philip Chou. "What about our guy? Didn't you put one of our agents on surveillance here? Why didn't he see anything?"

"I don't know." Stephanie set her coffee down and pulled a pair of gloves from her pocket. "I sent him back to the office and told him to explain himself to Rob directly. I didn't trust myself not to shoot him."

"Now you sound like the Black Widow," John told her with a grin, pulling on his own gloves and turning his attention to the grass around the tree. "Did we send for our techs, or are they all incompetent as well?"

"Keep it up, Smithe, and I'll send you home too," Stephanie snapped.

John grinned and fell silent, bending down to examine the ground. The lack of rain had left it hard, making it impossible to see imprints in the hard-packed dirt.

"The ground's too hard to get any prints off it," he said, glancing up at the body. "We'll need the techs to check for any stray DNA."

"They're on the way," Stephanie mumbled, her hands on Chou's legs. She held him steady as she stared at something on his head. "Does that look like a bruise to you?"

"Where?" John asked, standing up and moving to her side.

"There, on his temple."

John looked at the discolored swelling near Philip Chou's left temple.

"It looks like he was hit on the head with something," he answered, tilting his head. "Maybe that's how they got him out of the building and into the van."

Stephanie nodded and let go of the legs, releasing the body back into the wind.

"Probably," she agreed. "Larry should be able to tell us more when he gets a good look at him."

"Where *is* our trusty ME?" John asked, looking around. "Usually he's right on time."

"He's on his way." Stephanie stepped back and stripped off her gloves. "The van popped a tire in a pothole on the way here. He called just before you got here."

John nodded and watched as Stephanie sipped her coffee and stared at the body pensively.

"What are you thinking?"

"Why are they going through all this trouble?" Stephanie asked, glancing at him. "Leaving bodies around the prison is risky and dangerous. Why bother?"

"To leave a message," John replied with a shrug. "Blake and the Black Widow both seem to agree that the Cartels have a dramatic streak in them. Gomez is leaving a message."

"For who? He's running out of audience members to intimidate."

"Not quite," John said slowly. "He still has Kwan."

Stephanie stared at John.

"Or Moon," she murmured thoughtfully.

John nodded and pulled off his gloves. His phone started ringing and he reached into his pocket, pulling it out.

"It's the agent we put on Kwan checking in," he said, swiping the screen and pressing accept.

Stephanie nodded, turning her thoughtful gaze back to Philip Chou's body as John turned and walked away, his phone pressed against his ear. She still stood, staring at the body absently, a minute later when John came back, his face grim.

"Looks like Kwan flew the coop," he told her. "Peter hasn't seen him since last night. He followed him out into the Pine Barrens, then lost him when his GPS went berserk on him. He went back to Lowell's apartment to wait for him, but he hasn't come back yet."

"The Pine Barrens?" Stephanie looked at John sharply. "Where?"

"Peter doesn't know," John replied. "You think he was going after Angela?"

"Call the Black Widow and find out," Stephanie replied, turning away from the body of Philip Chou. "If he did, he may not be running. He may have just run into Viper."

"In which case, we may be looking at another body soon," John muttered, looking up Alina's number in his phone. "What if he didn't?"

"We'll get another damn BOLO out," Stephanie replied grimly. "This is getting to be ridiculous. How many BOLO's can we possibly put out in the space of a couple days?"

"I don't know, but I'm pretty sure you've already broken the department record," John answered with a grin.

Alina reached into her pocket and withdrew her silently vibrating phone. She glanced at the screen and raised an eyebrow slightly when she saw John's number flashing.

"Yes?" she answered shortly, returning her gaze to the large, gray building across the road. Police tape roped off the front yard and she watched the swarming activity, centered around a white screen concealing the body blowing in the breeze.

"Hey, you got a minute?" John asked.

"For you? Not really," Alina replied, raising her scope to her eye and studying the white screen. John appeared from around the screen, walking away with his phone against his ear. "But talk."

"We just got word Lowell Kwan never went home last night," John told her. "He was last seen heading into the Pine Barrens. You know anything about that?"

Alina shifted the scope from John's profile to the group of local police officers standing in a group near the Warden's House, well out of the way of the hubbub.

"Possibly," she murmured. She turned her head to watch as the ME van turned down the side street next to the prison and stopped near the curb.

"Let me put it this way, Lina," John said, a note of steel threading into his voice. "Tell me what happened last night or I'll charge you with impeding a federal investigation."

"How ambitious of you!" Viper retorted. "Did you put an extra shot of espresso in your coffee?"

"Lina!"

Alina chuckled and watched as the ME and his assistant got out of the van.

"Kwan came after Angela," she relented. "He showed up in my security perimeter around 2100 hours. Michael and Damon went out, intercepted him, and Damon convinced him he was better off leaving Angela alone."

"Then what?" John asked after a brief silence.

"Nothing." Viper lowered the scope and pursed her lips thoughtfully as she watched the activity across the road.

"Nothing?" John sounded incredulous. "He just left and you went about your business?"

"For the most part," Alina agreed. "You say he didn't go home?"

"No."

Alina paused for a long moment, then her lips twitched.

"Are you telling me you guys lost another witness?" she asked in amusement.

"I wouldn't get too cocky," John snapped. "You're the last one to see him, so that makes you a witness now."

"Hmm." Alina grinned. "I guess I better be careful. I might disappear."

"Keep it up and I'll take care of it myself!" John threatened.

Alina burst out laughing.

"Don't get your panties all in a bunch, John," she advised, still chuckling. "Go finish your coffee and tell Stephanie I still have the tracking dot on his car. I'll find him for you."

"We don't need you to find anything for us," John informed her.

"Oh really? Are you sure? Because you don't seem to be having much luck finding your witnesses while they're still alive."

John was silent, speechless either from chagrin or anger.

"Good. Now that's settled, I have things to do," Alina said. "I'll be in touch with Stephanie as soon as I get his location."

Viper disconnected the call and slipped the phone back into her cargo pocket. Glancing at her watch, she got up and moved toward the fire escape at the back of the roof. She dropped her scope into her pocket, swung onto the ladder and disappeared over the edge of the roof.

John put his phone away and turned to go back to Stephanie with a scowl. Larry and his assistant were walking up to the screen as he approached and he watched as Stephanie turned to greet Larry, her phone in her hand. She waved Larry behind the screen and turned to meet John, her expression grim.

"Blake just called. Ramiero Losa turned up," she told him.

"Ramiero Losa of the cigarette butt in yonder maze?" John asked.

"Yep."

"That's good news!" John said. "Where is he?"

"In Mt. Laurel, with a bullet in his skull," Stephanie replied, turning to walk toward the Warden's House.

"*Not* good news," John sighed. "Where?"

"Oh, that's the fun part," Stephanie told him. "Next to a lake behind the IT building of One District Bank."

John stared at her.

"Where Kwan works?"

Stephanie nodded.

"Did you get hold of Lina?" she asked, glancing at him.

"Yes. Kwan went after Angela last night," John said.

Stephanie stopped walking and looked at him.

"Well?"

"She says Michael and Damon intercepted him and convinced him to leave Angie alone, then he left," John told her. "She said to tell you she still has his car tagged and she'll let you know when she has a location on him."

"Well, that's something at least," Stephanie muttered and started to move again. "We know he wasn't running last night. Whether or not he is now, after his run-in with them, is another question. Let's get the BOLO out anyway, just in case. I don't like that he's the last one standing at this point. I'll head over to Mt. Laurel and see what the story is with Ramiero while you stay here and supervise this mess. When Larry's done here, tell him to get over to Mt. Laurel. I'm sure he already got the page."

"You got it." John nodded and turned to head back toward the white screen.

Stephanie rounded the corner of the Warden's House and strode toward the small parking lot behind it. With everyone turning up dead, Lowell was her last chance to salvage this case. If she lost him, she lost all hope of finding the virus.

She had to find Lowell Kwan before he turned up dead as well.

The scar on Jenaro's face   paled against his dark skin as he stared at Turi.

"Are you sure?" he demanded.

Turi nodded solemnly.

"His body was found at a marina yesterday afternoon," he said. "He was shot in the head."

Jenaro swung around and strode to the window of the living room. "Have you heard from Ramiero yet?"

"Nothing."

Jenaro turned his attention to the street below, his jaw twitching. Turi waited silently, loathe to say out loud what both men were thinking. When the messenger came to him last night with the news of Lorenzo's death, Turi postponed telling Jenaro, hoping there had been some kind of mistake. When he saw the papers this morning, he knew there was no mistake.

"Find Ramiero and get him back here." Jenaro finally spoke, his back still to Turi. "It must be the Hawk. He's the only one stupid enough to do this thing."

Turi nodded and turned toward the door.

"Turi?" Jenaro turned his head and glanced at him. "Get everyone ready to travel. We leave tomorrow."

"What about the boy?" Turi asked with his hand on the door handle.

"We take him," Jenaro said shortly, turning his attention back out the window. "I have a buyer willing to pay more than I expected for a seven-year old boy."

Turi nodded and disappeared out the door, closing it softly behind him.

Chapter Twenty-Seven

Stephanie got out of her car and looked around. A parking lot ran behind the IT building, running the length of the long structure. Behind it, a stretch of grass led to a heavily wooded area. Blake's SUV was parked on the grass, pulled up near a break in a row of trees, and Stephanie started towards it. A uniformed police officer came toward her, holding out his hand to stop her, and she showed him her badge tiredly.

"Right through there, Agent Walker," he said, nodding to the break in the trees.

Stephanie nodded and continued across the grass. She could see the glint of water through the trees, and a couple of geese honked as they glided overhead. Stepping past the trees, she saw a small lake nestled in the middle of the wooded area. The morning sunlight filtered through the branches and shone brightly across the water, dappling the mossy grass beside the lake with speckled bands of light. It would have been a picturesque setting had it not been for the flurry of activity taking place to the left side of the lake, near a dense copse of thickets.

Blake looked over from where he crouched beside a figure on the ground and waved her forward.

"Busy morning!" he called, standing up as she approached. "I heard you found Chou."

"Yes. He's hanging from a tree outside the Prison," Stephanie told him, looking down at the body stretched out on the ground. "Larry will be along as soon as he's finished there."

"Meet Ramiero Losa, formerly of the Casa Reino Cartel," Blake told her.

"He wasn't in the water, I see," Stephanie murmured.

"No. Some employees found him in the thicket while they were having a cigarette," Blake said. "They pulled him out, thinking he was just passed out, but then realized he wasn't breathing."

"Any of them ever see him before?" Stephanie asked, glancing at

263

Blake.

He shook his head.

"No." Blake crouched down and turned the dead man's head so she could see the small hole near the temple. "Your ME will confirm, but it looks like the same size hole as Lorenzo."

"Poor Larry." Stephanie pulled on gloves and crouched down on the other side of Ramiero. "I don't think he's finished with Lorenzo yet, and now he has two more."

"He hasn't. I already talked to him," Blake told her. "All he could tell me was it was .22mm shell."

Stephanie nodded and studied Ramiero. The small hole near his temple barely marred the side of his head, with only a thin line of dried blood coming from the wound.

"That would explain the small entry wounds," she murmured.

"Nasty things, .22s. They bounce around inside the skull like a pinball," Blake agreed. "Other than the hole in his head, there doesn't seem to be any sign of struggle."

"You think he knew his attacker?" Stephanie glanced at him sharply.

Blake shrugged.

"Don't go putting words in my mouth," he replied with a grin. "All I'm saying is there doesn't appear to have been a struggle. That could mean he was taken by surprise, knew the attacker, or just plain didn't expect to get shot."

"Fair enough," Stephanie agreed and turned her attention back to the body. "Are you still standing by your statement that this isn't Gomez?"

"I think so," Blake said thoughtfully. "There's no reason for Jenaro to be killing off his crew, especially so far from home."

"Who else would know where they were? Or even *who* they were?" Stephanie murmured more to herself than to him. Blake answered her anyway.

"Well, that's the big question," he said. "If we knew the answer to it, we'd have a good idea who wants them dead."

"Aside from half of Mexico, you mean?" Stephanie stood up and looked around the isolated lake. "What was he doing here?"

"Now, *that* I think I can answer," Blake said, standing up and motioning her away from the body. Stephanie followed him a few feet away from the techs and police officers. "One of the guys who found Ramiero said he was pulling into work early this morning when he saw a man coming out from the trees."

"Did he now?"

"Yes. Now, he says the man came out further down there, toward the other end of the building." Blake pointed in the opposite direction. "Apparently, this is a fairly common area for hunting and the employees here do occasionally see hunters and fishermen early or late in the day. He didn't think anything of it until they found the body a few hours later."

"Where is he?" Stephanie asked.

Blake nodded to the police officer on the other side of the trees.

"The officer out there has him waiting for us," Blake told her.

Stephanie nodded and glanced back to Ramiero.

"You ok here while I go see if I can get a description?" she asked.

Blake nodded and turned back to the body.

"Absolutely."

John watched as Larry drove away, Philip Chou's body in the back of the van, before he turned to head towards his motorcycle. Two techs were finishing up with the pictures, and he had all the evidence bags in their SUV, ready to go back to Matt. He glanced at his watch and sighed. It was almost ten. Another morning spent at this prison. John glanced up at the dark building and scowled. If he never saw the place again, it would be too soon.

He brought his gaze back down and glanced at a policewoman heading towards him. She was dressed in uniform, a standard issue on her hip, and her hair pulled back into a ponytail at the back of her head. Large sunglasses shaded her eyes from the bright morning sunlight and an FOP baseball cap cast shadows across her face. Smiling at him cheerfully, she headed toward the two officers at the front steps of the prison. He nodded back as he passed, reaching into his pocket to pull out his phone when it started to ring.

"Yo," he answered, walking up to his motorcycle.

"Are you almost finished there?" Stephanie asked.

"Just finishing now," John said. "Larry is on his way over there. He said to tell you Ramiero will take up his last open table, so if any more show up, you'll have to call the city ME."

"Ha!" Stephanie chuckled. "He should be so lucky. Did you find anything interesting after I left?"

"Not a thing." John got on the bike. "What's the story over there?"

"Ramiero was shot in the head with what looks like the same type of weapon used on Lorenzo," Stephanie told him. "Larry told Blake it's a .22."

"That explains the small entry wound," John said thoughtfully, unconsciously echoing her words. "Any leads?"

"Glad you asked," Stephanie replied. "As a matter of fact, yes. Lowell Kwan was seen leaving the area around six-thirty this morning."

"What?!" John exclaimed.

"I thought you'd like that," Stephanie said with a slight chuckle. "A witness described him and when I showed him his picture, he confirmed it. As a matter of fact, as soon as I showed him the picture, he recognized him as the "crazy smart analyst" who works on the other end of the building."

"He didn't recognize him when he saw him this morning?" John asked.

"Apparently, it was still somewhat dark and Kwan looked a mess. The witness thought he was a hunter. He was covered in leaves and brush and was favoring his right hand." Stephanie stifled a yawn. "So, as of six-thirty this morning, Kwan was here."

"You think he's the one knocking out Jenaro's guys?" John asked with a frown.

"I don't know," Stephanie answered. "Why don't you head over here and bring coffee and bagels with you? I'm starving and running low on caffeine."

"On my way," John agreed and disconnected.

The policewoman glanced back briefly at John's retreating back before approaching the two officers at the front of the prison. She nodded to the senior officer.

"Agent Smithe wants me to check inside once more," she told him, placing one foot on the bottom step.

"Again?" he asked, rolling his eyes. "I think the Feds are getting a little paranoid."

"Tell me about it," she agreed with a grin. "I heard they think a ghost is doing all this."

"Wouldn't be surprised," he chuckled. "Karl was busy filling their heads with ghost stories their first day here."

"Hey, are you the rookie from Mt. Laurel?" the other officer asked, putting a hand on her arm as she started up the steps. She glanced at him.

"Yeah. Sandy Whitaker," she replied, holding out her hand.

"Joey Miller," he introduced himself. "And that's Donnie. Welcome to Prison."

She pulled her hand away and chuckled.

"Thanks, I think," she murmured. She glanced back to the

motorcycle, where John had his phone pressed against his ear. "I better get in there. He looks like he's watching me."

"If you need anything, give a yell," Joey told her, watching her as she continued up the steps. He caught Donnie's grin and grinned back. "What?"

"Hitting on the rookie already?" Donnie demanded as she disappeared inside the prison. "She just got here!"

"So what?" Joey shrugged. "Did you see the rack on her?"

"Yeah, I saw," Donnie retorted. "I also saw the way she carries herself. Do yourself a favor and don't piss her off."

"What can I say? I like it rough."

Viper slipped silently down the steps to the basement of the prison in her stolen uniform. She shook her head over how easily she had walked into the prison, then grinned. John had looked right at her and not recognized her. People only ever saw what they expected to see, and that one simple fact never failed to amaze her. John expected to see a stranger, and a stranger was what he saw.

The chill in the basement of the old prison crept into her bones and made her muscles ache for the warmth of sunshine. Viper paused at the bottom of the steps for a moment and looked down the long, narrow corridor. It was empty and the silence seemed oppressive. A chill snaked down her spine and her lips tightened as the hair on the back of her neck rose. Reaching out her gloved hand, she rested it on the stone wall lightly. The cold from the stone seeped through her black gloves and the chill spread down her arm.

"Whatever you are," Alina murmured, her voice a mere breath, "I'm not here for you."

The cold increased and Viper slowly pulled her hand away from the wall, trying to ignore it. The track lighting in the corridor shone brightly, casting a yellow glow over the old curved walls with their crumbling whitewash, and she sent another glance down the long hallway, searching for shadows. There was nothing, but all her senses were screaming that she was not alone.

Turning, Viper slipped around the corner and opened a storage closet, glancing inside. Boxes and tubs filled the small space, labeled neatly on the outside in black marker. There was no room for anyone to fit in the closet with the containers, so Alina silently closed the door and moved on to the next room. She quickly went through every room and closet at this end of the basement, ever conscious of the cold following her. When she finished, Alina faced the long corridor again with a sigh.

She began to move down the main corridor, glancing into the museum rooms along the way. The basement housed the kitchens and tooling rooms for the prison, and she scanned each room cursorily. What she searched for would not be found in the public display rooms of the prison, and her searching glances were focused on windows and doors, not the artifacts themselves. She moved down the hall quickly until she reached the last room in the corridor. Larger than the others, it boasted a huge fireplace and a fairly large window at ground level.

Viper's lips curved coldly in satisfaction. The window was ajar.

She entered the room, crossing swiftly to the large window. An old, large metal shelving rack on wheels stood in front of the window and Viper examined it carefully, noting the small clumps of dirt on the top shelf. She eased it away from the wall slowly, cringing at the loud screech the old wheels made in protest as they moved slowly across the worn stone floor. Slipping behind the rack, Viper scaled the brick wall easily, holding on to the window sill above her head. She pulled herself up and glanced at the narrow, stone sill. It was covered with dirt and dried leaves from outside. Reaching out, she touched one of the iron bars and it slipped sideways against the window. It had been sawed at both ends.

Viper dropped back down onto the floor and smiled.

Now she knew how he got in and out.

She just had to find where he was being hidden.

Damon stretched and yawned, glancing at the security monitor that showed him the kitchen and living room above. Still ensconced in Viper's command center, a large bottle of water sat at his elbow and a breakfast plate lay empty beside it. Viper left him there, under strict instructions to stay put until Michael and Angela were not there to see him sneak out. He had watched on the security camera as she left over two hours ago, leaving Angela settled at her dining room table with her laptop and Michael outside, tinkering with his truck.

Damon turned his attention back to the computer in front of him and looked at the hotel call logs streaming onto the screen. He raised an eyebrow as one from the penthouse suite caught his eye, and he checked the log time with a frown. Placed twenty minutes ago, the call had been outgoing to the Rittenhouse Hotel in Philadelphia. Hawk refreshed the call logs and pursed his lips when he saw another outgoing call from the same suite to a cell phone. He turned to his laptop and opened a special database, plugging in the cell number swiftly. He smiled slightly when he got a hit back on a name he recognized.

Turning back to the computer, Hawk opened another browser, pulling up the Rittenhouse Hotel main number. He picked up his cell phone and dialed, sitting back in his chair while it rang. His gaze wandered back to the security camera and he watched as Angela stretched and then hunched over her laptop again.

"Good Morning! Thank you for calling the Rittenhouse. How may I assist you?" a female answered the phone, her voice a perfect blend of efficiency and friendliness.

"Heavens! Is it morning there? Yes, I suppose it is," Hawk's voice slipped into an effeminate tone with a crisp British accent. "Sorry. I'm calling from London. It's the middle of the night here."

"And how can I help you, sir?"

"I'm calling to confirm a reservation for Jin Seung Moon," Hawk told her, throwing in a yawn for good measure. "I'm told it was called in a few moments ago."

"Hold just one moment, sir," the woman said politely, "and I'll take a look."

She placed him on hold and Hawk's eyes strayed to the outside camera where Michael had his head under his truck hood. As he watched, Michael pulled his head out and wiped his hands on a rag laying nearby.

"I have it here, sir." The efficient woman was back on the phone, drawing Damon's attention from the security cameras. "One of our Parkview Suites for two nights, checking in tomorrow. Is there a problem?"

"Problem? No, not at all. Mr. Moon simply likes to be assured that everything will be as he requested," Hawk told her cheerfully. "We've learned to confirm and re-confirm everything before he arrives."

"I understand, sir," the woman said, allowing a smile into her voice now that the threat of losing the reservation was laid to rest. "We'll be ready for his arrival at five-thirty."

"Wonderful! Then I can go back to sleep in peace for a few hours," Hawk announced. "Thank you so much."

"Not at all."

Hawk disconnected the call and set the phone down, smiling slowly.

"Gotcha," he whispered.

269

Viper straightened up from where she crouched in front of the window outside and glanced around her. All the bars had been sawed, then placed back in position as if nothing was out of the ordinary. The ground around the window was disturbed and Alina fingered the scrap of white tee-shirt she pulled off a jagged piece of stone in the corner of the window frame. Frowning thoughtfully, she tucked the fabric into one of her pockets and turned to move along the path of the haunted maze.

Her gut told her that Jenaro was hiding the boy close-by, and her bet was on the prison grounds. She was pretty sure the guide had been kidnapped to take care of the boy, and when Karl disappeared, Viper gathered the two were becoming a handful. She had already checked the inside of the prison, so that just left the exercise yard and the Warden's House. Too many people were coming and going from the Warden's House. The FBI were using it as a work center, causing Viper to bet heavily on the odds of the exercise yard.

Somewhere out here, a small boy was being held captive.

Rounding a bend in the path, she paused as she passed a flight of steps that led to a locked door in the prison. Alina glanced at it, recognizing it from when she walked through the haunted maze as a paying spectator. She pursed her lips and turned to continue walking, following the maze through a section of corrugated metal walls housing mock hospital rooms and cells. Halfway through the section, Viper stopped and swung around as an icy chill ran down her spine. Her eyes narrowed and she cast a searching glance up to the forbidding prison looming over the maze.

Without knowing why, she began walking back toward the steps leading up to the locked door. The chill on her back remained, growing stronger as she drew closer to the steps. Viper ignored the cold, her eyes fixed on the small window high above her: the window she now knew belonged to the Dungeon.

She reached the steps and put her foot on the bottom one, intending to go up to the door, but as soon as Alina set her hand on the railing, the icy chill disappeared. Frowning, she glanced up the sheer wall to the dark window. The feeling of awareness was gone.

Viper turned around to step off the step and glanced up, looking straight-ahead. Her breath stilled. Up ahead, where the path veered into the hospital ward section of the walk, ten-foot tall pieces of plywood lined the left-hand side of the walkway. Alina had assumed the pieces of wood were leaning directly against the prison. However, looking straight from the steps, she could see a narrow opening between the wood and the wall creating another walkway behind the maze.

Viper stared at the opening for a beat, then glanced back up at the Dungeon window. With a slight nod of her head, she turned and strode forward into the narrow walkway, following it behind the maze. It ran parallel with the prison, but when the maze turned inward, the outer walkway got wider, turning into a "backstage" section for the actors in the haunted maze.

Alina stepped over an upside-down metal barrel and followed the path around the outer wall. About halfway around, she stopped and her lips curved into a smile. Straight-ahead in the corner, up against the wall of the prison yard, stood a large, 2-story shed. It looked as if it was a temporary garden shed, probably rented to help house all the extra paraphernalia the haunted walk required. A padlock hung on the door and black paper covered the inside of the windows on the ground level.

Viper glanced around, listening to the silence around her before turning to her left and moving over to the wall. She quickly and silently scaled the wall, pulling herself onto the top a few moments later. She paused, taking a moment to catch her breath, and looked down on the other side. The wall over-looked a small parking lot and half a dozen cars were parked below her. Viper shook her head slightly, wondering why on earth she risked exposing herself like this for a small boy, before moving swiftly along the wall toward the shed. No sooner had the thought entered her head then she knew the answer.

She did it because there was no one else.

And men like Jenaro Gomez couldn't be allowed to win all the time.

Chapter Twenty-Eight

Viper slipped through a small window and dropped silently into the shed. She found herself in the center of a large loft packed with plastic boxes and tubs, electric cabling, and spare outdoor light fixtures. A narrow aisle wound its way through the storage area to the edge of the loft, where the top of a fixed ladder peeked a few inches above the loft floor. She crouched, silent and still, her eyes narrowing at the muffled sobbing coming from below.

She had found Marcus Nuñez.

Viper crept forward silently until she reached a large wooden crate near the edge of the loft. Concealed behind its solidness, she peered over the edge. Murky shadows cloaked the ground floor of the shed, with the only light being that which filtered down from the two windows above. Marcus huddled in the corner to the left of the door, his head on his knees. His black running pants were covered with dust and dirt, and a grime-streaked white tee-shirt hung from his bony shoulders. Next to him on the floor lay an empty McDonald's bag with some crumpled hamburger wrappers and an old pillow with a thread-bare blanket. It was clear that the boy attempted to muffle his sobs as he buried his face in his knees, his arms over his head.

Alina scanned the rest of the floor slowly. The storage boxes had been pushed to the other side of the shed, leaving no room for anyone to move on the right side of the shed. There was no sign of anyone else in the front of the lower level, but Viper knew they were there. They would never leave the boy alone, even locked in. They had to be toward the back of the shed, below her.

Even as she thought it, Alina heard movement directly below her. The top of Karl's head came into view as he moved out from under the loft, cursing.

"Shut up!" he yelled as he moved towards Marcus. "I'm tired of listening to you!"

Next Exit, Dead Ahead

Marcus didn't raise his head, but Alina heard him take a gasping breath as he tried to control his sobs.

"Stop it, I said!"

Karl kicked Marcus's feet, causing his legs to fly out in front of him.

"Leave him alone!" a female voice cried from underneath Alina. "He can't help it."

"He can, and he will," Karl snarled. "What a useless piece of shit. All he does is cry and eat."

"He's a little boy, not a piece of shit," the woman retorted, coming into view from the back of the shed. "He misses his family and he's scared. What do you expect from him?"

Her brown hair was pulled into a ponytail and she still wore the white nurse's scrubs smeared with fake blood that she had been wearing in the haunted walk the night she disappeared. She hurried across the floor as Marcus scooted as far back into the corner as possible, pulling his legs back up to his chest. He looked up and Viper saw huge, frightened eyes in a thin face before the woman hid him from view. She turned to face Karl defiantly and Viper's lips tightened grimly as she got a good look at the missing guide and Jessica's friend, Rachel. One black eye was completely swollen shut, while the other side of her face displayed a variety of multi-colored bruises and welts, making her skin tone indeterminable. Her bottom lip was split open in three different places and blood caked the side of her mouth. It looked like she had tried to clean it the best she could, but whether or not it had been split open again or had never stopped bleeding was up for debate.

Viper cut her gaze to Karl, the flirtatious night guard Stephanie thought so charming, and her eyes dropped straight to his hands. Red, angry wounds stretched across his right knuckles.

Anger burned inside Viper, hot and intense, and she watched through narrowed eyes while Rachel stood between Karl and the boy. She couldn't see out of one eye, but her chin pointed upwards and Viper had to admire her obvious commitment to preventing him from laying a hand on the boy.

"I expect him to shut up when I tell him to," Karl retorted. "Get out of the way. Or do you want me to close your other eye?"

"Will that make you feel more like a man?" Rachel shot back, scorn dripping from her lips.

Viper kept her eyes on the trio in the corner as she swung her legs over the edge of the loft. Reaching down, she undid the holster holding her military knife strapped to her ankle. Marcus caught sight of her then, his eyes getting even wider in his face as he stared at her. Viper raised a finger to her lips before dropping out of the loft and landing softly on the floor below. Neither Karl nor Rachel heard, so intent as they were on each other, and she moved across the floor silently.

"You can't protect the kid for much longer," Karl hissed. "Jenaro is taking him with him tomorrow. Then you'll have no purpose here and nothing to bargain with, bitch."

Karl raised his fist and Rachel braced herself for the hit.

It never came.

Viper clamped two fingers on Karl's shoulder near the base of his neck and swung him around effortlessly, using his own pressure point to propel him around.

"Why don't you try that with me?" Viper purred, her cold eyes meeting his.

"What the...who the hell do you think *you* are?!" Karl demanded.

"Your worst nightmare."

Stephanie pulled into the parking lot behind the Warden's House and slammed on her brakes. Jumping out of the car, she hurried around to the open door of the house and climbed the steps. A policewoman stationed just inside saw her and came forward, holding out her hand.

"Agent Walker?" she asked.

"Yes."

"They're right through here," she told Stephanie with a smile. "They're going to be fine, but the guide is pretty beat up. She wouldn't go to the hospital until you got here."

"And the boy?" Stephanie asked, following the policewoman through the front room of the Warden's House.

"He's frightened and wants his mother, but he's fine," she said, motioning Stephanie into a small make-shift office.

Stephanie stepped into the small room and her eyes went straight to the two figures huddled under police blankets, sitting close together on the window seat. The guide had her arm around the boy and their heads were close together. When she entered, Rachel looked up and Stephanie gasped. The pretty young woman whom she had interviewed four days before had disappeared completely. The damage to her face was extensive, leaving her unrecognizable, and if it weren't for her unique, aqua-colored eyes, Stephanie would have questioned if it was even the same woman.

"Oh my God," she breathed involuntarily.

"They won't give me a mirror," Rachel said ruefully, speaking slowly around her swollen lips. "I guess I don't need one now. Your face says it all."

"Who did this?" Stephanie asked, fury making her voice shake as she crossed the small space.

"Karl," Rachel answered, squeezing Marcus's shoulders as Stephanie approached. "It's ok, mi cielo, she's a good woman. She is here to help."

Stephanie crouched down before Marcus and glanced at Rachel. At her nod, she reached out and took his small, thin hands into hers.

"Hi Marcus," she said softly. "We've had a lot of people looking for you. I'm glad you're safe. I'll make sure we get hold of your mom, ok?"

Marcus raised huge, brown eyes to hers.

"You'll call my mom?" he asked hopefully.

"Absolutely," Stephanie promised. *Just as soon as I can get hold of the woman holding her,* she added silently.

"See? I told you she could help," Rachel told him. She looked at Stephanie through her one good eye. "He's been worried they would hurt her."

Stephanie paused, then sighed.

"They tried," she admitted softly. Marcus looked at her in alarm and Rachel squeezed his shoulders again. "A very strong woman saved her," Stephanie told him, squeezing his hands gently. "She put her somewhere safe."

"Was it the lady in black?" Marcus asked, his eyes brightening. Stephanie glanced at Rachel uncertainly, but before she could speak, Marcus continued, "She said she knew my mama. She said my mom was brave, almost as brave as me. And she said she would make sure I saw my mama soon."

"Lady in black?" Stephanie repeated, looking to Rachel for clarification.

"She never gave her name," Rachel told her. "She appeared out of nowhere, in the shed where he kept us. She...well, she stopped Karl from hurting us."

"Sounds like the same woman," Stephanie said dryly, her lips curving. "Scary, intimidating, and not someone you would mess with?"

"Yes."

Gathering from this exchange that Stephanie did, indeed, know the lady in black, Marcus leaned forward, his little body wriggling with excitement.

"She made Karl stop hurting Aunt Rachel," he announced confidentially, "and then she went like this," he chopped his hands in the air dramatically, narrowly missing Stephanie's head, "and *he* went like *this*!"

Marcus jumped up and pushed past Stephanie to stand with his fist

275

raised as he remembered seeing Karl raise his, then he dropped straight back to land flat on his back and lay completely still. Stephanie gasped and moved toward him, but a surprisingly firm hand came down on her shoulder to stop her.

"He's acting," Rachel whispered. "He's very good, actually."

Stephanie nodded and stopped, watching as Marcus opened one eye to peek at her. When he found her still watching, he grinned a big grin, showing off a wide gap where he was missing a baby tooth, and jumped up.

"She was awesome!" he cried, his dark eyes shining. "When Karl went down, she turned to Aunt Rachel and made her sit down! Then she came over to me and picked me up and took me outside. The door was locked, but she went right through it. It was magic!"

"It was?!" Stephanie exclaimed. "How do you think she did it?"

"I asked her, but she said it was a secret," he informed her solemnly. "She said it was an ancient secret and if she told anyone, she could die."

"I bet it was," Stephanie murmured, smiling despite herself. "What happened then?"

"Well," Marcus said, going back to the window seat and settling himself next to Rachel, "then she tried to carry me away, but I said we couldn't leave Aunt Rachel with Karl. He would hurt her again."

"I was perfectly fine," Rachel interjected, smoothing his hair back from his forehead.

"Well, you don't *look* fine," Marcus informed her with the kind of bluntness characteristic of children. "And I was afraid he would wake up and really hurt you then. But the lady in black, she said he wouldn't wake up for a long time. I asked her if she was a doctor and that's how she knew, but she just smiled at me and said in her business, she knew more than doctors. What does that mean, Aunt Rachel?"

"I don't know, mi cielo," Rachel said with a sigh. "There's a lot I don't know right now."

"Well, then she asked me if I thought the haunted maze was scary," Marcus moved on, losing interest once he couldn't get a satisfactory answer, "and I said, no. It was all acting and sets and one day, I would be acting on sets too!"

"Really!" Stephanie sat back on her heels and smiled at the little boy. "Can I come see you?"

"Sure!" he said with another toothless grin. "She asked the same thing! I told her yes, but she would have to leave the knife at home."

"Knife? What knife?" Stephanie asked, her ears perking up.

"The one she threatened Karl with," Marcus said cheerfully. "It was awesome!"

276

"But...I thought you said she hit him and knocked him out," Stephanie reminded him.

"That was after she pulled out her knife," Marcus told her. He looked up at Rachel. "Wasn't her knife cool? I've never seen a knife like that!"

"Neither have I," Rachel agreed, resigned. "It was very cool."

"It was awesome!"

"I'm sure it was," Stephanie murmured, turning to look at Rachel. "Did she come back?"

"Yes." Rachel nodded. "Once she had Marcus away and safe, she came back for me."

"Did she...say anything?"

"She told me that she had called you," Rachel said slowly, "and I could trust you."

"You can," Stephanie said quietly.

Rachel nodded, studying her thoughtfully through her one eye.

"I know," she said simply. "When she came back for me, she told me where to find Marcus and told me not to release him to anyone except you. She said you would keep him safe until she could get his mother to him."

"I will," Stephanie promised. "What happened to the bastard who did this to you?"

"The lady in black took him!" Marcus answered brightly, anxious to be part of the conversation again.

Stephanie looked at him and raised her eyebrows.

"She did?" she exclaimed. "Where did she take him?"

"She didn't say." For a moment Marcus looked crestfallen with that realization, then he perked up again. "But she did say he would never be able to touch me or Aunt Rachel ever again."

"I bet that made you very happy," Stephanie said.

Marcus nodded and suddenly buried his head into Rachel's side and wrapped his arms around her.

"He hurt Rachel," he told Stephanie plaintively, and she nodded gravely.

"Yes, he did," she agreed.

"She let him so he wouldn't hurt me."

"Yes, I know," Stephanie said, her heart breaking at the look in his eyes.

"The lady in black said he won't hurt anyone ever again," Marcus said, squeezing Rachel tightly. "I'm glad."

Stephanie glanced up at Rachel.

"Did she tell you anything else?" she asked her quietly.

Rachel met her gaze steadily.

"She told me to tell you everything I know," she said calmly, "and no one else."

Stephanie nodded slowly and glanced at Marcus.

"Let's start with him," she said softly. "What did they do with him?"

"They used him to move around the museum," Rachel told her, smoothing the boy's hair. "He could fit through the prison windows, you see. He's very athletic and they exploited that fact."

"What did they make him do?" Stephanie asked.

"They made him go through the dungeon window on the night before you found the arm," Rachel told her as Marcus buried his head in her side again. "He went in and moved the arm out from behind the dummy. They used some kind of cross-bow to shoot a zip-line in the window from the top of the wall. Then, they lowered him down from the roof and he slid in through the window. When he got inside, he took the end of the line from where it had latched onto the gate and moved it to the hook in the floor. He used it to climb out the window when he finished, sliding down the zip-line to the wall where Turi was waiting for him."

"The alarms!" Stephanie breathed and Rachel nodded.

"The grappling hook shot out of the gate, setting off the motion detector before it came back in and clamped onto the bars," she explained. "When Marcus got in and moved it to the hook in the floor, he set it off again."

Stephanie glanced at Marcus.

"It took him an hour and a half to get into the cell?" she whispered.

"He was terrified," Rachel replied. "He doesn't like heights. They told him if he didn't do it, or if he fell, they would kill Jessica."

"Karl said I'm going to jail," Marcus whispered. "He said I'm a cri...cri...a bad person now."

"No baby, you're not a bad person," Stephanie assured him, reaching out and taking one of his hands again. "You're very brave." She looked at Rachel. "Was that all he did?"

"No." Rachel shook her head. "They also made him put the blue box on the front steps."

"How did you do that?" Stephanie asked him.

Marcus peeked at her.

"I went in through the basement window in the back," he whispered. "If you go across the basement, there's another window. I went through it, put the box on the steps, and came back."

"And did Karl open those windows for you?" Stephanie asked.

Marcus nodded.

"What about..." her voice trailed off, not knowing how to ask if the boy had seen Rodrigo's remains or Philip hung up outside.

"He didn't see anything else," Rachel told her softly, seeming to know what Stephanie hesitated to say. "I made sure of that."

Stephanie glanced at her mutilated face and had no doubt as to how she had ensured the boy didn't witness a mutilated, headless corpse or a full dead body.

"Do you know why they chose this museum?" Stephanie asked Rachel. "Why all the elaborate displays?"

"Karl's been bringing drugs into Mt. Holly for them for about a year now," Rachel told her. "When Jenaro showed up and saw where he worked, he wanted to use it for the shock and fear value. Karl said the Cartel was intent on instilling fear in the area because they wanted to expand their reach to this state."

"What do you mean?" Stephanie asked.

"The Casa Reino Cartel is responsible for about thirty percent of the drugs on the streets from Florida up to Maryland," Rachel explained.

Stephanie blinked, shocked.

"What?!" she exclaimed.

Rachel nodded.

"Why do you think Jenaro came here himself?" she asked. "He wanted to set up operations in New Jersey, using Karl to run them. Karl said someone here owed the Cartel a lot of money and Jenaro was going to take care of that as well, but he was more focused on getting their operation started."

"This was all a tactic to bring fear into the area?" Stephanie repeated, shaking her head. "How?"

Rachel gazed at her steadily.

"After all the displays at the prison, they were going to start kidnapping children and threatening the parents," she said, "starting with the Nuñezes."

"And Marcus?"

"They were going to sell him in Mexico."

Stephanie closed her eyes briefly.

"All to bring the fear of the cartels to Jersey," she murmured. "What evil mind thinks this stuff up?"

"Jenaro Gomez."

"Don't let them take me!" Marcus suddenly cried, lifting his head.

"No one's taking you anywhere," Stephanie promised him.

"That's what the lady in black said, too," he said, settling back against Rachel. "Do you know her? Will she keep Karl away from me?"

"I know her well," Stephanie murmured grimly. "You won't have to worry about Karl ever again."

Viper straddled the rickety, old ladder-back chair and rested her chin on the back, watching as Karl started to come around. He lay on a drift of dead leaves, his wrists bound with wire behind his back, in front of a rotted out log in the woods. Her Jeep was parked in the trees behind him a few feet away, and she sat in the back-door of an infrequently-used hunting blind buried in the depths of the Pine Barrens. The hut sat on the edge of a large clearing, and the afternoon sun glared high in the sky, casting her in shadows. She sat perfectly still, watching as Karl groaned and turned his head, his eyes flickering open.

"What the..." he mumbled thickly, squeezing his eyes shut again for a moment against the bright sunlight. He winced as he tried to struggle into a sitting position. "Where the hell am I?"

"Somewhere no one will hear you scream."

Karl started and looked toward her voice, squinting against the sun and trying to see her in the shadows.

"I remember now," he said slowly.

"Good. That will save time," Viper replied, lifting her head from the back of the chair. "Tell me about the boy."

"Bite me," Karl spat, leaning back against the log.

Viper shook her head and clucked her tongue, calmly reaching down to pull her military knife out of her ankle holster. She flipped it in the air and the sun glinted off the serrated blade brightly before the handle landed comfortably in her hand. Karl stared at it uncomfortably.

"Now, that's no way to talk to a lady," she purred softly. Getting up, she moved the chair out of the way. "I heard you were quite the flirt. I should have known something was off when you impressed Agent Walker. She's always been a sucker for creeps."

"You're the one she brought into the prison that day!" Karl exclaimed, recognition dawning as Viper moved out of the shadows. His eyes went to her black boots. "You're the one with the boots."

"Congratulations," Viper murmured. "You remembered the shoes."

"Who the hell are you?" Karl asked, tilting his head back. "Why do you care about the boy?"

"I don't," Viper answered, her voice still soft and cold. "I care about you and the man who's paying you."

"I'm flattered."

"Don't be." Viper moved around behind the log and Karl twisted his head to watch her. "Where's Jenaro?"

"I don't know what you're talking about," Karl said, turning his head back around and testing the wire holding his wrists together. He grimaced when the wire cut into his skin.

"Yes, you do." Viper sighed, crouching down behind him. She draped one arm over his left shoulder and pressed the tip of her blade into the right side of his neck. He flinched and blood appeared, pooling around the blade tip before trickling down his neck. Her voice continued, an icy wave that made Karl freeze, "You're going to tell me everything you know about Jenaro Gomez."

Alina watched as beads of sweat broke out along Karl's temple and his breathing became shallow. He would break sooner than she expected.

"You can suck my..."

Viper pressed the knife further into his neck, stopping him mid-sentence. She twisted her blade and he whimpered in response.

"No, thank you," she murmured. "Where is he?"

"I don't know," Karl said, swallowing.

"I don't believe you."

Viper pulled the knife out of his neck. He sighed a deep breath of relief, but it cut off when she wrenched his head back at an extreme angle and pressed the blade against his esophagus.

"Let me put it this way," Viper hissed, "you can tell me now, or I can leave *your* head on a pole outside the shed where you mutilated the face of a young woman and terrorized a small boy. You have three seconds to decide. One..."

"*You* left Rodrigo's head there?" Karl gasped.

"Two..."

"Gomez thought it was someone called The Hawk."

Viper paused and her hand stilled on the knife at his throat.

"Is that so?" she asked softly.

"He said the Hawk was becoming a nuisance," Karl said, taking a quick breath as she paused. "I thought he was being paranoid, until I heard Lorenzo turned up dead."

Viper kept her knife against his throat, but pursed her lips thoughtfully.

"Paranoid how?" she asked, diverted.

"He said the Hawk would come after him. He said the head outside the prison was a warning." Karl stared up at her, sweat pouring down his face. "I thought anyone would be suicidal to go after Jenaro Gomez, but then Lorenzo turned up dead and now here you are."

281

"How did you find out about Lorenzo?" Alina asked.

"Turi brought me food and beer every day, along with instructions," Karl said. "He told me this morning Lorenzo was found with a bullet in his head, and now Ramiero's missing. Jenaro is nervous, and that makes Turi nervous. He said he's never seen Jenaro afraid before now."

"And where is he?"

"I don't know, I swear!" Karl gasped as the knife pressed against his esophagus and broke the skin. "He always came to me. I never went to him."

Viper's eyes narrowed as she stared down at him coldly.

"I thought you might be useful, but it turns out you're just a rent-a-cop who likes to beat up people weaker than yourself," she said, her eyes black pools of darkness that made him shiver involuntarily. "You're no use to me at all."

"Wait!" Karl cried out. His eyes flared in terror as her hand shifted on the knife. "He knows you're coming! He's waiting for you. I don't know where he is exactly, but I know he's close to Riverside. He's close to the river. And he's waiting for you. He's waiting to kill the Hawk."

"Oh, I'm not the Hawk," she told him, smiling a smile that made Karl's blood run cold.

"But...then...who are you?" Karl stammered.

"I already told you," Viper purred, raising the blade above his neck. "I'm your worst nightmare."

Chapter Twenty-Nine

John leaned against the side of the SUV with his arms crossed and watched Blake stride up the cement sidewalk to the two-story, dilapidated Cape Cod. The house had seen better days. Its paint was no longer white but dingy gray, peeling in places to reveal weather-worn siding underneath. The windows were all intact, but some were missing one shutter while the others were missing both. The front porch sagged with age, and the railing was long gone, leaving posts where it used to sit. Trash collected along the base of the front porch, banding together in the dirt like so many tumbleweeds, and any grass that had once graced the small, postage stamp front yard had given up, strangled out by crabgrass and weeds.

John kept one eye on Blake and one eye on the front windows, his hand near his holster with his 9mm. He didn't like the fact that Blake was going to the door alone, but Blake had been adamant. How he intended to get the inhabitants of an alleged crack house to talk wasn't clear, but John stayed alert near the SUV, ready to intervene if necessary.

The front door cracked open and a face peered out cautiously, providing the only opening Blake needed. He never broke stride as he slammed the door open with his shoulder, driving it into the person inside. He reached around the door, ripped a shotgun out of the man's hand, and tossed it outside into the barren yard as he disappeared into the house. The door slammed shut and John blinked at the speed with which it had been accomplished, his lips curving into a reluctant grin.

He was still grinning about ten minutes later when Blake came out the door again, strolling down the sidewalk and ignoring the shotgun laying in the yard.

"He wasn't here," he said, coming up to the SUV and going to the driver's door. John nodded and turned toward the passenger's door. "But they told me somewhere else to try. It's a few blocks away."

"Just like that?" John asked in disbelief, getting into the SUV.

Blake slammed the door and started the engine, glancing at him

283

with a grin.

"I may have...encouraged them a little," he said with a shrug, pulling away from the curb.

"What makes you so sure Lorenzo was at a crack house, anyway?" John asked.

"I've been studying these guys for over three years. I know them like I know my own family," Blake answered. "Larry hasn't had time to run the tox screen, but he said the marks on the inside of Lorenzo's arm are consistent with a needle. I don't need the tox screen to tell me Lorenzo fell off the wagon again."

"Ok." John nodded and watched out the window as they rolled through a stop sign and into another depressed neighborhood of old, deteriorating row homes. "You said he was diabetic. Could it be from insulin?"

"Lorenzo takes insulin pills, not needles," Blake replied. "Besides, you don't inject insulin into your arm. Don't you know any diabetics?"

"No," John answered with a grin. "And I'm not much of a fan of needles, so I wouldn't know where they stick themselves."

"Better watch your sugar intake, then," Blake warned. "Lay off the soda pop."

"Did you just call it...soda pop?" John demanded.

"Yeah. So?"

"Do me a favor and never say that again," John told him. "I can't work with someone who calls it pop."

"What do you call it?"

"Soda," John said emphatically. "Just soda."

Blake glanced at him as he pulled over in front of a gray row home, flanked on either side by an empty lot where the neighboring houses had long since burned down.

"You need to learn to not sweat the small stuff," he told him. "You'll have a heart attack before you're forty."

"I live in Jersey," John retorted. "If I only have a heart attack, I'm in good shape!"

Blake chuckled as they got out of the SUV, glancing around as they slammed the doors.

"Think they know you're coming?" John asked, looking at the forbidding gray house.

"Undoubtedly," Blake answered.

"Want company this time?"

"Nope." Blake started up the sidewalk. "You just watch my car."

John opened his mouth to toss a smart comment back, but the words died on his lips as the front door of the house swung open and two immense Latino men stepped onto the cement stoop. They crossed their arms over their barrel chests and scowled at Blake, standing shoulder to shoulder and blocking his advance.

"You sure about that?" John called.

"Yep!"

Blake rolled his shoulders and eyed the two behemoths before him, sizing them up. He smiled.

"You can make this easy on yourselves and just tell me what I want to know," he told them, speaking in Spanish just to be sure they understood. They looked surprised, but then grinned in amusement and uncrossed their arms. Blake let out an imperceptible sigh. "Or we can all get our workout in for the day," he added in resignation, flexing his hands.

John watched from the curb as the two gorillas charged Blake simultaneously. The scuffle lasted all of maybe two minutes and when it ended, Blake was the only one rising from the pile of bodies on the ground. John was impressed, despite himself. He moved forward, clapping as Blake brushed dirt and dead weeds off his jeans.

"That wasn't agency training," he said, nudging one of the unconscious men with his foot.

"No, it wasn't," Blake agreed with a quick grin. A gash on his forehead above his right eye oozed blood and his lip showed a tendency to swell, but he looked none the worse for it. "Do me a favor and make sure they don't wake up before I'm done in there. As fun as that was, I'm not feeling a round two."

John chuckled.

"I don't blame you," he said, watching as Blake stepped onto the stoop and disappeared through the door.

Stephanie hit speed dial and held her phone to her ear, watching as Rachel climbed into the back of the ambulance. Marcus held tightly to her other hand, waving to Rachel from beside Stephanie. Rachel waved back as the paramedic closed the door and the ambulance pulled away from the curb, the lights flashing above.

"I have Marcus Nuñez," Stephanie said without preamble as John answered. "He's fine. Rachel isn't. She's on the way to the hospital now."

"The guide?" John asked. "What happened? Where were they?"

"Karl was holding them in a shed behind the maze at the back of the prison," Stephanie told him grimly, turning to walk toward her Mustang. Marcus skipped along next to her, holding her hand with a death grip. "Jenaro was paying him to keep them in line. He kidnapped Rachel that night after the haunted maze closed, with the intention of having her help control Marcus. He called in Karl when it became apparent Rachel wasn't going to play ball very easily. They were right under our nose the whole time."

"Wait, so let me get this straight," John said. "Jenaro kidnapped the boy, realized he needed a nanny and kidnapped Rachel, who refused to...to do what, exactly?"

"Instill the fear of God into him," Stephanie answered. "I gather Jenaro thought he could control her the way he controlled Jessica. He didn't take into account that Rachel wasn't raised in fear in Mexico."

"What happened to her?" John asked. "You said she's on her way to the hospital."

"Karl beat her beyond recognition," Stephanie told him. "It's bad. I wouldn't have recognized her."

John remained silent for a long moment.

"How did Karl come into it?" he finally asked, his voice tight.

"Rachel says Karl's been bringing drugs into the area for the Cartel for a while now," Stephanie replied, walking Marcus around to the passenger's door of her car. "When Gomez saw the museum, he decided to use it, with Karl's help."

"How did we find them?" John asked.

Stephanie watched Marcus climb into the backseat and reach over to grab the seat belt himself. She smiled at him and closed the door before answering John.

"We didn't. The Black Widow did."

"*That's* who called you at the IT building," John said. "So that's why you took off so fast."

"I didn't have time to explain," Stephanie said, circling to the driver's door. "As it was, I got here too late. She was already gone...with Karl."

John cursed.

"Of course she was!" he muttered. "Hey! Hold on..."

Stephanie slid behind the wheel, raising an eyebrow slightly as she heard a grunt and a muffled thump over the phone. She listened to another thump, then John was back.

"Sorry," he apologized. "Where are they now?"

"I don't know. Where are *you*?" Stephanie asked, starting the engine.

"Babysitting," came the cryptic reply. "I'm with Blake. He thinks he can get a lead on Jenaro's location. What are you going to do now?"

"Try to find Kwan," Stephanie replied.

"Do you need me?" John asked. "I can be done here shortly."

"No, you go ahead and help Blake. I have a mini-partner for the afternoon," Stephanie told him, glancing at Marcus. "Be careful. If you guys think you found him, call me before you do anything."

"Of course," John agreed. "You know, Lina said she had a tracking dot on Kwan."

"Oh, I haven't forgotten," Stephanie assured him. "I've already got three calls into her voicemail."

"What do you think she's doing with Karl?" he asked after a moment.

"I don't think I really want to know," she replied honestly. "I just hope she leaves him alive so we can question him."

"Good luck with that," John murmured. "If the guide looks as bad as you say, and she knows Karl's responsible, I wouldn't place any bets on ever seeing him again."

"Stephanie has the Nuñez boy," John told Blake as he emerged from the house, stepping over one of the freshly-unconscious guards.

"Wonderful!" Blake exclaimed, a big smile breaking over his face. "How is he?"

"She says he's fine. The guide was with him, but she's not so good. They took her to the hospital. Steph said she's beaten up pretty bad."

Blake glanced at John as they walked toward the truck.

"Jenaro?" he asked.

"No. Karl Didinger, the missing night guard," John told him.

"So you got back two of your witnesses," Blake said, climbing into the SUV. "That's good news!"

"Well, not exactly," John replied, getting in next to him and reaching for his seat belt. "We have the guide, but not Karl."

"What do you mean?" Blake demanded, starting the engine.

John glanced at him.

"It's complicated," he murmured, wincing inwardly at his response. It drove him insane when Damon or Alina said those words, yet here he sat, using the same phrase.

Blake raised an eyebrow.

"That seems to be an ongoing theme with you guys," he observed. John nodded glumly.

"I know," he agreed. "Don't hold it against us. It's not our fault."

"I've noticed that too," Blake said with a chuckle.

"Where are we headed?" John asked as Blake pulled a U-turn and hit the gas.

"An old abandoned factory near the train tracks," Blake told him. "I found an informative, if not very bright, witness who was there when Lorenzo stopped in. Our witness remembered that a friend of his got kicked out of an abandoned factory, along with some other squatters, not too long ago by some mean Mexicans. Turns out Lorenzo mentioned this old factory that night."

"That's convenient."

"Isn't it? That's not all. According to my new best friend, Lorenzo was alive and well when he left the house, all accounts paid and no one unhappy with him. In fact, it seems like he was something of a hit with them all."

"And you trust this information?" John asked, looking at Blake doubtfully.

Blake nodded.

"He was too far gone to make it up," he said.

"So, where's this abandoned factory?" John asked.

Blake glanced at him.

"Along the train tracks, about ten minutes from here," he said. "He said it's a ways back from the road, but you can see what's left of the roof through the trees."

John frowned thoughtfully.

"I might know it," he said slowly. "If it's the place I'm thinking of, the train goes right by it. It's a shell of a building, over-grown, and it's been empty for years. It's uninhabitable. Jenaro can't be staying there."

"Well, it's all we've got," Blake said. "Let's see if it leads anywhere."

Stephanie rubbed her eyes and picked up her cell phone from where it vibrated on her desk. Marcus sat in John's chair, playing on Rob's iPad, and sipping hot chocolate that another agent had bought him from the vending machine. The kid was in spoiled heaven, soaking up every second of fussing attention he got as people stopped by to congratulate Stephanie on finding the boy.

"Hello?" she answered, glancing at her watch.

"Three voicemails?" Alina asked, sounding amused. "One would have sufficed."

"I wanted to make sure you got the message," Stephanie retorted.

A soft chuckle came from the other end of the phone.

"Oh, I got the message," Alina murmured. "I'll send the tracking software to your phone. I've already unlocked it so you can access his location. Just install it like any other app. It will alert you when he's moving. He's at an urgent care clinic in Mt. Laurel right now."

"Any idea why that might be?" Stephanie asked.

"At a guess, I'd say he needs urgent care," Alina retorted dryly.

"Funny." Stephanie stretched and reached for the cup of coffee on her desk. "What about Karl?"

"What about Karl?"

"Is he in need of urgent care, too?" Stephanie demanded.

"Oh, I don't think urgent care would do much good," Alina answered, sounding downright cheerful.

"Lina, I need to bring him in!" Stephanie hissed, lowering her voice. "Am I going to need Larry to do it?"

"Is that your ME?"

"Yes."

"Not just yet."

"Thank God!" Stephanie breathed a sigh of relief, but Alina's next words made her head drop onto the desk with a thud.

"But I can't guarantee how long you have."

"For the love of...where is he?" Stephanie asked tiredly.

"In his apartment. You'll want to take the medics with you," Alina told her cheerfully.

"Did you at least find out what you wanted to know?" Stephanie asked. "I know you didn't take him just to avenge a complete stranger, even if she *was* brutally beaten."

"Oh, I got everything I needed," Viper answered softly. "He's all yours now...what's left of him."

Chapter Thirty

Alina unlocked the door to the condo and stepped inside, closing the door behind her silently.

"Jessica?" she called.

Movement came from the kitchen and Jessica poked her head out, a coffee pot in her hand.

"Si?"

"I have good news," Alina told her in Spanish, moving forward toward the kitchen.

"I just made coffee," Jessica offered, holding up the coffee pot. "Would you like some?"

"I'd love some."

Alina followed her into the kitchen and watched as Jessica pulled a second mug from the cabinet. She glanced around, noting the spotless counters and sink, and raised an eyebrow.

"Haven't you been eating?" she asked as Jessica poured coffee into the mug.

"Yes, but I have nothing to do all day but worry," Jessica replied. "So I clean. Do you take cream or sugar?"

"Nothing, thank you."

Jessica nodded and handed her the mug of black coffee before setting the pot back into the machine and reaching for the milk for her own coffee.

"What's this good news?" she asked, glancing over her shoulder. "Have you found Jenaro?"

"Yes." Alina sipped her coffee. "I know where he is and soon he won't be a threat to you anymore."

"I can go home soon?" Jessica asked hopefully, turning to face her.

Alina looked at her, her lips curving slightly.

"You can come with me now," she told her softly. "You see, I also found Marcus."

Jessica gasped and set her coffee down, her dark eyes flaring wide as a big smile crossed her drawn, tired face.

"Is he ok? Where is he? Is he hurt?" she asked, the questions rolling off her tongue in rapid-fire Spanish. "When did you find him? Does Jenaro know he's gone?"

Alina waited for her to finish, sipping her coffee. When Jessica finally ran out of questions, she glanced up.

"He's fine," she told her. "Jenaro doesn't know he's gone yet, but he will. Marcus is safe right now. I can take you to him, but you will have to answer questions."

"Where is he?"

"With the FBI," Alina said, setting her mug down on the counter. "They have a lot of questions for you, I'm sure. I've given them the transcript we agreed on of what you told me, but if I know Agent Walker, she'll have a lot more that she wants to know."

"You trust this Agent Walker?" Jessica asked.

"I do."

"Then we shall go," Jessica announced.

Alina nodded.

"There's something else," she murmured. "Rachel was with Marcus when I found him."

"Rachel?" Jessica exclaimed.

"Jenaro took her to control Marcus," Alina explained slowly. "When she wouldn't discipline him for trying to escape, and actually helped instead, Jenaro decided additional help was needed."

"Oh God." Jessica leaned against the counter, her face paling. "I know Jenaro. I know what that means."

"Rachel is...not recognizable right now," Alina said, trying to be tactful. "She'll be ok, but I want you to be prepared. She placed herself between Marcus and the bastard sent to keep them in line."

"How bad is she?" Jessica asked.

"Pretty bad," Alina answered truthfully.

"And the man?"

"Worse," Viper said softly.

Jessica shivered at the calm chill in her voice, but she nodded in satisfaction.

"Good. Does Marcus blame himself?"

"I think so." Alina shrugged. "I'm not used to children, but I know I'd blame myself. Agent Walker will be able to tell you more. I took him to safety, then left him with Rachel while I attended to Karl."

"Karl!" Jessica cried in surprise. "The nice guard from the museum?"

"Yeah, he had everyone fooled," Alina said, glancing at her watch. "Come on. If I'm going to get you to your son today, we have to go now."

"I'm ready now," Jessica announced, running out of the kitchen and grabbing her purse from the living room.

Alina nodded and walked over to turn off the coffee pot. She did a once through the apartment, then went to the door and opened it, stepping outside into the plush hallway. Jessica followed her and Alina locked the door behind them. She smiled at Jessica.

"Soon, you and your family will be free of the Casa Reino Cartel," she said softly.

Jessica's eyes suddenly swam with tears.

"I prayed to the Virgin Mary every day since Gomez came back. I knew she would send us help," she whispered. "You're an angel, sent from the Holy Mother."

Viper blinked and turned to walk down the hall.

"God help us all if that's true," she murmured under her breath.

John got out of the SUV, taking in the abandoned shell of a building before them. The old factory was almost part of the landscape now, with ivy growing up the sides and creeping along the edges of the roof. What used to be the parking area was completely overrun with weeds and grass that erupted through the old, cracked cement, and the road leading there was little more than a path now. The old building had every indication of being forgotten by man, the space reclaimed by nature.

"I see what you mean about it being uninhabitable," Blake murmured, joining him in front of the SUV. "Why is this even still here?"

"Who knows," John said, shaking his head. "Probably cost too much to take it down when it closed, then it got forgotten over the years."

He looked around and paused, his eyes narrowing at the sight of several red mulberry trees at the side of the building. John pressed his lips together, staring at them thoughtfully until Blake pulled his attention away.

"We're not the first visitors," he said, nodding to some fresh tire tracks a few feet away.

John glanced at them and went over to get a closer look.

"There are two sets here," he called, bending down. "Definitely recent."

"Well, that's a good start," Blake answered, pulling out his gun and flipping off the safety. "You want to take the back, or go in together?"

John straightened up and pulled out his 9mm, glancing around the deserted wilderness.

"Let's go in together," he said.

Blake nodded and they started across the crumbling cement walkway toward the entrance of the factory. The bottom of the old front door had been painted at one time, but now it was just a rusted, steel half-door with broken glass in the top and a broken lock. Blake pushed the door open and stepped inside. John followed, holding his gun up near his shoulder, his eyes scanning the entryway they found themselves in. The front area was surprisingly intact, with a counter dividing the area in half. A door behind the counter led to the factory floor beyond, visible through a long, empty section that presumably held plate glass when the building was in use. Blake glanced down the short hallway at the other end of the entryway and then looked at John. John nodded and they moved down the short hallway. Three doors in the hallway were ajar. Two were restrooms and the third led to a stairwell, covered in graffiti and layered with dirt and dead leaves that had blown in through a gaping hole in the outer wall where a window used to be.

"Do you think the stairs actually go anywhere anymore?" Blake asked, peering up the steel stairs to the closed door at the top.

"If they do, I can guarantee the floor won't hold you," John answered. "It has to be rotted away. There's hardly any roof left."

Blake nodded in agreement.

"Let's check out the factory floor," he said, turning to go back down the short hallway.

"What would Gomez want with an old empty building like this?" John wondered out loud.

"Any number of things," Blake answered, ducking under the counter. "If it was closer to home, I'd say he was using it to run contraband, but this is a long way to go."

"Could they be considering expanding their operations to the northeast?" John asked, swinging his legs over the counter and sliding across.

Blake glanced at him.

"If they are, then we have a much larger problem on our hands," he murmured. "It's bad enough that we can't keep them out of the border states. The last thing we need is a two-front war with these guys."

Blake passed through the door to the factory floor, his gun securely in his hands, glancing to the left as John followed him and went to the right. They moved apart silently, eyes ever watchful, and began to move around the perimeter of the old floor. After checking the floor above and finding it non-existent between the support beams, Blake tucked his weapon back into its holster. He looked around, taking in the old graffiti on the walls and the swept out floor.

"Looks like they've cleaned it out," he called across the floor to John. "They're using it for something. They took the time to get out all the trash."

John nodded and looked across the huge room to the one corner that didn't seem as desolate as the rest of the building.

"What's that?" he called, nodding to the back corner closer to Blake.

Blake turned his head and frowned, moving forward. Shadows hung heavily over the corner, partially concealing a folding camping table and two folding chairs. A tall tripod held a huge spotlight pointed into the corner, and an orange, all-weather extension cord ran across the floor to a portable, battery generator near the wall.

"They have a generator to run a light," Blake replied, crossing the large space.

"Free office space?" John asked, crossing over from the other side.

Blake stopped dead when he got a whiff of the sour smell hanging over the corner. His eyes narrowed sharply.

"Not quite," he muttered, moving forward and going over to the spotlight. Reaching out, he flipped it on, illuminating the corner.

John stopped dead beside him and they both stared at the blood stains splattered all over the walls and the darker, deeper stains covering the floor.

"Oh my God," John breathed.

"I think we just found where Rodrigo was hacked to pieces," Blake said grimly.

Angela stretched and looked around the dining room. Finding herself alone, she glanced at her watch and yawned, closing her laptop with a snap. Michael wasn't in the living room and silence filled the house. She went into the kitchen to get a soda out of the refrigerator, popping open the tab on the can and lifting it to her lips before the door had even closed.

Restlessness surged through her and Angela suddenly couldn't wait to get back to her own house. She wanted her own bed, her own kitchen and, most of all, her own food. There was nothing to snack on in this house except dried fruit and nuts.

Angela crossed the kitchen and strolled past the bar and over to the sliding doors. She sipped her soda while she looked out. The sun gleamed high above, shining brightly through the tops of the trees, the sky a bright, clear blue. Squirrels scampered over the grass, frantically searching for more nuts to store for the winter while birds flitted cheerfully through the air, singing loudly to each other as they enjoyed the fall day.

Shifting her gaze to the driveway, she watched as Michael pulled his head out from under his hood and wiped his hands on a rag. Angela opened the door and stepped outside, sliding it closed behind her.

"Hey!" she called, crossing the deck and tripping down the stairs. "Have you heard from Lina?"

Michael glanced over and shook his head.

"Nope."

"Where did she go?" Angela asked, joining him next to his truck. Her chin stood level with the engine and he grinned.

"Damn, you're short," he told her.

Angela's eyes narrowed and she glared at him.

"Excuse me?"

"I said you're short," Michael answered cheerfully. "Look at you. You can barely see into the engine."

"You shouldn't drive monster trucks," she retorted.

"Babe, this isn't a monster truck," he said, picking up a half-empty water bottle from the ground and raising it to his lips. "It's just a regular F-150 pickup."

"It's a hillbilly car," Angela shot back with a sniff, "and you didn't answer my question."

"I don't know where she went," Michael said after taking a long drink of water. "She said she had some things to take care of."

"Do you think Kwan was one of those things?" Angela asked, leaning on the side of the truck.

"Why would you think that?" Michael asked. He shot her a glance out of the corner of his eye as he leaned back over the engine.

"I don't know." Angela shrugged. "I just think she's doing more than she says. She didn't seem at all concerned that Damon went walking off into the woods last night with Kwan draped over his shoulder. In fact, she seemed to think it was funny."

"How does that translate into her doing something about him today?" Michael asked, his voice muffled as he reached deep into the bowels of the engine.

"She wasn't happy about staying behind while you two went out there," she answered.

Michael lifted his hand out of the engine and turned his head to look at her, trying to follow her train of thought.

"Again, why does that make you think she's doing something about him today?" he asked with a frown.

295

"It doesn't," Angela said, looking confused.

"Then why did you bring it up?"

"Because you asked why I thought she was taking care of Kwan," she answered calmly.

Michael stared at her.

"You realize you're making absolutely no sense, right?" he asked.

"I make perfect sense!" Angela exclaimed, her eyes flashing. "Lina is supposedly in security consulting, and while I know that's a euphemism of some sort, I'm perfectly willing to play along. If she doesn't want me to know what she does for a living, that's fine. I have my theories, and if they're anywhere close to the truth, I don't think I *want* to know what she really does. Last night she was way too calm and in control to not have done stuff like that before. Granted, she was in military intelligence in the Navy, but I still think she did a heck of a lot more than just codes and ciphers. First, she got her panties all in a bunch because you and Damon went out into the woods to confront Kwan, when really she should have been thankful not to have to go out there. Then, once you guys were out there, she monitored your every move on that security system of hers, for all the world like she knew how to do it better than you. And, after all of that, when Damon disappeared with Kwan, she outright laughed. Laughed! And it was a satisfied laugh, like she was happy with the fact that Mr. Hunk O' Mysterious walked off with Kwan. It was almost like she knew he would do something you couldn't do. So, of course I think she's doing something with Kwan today. Why wouldn't I?"

Michael rubbed his forehead, a reluctant grin breaking across his face.

"Ok, then," he said, turning back to his engine. "That makes sense."

Angela's mouth dropped open and she stared at him, flabbergasted.

"That's all you have to say?!" she demanded. "I say all that and all you can say is," she lowered her voice to imitate his, "'That makes sense?'"

"Oh, I could say a lot more, but I don't see the point," Michael replied, glancing at her. "You seem to have it all figured out in that convoluted head of yours."

"GAH!" Angela swung around to stomp away. "You're infuriating! I don't know why Lina thinks you're so great. I think you're a jerk!"

"What?" Michael's shoulders were shaking as he watched her flounce away. "I was agreeing with you!"

A sound reminiscent of a cat being strangled made its way back to him and a chuckle escaped him.

"Will you agree with me when my foot's up your ass?" Angela muttered to herself, stalking away. "Jerk. Typical, dumb, male jerk."

"I can still hear you," Michael's voice shook, "and you're too short to put your foot up my ass."

"I'm *not* short!" Angela yelled over her shoulder. "I'm fun-sized!"

Michael burst out laughing, the sound echoing through the yard. Angela ignored him as she stalked up the deck and through the sliding door, closing it behind her viciously.

Neither of them noticed Hawk slip around the corner from the front of the house and disappear into the trees.

"Make sure you get plenty of good shots of that blood," John instructed the photographers, motioning to the blood stains. "You know Agent Walker is going to want all angles since she can't be here."

"Got it," the photographer answered with a nod. "I'll get it all."

"Good."

John turned away and watched as the forensics team bore down on the corner of the factory. As soon as they realized what they were looking at, he had called in reinforcements. The building now crawled with techs and junior agents and he surveyed them all like a watchful mother hen.

"Ms. Walker can't make it?" Blake asked, pausing next to him on his way across the building with a handful of sealed evidence bags.

"She has the boy with her," John replied. "After she heard what we found, she decided it was best not bring him along."

"Good call," Blake nodded, glancing back at the gruesome corner.

"You know, technically we still don't have anything to tie Jenaro to this place except the word of a high drug addict," John remarked, walking with him toward the makeshift evidence pool they had set up near the front door. "It will take the lab days to process all this blood, and unless one of those cigarette butts in that bottle are an exact match to the one we found at the maze, those will take days as well."

"That's why I'm still looking," Blake retorted. "With any luck, we'll find something conclusive we can use now."

"What do you want me to do?" John asked. "I've got half the techs collecting all the samples now, and the other half going through the building with a microscope."

"Let's start outside." Blake dropped his evidence bags into the box and turned to head out the door. "You take one side and I'll take the other. We're looking for anything that looks like it's only a few days old. That should narrow it down considerably."

"You got it."

John followed him outside and turned right while Blake went left. FBI vans and cars filled the overgrown parking lot, and police tape draped the lane leading to the factory. Jenaro wouldn't be returning any time soon. They had the whole area locked down.

John moved along the front of the building slowly. Weeds and ivy stretched along the base of the building, choking out any grass that used to grow there, and the amount of debris laying in the greenery was staggering. Old beer bottles, wine bottles and beer cans lay half-buried alongside more sinister items like old, broken syringes and rusty metal spoons. Plastic bags and half-deteriorated fast food wrappers peeked out from under drifts of multi-colored leaves and John shook his head. The waste depressed him and he sighed, nudging a newer-looking plastic bag with the tip of his shoe. After a few minutes of searching, he didn't find anything newer than a week old. He moved on.

"Smithe!" Blake yelled from the corner of the building at the other end.

John looked up to see him motioning to him. The big grin on Blake's face told him their search was over. John turned and jogged down the length of the building, gratefully leaving the waste and debris behind him.

"We've got him," Blake told him as he grew closer, holding up an evidence bag. Inside lay a pill bottle.

"What is it?" John asked, stopping and reaching out a hand for the bag.

Blake handed it to him and John turned it over, tilting his head. The empty pill bottle was missing its lid and covered with dirt on one side where it had been laying on the ground. John shook the bag to turn the bottle so he could read the label.

"Juan Phillips?" John read, glancing up at Blake.

"Look at the medication," Blake told him. "Forget about the name."

"Amaryl?"

"It's Lorenzo's diabetes meds," Blake explained. "Same drug, same dosage he's been taking for the past year. Look at the date."

"It was filled two weeks ago," John said, looking up.

Blake nodded, his eyes alight with the scent of the trail.

"And it has an address in Riverside."

Chapter Thirty-One

Alina glanced at her watch and leaned against the cool, marble stone of the building while she watched the river of human traffic flow by. Even after all her globe-trotting, Philadelphia still remained one of her favorite cities. It had all the hustle and bustle of other major cities, but it also had a small community feel to it that made everyone feel at home on her streets. There was a reason it was called the City of Brotherly Love, even if its sports fans *were* notorious for being the worst behaved in the nation. Possibly the world.

Stephanie had met them at the door to the FBI building, whisking Jessica away to be reunited with her son. Viper refused to enter the secure building, not willing to part with the gun at her back or knife at her ankle. Stephanie shook her head slightly, as if she knew exactly why Alina was unwilling to enter the lobby and go through the metal detector. Promising to come back down in a few minutes, she took Jessica into the building and left Viper to wait in the alcove outside the gleaming glass doors. If the security guards inside thought it odd that she chose to wait outside rather than in, they knew better than to ask questions.

Alina frowned slightly when her phone started vibrating against her thigh and she reached into her cargo pocket.

"Yes?"

"Do you have an update?" Hawk asked.

"It's clear. I found the boy," Viper told him. "He's with Stephanie now."

"And the mother?"

"Stephanie just took her to her son. You're good to go."

Hawk disconnected and Alina dropped the phone back into her pocket, glancing behind her as one of the glass doors swung open.

"I don't think I'll ever get over the feeling of seeing family reunited," Stephanie said, joining her in the alcove. "They're in a conference room. I'll give them some time together before I go up and get the whole story."

"I told her you would have questions," Alina said with a slight smile.

"Do you want me to tell you when I'm finished with them?" Stephanie asked, looking at her. "Blake hasn't found Gomez yet, so it's still not safe for them to go home. I have two agents with her husband, but I'd rather not risk it. Will you take them back to wherever you had her stashed away?"

"If needed."

"What's that supposed to mean?" Stephanie demanded.

"I have some things to take care of," Alina replied. "If the situation is still the same when I'm done, I'll take them somewhere safe."

Stephanie studied her thoughtfully.

"You have something up your sleeve," she accused her softly. "What is it?"

"Plausible deniability is a wonderful thing, Steph," Alina answered, her eyes glinting. "You know that."

Stephanie sighed.

"I'm giving you way too much freedom on US soil, *and* in my jurisdiction," she muttered. "Don't make me regret it."

"It worked out ok for you last time," Alina pointed out with a grin. "You got a promotion out of it."

Stephanie rolled her eyes and shook her head, but changed the subject.

"I have another problem," she told her. Alina raised an eyebrow questioningly. "Kwan ditched the car."

"What?"

"I had someone waiting for him when he finished at the Urgent Care facility," Stephanie explained tiredly, leaning on the wall next to her. "He tailed him to a pharmacy and then to the Cherry Hill Mall. He lost him in the mall and the car hasn't moved since. I doubt he's hanging out in the mall, gnawing on a pretzel and browsing in The Gap."

"No. He's gone," Alina agreed. "He spotted your tail. You need to train your people to be more discreet. Hell, they're like Godzilla out there. A two-year-old could spot them a mile away."

"That's helpful," Stephanie muttered. "Without Kwan, I have nothing. Everyone else is dead."

"Well, you know he can't travel easily because of your BOLO, so I'd start watching the bridges and trains," Alina said with a shrug. "I can tell you this much, he has a broken hand. He probably has a couple other broken things, but the hand will be easy to spot."

"Thank you." Stephanie nodded. "*That* is helpful."

Next Exit, Dead Ahead

"I'll let you know if I come across anything," Alina promised, feeling a little guilty about keeping so much from her friend. "It's complicated with Kwan."

"Oh, I know," Stephanie retorted. "Your agency gave Rob a hell of a headache when his name came up, but they finally backed down. I'm not sure if that's a good or a bad thing."

"That's a "be very careful how you handle him" thing," Viper told her, her eyes serious. "They don't usually back down unless they already have another plan in place. They flat-out stonewalled Michael when he started to poke around for information."

Stephanie stared at Alina.

"What do you think is going on?" she asked in a low voice.

"I think Kwan is a pawn in something bigger and they're using the FBI to manipulate a situation," Viper said, choosing her words carefully.

"You think they planned it from the very beginning?" Stephanie asked after a long moment of silence. "Did this whole case get assigned to me by design?"

Alina was silent.

"Well, hell!" Stephanie exclaimed, throwing up her hands in exasperation and causing Alina to chuckle despite herself. "You're telling me I've been a puppet on a string for over six months!"

"You should be flattered," Alina told her with a grin. "You got the CIA's attention. That's no small feat."

"No offense, but I can do without their attention," Stephanie informed her roundly. "They bring trouble wherever they go!"

"Just tread carefully with Kwan. I can at least make sure he doesn't slip away from you," Alina said.

Stephanie frowned and glanced at her.

"Not if doing so will compromise you," she said. "I'd rather lose him altogether then go through another Washington, DC."

Alina smiled faintly, her dark eyes unfathomable.

"I wouldn't worry about that," she murmured. "I know how to be discreet...unlike your tails."

"Ha!" Stephanie grinned at the shot, then sobered. "What the hell am I going to do with Jessica and Marcus when I'm finished debriefing her?"

Viper glanced at her watch.

"Take them out to a late dinner," she advised obscurely, her lips curving into a cool smile.

The last of the sunlight had disappeared and night had fallen, cloaking the narrow street in the shadows Viper knew so well. She raised her military binoculars to her eyes and scanned the pavement, watching as the nightlife stirred and slid out into the streets. Most got into their late model Mercedes with their tinted windows and slid silently out of the neighborhood, heading to more lucrative endeavors. Some walked quickly down the sidewalks, their hoods pulled up over their baseball hats, trying to get to their destinations as unobtrusively as possible; while others swaggered from their souped-up Mazdas to their doors as if they owned the world. All told, it was a quiet neighborhood and Viper turned her attention to the corner row home next to the narrow alleyway across the street.

Karl had ended up knowing much more than he was aware of, and Viper had no problem locating the house Jenaro Gomez was using as a temporary base of operations. She studied it thoughtfully, noting the black pickup with the shattered windshield backed into the alleyway. Behind it, concealed from the road, she could just make out the front of Jessica's putrid green crossover.

A light flashed on in the front window on the second floor and Viper shifted her gaze to the bare window. The glow seemed bright after her study of the darkness and she blinked, her eyes adjusting easily through the binoculars. A male figure crossed the room and Viper zoomed in expertly, watching. When the man turned around to move toward the window, she smiled coldly.

Jenaro carried a metal case in his hands and, as she watched, he set it onto a folding table in front of the window. He turned his head, speaking to someone out of sight in the room. There were at least two of them, then. Flipping a switch on the binoculars, she switched modes and watched as the binoculars picked up body-heat signatures in the room. There were four others in the room with him.

Viper was in the process of lowering the binoculars when she thought she caught sight of a shadow moving on the roof of the house. She quickly raised the binoculars again and scanned the roof directly across from her searchingly, but she didn't see anything in the darkness. After a moment of fruitless study, Viper lowered the binoculars, her lips curving slightly.

Hawk was there.

Standing, she turned and moved toward the back of the roof swiftly, disappearing into the shadows. Reaching the edge of the building, Viper grabbed the edges of the fire escape ladder and swung herself over the edge. Gripping the rails with her black gloved hands, she moved her feet to the side railings and allowed gravity to pull her downwards. She slid down the ladder swiftly, landing on the ground silently a few seconds later. Rounding the corner of the old, dilapidated building, Alina moved in its shadows to the edge of the street. She paused at the curb, glancing back up to the window across the street. There was no sign of movement, and from the street level she could only see the ceiling of the brightly-lit room.

Viper ran swiftly across the momentarily deserted road, disappearing into the shadows of the narrow alley just as a low-slung Acura turned the corner. Bass blared from its speakers and shook the ground. Alina ignored it, slipping behind the pickup and moving swiftly along the side of the building until she came to the back corner of the alley and the building. She smiled when she saw the black nylon rope hanging just above her head in the corner. Reaching up, she grabbed the rope Hawk had left for his descent and, hand over hand, started to climb up the side of the building. When she reached the top a few minutes later, Viper glanced around the huge, pitch-black expanse of roof and crouched, still and silent, listening. She was alone.

She reached into her pocket and withdrew a thin maglite. Switching it on, Alina shone it quickly around the roof. She stood on a crumbling, weather-worn surface in desperate need of resurfacing. The roof sloped upward a few feet in front of her, flattening out for a couple of feet before sloping down again toward the front of the building. A brick chimney stack protruded from the center of the roof and Viper's eyes went straight to the blind spot behind it. Switching off the light, she moved swiftly along the back of the roof before running silently up the slope to the chimney. She peered around the blind side, clicking on her light again to shine it across the roof. No one lurked in the dark shadows between this roof and the adjoining roof of the next house and she clicked the light off again, glancing back towards the front of the building.

Viper dropped the Maglite back into her pocket and pivoted on her heel, going back the way she came. She moved swiftly and silently along the flat-topped roof until she reached the edge, high above the alley. Looking over the ledge, Viper smiled when she saw the small, dark open window a few feet below her. Without a second thought, she grasped the edge of the roof above the gutter and swung her legs over the edge.

A second later, she slid through the open window silently, following the path she knew Hawk must have taken. She landed on a linoleum floor, between a toilet and a bathtub, wincing as her hand brushed a can of shaving cream balanced on the edge of the tub. She caught it swiftly before it clattered to the floor and set it back gently, listening intently. A muffled crash came from the far end of the hallway outside the bathroom and Alina moved to the door, pausing to peer around the edge.

Shadows cloaked the hallway, concealing cracked and naked walls. Alina raised an eyebrow as her eyes fell on a woman, slumped on the floor against the wall. Dressed in black leggings and a red shirt, a black gag was tied across her mouth and her hands bound behind her. A wooden baseball bat lay on the carpet nearby.

Viper moved out of the bathroom silently and down the hall, pausing near the woman. She slid off her glove and bent down, pressing two fingers to the side of the woman's neck. When she felt the faint pulse, she glanced at the bat again, her lips twitching. She knew from experience that it was damn near impossible to catch Hawk unawares, and clearly this woman had discovered that for herself. She probably didn't even know what hit her.

Alina replaced her glove and stood up swiftly as another crash, louder than the first, sounded from the living room, followed by the unmistakable pop of suppressed gun fire. Viper pulled her .45 from her back holster, flipping off the safety as she ran down the hallway silently. As the living room came into view, she watched a medium-height, dark-skinned man slide down the back wall, blood spreading over his chest. A machine gun lay on the floor nearby, dropped when the bullet ripped through his body.

Viper paused and pressed against the wall, leaning forward and peering around the edge of the wall toward the front of the living room. A smile crossed her face when she saw Hawk standing over an inanimate Jenaro Gomez. Three other Cartel soldiers were littered around the living room, dead. After scanning the room, she tucked her gun back into her back holster and stepped out of the hallway. Hawk didn't even glance in her direction.

"Is the woman still out?" he asked, bending over Jenaro.

Viper smiled.

"Yes," she answered, glancing at the man on the back wall as she passed. "How did you know I was here?"

"How did you know I was in the room the other night?" Hawk retorted, pulling a wallet and set of keys out of Jenaro's pocket.

"Is the rest of the place clear?" Viper asked, her lips twitching.

"Yes." Hawk straightened up and finally looked at her, his arctic blue eyes glinting. "Welcome to the party."

Alina began to return the smile when a click sounded from the direction of the front door on the other side of the living room. Hawk's head snapped around, but Viper was already halfway to the door. He watched as she reached down and pulled out her military knife from her boot before silently wrenching the door open.

Next Exit, Dead Ahead

A broad-shouldered, stocky man turned away as Viper opened the door. She smiled coldly.

"Going somewhere?" she demanded, her voice like ice.

The man swung around and Alina found herself facing a younger, unscarred version of Jenaro Gomez. His eyes flashed and a Beretta glinted in his hand as he raised his arm.

The heel of her boot caught his wrist, snapping it effortlessly, and the gun fell harmlessly to the floor as her knife embedded itself in his opposite shoulder. The man began to howl with pain and Viper moved forward swiftly, cutting off the sound with a blow to his throat from her left elbow. He choked, doubling over, and she raised her right arm, bringing her elbow down unerringly. The man fell into her waiting arms, unconscious.

Alina caught him and glanced around quickly. Only one other apartment graced this floor, and the door was closed tight. If the neighbors heard his split second cry, they had wisely decided to ignore it. She backed up, dragging him through the open door behind her. Kicking the door closed, she hauled him over to the couch, pushing him onto it with a huff.

"Was he the only one out there?" Hawk asked, coming over to the back of the couch.

"Yes."

Viper reached down and pulled her knife out of his shoulder, wiping it clean on his chest.

"Good."

Hawk turned back to Jenaro and Viper rounded the couch to join him. Jenaro lay on the floor, unconscious, with blood dripping from a gash above his temple. She glanced at Hawk.

"You know that's cheating, right?" she asked breathlessly. "They have to be conscious when you kill them, or it doesn't count."

"Just because you're impatient and strike instantly doesn't mean I'm cheating. I'm not leaving his body here, where Hanover can take the credit," Hawk retorted, tossing her a roll of duct tape. "Do you mind?"

"Not at all," Viper answered, catching the tape with one hand and turning to her right at the same time. With one smooth movement, she pulled her back-up pistol from her leg holster and fired a single shot behind her. Hawk looked up, watching in surprise as the man with the bullet in his chest fell back again, her bullet in his forehead. The automatic dropped from his lifeless fingers, falling harmlessly to the floor again. "I thought you killed him already?" she demanded, snapping her head back to Hawk.

He shrugged.

"I thought I had."

"Should I check the rest? Did you miss anyone else?" she asked, raising an eyebrow.

"I didn't miss," Hawk retorted.

"Oh really? Have you thought about glasses?" Viper asked, bending over Jenaro and securing his mouth with the tape.

"No, you didn't just go there," Hawk muttered. He picked up Jenaro's phone from the floor and tucked it into his pocket. "Don't make me bring up why you favor your right side."

"I don't favor my right side," Alina snapped, wrapping tape around Jenaro's wrists swiftly. She scowled at Hawk. "That was a temporary thing, and it healed years ago."

"Uh-huh." Hawk turned to grab the metal case from the table. When he lifted it, he found a handgun and grabbed it. "Whatever lets you sleep at night."

"Oooh," Alina growled, her eyes flashing as she turned her attention to Jenaro's feet. "Come over here and I'll show you."

"Baby, we're busy." Damon winked and tossed her the extra gun. "Work now, play later."

"You're lucky I like you," Viper muttered, catching the gun with one hand and tucking it into her cargo pocket while she finished securing Jenaro's ankles with the other. "But don't push your luck."

"I wouldn't dream of it," Hawk murmured, coming over to her. He looked down at Jenaro Gomez, unconscious and trussed up with duct tape. "We need to get him out of here."

"We need to do it fast," she agreed, glancing up at the sound of a helicopter. A spotlight appeared on the horizon through the window as sirens sounded a few blocks away. "Looks like Hanover is on his way. Roof?"

"No time." Hawk glanced at Jenaro, then at Viper. "Babylon."

"Oh, you're an ass!" Viper exclaimed.

Hawk burst out laughing.

"It's Babylon or Gomorrah. Take your pick," he told her.

"You're going to pay for this," Alina informed him, dropping Jenaro's ankles unceremoniously. She rapidly pulled her knife out of her boot again and reached into her back holster for her .45. Damon held out his hand and she handed them to him before unstrapping her leg holster and passing it to him.

"Don't forget the one I just gave you," he reminded her and Viper nodded, pulling it from her pocket and handing it over.

"I don't know when, or how, but I will personally make sure I get you back for this!" she said, turning toward the hallway.

"Looking forward to it," Hawk retorted with a grin, stowing her weapons away in his own cargo pockets before bending down and hoisting

Jenaro's motionless body over his broad shoulder. He followed her into the hallway and kept going when she stopped in the door to a bedroom. "Until then, happy trails."

Alina glanced over her shoulder at Damon, striding away with Jenaro tossed over his shoulder like a sack of grain. She paused, watching as he headed toward the kitchen. When she didn't answer, Hawk turned his head. His eyes met hers. She smiled slightly, her eyes softening, and Damon felt as if she was sucking his soul right out of him.

"Take care of you," she murmured softly.

Hawk lowered one eyelid in a slow, sexy wink.

"Break a leg," he replied.

Viper grinned as he disappeared into the kitchen. A few seconds later, she heard him open the window and drop onto the fire escape. She turned back into the bedroom and went straight to the closet, pulling out a variety of women's clothing at random.

When the banging began at the door a few moments later, Viper was ready. She slipped out of the bedroom and into the living room, sliding down onto the floor as the front door crashed open.

Chapter Thirty-Two

"You mean to tell me the only ones left are two women, and neither of them can tell us anything?" Blake demanded, striding up the stairs to the second floor furiously.

"Pretty much," John answered, keeping pace with him stride for stride. "A man too short to be Jenaro ran out the front door as we pulled into the street, but he's long gone. He disappeared into the woods along the river before we even stopped."

"And the women?"

"One was found in the hallway, unconscious and tied up. She says she heard a noise, came out of the bedroom with a baseball bat, and that's all she remembers. She didn't see the person who hit her."

"Typical." Blake reached the top of the stairs and started down the hallway. "What's the story with the other one?"

John grinned as they approached the open door to the apartment. "See for yourself," he said, waving Blake forward.

Blake glanced at him, raising an eyebrow, and strode into the apartment. He stopped abruptly, taking in the scene before him. SWAT agents were milling around securing the apartment, while a woman sat on the couch, rocking back and forth. Her dark hair hung around her face in long, unkempt clumps, and a dark, fading bruise covered half her face. Swollen and heavy-lidded eyes gazed blindly ahead while she muttered to herself continually in Spanish.

John came up behind him and Blake glanced at him, startled.

"She was unconscious on the floor when SWAT came in," John told him. "They checked her for weapons, then brought her around. Apparently, she woke up yelling in Spanish and hasn't shut up since."

"Do you speak Spanish?" Blake asked John, studying the woman.

She wore a long, black skirt and bright turquoise shirt. Black boots graced her feet and the shirt hung off one shoulder, revealing a black tank top strap. She seemed to be dressed at random, as if she had just thrown on the clothing without regard to color or style.

"No," John answered. "One of the agents downstairs does, but he said he couldn't make out more than a few words."

"That's because her dialect is unusual," Blake murmured, tilting his head. "She's from one of the Southern regions of Mexico."

"You can tell that just from listening to her?" John asked, looking at him in surprise.

Blake grinned.

"I've spent some time in Mexico," he replied. "She's from the same region as Jenaro."

He glanced around the living room, noting the four bodies, and turned his attention back to the woman on the couch. She stared straight-ahead, her swollen eyes glazed over.

"Find me a blanket," he told John. "She's in shock."

John nodded and disappeared out the door. A moment later, Blake heard him yelling from the top of the stairs for a blanket. He moved forward slowly, heading for the couch. As he grew closer, the woman suddenly started and raised her head, directing that startled gaze on his face. He only had time to notice that her eyes were as dark as her hair before she started shaking her head violently back and forth.

"No, no, no, no, no, no," she cried out.

Blake held his hands up non-threateningly and stopped moving toward her.

"I'm here to help," he told her, speaking in the same dialect of Spanish.

Surprise crossed her face and she stopped shaking her head, falling silent as she stared at him. She still rocked back and forth and Blake found himself starting to sway with her before he caught himself.

"I won't hurt you," he told her gently. "You look like you've been hurt enough. I just want to ask you some questions."

"Careful, Hanover," someone called from across the room. "She's on something. Look at her eyes!"

"I see," Blake answered in English. "Where's the other woman?"

"In the kitchen. We kept them separate so they didn't even see each other."

"Good." Blake nodded in approval. "Are these the only bodies? The ones in here?"

"Yeah. Rest of the place is clear."

Blake nodded again and turned his attention back to the couch, moving closer.

"Did you see this happen?" he asked the woman, switching back to Spanish. "Did you see who did this?"

"La Calavera Catrina," she said shrilly.

Blake stopped moving and raised an eyebrow.

"La Catrina?" he repeated.

The woman nodded, her hair falling across her eyes. She brushed it out of her eyes with a hand shaking violently.

"She comes to guide us to the afterworld," she told him. "She came to take Jenaro to his father."

Blake sighed and rubbed his forehead, looking down at the woman on the couch.

"La Catrina is a symbol, a deity, a representation of The Day of the Dead," he told her. "She is not real."

"HA!" the woman let out a loud, shrill laugh, her eyes wild. "You think what you will. I *saw*! I *saw* death! She was dressed in a flowing black dress and she came for Jenaro!"

"Why would she do that?" Blake asked in resignation.

"He would not pay tribute to his father," the woman whispered, her eyes dropping again.

"Jenaro Gomez's father died fifteen years ago," Blake said impatiently.

The woman raised swollen dark eyes to his face.

"I know. La Catrina came to take Jenaro to him, so he can learn from him," she told him. "He would not pay tribute! Look!" The woman swung her arm out, indicating the living room. "There is no alter! There is no place for the ancestors to eat. There is no tribute here."

"Yes, ok." Blake shook his head and turned as John came up behind him with a red blanket in his hands.

"What the hell is she going on about?" John asked under his breath.

"She thinks Jenaro was taken away by a female skeleton who guards over the festival, The Day of the Dead," Blake answered shortly, taking the blanket from him.

"Say what?"

John stared at him blankly and Blake smiled reluctantly.

"The Day of the Dead is a festival, still very prominent in her region of Mexico," he explained quietly. "The story goes that for two days, the dead are allowed to come back to earth to eat and drink with the loved ones they left behind. However, they have to be guided back. The living do that by building alters on the eve of the festival to invite the spirits back. In her region, they play music at the alter to guide the dead back."

"You're kidding, right?" John demanded.

"No." Blake shook his head. "She says La Catrina came in here to take Jenaro to the afterlife because he didn't invite his father back."

310

"For the love of...she's crazy!" John exclaimed. He watched as Blake moved forward and draped the blanket around the woman's shoulders. The woman had returned her gaze to the opposite wall and resumed muttering to herself. "What's she saying?"

"She's praying to the Holy Mother," Blake answered, straightening up turning away. "She's praying for Jenaro's soul."

"Good Lord." John shook his head, staring at the woman on the couch as if she was a huge python curled up on the cushions.

"Quite," Blake murmured. "You'd better get her down to the paramedics. Judging by the size of the bruises on her face, she's been used pretty hard by Jenaro."

"You think her mind snapped?"

Blake glanced at him.

"She just told me that a female skeleton, dressed in a flowing black dress, came in here and did all this, then took Jenaro with her to the afterlife," he told him. "What do *you* think?"

Stephanie glanced down at her phone when her text alert dinged. She picked it up and swiped the screen. The text was short and to the point.

The Nuñezes are safe now.

Stephanie glanced across the living room to where Jessica sat on the couch with her son next to her, watching a Disney movie. She had taken Alina's suggestion and took them out to a late dinner. Then, not knowing what else to do with them, she brought them back to her apartment.

She opened her mouth to tell them she could take them home, but before she got a word out, her phone started vibrating in her hand and Led Zeppelin started playing.

"Hello?"

"We secured Jenaro's place," John told her. "Four of his men were dead when we got here."

"And Gomez?" Stephanie asked.

Jessica looked over sharply on hearing the name.

"Not here."

"Shit!" Stephanie exclaimed, standing up impatiently and heading into her kitchen. Once there, she spoke quickly, lowering her voice. "I just got a text from the Black Widow, saying the Nuñezes are safe. Where is he?"

"Given that little bit of information, I would guess with her," John

311

replied, also lowering his voice. "Here's what I know. When SWAT pulled up to the house, a man too short to be Jenaro was running out the door. He disappeared into the trees across from the river and was long gone. When we got up to the apartment, four of his men were dead, two women were unconscious, and there was some blood on the floor in an area where there were no bodies."

"Meaning?"

"Blake thinks Jenaro *was* here, but either injured or killed, and then removed," John told her. "I'm inclined to agree with him, especially after what you just told me. The blood pattern isn't consistent with spatter from any of the bodies we have here."

"John!"

Stephanie heard Blake's voice in the background.

"Hold on, Steph," John said.

Stephanie leaned on the counter, listening as John went into an area with a lot of background noise. She tried to make out the sounds, but they all blurred together until she clearly heard Blake's voice again.

"Look at this."

"More blood?" John asked after a moment. "Isn't this where Death Chick was sitting?"

"She was sitting next to it, but yes," Blake answered. "So, we have at least two missing bodies. Is that Stephanie on the phone?"

Stephanie glanced up as Jessica appeared in the doorway of the kitchen.

"Ms. Walker?" Blake spoke into her ear.

"Yep," she answered as Jessica leaned against the door frame, watching her.

"Do you still have Mrs. Nuñez and her son with you?" he asked.

"Yes."

"Jenaro is missing," Blake told her. "I don't think he's still a threat, but you may want to set a couple of good agents on the Nuñez family to be on the safe side."

"Already done," Stephanie told him. "I've had a pair with her husband and daughter since this all began, and she's still with me. Tell me what happened."

"I don't know yet, but I can tell you this, he was here."

"How do you know?"

"There are too many of his entourage here, dead," Blake answered bluntly. "This many of his men wouldn't be in one place if Jenaro hadn't been here. There's some blood on the floor, consistent with a small wound, and now I just found a much larger stain on the couch. This, I would say, is consistent with a much deeper and more serious wound."

Next Exit, Dead Ahead

"I'll call Matt and get him into the lab," Stephanie told him, glancing at her watch. "Get swabs of all the blood and give them to John. Tell him to get them over to Matt immediately. Let's see if we can get confirmation tonight."

"Your basement gnome will be willing to go in at...ten o'clock at night to run DNA?" Blake asked incredulously.

"He will for me," she assured him.

"I'll get the samples together."

Stephanie disconnected and looked across the kitchen at Jessica. "It looks like you're free of Jenaro," she told her.

"Then why aren't you smiling?" Jessica asked softly.

"Because we don't have a body yet," Stephanie said, hitting speed dial on her phone.

"Then I'm not free of him yet," Jessica told her grimly. "I know this man. Many have thought they killed him before, only to find out they were wrong."

"You know that woman who saved your life?" Stephanie asked her, putting her phone back up her ear as it started to ring on the other end. Jessica nodded. "Well, she's the one who says you're safe."

Jessica stared at her for a beat, then a slow smile spread across her face.

"Then we just may be free," she breathed.

Stephanie shook her head, smiling reluctantly at Jessica's absolute faith in Viper.

"Matt!" Stephanie said as a male voice answered the phone. "I need a huge favor."

"I'm not going into work," Matt told her. "I'm beat. I'm going to bed."

"Please? I need you to run a DNA sample," Stephanie said, drawing a loud sigh from him.

"Running DNA samples isn't like running a social security number," he informed her. "It takes time. A lot of time."

"Even if you're comparing it to DNA you already know?" Stephanie asked.

After a moment of silence, Matt sighed.

"You're checking to see if it matches someone?" he asked.

"Yes."

"And we know that someone has their DNA on file?"

"Yes."

"Who?"

"Jenaro Gomez."

There was a heavy sigh on the line and Stephanie knew she had him.

"I'll be there in twenty minutes," Matt said tiredly, "and you owe me huge for this."

"Agreed."

John jogged down the stairs of the row home, two evidence bags in his jacket pocket. Stepping out into the night, he glanced around. They had the street blocked off and coroner vans were pulled up onto the sidewalk, ready to take charge of the four bodies upstairs. The neighbors were huddled on their stoops, watching the activity with wide eyes as agents and techs swarmed in and out of the end house like so many flies at a picnic. An ambulance idled in the street, its lights still flashing, and John glimpsed one of the women sitting in the back, a blue blanket around her shoulders. He frowned and walked over to the ambulance, glancing inside. She was the only one sitting there.

John spun around, looking for the paramedic he had summoned earlier. He spotted him a few feet away, talking with one of the SWAT team.

"Hey!" he called, waving a hand.

The paramedic looked up and came over.

"Yeah?" he asked, glancing in at the woman in the ambulance.

"Where's the other one?" John asked.

The paramedic looked at him, confused.

"What other one?"

"The other witness," John replied impatiently. "The other woman!"

"There wasn't another woman," the paramedic answered. "Just her. I thought she's who you meant."

"There was another woman," John told him harshly. "She was sitting on the sofa up there."

"Agent Smithe, there was no one on the sofa when I went up there," the man told him, shaking his head. "I stopped one of the agents and asked where the woman was, and they took me to her."

John stared at him speechlessly and the paramedic stared back, nodding.

"Well, where the hell did she go?" John finally demanded.

"I have no idea," the paramedic replied with a shrug.

John turned away and ran a hand through his hair, looking around the busy street hopelessly. Another witness gone. Although, he admitted to himself as he turned away and headed toward his car, she was certifiably bat-crazy, so she wouldn't have been much of a witness. He shook his head, looking around again as he reached his car.

But where had she gone?

And how the hell had she disappeared from a room full of FBI and SWAT?

Chapter Thirty-Three

Alina sat with her back against a tree trunk, one leg bent, and her head resting against the bark. The woods were pitch-black around her and the sounds of the night creatures filled the air. The temperature had dropped and the bite of fall hung in the air, bringing with it the crisp clean scent of impending frost. Taking a deep breath, Alina closed her eyes, her senses tuned to the sounds around her, perfectly comfortable.

She smiled.

Blake and John had fallen for her performance hook, line, and sinker. She didn't have time to be as thorough as she would have liked with her disguise, but what she managed had apparently sufficed. The skirt and top went over her own clothes comfortably enough, hiding everything except the boots. Oddly enough, though, no one seemed to notice the boots. In the bedroom, on the dresser, Viper found enough make-up to hastily create a bruise to cover half her face, blending it to make it appear as if it was fading. Using red lip liner on her eyes, she smudged it in with her fingers to make them look red. At the last minute, on her way out of the bedroom, she spied some vapor rub. She rubbed it under her eyes and they swelled up, adding to the redness. Over all, she hadn't been entirely happy with the results, but it did the job. John hadn't looked twice at her, except to think she was crazy.

Viper shook her head slightly, her eyes still closed. She had been expecting Blake, but not John. That was a larger risk than she would have been willing to take, just to give Hawk an extra few minutes to clear the building with Gomez. However, it all worked out in the end.

Who knew Blake Hanover would turn out to speak the odd Spanish dialect unique to a tiny, southern region of Mexico? Alina smiled ruefully. He had genuinely surprised her, and that was hard to do these days. He had been thorough in his pursuit of the Cartel, she would give him that. He must have spent time in Mexico, tracking them and learning everything about them. Blake Hanover was not a common federal agent.

Alina supposed she should have expected that. He was a Marine. They were all unpredictable.

Viper opened her eyes at the faint and distant sound of a motorcycle. She listened intently for a moment, then yawned and zipped up her jacket against the chill in the air. An owl hooted nearby and something went scurrying under some leaves behind her. The motorcycle grew louder as it came closer and little by little, the forest creatures around her stilled, hiding from the intruder heading in their direction. A few minutes later, the bike splashed into the creek and roared up the bank.

Alina blinked as it broke through the trees and caught her with its headlight. She didn't raise her hand to shield her eyes, but simply kept her eyes down until the light veered off her face as Hawk turned the bike. He pulled up in front of her and switched off the engine.

"How long have you been here?" he asked, pulling off his helmet.

"Not long," Viper answered, standing. "Did you make it out ok?"

"Piece of cake," Hawk replied, kicking down the kickstand and getting off the bike.

"And Jenaro?"

"Taken care of."

Alina nodded and studied Hawk in the darkness thoughtfully.

"So, it's over then," she murmured.

Hawk turned toward her, dark and forbidding in his black jacket and clothes. He reached into his pockets and pulled out her pistol, handing it to her. Viper took it and tucked it into her back holster.

"As far as the Casa Reinos are concerned," he said. "If there are others out there considering trying to find me, this might make them think twice."

He pulled out her leg holster and knife, handing them to her. She slid the knife back into her sheath on her ankle and tucked the leg holster into her pocket.

"Have you briefed Charlie?" Alina asked, watching as he pulled the bike cover out from under its pile of leaves and tossed it over the bike.

"Not yet," Damon answered, securing the cover. "I will."

"He needs to know you're compromised," she said softly.

Damon glanced at her silently as he finished securing the bike. When he turned back toward her, he looked every inch like the dangerous assassin he was.

"I'm only compromised if they find me," he told her steadily. "Jenaro's the first one who did, and he's not a factor anymore."

"But he found you," Viper pointed out, her eyes locking with his. "Don't make the mistake of thinking you're invincible. Regina compromised you, and you're still at risk. Charlie needs to know how close they got."

"I'll handle it," Hawk said shortly.

Alina pressed her lips together and clamped her back teeth together with a snap, but let the subject drop. She turned and walked away, heading through the trees toward the house. Hawk would do what he wanted, regardless of what she said, but she had voiced her concern. The rest was up to him. It was his life.

Hawk followed silently, a frown on his face. Viper worried he was no longer invisible in the world arena. Their anonymity was their greatest weapon, and Regina stripped his away when she circulated his photo. Charlie was perfectly aware of the risk in continuing to send him out into the field, but Hawk knew he had weighed those risks against real-time analysis of how many people actually saw the photograph. Harry had alerted Charlie as soon as Regina sent the communications, allowing him to get a good jump on containing the damage. Only Charlie knew just how much damage had actually been done, and he seemed to believe it was minimal.

The fact that Jenaro recognized him in Jersey was unfortunate, but Damon knew now it was a freak accident that he had ended up in the same area as Jenaro. Viper clearly thought it was more than just a coincidence.

Hawk studied the back of her head thoughtfully as they wound their way silently through the woods towards her house. They were both still alive because neither of them took anything at face value, and they were habitually suspicious of anything hinting of coincidence or accident. Even though he believed it really *was* just coincidence that Jenaro had recognized him, perhaps he should have Charlie look into it just to be safe.

If there was one thing he had learned over the years, it was that Viper's instincts were never wrong.

Alina sipped her coffee and stared out the sliding door, waiting for the red Mustang to make its way through the trees and around the driveway to the back of the house. The security cameras had picked Stephanie up as soon as she turned off the road, and Alina knew why she had come. She wanted answers, and understandably so.

Alina watched as two squirrels chased each other across the deck, chattering loudly. She had been up since dawn, practicing Yoga on the deck before descending downstairs to try to find something that would help Stephanie with Kwan. The fact that Lowell Kwan was somehow part of a bigger operation than a hacking ring was obvious. What, exactly, that operation was had Viper digging through classified files all morning, only to come up empty.

Her eyes narrowed now as she lifted her coffee cup to her lips again. Kwan's digital record was being protected for a reason, and the more she dug, the more she didn't like it. Viper had been trained to find information, and she excelled at it. Yet, she wasn't able to find anything on Kwan that wasn't general information. Someone had taken great pains to make sure the agency's interest in Kwan was concealed, and they had succeeded. If it weren't for the fact that Michael had been stonewalled, Alina would be inclined to believe the agency had no interest in Kwan at all. But someone warned him off, and that made all the difference. What was Kwan really doing?

The Mustang roared around the corner of the house and pulled up behind Michael's truck, pulling Alina's attention back to the driveway. She watched as Stephanie got out, carrying a white bakery bag in one hand. Shaking her head slightly, Alina slid open the door and stepped out onto the deck.

"You always come bearing unhealthy food," she said as Stephanie walked up the steps.

Stephanie grinned.

"You need good, old-fashioned starch in your diet," she retorted. "Is the coffeemaker still on?"

"Yes."

Alina motioned Stephanie inside and followed her into the house, sliding the door closed behind her. Stephanie walked over to the bar and dropped her purse and keys on the granite counter, setting the bag down.

"Are Michael and Angela still sleeping?" she asked, glancing at the clock. It was just past eight.

"I think Angie's in the shower," Alina replied, circling the bar and heading to the coffeemaker with her mug. "Michael went out for a run."

"How are you holding up having them here?" Stephanie asked, perching on a bar stool and pulling of her sunglasses.

Alina glanced over her shoulder.

"I haven't killed them yet."

She opened a cabinet and got a clean mug for Stephanie, placing it under the coffee spout. Stephanie chuckled and opened the bakery bag, pulling out two toasted bagels with cream cheese.

"That's a good thing," she murmured, getting up and joining Alina in the kitchen. "Plates?"

"In there," Alina said, pointing to another cabinet.

Stephanie nodded and turned to get two plates out of the cabinet.

"So, tell me about Jenaro," she said, glancing at Alina.

Alina's lips twitched.

"Jessica's safe," she replied.

Stephanie's eyes narrowed and she went back to the bar with the plates.

"That's what you said last night." She sat on the bar stool again and cast a searching look at Alina. "Blake and John were there. They found four bodies, none of which were Gomez."

Alina's face didn't give anything away and Stephanie sighed at the shuttered look.

"I can't release the Nuñezes from agency protection without knowing for sure they're safe," she told Alina, picking up one of the bagels. "Give me something I can work with here."

Alina considered Stephanie for a long moment thoughtfully before she turned and withdrew the full coffee mug from the machine. She carried it over and set it in front of Stephanie.

"What I tell you cannot go beyond the two of us," she said quietly, her voice like steel.

Stephanie looked up in surprise to find Viper looking at her, her dark eyes cold and distant. She nodded mutely, her heart thudding in her chest despite herself. Viper held her gaze for a second longer, as if searching her soul, before turning to go back to the coffeemaker. She set her own cup under the spout and hit the button to brew another cup. Stephanie breathed a silent sigh of relief when she turned away. The stranger that lived inside her friend terrified her, and Stephanie still remembered vividly what that stranger was capable of.

When Alina returned a few moments later with her coffee, Viper had disappeared. The dark eyes were still shuttered, but the danger had passed, and Stephanie relaxed.

"Two months ago, before Regina died, she put out a hit on Damon," Alina said quietly, seating herself next to Stephanie at the bar. "She included a photo and sent it to all the top mercenaries, assassins, and guns for hire in the world."

Stephanie's mouth dropped open and she stared at Alina. "What?!"

"She also sent it to three Mexican cartels," Alina continued, sipping her coffee.

"Oh my God," Stephanie breathed. "Jenaro Gomez."

"You asked me how I knew about the Cartel before you did," Alina reminded her, glancing at her. "I knew because they put Rodrigo's head outside Damon's condo as a warning."

"Damon's? But....we found it outside the prison!" Stephanie exclaimed, the bagel forgotten. "How did it get to the prison if they left it..."

Alina's lips twitched as Stephanie's voice trailed off.

"Damon sent the warning back," she said softly.

Stephanie dropped her forehead into her hand with a groan.

"Do you have any idea what kind of penalties there are for tampering with evidence in a federal investigation?" she demanded, glancing at Alina. "Are you *laughing*!?"

"No." Alina swallowed her grin and picked up her bagel, tearing a piece off. "I would never find relocating a human head on a stick amusing."

Stephanie lifted her head and looked at Alina suspiciously, but her friend chewed her bagel innocently.

"So, Jenaro's apartment last night," Stephanie murmured, "that was Damon?"

"Let's just say the Casa Reinos went after the wrong man," Alina answered.

Stephanie sat silently for a moment before picking up her forgotten bagel and biting into it. The two women ate quietly for a moment. One was processing the knowledge that a government assassin, protected at much higher levels than her, had single-handedly taken on a Cartel. The other was pondering the wisdom of telling a federal agent the truth.

"Lorenzo and Ramiero?" Stephanie finally asked.

"Remember how Dimitrius took out the members of Johann's network to instill the fear of God into him?" Alina asked.

"Do they train you people to be so messed up, or does it just come naturally?" Stephanie demanded.

Alina burst out laughing.

"Fear is one of the biggest weapons you can wield," she told her, still chuckling. "We don't think of it as messed up. We think of it as tactical advantage."

"So, where's Jenaro now?" Stephanie asked. Alina gave her a look and she sighed. "Will we ever find his body?"

"Doubtful," Alina answered calmly.

"Blake won't be happy," Stephanie said, sipping her coffee. "He's spent over three years trying to get Jenaro Gomez. This is the closest he's come, and now he won't have anything to show for it."

Alina smiled faintly and Stephanie shot her a look.

"What?" she demanded. "I'm getting to know that smile. What do you know?"

"Blake won't leave empty-handed," Alina promised. "I owe him."

"Owe him? Owe him for what?" Stephanie stared at her. "How do you even know him?"

Alina finished her coffee and stood up.

"Steph, finish your breakfast," she advised.

"God! I hate it when you do that!" Stephanie exclaimed, making a face at Alina's back. "At least tell me this, who's going to take the fall for all these dead Cartels I have cluttering up the place?"

Alina glanced over her shoulder, her lips twitching.

"What dead Cartels?" she asked.

Stephanie stared at her.

"Lina, even *you* can't make six bodies disappear from the morgue," she stammered.

Viper raised her eyebrow.

"Are you sure about that?" she asked softly.

Blake rode the elevator down to the basement level, watching the numbers decrease above his head. He met Rob in his office first thing this morning, filling him in on the events from last night. Rob had not been happy when he heard four dead bodies were recovered and none of them were Jenaro. In fact, he hadn't been happy that someone beat them to the Cartel at all. Blake grinned, recalling Rob's inventive vocabulary. He sent Blake off to see what Matt had been able to find out with the blood samples, still fuming as Blake went out the door.

The smile on Blake's face faded as he sipped his coffee. He wasn't happy himself. Three years of work trying to nail these bastards, and now he got this close only to have them start turning up dead everywhere. Who the hell was doing it? And how? He went over that apartment twice last night, examining every crack and every inch of floor. He hadn't found any evidence of forced entry or anything that could have been left behind by whoever killed those men. Hell, there hadn't even been a scuff mark anywhere. If Blake didn't know better, he would consider the possibility Jenaro killed them all himself.

The elevator dinged and Blake raised his eyes as the doors slid open. He stepped out of the elevator and looked around, following the loud, pulsing music coming from an open doorway a few feet away. He raised his eyebrows when he entered Matt's lab, his eyes widening as he looked around slowly. Computers and monitors lined one side of the large room, while mysterious-looking machines and big refrigerators lined the other. The space between was filled with two long tables holding just about every device used for testing known to man. Old-fashioned chemistry equipment jostled for space with state-of-the-art technology. A faint smell of burning hung over the room, indicating that the chemistry equipment had been in use recently.

Next Exit, Dead Ahead

The master of this world of chaos stood near one of the large machines at the side of the room, watching the digital readout on the machine as it hummed loudly. Dressed in wrinkled khakis, Matt looked like he had never heard of an iron and his lab coat had seen better days. His sandy-colored hair stuck up in the back, and glasses perched on his nose, lending him an air of educated insanity. He looked up when Blake appeared, pushing the glasses up and tilting his head slightly to study him.

"Agent Hanover?" he called over the noise blaring from surround-sound speakers in the corners of the room. Blake nodded, speechless. "Good! You're just in time!"

Matt picked up a remote and the music stopped suddenly. Someone made a snorting sound in the corner behind Blake and he swung around to find John lifting his head from a pillow on the floor. He blinked up at Blake sleepily before launching into a wide, jaw-cracking yawn.

"Is it that time already?" he mumbled.

"Rise and shine, John," Matt called, tossing the remote back on the table.

"Did you sleep here?" Blake asked, watching as John sat up and rubbed his face.

"I didn't see much point in going home," John retorted. "The mad scientist over there was still running the blood samples at three. I figured I might as well stay."

Blake turned to look at Matt.

"Did you find anything?" he asked.

Matt looked at him and picked up a can of Red Bull, chugging it down before answering.

"Of course I did," he finally answered, tossing the empty can into a recycling bin under one of the long tables. "Come over here and I'll show you."

John struggled to his feet, stretched, and ambled over to where Matt stood near one of the long tables. Blake followed, glancing at the readouts and photographs littering the table.

"You gave me two blood samples, right?" Matt asked rhetorically. "You wanted to know if one of them matches Jenaro Gomez. Lucky for you, Jenaro's DNA is in the database."

"I know," Blake said. "It was entered two years ago when he was convicted of manslaughter. He only served six months of his fifteen-year sentence in Mexico."

"I know. What I meant was, lucky for you it was entered into the database. Otherwise, I would *not* have come in last night to try to run cold DNA searches," Matt told him. "As it was, I ran into problems running these against the DNA we have."

"Why?" John asked, stifling another yawn. Blake handed him his coffee. "Thanks."

"Please observe sample A," Matt said. He pulled out a sheet of paper and handed it to them. "This is the sample taken from the floor."

"What am I looking at here?" Blake asked, peering at the graph.

Matt sighed.

"The DNA from the database is in blue," he explained. "That's Jenaro's DNA that we have on file. Sample A is in red."

"They're almost identical," John said, glancing up from the sheet.

Matt nodded.

"It's a 97% match," he agreed.

"Then we know he was there!" Blake said, grinning.

"Oh, he was there all right, but hold on," Matt cautioned him, pulling out another sheet. "This is what took me all night. This is why you're lucky I came in." He handed them the sheet. "That's sample B, the blood you took from the couch."

Blake and John stared at the sheet in silence.

"I don't understand," John finally said, looking up in confusion.

"Sample B is a 27% match," Matt told them.

"How...how is that possible?" John asked.

"It can only be possible if the sample came from..." Matt began.

"...a half-sibling," Blake finished.

Matt nodded.

"Exactly."

John looked at Blake questioningly.

"Turi," Blake told him. "His name is Turi Alvarado. He's Jenaro's half-brother."

"I spent all night trying to match his DNA," Matt said. "It's still searching."

"You won't find a match," Blake said, shaking his head. "Turi has never been convicted of a crime. His brother gets him off every time, so his DNA has never been entered into the databases."

"So, let me get this straight," John finished Blake's coffee and shook his head. "We're missing both Jenaro *and* his brother?"

"Something like that," Blake replied.

"Well hell, then the Nuñezes aren't safe yet!" John exclaimed.

Blake shook his head grimly.

"Not yet," he agreed. "Given the amount of blood on that couch, Turi is hurt pretty bad. Now we know who we're looking for, let's start with the area hospitals and clinics and hope for some luck. He couldn't have gotten far."

John nodded and turned toward the door.

"I'll get on it," he said. "What about Jenaro?"

Blake frowned thoughtfully.

"I'll worry about him," he said. "You just find me Turi."

Chapter Thirty-Four

Stephanie dropped her purse into her desk drawer and slammed it shut. She fell into her chair and glanced over at John. He was on the phone at his desk. She had just got to the office and already felt tired. She spent the entire drive into the city wondering how Alina and Damon had managed to take over and run riot all over South Jersey and where, exactly, she had lost control of the two assassins. Stephanie was pulling into the parking garage at work when she realized she never *had* control of them. They did what they wanted. She supposed if she kicked up a fuss, she could get them reprimanded and maybe even pulled from the field. If it was anyone else, she would try to prosecute them with impunity, but they weren't anyone else. They were the people who had saved her life more than once, and she knew they were the good guys. These days, it was getting harder and harder to tell who the good guys were. Stephanie wasn't about to punish two of them.

"And what took you so long to get here?" John demanded, hanging up and rolling over to her desk in his chair. "It's almost ten!"

"I had breakfast with Lina," Stephanie answered, glancing at him.

"And what does the Widow have caught in her web today?" he asked with a teasing grin.

"Jenaro Gomez," Stephanie told him.

The grin disappeared and John stared at her.

"What?!" he yelled.

Stephanie hushed him, rolling her eyes and glancing around. A few people glanced over and John lowered his voice.

"Explain!" he hissed.

"I can't," Stephanie answered. "Let's just say he's not going to be our problem for much longer."

"Oh, you have to explain this," John said, leaning forward in his chair imploringly.

"I can't," Stephanie insisted. "I only told you so you wouldn't waste too much time on him. He's gone."

"Well, I know he's gone," John muttered. "Is he gone and might come back?"

"Highly unlikely," she murmured, "unless he learns the art of reincarnation."

John sat back in his chair.

"So that's it," he said. "Are we telling Blake?"

"No." Stephanie shook her head. "I have a feeling we won't have to."

"How so?"

"Just call it a hunch."

"You know, you're picking up her bad habits," John informed her, sliding back to his desk.

Stephanie grinned and turned to face him.

"Tell me about the blood samples," she said.

John grabbed the papers Matt had giving him and got up to go over to her desk, perching on the corner.

"One is a 97% match to Gomez," he told her, handing her the read-outs. "The other is a 27% match."

Stephanie looked up sharply.

"Family?"

"Half-brother," John said. "Blake says his name is Turi Alvarado."

"So it was Turi who ran away from the house?" Stephanie asked. "Is that what we're thinking?"

"Yes, and he was wounded pretty badly. There was a lot of blood on the couch."

"Are you checking the hospitals?"

John nodded.

"And the clinics. We should be able to find him."

Stephanie nodded and dropped the read-outs on her desk, leaning back in her chair thoughtfully.

"If Turi is still alive, Blake won't go home empty-handed," she murmured. A slow smile curved her lips. "She said she owed him."

"Who?" John raised a sandy eyebrow. "What are you talking about?"

Stephanie shook her head, looking up as Rob yelled her name from his office door.

"Nothing," she said, getting up. "Where *is* Blake?"

"He went to get some coffee from the shop on the corner," John said, going back to his desk as she turned to head towards Rob's office.

Stephanie nodded and strode down the aisle to her boss's office. She stepped into the open door and glanced around the small office.

"Morning, Rob!" Stephanie said cheerfully.

He nodded to her as he rounded the corner of his desk and settled into his chair, waving her into one of the seats in front of the desk.

"Morning," he replied. "Blake told me about last night. Have you spoken to him yet?"

"Briefly, last night," Stephanie answered, sitting down. "John just filled me in on the blood samples."

"Well, first things first, where are the Nuñezes?" Rob asked, sitting back in his chair.

"At home, with their family," Stephanie told him. "I took them there this morning. I have two agents in the house with them, and left two more outside down the street."

"Jenaro and Turi are still out there," Rob pointed out. "Why aren't you putting them somewhere safe?"

"I don't think there's a real need," Stephanie replied carefully. "Jenaro wasn't here for them. The Nuñezes were just a tool to him. Now his soldiers are dead and someone is going after him, I don't think he's going to worry about them." *I don't think he's ever going to worry about anything again,* she added silently to herself.

Rob studied her for a long moment.

"That's a mighty big risk to take with four lives, when he already kidnapped the boy and tried to kill the wife," he finally said. "Please tell me you're basing your decision on more than just a hunch."

Stephanie squirmed a little in her seat.

"I would say it's more than just a hunch," she murmured. "If we don't have any answers in the next twenty-four hours, I'll see if they'll consider protection. However, I don't think it will be necessary."

"Stephanie, I've trusted you before and you haven't let me down," Rob said slowly. "For God's sake, don't start now."

"I'll try not to."

"Well, then, that brings me to what happened last night," Rob said, moving on. "Do you have any idea who may have gotten to Jenaro before us?"

Stephanie swallowed and resisted the urge to cross her fingers.

"Someone who had more information than we did," she replied briskly. "I've been concentrating on Lowell Kwan, but Blake was making good progress on Gomez. I have no idea what happened."

"Blake thinks it was a professional hit," Rob told her, absently picking up a pen from his desk and turning it over in his fingers.

"Professional?" Stephanie raised an eyebrow.

"He couldn't find any trace of the attacker, either inside the apartment or out," Rob explained. "He thinks they came and went by the fire escape, but there was nothing to confirm it. No witnesses, no fingerprints, not even a footprint."

"What about inside?" Stephanie asked with a frown. "There's *always* something."

"Not this time."

Blake spoke from the doorway behind her and Stephanie turned around sharply. He smiled and came into the office carrying a coffee carrier with three cups in it.

"I brought coffee for everyone. I figured we needed it," he continued, walking over to Rob's desk. He pulled out one of the cups, handing it to him. Rob nodded in thanks. "There were four bodies inside the apartment, two with broken necks and two with gunshots. It's the bullet wounds that make me think we're dealing with a professional."

Blake handed Stephanie a coffee and held the carrier out for her to pick up some packets of sugar and a few creamers from the stash in the extra cup slot.

"What was different about the bullet wounds?" Stephanie asked, smiling in thanks as she took two sugar packets and two creamers. "I haven't had time to look at the crime scene photos yet."

"One body had one shot, perfectly through his heart," Blake told her, sitting in the other chair across from Rob's desk. He pulled out the last remaining coffee from the carrier and dropped the carrier onto the floor. "The second body had a gunshot through the chest, but he also had one perfectly centered on his forehead. The precision of the shots was remarkable. Not many people have aim that good."

"Same caliber?" Rob asked, pouring sugar into his coffee.

"I don't know yet," Blake answered. "Larry almost had my head off this morning. He has bodies lined up outside autopsy and he told me he's getting a deli ticket machine for the door."

Stephanie chuckled despite herself.

"Poor Larry," she murmured.

"So, we have precision shooting and broken vertebrae," Rob said. "What about the blood stains?"

"The one matching Jenaro's DNA was on the floor, behind the sofa," Blake said. "There was no blood trail, so he was probably dropped there and then picked up. The other one, the one we believe is from Turi, was on the sofa. That had a history. He was wounded outside in the hall, then dragged into the apartment and put on the sofa."

"Blood trail?" Stephanie asked, glancing at him.

Blake nodded.

"And not a very long one," he told her. "If he was trying to get away, he didn't get far. Only a few feet. We found minute splatter on the wall outside, but only a few drops on the floor leading to the couch."

"Sounds like a stab wound," Rob said thoughtfully, sipping his coffee and sitting back in his chair. "If he was stabbed in the hall and dragged inside with the knife still in, there would be little blood."

"Exactly," Blake agreed. "I think they pulled him in, put him on the couch, then pulled the knife out. The amount of blood soaked into the couch is consistent with a deep wound."

"And, in all of this, they didn't leave any trace of themselves?" Stephanie demanded, raising her eyebrows. "How is that possible?"

"I don't know." Blake shook his head. "A few techs are still there, trying to find something, but I'm not optimistic."

"Why would they take Jenaro?" Rob wondered. "Why not just kill him there?"

"That's the million-dollar question," Blake said. "And why leave Turi alive?"

"And the two women didn't see anything?" Rob shook his head. "Unbelievable."

"What two women?" Stephanie asked, looking up sharply.

Blake looked at her.

"There were two women in the apartment when we got there, both unconscious," he explained. "Neither of them saw anything."

"Well, that's not entirely true," Rob murmured, a grin breaking over his face.

"I don't think hallucinations of a female skeleton in a black, flowing dress qualifies as reliable evidence," Blake retorted. He looked at Stephanie. "One of the women was convinced it was La Catrina, the skeletal Goddess of Day of the Dead, who went in and took Jenaro."

"Wow."

"Ok!" Rob sat forward and put his coffee down. "Let's get away from Jenaro for a minute. What's going on with Kwan?"

"He's ditched his car and disappeared," Stephanie said, "but I don't think he's going far yet."

"Why?"

"Because of the virus," she told them. "If Matt is right about the way the virus works, it's still in the mainframe of the banks. We haven't had any word that millions of dollars have suddenly gone missing. Kwan isn't going anywhere until he gets paid. In the meantime, we're looking for him."

Rob nodded.

"Any thoughts on whether he could have been involved last night?" he asked, glancing from Stephanie to Blake and back again.

"He doesn't have the training for that," Blake said, shaking his head.

"No, but..." Stephanie started, then stopped.

"But what?" Rob asked, looking at her.

Stephanie hesitated, glancing at Blake, then sighed. Getting up, she went to the office door and closed it before going back to her seat.

"Jin Seung Moon," she said simply, seating herself again.

Rob sat back and studied her.

"What about him?"

"Lowell Kwan has been a follower of Moon since college," Stephanie told them. "He made no secret of this. We have a direct link between Kwan and Moon, Moon is in New York, and Kwan just inserted a virus capable of crashing whole economies into a bank mainframe. If Kwan is selling the virus to Moon, and Moon found out Jenaro Gomez wanted the money, is it too far-fetched to think Moon could have sent *his* men after Jenaro?"

Rob and Blake both stared at her in silence.

"If he did, we can't prove it," Blake finally said.

"Even if we could, we can't touch him," Rob muttered.

"I'm not saying that's what happened," Stephanie said, "but it's a theory."

"It's a good one," Blake muttered. "Damn."

Silence fell in the office as Blake and Rob mulled over the ramifications of Moon being involved while Stephanie silently prayed to God for forgiveness in deliberately misleading her boss. Rob's phone rang suddenly, making her jump, and he grabbed it.

"Hello?" Rob answered impatiently, then grew still while he listened. "Are you sure?" he finally demanded, his tone grim.

Stephanie glanced at Blake, who was watching Rob with a slight frown.

"Ok. I'll send over our analysis team with the agent," Rob said after another lengthy silence. "Try to keep the press out of it for as long as you can."

He hung up and looked at Stephanie.

"The virus just did its thing," he told her. "Between One District Bank and New Federal, $57.6 million just disappeared."

Alina looked up sharply at the gasp of shock from the dining room table. Angela was ensconced in her chair, laptop and blackberry set up in what Alina gathered was her daily workstation. Right now, she stared at her laptop screen, a look of pure shock on her face.

"What's wrong?" Alina asked sharply, closing her laptop and getting up from the sofa.

"The bank..." Angie mumbled, fumbling for her blackberry.

"What about the bank?" Alina demanded.

"He did it." Angela sounded stunned. "It's been robbed."

Alina frowned and rounded the table to look over Angela's shoulder.

"How much?" she asked.

"Well, the system thinks $28 million is missing, but that's not possible," Angela said, hitting speed dial on her blackberry and hooking her blue-tooth onto her ear. "It's not possible that he could have hacked the system and taken that much without any red flags going up."

Alina straightened up slowly, her eyes narrowing thoughtfully. She turned away from the dining room as Angela started talking urgently on the phone. Crossing the room to the living room, she picked up her phone and sent a text to Stephanie.

Kwan just extracted the virus.

Alina sank onto the couch, her lips pursed. If Kwan had the money now, he was free to run. He would want to get as far away as quickly as possible. He knew the FBI was on his tail. Where would he go? Where would he run?

I know. We're on it.

Alina glanced at Stephanie's message and stared at the phone thoughtfully. After a long moment, she reached out and pulled her laptop onto her lap, flipping it open. She glanced behind her, making sure Angela was still engrossed on her blackberry, then turned her attention to the screen, pulling up a portal and typing in her credentials. A few seconds later, she paused, the cursor blinking on a search box.

Viper lifted her eyes and stared across the living room at the fireplace, her fingers still poised over the keyboard. Charlie would have her head on a platter, sliced off and served with caviar. Hawk was right. He wasn't her target, wasn't her responsibility. If Kwan ran to him, it was up to the Fearless Feds to handle it.

Viper's eyes narrowed. Her lips compressed grimly and, for the briefest of seconds, a glint of uncertainty flashed in her dark eyes. In an instant, it disappeared and she lowered her gaze to the screen, typing a single name into the search field.

Jin Seung Moon.

Next Exit, Dead Ahead

Stephanie strode into Matt's lab and went straight to the remote on the far table. Picking it up, she turned off the loud, god-awful music blaring from the hidden speakers and dropped the remote back on the table. She ignored Matt's indignant protest and turned to face him.

"The virus was activated," she told him bluntly.

Matt stopped what he was doing and stared at her.

"When?"

"Twenty minutes ago," Stephanie said. "You need to get the analysts who worked with you and come with me now. You have your free pass into One District Bank's mainframe."

Matt shoved his glasses up on his nose and turned to grab his backpack from under one of the long tables.

"How much money is missing?" he asked, tossing the bag onto a table and crossing the room to grab a laptop.

"$56.7 million between One District and New Federal," Stephanie told him, watching as he opened a drawer and fished for a flash drive. "One District Bank is reporting $28 million."

Matt whistled and stuffed the computer and flash drive into his bag.

"I bet they're panicking like never before," he chortled.

"You'll be panicking if you can't find the money," Stephanie retorted.

Matt looked at her.

"We might be able to find where the money was taken from, which accounts, but if the virus worked the way I think it did, I'll never find the money," he told her.

"You better hope you're wrong, then," Stephanie said grimly. "Who are the analysts who helped with Rodrigo's computer?"

"Terry and Anna," Matt said, grabbing his cell phone. "I'll text them and tell them to meet us in the parking garage."

"Do you think you'll be able to do this?" Stephanie asked.

Matt glanced up at her.

"I don't know," he answered honestly. "It all depends on whether or not I can locate where the virus stored the money. I'll do my best."

"What will it take to get the money back?"

Matt shrugged.

"The virus itself," he answered. "If I have the virus, in theory, I can reverse it and find out where the money was transferred. Unless they used a different algorithm for the transfer, in which case, it could take months."

"We don't have months," Stephanie muttered.

Matt grabbed a four-pack of Red Bull out of one of the huge refrigerators used to store samples and tissues and tucked it into the backpack. Stephanie grimaced.

"What?" he asked, catching the look.

"You keep your Red Bull in the same fridge you keep blood samples," she said.

Matt grinned.

"So? It's not like the samples are touching the cans."

"It's just....gross." Stephanie shook her head and turned to leave the lab.

Matt slung his bag over his shoulder and followed her.

"This is really bad, isn't it?" he asked seriously as they stepped into the elevator.

Stephanie glanced at him grimly.

"It's certainly not good," she retorted. "If we don't find the money, we can kiss our jobs good-bye."

Chapter Thirty-Five

Hawk slid his pen into his uniform shirt pocket and tucked his clipboard under his arm.

"I'm glad you made it over so quickly," the assistant manager of the Rittenhouse Hotel told him, coming out from behind the counter and leading Damon across the marble floor to a back hallway marked Employees Only. "I have three suites with no air. We had the air conditioner guys out, but they think it's the wiring."

"No problem," Hawk replied easily, his blue eyes noting the position of all the security cameras in the lobby as he followed the manager. "You ever have problems with the wiring before in that section?"

"Not since I've been here," the man answered. "I'm Paul, by the way."

The opulent luxury present in the lobby disappeared as they entered the employee hallway. The wide, long corridor had multiple doors on either side and was painted a pale taupe color. It was lunchtime, and the smell of food coming from one of the break rooms seemed to permeate the entire hallway.

"Jerry," Damon introduced himself. "Well, here's hoping it's just a short."

"That would be great," Paul said, leading him down the hallway toward a service elevator at the end. "I've got a hectic day. This is the last thing I need, what with three VIPs coming in today, and one of them in that section."

"Has the guest checked in already?" Hawk asked, his eyes never still, noting the cameras, doors and exits around them.

"No. You have a few hours yet," Paul replied. "He's expected around five-thirty. Hopefully, it won't take that long."

"I hope not," Damon said with a grin. "I have a date tonight."

Paul laughed and stopped outside the service elevator. He pressed a button and the doors slid open. As he prepared to get into the elevator, his phone started vibrating. Sighing, he pulled it out of his inside suit pocket.

"I'm sorry. I have to take this," he told Damon. "Are you okay on your own?"

"No problem," Damon said, getting into the elevator. "Do what you gotta do."

"If you need anything, call down to the front desk," Paul told him. "They'll find me. Anything you need, just let me know."

"Will do," Damon agreed cheerfully as the doors slid closed.

As soon as the elevator doors were closed, he glanced out of the corner of his eye at the camera in the upper corner of the elevator. Crossing his hands in front of him, Hawk rode the elevator up to the Parkview Suites. At the third floor, the doors slid open and he stepped out of the elevator.

Hawk glanced around the alcove and moved out into the plush corridor, glancing up and down the deserted hallway. Looking down at his clipboard, he headed for the electrical closet a few feet away. A few seconds later, he disappeared inside, the door closing softly behind him.

He flipped on the light and looked around. Breaker boxes and neatly tied bunches of multi-colored wires lined the small closet . He set his clipboard down and pulled out his phone, swiping the screen and pulling up the electrical schematics for the floor. After studying them for a minute, Hawk turned and scanned the boxes on the other wall. Finding the one he wanted, he set his phone down and pulled out a flat-headed screwdriver, popping open the box. Working quickly, Hawk separated some wires inside and clamped them off, attaching a small device before tying them back up with the others. He closed the box up again and turned to do the same to another box on the other side of the room. Once he finished, he slid his phone back into his pocket, picked up his clipboard and exited the closet.

Turning left, he moved down the thickly carpeted hallway, past doors widely spaced apart, until he came to the last suite on the left. Glancing around, he bent over the door briefly and disappeared inside a second later.

The suite was silent and empty, the air still. Hawk scanned the entryway and the main room, then went over to the window swiftly and glanced out. It overlooked Rittenhouse Park with a stunning view of the autumn colors taking over the park. Turning his head, Damon scanned the large sitting room searchingly. His eyes lit on a modern, geometric sculpture gracing the small display table at the front of the room. He smiled slightly and went over to it, pulling a small, wireless camera from a compartment on his tool belt. He slid the camera into one of the many crevices and turned the sculpture slightly so the angle would capture the entire room. Once he was satisfied, Hawk moved back to the door, slipping out of the suite as silently as he had entered.

He went back to the electrical closet and flipped open one of the breaker boxes. Removing one of the breakers, he pulled out a probe and slid it into the opening. He attached it to a wire and pulled a small box from his tool belt. Inserting the wire, he pressed a button. A light glowed green and he smiled. Removing the probe, he replaced the breaker and closed the box, turning to leave the closet. As he walked back to the service elevator, Damon heard a distant groan as the air conditioner switched on in the wing to the left.

Ten minutes later, Hawk sat at the wheel of his borrowed white electrical van in the parking garage, opening up a small laptop and checking the camera in the Parkview Suite. He smiled. It was working perfectly. He opened up another program, typing rapidly. A moment later, the security cameras in the employees' hall, service elevator and the corridor leading to Moon's suite came online. He had full control over them. Hawk nodded in satisfaction and closed the laptop. It had been an hour well spent.

He pulled out of his parking spot and drove through the underground parking garage, turning to go up the ramp to the exit. He was just pulling out of the exit when a Ducati flew around a car in traffic and pulled right in front of him. Damon slammed on the brakes, jerking the van to a stop inches from the bike.

The rider wore full gear, from black motorcycle pants to a red jacket to a red and black helmet. He looked at Hawk from behind a full, black-tinted visor and Hawk glared back. After staring at each other for a beat, the motorcycle pulled forward into traffic, weaving its way down the block.

Hawk shook his head and pulled out into the traffic, driving away from the hotel. Two blocks up, he passed the Ducati. It was pulled to the side of the road and the rider was getting off. Damon shook his head again and rolled through the green light. Some people should never be allowed on a bike.

Viper watched the white electrical van continue down the road with narrow eyes. When she pulled into the narrow spot in traffic, she hadn't been expecting to almost get hit by a van pulling out of the underground garage. She most definitely hadn't expected Hawk to be driving that van. Alina's lips twitched. She was so surprised to see him, she just stared at him, thankful for the black-tinted helmet concealing her face. The slight smile disappeared from her lips as she watched the van turn the corner on the next block.

What the hell was he doing?

Viper turned away from the bike and crossed the narrow sidewalk to the store in front of her, setting Hawk out of her mind. She pulled off her helmet as she entered, shaking out her hair and looking around. The store combined a mini-mart and delivery service. Heading to the counter at the back, she tucked her helmet under arm and grabbed a Slim Jim off a display rack on the way.

"I'm from Speedy," she told the woman behind the counter. "You called for an extra courier."

"It's about time you got here," the frazzled woman told her. "You're late."

Alina shrugged.

"So sue me," she retorted. "Some asshole just almost hit me, flying out of a parking garage. There's never a cop around when you need one."

"Oh, I hear that," the woman said, turning to reach down under the counter. "It's getting worse every day. Yesterday, one of my regular delivery girls broke her arm when a cab flew around the corner and clipped her as she stepped off the curb. No cop around then, either." The woman straightened up with a huge, cellophane-wrapped wine and cheese basket in her hands. "Luckily, a guy standing on the sidewalk got the cab number."

"Well, that's good. She's lucky she just broken her arm," Alina said, eyeing the basket. "Is that what I'm delivering?"

"Yeah. Here, I'll put it in a box for you," she said. "Will it fit on the back of your bike?"

"Yeah. I have a rack." Alina watched as the woman lifted the basket into a box and tied it up with string. "Where's it going?"

"Rittenhouse Hotel. The woman was very clear. She wants it delivered to one of the Park Suites. Name is...Moon," the woman said, checking her computer screen. "She said to make sure they place it directly on the coffee table in the suite sitting room."

"Not the bedroom?" Alina asked dryly with a grin.

The woman grinned back.

"Supposedly this Moon guy is picky," she told her. "He likes things to be perfect."

"Well, I guess if you're paying three grand a night for a room, you can afford to be picky," Alina said. She held up the Slim Jim. "How much for this?"

"Honey, you came all the way across town to help me out in a jam," the woman told her, shaking her head. "Consider it a tip."

"Thanks!"

Alina put her helmet back on and grabbed the box, turning to leave. After securing the package on the rack at the back of the bike, she got on and pulled into traffic. She rounded the corner and drove down a block before pulling off to the side. Leaving the engine running, Alina twisted in the seat and swiftly undid the string and opened the box. Reaching inside her jacket, she pulled out a minuscule wireless camera. She pressed the button to turn it on and examined the cellophane wrapping. Pulling her knife from her boot, she cut a slit into one of the folds and reached in, attaching the camera to some of the fake moss in the center of the basket.

Viper slid her knife back into her boot, replaced the lid to the box and retied the string.

A few seconds later, she pulled back into traffic and turned down the next block, heading back towards Rittenhouse Hotel.

Stephanie looked up as Blake came outside, sliding his sunglasses onto his nose and squinting against the late afternoon sun. He spotted her, leaning against her car, and ambled over.

"Matt thinks he found the accounts the money came out of," he told her, leaning next to her.

"Great! Now we just have to find where it went," Stephanie replied.

"Well, the good news is that Matt and his team of Super Geeks are confident they can back-track the money trail if we can get him the virus," Blake said, crossing his arms over his chest.

"The only way we can do that is to find Kwan," Stephanie said tiredly. "Given the amount of interest he seems to be garnering, I'm starting to think even if we find him, we won't get the virus."

"Why do you say that?" Blake asked, glancing at her.

Stephanie shook her head.

"This whole investigation has been one big nightmare," she murmured. "I can't shake the feeling I've been manipulated through the whole thing."

"Explain."

"I can't," Stephanie said with a sigh. "Not without sounding like a crazy conspiracy theorist."

"Oh, trust me, you can't possibly say anything as crazy as what went on in Washington two months ago," Blake informed her and Stephanie grinned reluctantly. "Come on. Spill it."

"Everyone who tries to find any information on Lowell Kwan runs head-first into the CIA," she said quietly, "everyone except me. Aside from one rather heated discussion between them and Rob, I'm the only one who has been allowed to pursue Kwan. It's like it was all planned out to come down to this."

"You think the CIA wants the virus?" Blake asked, trying to follow her train of thought.

"Wouldn't you?" she replied. "If it does what Matt says it does, it's a world economic crisis waiting to happen."

Blake nodded and stared across the parking lot thoughtfully.

"Let's say the CIA wants the virus," he said slowly. "Let's say they knew Lowell Kwan was here and hacking into mainframes. If they knew that, then they also know who he's going to sell it to."

"Moon."

Blake nodded.

"If that's the case, though, why involve the FBI at all?" Blake asked. "They could get the virus from Kwan at any time."

"Not really," she said. "He had it in play in the mainframe, and there were three of them who had to insert it and extract it. They would have to wait until they were finished."

Blake shook his head.

"So you think they manipulated this whole investigation from the beginning so you would lead them to the virus before it got to Moon," he mused. "That's pretty out there, Steph."

"I know."

"But not anymore out there than them trying to kill their own agent," Blake said, looking at her. "If this is all true, then I can see why you don't think you'll ever get your hands on the virus."

Stephanie nodded glumly.

"The best I think I can hope for is that we can get Kwan and convince him to tell us where the money went," she said.

"You find Kwan, and I'll convince him to talk," Blake told her.

Stephanie grinned.

"I believe you," she said. "What about you? Any word on Turi yet?"

Blake smiled down at her.

"That's where I was going when I came out here," he said. "I got hold of an old photo of him and John faxed it to all the hospitals. He just got a call back from Virtua in Mt. Holly. Turi was admitted early this morning with a severe stab wound and concussion."

Stephanie grinned.

"Well, don't let me hold you up any longer," she said and waved him away.

Blake laughed and turned to walk toward his truck. He went a few steps, then turned back.

"Don't go having any fun without me," he told her with a smile. "If you find Kwan, I want in on it. I feel invested now."

Stephanie laughed.

"I'll let you know," she promised.

Viper sipped her bottled water and glanced at the large, flat-screen TV hanging on the wall. The camera she inserted into the wine and cheese basket was transmitting clearly from the Park Suite six floors below her. She watched as one of Moon's bodyguards crossed the large sitting room to go into the adjoining dining room. His tailored black suit did nothing to conceal the bulging muscles beneath and Viper thought he looked like a casino pit boss. His two counterparts looked just as silly to her and she shook her head, returning her attention to the back-up Glock she had apart on the table before her. She picked up a small brush and inserted it into the barrel, gently cleaning it.

She checked into the Rittenhouse late in the afternoon, taking a deluxe room on the ninth floor overlooking the park. The view was outstanding, but after one glance when she arrived, Viper hadn't paid it any more attention. She set up her laptop, hooking it into the flat-screen TV, and then wandered down to the lobby. Viper had been in the lobby when Jin Seung Moon arrived at five-thirty precisely.

He had arrived with his entourage, striding into the lobby wearing a tailored charcoal suit and carrying a briefcase. The speed with which he checked-in was noteworthy, and Alina had watched surreptitiously as his bodyguards ushered him into an elevator moments after his arrival.

Viper set the little brush down and peered into the barrel briefly before setting it down with the rest of the gun. Her lips tightened slightly. She had been turning toward the elevators herself when a tall man with a dark, shaggy beard entered the lobby carrying a black guitar case. He was dressed in black slacks and a blue button-down shirt. The shirt had been what caught her eye. It made his eyes glow an unusual shade of cobalt.

Alina had watched from behind a potted fern as he ambled up to the desk. He spoke briefly to one of the women and she motioned him toward the bar. He smiled, nodded in thanks, and turned to stroll toward the bar, just another musician showing up early for a gig. He had passed right by her on his way.

Frowning, Viper started to reassemble the 9mm handgun. Hawk

hadn't even glanced in her direction before he disappeared into the bar. He had no idea she was here. That would normally give her an advantage, but not with Hawk. They were too evenly matched. His presence here simply put her on her guard, nothing more.

Knowing *why* he was here infuriated her.

Alina took a deep breath when she realized her hands were shaking slightly. She slid the chamber in place, willing the familiar task to soothe her. There could be absolutely no doubt about why Hawk was in the hotel. Her lips tightened and her eyes narrowed. He had no more come back to Jersey for her then she was Mary Poppins. He had played her, plain and simple.

Worse, she had fallen for it.

Viper let out a sound suspiciously like a hiss and finished putting her gun back together swiftly. She tucked it into her leg holster and got up impatiently, taking a turn around the spacious hotel room. She didn't see the luxury around her, but instead saw a pair of tired blue eyes as they had looked the night Damon showed up. She recognized that look around his eyes at the time, but had ignored it. It was the look of the hunt. She had seen it enough times in her own mirror to recognize it, but Alina had chalked it up to jet lag, choosing not to see the truth that was there from the beginning.

"Gah!"

Alina spun around and stalked over to the bed, reaching down to pull out her rolling suitcase from underneath. She swung it onto the bed and it bounced twice with the force behind her arm. Unzipping it, she pulled out the clothes folded neatly into the case and lifted the false bottom to reveal a specially-lined compartment. Nestled in the custom-fit, foam slots were the pieces of her rifle. Viper pulled out the sections and carried them over to the table, setting them down so she could go over them and make sure they were spotless. She would worry about what an idiot she had been later, after it was over.

Movement on the TV made her glance over and Viper watched as the guards went over to the door. She paused, her eyes narrowing as Moon came out of the bedroom, still dressed in his charcoal suit, and waited in the living room with his eyes on the door. Frowning, Viper glanced at her watch and shook her head. It was too early for Kwan to have arrived. He would wait until after dark to give himself more protection from watchful eyes. She returned her gaze to the screen, her hands and breath still. When the door opened, she breathed a small sigh.

Moon was having an early dinner in his suite. Viper watched as the room service table rolled into the dining room, followed by two waiters. She scanned their faces and dismissed them, turning back to her rifle.

Next Exit, Dead Ahead

She had plenty of time.

Chapter Thirty-Six

Stephanie rubbed her eyes and glanced at her watch. It was almost five-thirty and Matt and his team were still working on the mainframe at One District Bank while they conferenced in Scott's team over at New Federal, walking them through how to find the accounts that were missing funds. Blake was still interrogating Turi. She seemed to be the only one not actively doing anything.

"You should eat," John said, digging lo mein out of his Chinese carton with chopsticks. "Staring at the clock isn't going to help."

Stephanie sighed and picked up her chopsticks and shrimp, sitting back in her chair and propping her feet on her desk.

"Have you heard from Blake yet?" she asked.

"Not since you asked me five minutes ago," John retorted around a mouthful of food.

Stephanie toyed with her shrimp and rice absently while John watched her.

"I hate waiting," she muttered.

"Any word from the agents with the Nuñez family?" John asked.

"They checked in an hour ago. Everything is quiet over there," she told him.

"Good. That's one less thing to worry about," he said.

Stephanie glanced at him. He didn't look worried. John was inhaling his dinner with all the abandon of a man whose appetite was as voracious as usual. She looked down at her own dinner and sighed.

Her phone started vibrating across her desk as Stephanie attempted another shot at her shrimp. She glanced at the incoming number and set the carton aside, snatching the phone off the desk quickly.

"Matt! Good news?"

"Not good, but better than I expected," Matt replied over the phone. "We figured out how the virus worked."

"And?"

Next Exit, Dead Ahead

"It's brilliant," he said simply. "It was in the mainframe for six months. In that time, it subtracted two dollars from every direct deposit that went into roughly 2.4 million checking accounts."

"Are you serious?" Stephanie demanded.

"Yep!" Matt laughed. "Brilliant, right? It's the same amount as a standard fee. No one would ever notice their paycheck was minus two bucks, and if they did, they'd just think it was a fee charged for an ATM withdrawal or something."

"Well, that explains why there's been no public outcry," Stephanie said, shaking her head. "None of the account holders know anything was taken."

"Exactly."

"Now we just have to find where it went," Stephanie murmured. "Thanks, Matt. You deserve a wild raise."

"Oh, trust me, I'll be addressing that when this is all over," Matt informed her with a laugh.

Stephanie hung up and looked over to John.

"Unbelievable," she said. "The virus took a grand total of two bucks out of every direct deposit that went into the accounts for six months."

"That's it?" John asked, his eyebrows soaring into his forehead. "Two bucks?"

"Those two bucks added up," she answered, picking up her shrimp again. "You figure most people get paid twice a month, sometimes three. Times it by two dollars over six months and it adds up fast."

"How many accounts?" John asked.

"2.4 million."

John whistled.

"That's insane," he exclaimed.

"Brilliant is what Matt said," Stephanie replied with a slight shake of her head. "I guess it really is."

"Well, at least we know how it works now," John mused.

Stephanie nodded.

"And how dangerous it is," she agreed. "Can you imagine if Moon gets it?"

John looked grim.

"You're convinced that's where Kwan is headed, aren't you?" he asked after a moment.

Stephanie raised dark eyes to his and nodded slowly.

"I am," she said quietly. "And we can't touch him."

"No, but we can watch him," John said, setting his carton aside and turning to his computer. "Let's find out exactly where Moon is and go from

345

there."

Hawk swiped the screen of his phone and touched an icon. Selecting the security cameras he had hacked into earlier in the day, he entered his access code and smiled when the application connected to his server controlling the cameras. A few more swipes and he had replaced the actual feed from the cameras with his own. Closing the application, he slipped the phone back into his pocket, picked up his guitar case and disappeared through the door into the employee hallway. He nodded to a baggage carrier on his way out, stepping aside so he could pass, then headed down the hallway. None of the employees he passed took any notice of him and he made it to the service elevator without incident. Using the edge of his guitar case, he pressed the button and waited, watching as the doors slid open. Stepping into the elevator, Hawk pulled tight-fitting black leather gloves from his pocket and slipped them on before he hit the button for the third floor. He glanced at his watch as the doors slid closed.

He was right on time.

Hawk's mind focused entirely on Jin Seung Moon as he rode the elevator up. He had been tracking him now for four weeks, following him all the way from Beijing. Four long weeks later, and after very strict instructions, it was finally time to slay the dragon.

The elevator stopped and the doors slid open. Hawk stepped into the empty alcove and glanced around the corner. Moving down the long, silent hallway toward the electrical closet, he pulled a tool out of his pocket. When he reached the closet, he bent over the lock. A few seconds later, a soft click broke the silence and he disappeared into the closet, closing the door silently.

Hawk set his guitar case down and pulled a small flashlight from his pocket, switching it on. Setting the light on the floor, he bent over the case and snapped it open. Inside was a change of clothes and gear belt, his rifle, and a box containing his modified Beretta, a back-up Ruger, and his military-issued knife.

Changing rapidly in the small space by the light of the flashlight, Hawk exchanged the black dress pants and blue button-down for black SWAT pants and black teeshirt. He strapped his gear belt on and then added his leg holster. His lips twitched as he slid his back-up Ruger into the leg holster and his knife into the special sheath on his belt. Viper wore her knife on her ankle, and always had, but he preferred to have it closer to hand.

Next Exit, Dead Ahead

The slight smile faded from his lips as he picked up his Beretta and tucked it into his back holster.

It was almost time.

Stephanie grabbed her standard issue Glock and tucked it into her side holster, looking around for John. He disappeared about ten minutes ago and still hadn't returned to his desk. She picked up her phone to call him as he appeared from the direction of the elevators.

"What's going on?" he asked, his eyes going straight to her gun. "Where are we going?"

"Moon checked in at the Rittenhouse Hotel," she told him. "I just got off the phone with the Delaware River Port Authority. They have a photo of Kwan passing through the tolls on Ben Franklin, taken about twenty-five minutes ago."

"We're going to Rittenhouse," John said. He opened the drawer of his desk and pulled out his holster and gun. "Do we know what room Moon is in?"

"One of the Park Suites," Stephanie answered, switching off her monitor and grabbing her purse.

"Of course he is," he muttered, putting on his holster. "He doesn't even try to be discreet."

"Why should he? He knows we can't touch him," Stephanie retorted, turning toward the elevators.

John glanced at her as they strode quickly to the elevators.

"Have you told Rob?" he asked and she nodded.

"He reminded me Moon is an internationally protected businessman visiting the US," she told him, pressing the button for the elevator. "So, I reminded him that we have proof Kwan was involved in the largest bank robbery in US history."

John grinned.

"And?"

"We're authorized to use all available force to get Kwan," she answered.

"That's my girl," John murmured with a chuckle as the elevator doors slid open.

Stephanie laughed and they stepped into the elevator.

"Call Blake and tell him where we're going," she said as the doors slid closed. "I promised him I'd keep him posted, and we can use all the help we can get."

Lowell Kwan entered the lobby of the hotel and looked around. He was in black dress pants and a casual shirt, and his right arm was in a cast with three of his fingers taped into splints. The swelling on his jaw had started to go down, but the bruising was out in all its colorful glory, drawing second looks from people who passed him. He ignored them, looking for the man who would take him to Moon. There were a few people seated on the plush, older-style chairs placed tastefully around the gleaming marble lobby, but none of them matched the description of his contact. Turning, he started to move through the lobby slowly, making his way past the front desk. He was strolling toward a set of shallow steps when he saw the large man in a suit moving towards him.

"Kwan?" he asked.

Lowell nodded and the behemoth in the suit nodded.

"Come with me. Mr. Moon is expecting you," he told him, turning to lead Lowell across the massive lobby toward the elevators.

Lowell followed him, slightly in awe of the hushed luxury surrounding him. They reached the elevators and Lowell's companion was joined by another massive gorilla in a suit. Lowell looked at him as the three men stepped into an elevator, oblivious to the dark eyes watching steadily from one of the seats in the lobby.

As the elevator doors slid closed, a woman got up unobtrusively and moved through the lobby swiftly. Later, as everyone present in the hotel racked their brains trying to remember everything they could about that evening, not one person would recall the tall, self-controlled woman dressed in black who disappeared from the lobby as silently as she entered, a soft instrument case hanging from her back.

Lowell watched the elevator doors close, sealing them in as the car began its short ascent. As soon as the doors were closed, the man who had met him in the lobby swung him around and pressed him against the wall of the car. He held him still with a beefy hand on the back of his neck while his companion frisked him, looking for weapons. Lowell tried to protest, but the hand on his neck pressed harder, cutting off the indignant exclamation. With his cheek pressed against the wall of the elevator, Lowell rolled his eyes. He had the worst virus the world's banking systems had ever seen on a flash drive in his pocket, and they were checking him for weapons?

"He's clear." The beast behind him straightened up and nodded to his captor.

Next Exit, Dead Ahead

The man released Lowell and stepped back. He made no apology, not even glancing at Lowell as the elevator came to a whispered stop and the doors slid open again. He stepped out into the hall and his companion motioned for Lowell to follow. Shaking his head and straightening his shirt, Lowell followed him out into a thickly carpeted hall.

Their footsteps made no sound on the carpet and the silence was almost eerie as they moved along the corridor. The doors were spaced widely apart and Lowell was led all the way to the end, to the last door on the left. His contact opened the door silently and motioned for him to enter the suite. The two men followed him in, closing the door silently behind them and staying near the door as Lowell moved forward into the main sitting room. Standing near the window, his hands crossed in front of him, was Moon.

Jin Seung Moon stood shorter than Lowell expected, but what he lacked in physical height, he more than made up for with a demeanor that commanded attention. Dressed impeccably in a dark charcoal suit with a steel gray shirt and charcoal tie, his gaze was sharp and direct. As Lowell entered the room, he was aware of the assessing look in those cold, dark eyes. Moon studied him in silence for a moment, watching as Lowell moved closer.

"You look like your father," he said finally, his voice strong. His accent blended a curious mix of Oxfordian English and North Korean lilt. "Do you remember him?"

Lowell started, his eyes widening.

"Not very well," he answered. "You knew my father?"

"Know, Lowell," Moon replied, moving forward and holding out his hand. "I know your father. He is looking forward to meeting you again after all these years."

Lowell grasped Moon's hand firmly.

"I'm honored to meet you at last, sir," Lowell said, bowing his head respectfully as he shook Jin's hand. "I've been waiting for this moment for a long time."

"The pleasure is all mine," Jin told him graciously. He motioned to the ornate sofa nearby. "Please. Have a seat. Would you like a drink?"

"No, thank you."

Lowell sank down onto the sofa and Jin nodded, moving to an adjacent chair. The round glass table before them was tastefully appointed, with an enormous wine and cheese basket sitting in the center. Moon seated himself, undoing the buttons on his suit jacket as he did so. He crossed his legs and sat back, studying Lowell.

"I understand you ran into some difficulties," he said softly. "I trust everything is as promised?"

"It is," Lowell assured him. "It's true I lost my two associates, but the fail safes we built into the system did their job. Philip was able to warn me before the operation was compromised."

"And the money?"

"Still transferring through the list of accounts you provided," Lowell told him. "It will deposit into your account in Beijing at nine o'clock tomorrow morning, our time."

Jin nodded, raising his hand and motioning to someone in the adjoining room. Lowell turned his head and watched as a slender man in black slacks and a black shirt came towards them, a laptop in his hands and thick glasses on his nose.

"This is Min-ho," Jin said, waving toward the young man. "He is going to verify that the money is in transit."

Lowell nodded and watched as Min-ho seated himself in the other chair, opposite Moon.

"While he is doing that, tell me of your mother," Jin invited him, his eyes dark. "She is well?"

Lowell swallowed, noting the suddenly ugly glint in Moon's eyes.

"I don't know," he answered truthfully. "I've had no contact with her since I went to Stanford. I don't even know where she's living now."

"Pity," Moon murmured. "I know your father would like nothing more than to settle the disagreement between them once and for all. I was prepared to assist."

"How do you know my father, sir?" Lowell asked.

"He has worked for me for many years," Moon answered easily. "You are like him. He is very proud of your intelligence and your work for our great cause."

Min-ho cleared his throat, glancing at Moon.

"The funds are currently in France," he told him. "It appears to be the full amount."

Jin looked at Lowell and smiled.

"I never doubted you, my young friend," he said. "You understand, of course, that I had to check."

"Of course."

"And do you have the flash drive?" Moon asked.

"I do," Lowell answered.

"And there is no other copy?"

"None."

Jin nodded to the bodyguards at the door and the one who met Lowell in the lobby moved forward, picking up a large briefcase on his way. He walked over and placed it on the sofa next to Lowell. Lowell reached into his pocket and pulled out the flash drive containing the only existing copy of the virus.

"If you wouldn't mind passing that to Min-ho," Moon requested with a smile. "He will verify the contents." Lowell passed the drive over to the young man and looked at Jin questioningly. He waved his hand royally. "By all means, check inside the case. You will find that all is in order."

Lowell unsnapped the case and opened it. Over six million dollars in cash lay inside with a manila envelope laying on top. Lowell lifted out the envelope and closed the case on the money. Opening it, he glanced inside at the passports and plane tickets.

"Your ticket back to your homeland," Moon told him with a small smile. "From there, you can watch as we bring the West to their knees and put an end to their international oppression." Lowell fastened the envelope again and replaced it in the briefcase, closing it with a snap. "The rest of your reward awaits you in Pyongyang."

"Thank you."

Moon nodded and made no move to end the interview. Lowell looked at him expectantly, wondering what else there was to say.

"There are no loose ends, nothing to assist the FBI with their search?" Jin asked softly, his eyes probing Lowell's.

Lowell swallowed, drowning in those dark eyes. His heartbeat quickened and he felt his palms grow damp. Jin Seung Moon frightened him. For all his civil politeness, Lowell knew what a cold monster Moon was capable of becoming. He had seen evidence of it in the past, and saw it in his eyes now. Lowell's mind shot to a pair of arctic blue eyes that were more frigid than anything he'd ever seen.

Moon frightened him, but the devil with the blue eyes terrified him.

"Nothing," Lowell assured Jin with a small smile. "The virus erases all trace of itself when it's extracted, and Philip and Rodrigo are dead. There's no way for them to replicate what happened."   .

Lowell held his breath as Moon studied him silently for a moment before turning his attention to Min-ho.

"Well?" he demanded, a note of impatience in his voice.

Min-ho looked up, startled, his eyes glittering behind his glasses.

"This is brilliant!" he announced, excitement in his voice. "Absolutely brilliant!"

"It is the virus, then?"

"Oh yes," Min-ho assured him. He looked at Lowell. "You're a brilliant man, Mr. Kwan."

Lowell nodded in acknowledgement, releasing his breath silently, and looked up to find Jin standing and buttoning his suit jacket. He got up, picking up the briefcase and Moon held out his hand, a smooth smile on his face.

"I look forward to working with you again, Mr. Kwan," he said. "Until we meet again."

Lowell shook his hand and turned to leave, relief rolling through him as the weight of the briefcase in his hand assured him he was on his way to his homeland. It was over and he had succeeded. Philip and Rodrigo were gone, but Lowell didn't feel anything apart from a passing melancholy.

Their cut belonged to him now, and he was going home to North Korea a rich man.

Chapter Thirty-Seven

Viper glanced behind her as she melted into the shadows engulfing the stone half-wall. Crowded during the day, Rittenhouse Park fell quiet after dark with foot traffic consisting mainly of the occasional couple or small group of friends moving between pubs or bars. The wide path winding around the park was lit at regular intervals with electric lamp posts, but she had managed to darken the two lights closest to her before any pedestrians came by, no small feat in the middle of a city. Sinking into the shadows, she glanced at the water fountain built into the stone wall. Carefully cultivated, large thick bushes, enclosed by a black wrought-iron fence, flanked the fountain on either side and lent their shadows to her, concealing her from anyone passing by in the darkness.

Right now, the path was empty of pedestrians and Viper swung the soft case from her back silently. Her hands were steady as she unzipped the case and pulled out the pieces of her rifle, assembling her old friend quickly and silently. She attached the night scope last and leaned the rifle against the wall, resting it on its handle butt. Pulling her military binoculars from the case, Viper turned and peered over the stone wall, adjusting the binoculars until the entryway to the hotel across the street came into sharp focus.

Under the overhang displaying The Rittenhouse in big, gold block letters, a low-slung, black Jaguar pulled around the curved driveway and up to the door. Viper watched as the doorman hurried to meet the driver, taking the keys from her and tossing them to a waiting valet before escorting her to the door. Viper tilted her head, studying the entrance to the hotel. The Jaguar pulled away, bound for the parking garage, and the doorman went back to his position near the door.

Alina pursed her lips and lowered the binoculars, glancing around the dark park. A couple strolled hand in hand away from her, and no one else was in sight. Reaching for her rifle, Viper rested it on the wall and peered through the night scope, adjusting it to the front of the hotel. She zoomed in on the doorman and then shifted to the valets, studying distance and angles before removing the rifle and lowering it beneath the wall again.

353

CW Browning

She reached into her bag and pulled out the suppressor, attaching it to the barrel with quick, practiced movements, her eyes on the driveway about 150 yards away. The location couldn't have been more perfect, with a straight shot to any point in the entranceway. This would be a piece of cake.

Movement in the shadows along the side of the hotel to the right of the door caught her attention and Viper's hands stilled. With a frown, she lifted her binoculars to her eyes and studied the shadows. A tall man dressed in jeans, with a soft guitar case over his back, leaned against the building. He talked with another man, dressed similarly, and Viper's eyes narrowed as she studied them thoughtfully. As she watched, one raised his hand and hailed someone passing by, greeting them briefly before the passerby continued on, turning to walk into the hotel.

Pressing her lips together, Viper lowered the binoculars thoughtfully.

A few moments later, her attention was arrested again, this time by a sudden procession of vehicles pulling into the driveway, led by a red Mustang. Viper watched as a black SUV turned in behind the Mustang, followed by two more government-plated, dark sedans.

"Shit," she breathed softly, watching as the Mustang stopped a few feet past the door.

Viper reached down and grabbed her rifle, resting it on the wall silently. Looking through the scope again, she adjusted the sight, focusing on the doorman moving toward the Mustang. She zoomed in on his face, over the roof of one of the sedans, then watched as Stephanie and John got out of the Mustang. Shaking her head slightly, Alina shifted the rifle to the right. She watched as the two musicians moved away from the wall and started toward the entrance of the hotel, watching the activity in the driveway. She was about to shift back to Stephanie when the taller musician reached into his bag and pulled out something small and compact, cradling it in his right hand. Viper exhaled sharply and moved her gaze to the entrance of the hotel, looking for what had the musician so transfixed.

Her cross-hairs centered on Lowell Kwan's face as he exited the hotel, a briefcase in his hand.

Everyone in the entrance-way to the Rittenhouse seemed to freeze at the same second. Blake had the door to the SUV open and paused, standing on the running board, staring over the roof of the vehicle at Lowell. Stephanie and John, wearing their FBI windbreakers, were already on the walkway leading to the door, their identities apparent. They hesitated while Kwan stopped dead, staring at them with wide, startled eyes. The doorman stopped, looking from the FBI agents to the young man and back again, somehow realizing that he stood in the middle of something with the potential to become very awkward. Even the valets seemed rooted to the

354

spot, waiting to see what would happen. Everyone was frozen in place for a few seconds, like a movie on pause, except the two musicians.

They were still moving steadily toward the door, their eyes fixed on Kwan.

Viper noted their controlled movements and probable military bearing even as she exhaled softly and squeezed her trigger.

The taller man fell to the pavement a second later, a semi-automatic dropping out of his hand. The second musician didn't hesitate. Breaking into a run, he charged at the stunned group before the door, heading straight for Kwan. The lights above the lobby door glinted off the long, dangerous blade in his hand before he, too, suddenly crumpled to the ground, a bare foot away from Lowell Kwan.

Viper took a deep, slow breath. She could almost hear the shocked silence that precedes an uproar, and she watched unemotionally as the small band of people stared at the dead men on the pavement. Alina exhaled softly, the familiar feeling of cold emptiness making her chest feel hollow. She watched as blood started to pool out onto the pavement, breaking the spell in the entryway.

Chaos erupted in an instant.

John yelled something and started toward the body near Kwan while the door slammed on the black SUV and Blake circled his truck, running toward the other one. Lowell Kwan let out a cry, shaking himself out of his stupor, and turned to run back into the hotel. Stephanie yelled to the doorman as she pulled her weapon, running toward Kwan. The doorman grabbed Lowell, wrapping his meaty arms around him and tackling him to the ground without any hesitation. The briefcase went skidding across the pavement, coming to rest near the doors as Stephanie advanced on Kwan.

Viper scanned the area around the entryway, and then the street. She examined the parked cars between her and the drama unfolding on the steps of the Rittenhouse. After a few seconds of searching, she cursed softly and pulled the rifle back, unscrewing the suppressor swiftly. She disassembled her rifle and slipped it back into the case. Tossing it over her shoulder, she moved out silently from the shadows of the stone half-wall. When the sirens of the first responders wailed around the corner, the fountain was deserted and the only trace Viper left behind were two dark lamp posts.

"Get your hands behind your head, Kwan!" Stephanie called,

advancing on the two men struggling on the pavement, her Glock trained on Kwan. "It's over. Don't make it worse than it already is!"

Lowell gave one final attempt to dislodge the large, heavy doorman planted on his back, then stopped struggling, raising his hands awkwardly to the back of his head in surrender. The doorman stayed put as Stephanie approached, keeping a wary eye on the suddenly quiet man beneath him. She eyed the cast on Lowell's right arm.

"Thanks," she said to the doorman with a nod, pulling out her handcuffs.

The doorman nodded and moved off of Kwan, watching as Stephanie placed her knee on the small of his back, taking the doorman's place. She kept her gun trained on the back of his head with one hand while she pulled his left wrist down behind his back with the other. Snapping one cuff on the wrist, she hooked the other cuff through his back belt loop, securing the arm to his own belt loop.

"What's your name?" she asked the doorman as he got to his feet, dusting off his uniform.

"Oliver," he answered, "but people call me Ollie."

"Well, quick thinking Ollie," Stephanie told him with a smile. She tucked her gun into its holster. "Thanks."

Ollie nodded.

"Yes, ma'am."

Stephanie turned her head and looked at John, kneeling beside the dead musician. He glanced up, saw the question on her face and shook his head, sitting back on his heels. Stephanie looked beyond him to Blake, further back. He also shook his head, straightening up from the other dead man. She cursed under her breath and turned her attention back to the man on the ground beneath her.

"Who were they?" she asked him. Lowell stayed silent, his cheek still pressed on the pavement. Stephanie's eyes narrowed at his silence. "John! Grab that briefcase!"

"Got it!" John was already moving toward the case. He pulled on gloves and reached down to pick it up.

"What's in the case, Lowell?" Stephanie asked, moving her knee off his back and pulling his casted arm down behind him. She got to her feet and pulled him up, one hand on his cuffed hand and the other hooked into his shirt at the back of his neck. "You might as well tell me because I'm going to open it and find out anyway."

Lowell's only answer was to spit on the pavement and try to pull his casted arm forward. Stephanie grabbed his thumb and wrenched it back, eliciting a sharp gasp of pain from him.

"Is it your payment for the virus you just sold to Jin Moon?"

Stephanie demanded, her voice low. She knew she guessed right when he shot her a startled look. "Oh, I know all about Mr. Moon," she assured him coldly. "Where's the virus? Does he have it?"

"You'll never get it now," Lowell finally spoke, his voice void of any emotion. "It's lost to you and your pathetic government. The next time you see it will be when your economy crashes and sends your country into the worse depression you've ever seen."

"If our economy crashes, so does the world's economy," Stephanie hissed. "You're a fool. Where is it? On a flash drive? On a laptop? Where?"

Lowell started to laugh mockingly, but it quickly turned to a howl of pain when Stephanie wrenched harder on the thumb of his broken arm.

"I'm getting impatient, Kwan," she growled. "Tell me!"

"F-f-f-flash drive," Lowell gasped, bending to the right almost double in an attempt to ease the pressure on his hand.

Stephanie immediately released his thumb and glanced at John.

"Take him!" she commanded, pushing Lowell towards him. "There should be something in one of the cars to restrain that cast." She turned her head. "Blake! You're with me! John, make sure our agents stay with the bodies. I want to know who the hell they were and why they were after Kwan!"

John nodded, but Stephanie didn't see. She was already halfway through the doors of the hotel, Blake close behind her. They strode into the lobby, flashing their badges to the security swarming toward the entrance. She stopped the most senior security officer as she passed, grabbing his arm.

"What's the quickest way to the Park Suites?" she asked urgently.

"The service elevator, in the employees' hall," he answered immediately. "Jimmy!" He motioned to another officer. "Take them there!"

"Thanks! Make sure no one leaves the building. Police are on their way," Stephanie told him, turning to follow Jimmy.

Blake glanced at her as they moved swiftly through the lobby, guests and employees alike staring at them as they went.

"Where are we going? Moon's suite? Because you know we can't touch him," he said.

"He's got the virus," Stephanie retorted. "He's not leaving here with it."

Blake grinned at the martial glint in her eyes.

"You know, Agent Walker, I kind of like you," he told her cheerfully.

Stephanie grinned and they followed the guard through a door marked "Employees Only."

"The elevator is at the end of this hall," Jimmy said over his shoulder, leading them down a wide hallway. "Park Suites are on the third floor. Moon is in the last one on the left."

"How do you know?" Blake asked him and Jimmy grinned.

"I'm in charge of security for the Park Suites," he replied, stopping as they reached the elevator. "Do you need me to come up with you?" he asked.

"No, go help secure the building," Stephanie said, pressing the button and watching as the elevator doors slid open.

Jimmy nodded and turned to run back down the hallway. Blake and Stephanie stepped into the elevator and he pressed the button for the third floor.

"What's the plan?" he asked as the doors slid shut. "We can't just knock on his door without a warrant and demand to search his suite."

"I haven't thought that far ahead yet," Stephanie retorted. "I'm still trying to figure out what just happened outside."

"Well, you better think fast," Blake said. "I'm not losing my job over an asshole like Moon. He's responsible for the death of three old combat buddies of mine. Nothing ever proven, of course."

"That seems to be a trend with him," Stephanie muttered. The elevator came to a stop and the doors slid open. "I'll think of something. Just let me to do the talking."

"Not a problem. You'll undoubtedly be much more diplomatic than I would," Blake said with a wink as they stepped off the elevator into a small alcove. They moved into the wide, hushed hallway and glanced up and down the deserted hall. "He said it's the last one on the left," he said, turning left and going around a corner.

The long hall had modern paneling and recessed lighting. Stephanie started down the corridor, her mind spinning. Who were the musicians-turned-killers who had tried to get to Lowell before them? Were they Moon's men? Had Moon received the virus and then tried to tie off the loose end? It all happened so fast. Stephanie shook her head, trying to remember what exactly had happened. One minute, the men weren't there at all, and the next they were dead. She didn't even know where the shots came from, let alone who fired them. If Moon had sent the men to kill Kwan after he got the virus, then who sent someone to kill Moon's men?

"Uh-oh," Blake murmured, snapping her attention back to the hallway. He reached for his holster, his eyes on the last door on the left. "This doesn't look good."

Stephanie followed his gaze and her heart plummeted. The last door on the left stood slightly ajar.

She reached for her Glock, pulling it out of her holster for the second time in less than fifteen minutes. Glancing at Blake, she motioned she would take point and he nodded, his own gun in his hands. Stephanie's eyes dropped to it and she raised an eyebrow at the blatantly modified Smith and Wesson. Blake saw her look and smiled, shrugging slightly. She shook her head, wondering if she and John were the only two people left in the country who carried standard issues.

Setting the thought aside, Stephanie moved to the left wall and approached the open door slowly, listening for any sound of movement inside the suite. The door was ajar by about ten inches and she looked down, checking for any shadows on the floor through the opening. Pausing when she reached the door frame, she glanced at Blake beside her. The easy-going cheerful look that characterized his face had disappeared, and his eyes were sharp and focused on the door. He caught her glance and nodded slightly.

Stephanie reached out her left hand and gently pushed on the door, keeping clear of the doorway as she did so. The door swung open silently, then stopped as it came up against something solid. Stephanie pulled her hand away and leaned forward, peering into the suite. All she could see was an empty section of the entry alcove. She glanced through the crack between the door and frame, trying to see what blocked the door from opening, and her blood ran cold.

A large, male head stared up at her sightlessly.

"Oh, please let that be attached to something," she whispered, pulling back against the wall.

She motioned to Blake and he crossed in front of her, moving to the other side of the door swiftly. He glanced inside the door, then moved into the doorway, his gun held up near his shoulder, eyes and ears concentrated in front of him. Stephanie watched him enter the suite, then followed, her hands gripping her Glock as if her life depended on it.

Blake stepped over a pair of feet and moved to the edge of the little entryway, peering around the corner into the rest of the suite. Stephanie glanced at the feet, then at the rest of the body, relieved to see the head was, indeed, still attached to the body. The man had to weigh at least 250 pounds of solid muscle, and yet he lay on the floor with his neck snapped like a twig. Swallowing, she stepped over the feet and moved around him, pressing two fingers against the side of his neck in vain.

"He's still warm," she whispered, standing.

Blake nodded to show he heard her and moved forward silently. Stephanie followed him into the suite living room, her heart thumping and her body tense.

A soft gasp escaped her as they stared speechlessly at the sight before them. She counted four bodies in the living room, not including the one behind her. The one closest to them, stretched out on the floor, was another large, solidly built bodyguard. He had no visible wounds, but his eyes were staring blindly at the ceiling. A third bodyguard slouched against the wall on the far side of the living room, near the door to an adjoining room, a gaping wound at the base of his throat. A semi-automatic still rested in his dead hand, and blood from the wound in his throat covered the front of his suit. The other two bodies were seated in opposite chairs, on either end of a glass coffee table. An expensive, top-of-the-line laptop had slipped to the floor, lying on its side beside the chair closest to them. The man had sagged sideways, his glasses askew on his face, and his head twisted at an impossible angle. The last body, however, held both Stephanie and Blake paralyzed.

Jin Seung Moon reclined in the other chair, a bullet hole through his left temple. His eyes stared sightlessly at the ceiling as a single rivulet of blood made its way down the side of his face to disappear beneath the collar of his tailored suit.

"Holy shit," Blake breathed softly, staring at Moon.

Stephanie nodded in agreement without realizing it, then started moving automatically to the left. Blake shook his head slightly and moved to the right, following the wall around to the adjoining room on the right while Stephanie moved toward the room on the left. The deafening silence hung over them as they separated and moved through the huge suite, checking closets and bathrooms, behind curtains and under beds.

Stephanie had just finished checking the master bath when she heard Blake call an all clear from his side. She stepped out of the bathroom and glanced around the bedroom, shaking her head. Nothing was out of place. A Rolex sat on the dresser and a gun lie on the bed. The killer hadn't taken anything.

"Clear," she called.

She met Blake back in the living room and tucked her gun back into her holster as he checked fruitlessly for a pulse on Moon.

"The blood is still trickling out," he said grimly, straightening up. "We just missed whoever did this."

"It couldn't have been Kwan," Stephanie said, checking the man in the other chair. She frowned at his youth, placing him somewhere in his early twenties. "He wouldn't have the skill to do this."

"No," Blake agreed, looking around. "This was a professional hit. Clean and quick."

"Did you see anyone when we came out of the elevator?" Stephanie asked, glancing up.

Blake shook his head.

"Nothing," he answered.

"They had to have left through the door," Stephanie said,

straightening up and looking around. "There are no other exits and the windows don't open."

Blake nodded, staring at the bodyguard with the wound in his throat.

"Definitely professional," he murmured. "They left Moon for last."

"How do you know?" Stephanie asked, watching as Blake moved to the entrance of the living room.

"By the way they were killed," Blake told her. "The killer entered through the door, surprising the bodyguard and snapping his neck. He moved into the living room, where he met the second guard and did the same thing." Blake moved forward to where the second bodyguard stretched out, then he pointed to the third guard. "By this time, someone, probably Moon, alerted the third guard, who came from that room with his weapon drawn. The killer didn't even have to move from this spot. He threw a weapon, cutting off any sound the guard was making. Judging by the size of the wound on his throat, it was probably a heavier knife with a wide blade. Once the bodyguards were down, the killer moved forward and killed the kid with the laptop the same way he had the first two guards."

Stephanie stared at the bodies, impressed despite herself.

"And all this would have taken...how long?" she asked.

"Less than a minute," Blake answered.

"And Moon?"

Blake looked across the room at the dead terrorist.

"The killer pulled out his gun and went over to him. Moon tried to get up, note the hands on the chair, but the killer shot him before he had time to move."

Blake went over to Moon's body and bent down to examine it. While he did, Stephanie looked at the laptop laying on the floor next to the chair. She pulled on gloves and bent down, turning it over. There was no flash drive plugged into the USB port. Frowning, she looked over to Moon.

"Hey, check his pockets," she told Blake.

Blake looked up, startled.

"What?"

"His pockets!" Stephanie repeated urgently. "Kwan gave him the virus not twenty minutes ago on a flash drive. There's no flash drive over here with the laptop, so check his pockets."

Blake pulled out a pair of gloves from his jacket pocket.

"The things I do for you," he muttered. "You're lucky you're cute, Agent Walker."

Stephanie just grinned and quickly went through the pockets of the kid in the chair.

"It's not here," she said, glancing at him.

Blake went through Moon's pockets quickly.

"Nothing here either," he said.

"That's not what I want to hear," Stephanie exclaimed, looking around the room. She glanced at the wine and cheese basket on the table and lifted it up, looking inside.

"You think he dropped it in the basket?" Blake demanded, his lips twitching.

Stephanie replaced the basket with a sigh.

"Do you think he had time to leave the room before our killer came in?" she asked.

"Doubtful," he said thoughtfully, still crouched next to Moon's chair. "Kwan left and we saw him as soon as he got to the front door. It couldn't have taken Kwan more than five minutes to get down the elevator and through the lobby, and that's being generous. It probably took less."

"So, Kwan left and the killer came in," Stephanie said thoughtfully. "The killer would have been in here while we were tackling Kwan downstairs." She shook her head. "You're right. Moon wouldn't have had time to leave the room, hide the flash drive, come back and sit down in the chair."

"The flash drive should still be here," Blake said, turning back to Moon.

He slid his hands down the sides of the cushions on the chair, careful not to move Moon's body too much as he felt between the cushion and the chair, checking to see if it had slipped down there. Blake quickly checked one side, then the other.

"Nothing," he said in answer to the question on her face. "It's not here."

"Shit!" Stephanie spun around and stalked a few feet to the door angrily. "The killer must have taken it!"

"At least you have Kwan," Blake remarked. "He can recreate it, with the proper encouragement."

"That will take weeks," Stephanie muttered. "I don't have weeks."

"Kwan should be able to tell you where the money went," Blake said, glancing at her. "But the thought of that virus out there in the open market makes me want to take all my money out of the bank and put it in my mattress."

"Tell me about it," she agreed, pacing in frustration.

Blake started to straighten up, then paused and looked again at the hole in Moon's temple. He leaned forward, taking a closer look.

"Looks like the same caliber that killed our Cartel friends," he murmured.

Stephanie stopped mid-stride and stared at him, her blood

pounding in her ears.

"What did you say?" she demanded breathlessly.

"The bullet," Blake repeated, glancing at her. "It looks like the killer used the same caliber as whoever killed Lorenzo and Ramiero. Looks like a .22."

"Oh my God!" Stephanie breathed. She spun around and headed for the door.

"What's wrong?" Blake called.

"I have to make a call!" Stephanie shot over her shoulder and disappeared out the front door.

Blake watched her go, his eyes narrowing thoughtfully. Turning, he went over to the third body guard and crouched down. He gently turned the guard's head and examined the wound in the neck closely. After a moment, he released the head and stood up, a thoughtful frown on his face.

Blake looked around slowly at the five bodies, killed with accurate precision. Only a professional with special training and nerves of steel would have been able to pull this off with such speed and accuracy.

Someone like a government-trained assassin.

"Oh Mikey, you really can pick them," he murmured under his breath, shaking his head slightly and turning toward the door.

Chapter Thirty-Eight

Stephanie strode through the lobby, her phone pressed to her ear. The other end rang a few times before switching over to voicemail. She pressed end with a low curse and dropped the phone back into her pocket. John, standing inside the door talking to another agent, glanced up and saw her coming. He frowned at the thunder on her face and started forward, meeting her halfway.

"What happened?"

"Moon's dead," Stephanie said shortly, "and the virus is gone."

"Where's Blake?" John asked, pulling out his phone and hitting speed dial to call it in.

"He's still up there." Stephanie stopped and faced John. "Where's Kwan?"

"In the back of Blake's car, under guard," John told her.

"And the mystery attackers?"

"No ID yet," John said. "Their prints aren't in our database."

"Of course not," Stephanie muttered, turning and continuing toward the door. She paused, then turned back. "The killer's long gone, I'm sure, but let's keep the building sealed off anyway. No one gets in or out until we sort this all out."

John nodded, turning away to give the report on the phone. Stephanie continued out the door of the hotel without looking back. Neither of them noticed the slim musician get up from a chair behind a potted fern nearby. He moved across the lobby, his soft guitar case over his back, heading for the hotel bar. As he walked, his head bent over the phone in his hands and he typed away on the screen. Anyone watching saw a sight they saw hundreds of time a day: a young man engrossed on his phone, oblivious to everything around him. The musician hit send and slipped the phone into his pocket as he wandered into the bar.

A few seconds later, 140 miles south of Philadelphia, a secured message came through on a tablet.

Next Exit, Dead Ahead

FBI have custody of Kwan. Moon is dead, and virus missing. Two agents down. Awaiting instructions.

The message elicited a soft curse and then long, deadly silence as the reader stared at the tablet, lost in thought. Finally, slowly, they answered:

Abort mission.

Viper was waiting for Hawk when he returned to his white electrical van in a parking garage a few blocks from the hotel. She was leaning against the side of the van, the hood of a black sweatshirt pulled up over her head and her arms crossed over her chest. One ankle was crossed over the other, and as he moved across the parking garage, she raised her head slowly, her face cast in shadows.

Damon didn't need to see her face to know she knew the truth.

Suppressing a sigh, he continued toward the van, watching her as he approached.

"Mission accomplished?" she asked when he came within feet of her, her voice a chilling caress on the breeze.

"How long have you known?" he asked.

"Does it matter?" Viper asked, her eyes glittering dangerously.

"I guess not."

Hawk pulled out his keys and beeped the van unlocked, moving to the back. Opening the back door, he tossed the guitar case inside and closed the door. Viper was on the other side, inches from his face. He hadn't heard her move from the side of the van.

"What's the story with Kwan?" she asked him, blocking his path to the driver's door.

Damon sighed and leaned against the back of the van, his blue eyes shuttered as he looked at her.

"I don't know," he told her. "I was sent for Moon. I didn't know anything about Kwan until I got here."

Viper stared at him for a long moment, her face unreadable.

"How long have you been tracking Moon?" she finally asked.

"Four weeks."

Alina's eyes narrowed and she shook her head slightly.

"Any ideas who was running Kwan?" she asked.

Damon shook his head.

"No," he said. "Do we know someone was?"

"Well, two spooks with government written all over them tried to

365

kill him tonight," Viper told him, leaning next to him and crossing her arms over her chest again. "So, someone was watching him."

"You were there?" Hawk asked sharply, glancing at her. He encountered a cold smile.

"Yes."

"You weren't..." Damon started, then stopped, his blue eyes searching hers.

"No." Alina dropped her eyes from his. "Your little speech about Moon not being my target did its job, even if it *did* have a hidden agenda."

Damon winced inwardly at the razor-sharp tone in her voice.

"Then what were you doing there?" he asked, ignoring the underlying barb for the time being.

"Kwan dropped off the grid after he extracted the virus," Alina replied. "I knew the only person he would sell the virus to was Moon. I also knew someone in the CIA was protecting him. I promised Stephanie I wouldn't let Kwan slip through the cracks."

"So you came to make sure he didn't disappear after giving the virus to Moon," Damon finished. He smiled reluctantly. "I hope the Fearless Feds realize what an asset your friendship is."

"They might not see it that way just now," she murmured ruefully. "I gave them two extra bodies."

"The spooks after Kwan?" Damon asked.

Viper nodded.

"They went for him in front of the hotel," she said. "The Fearless Feds seemed paralyzed, so I took matters into my own hands. There were three of them. I got two, but the third went into the hotel and never came back out."

"Any scouts?"

"Not that I could see," Viper said. "If there were, they were in the park with me."

Hawk stared across the garage thoughtfully.

"You think another section of the agency wanted the virus?" he asked.

"I can't image what else they would have wanted with Kwan."

"Well, they didn't get it," Damon said softly, pulling a flash drive from his pocket. "I did."

"Did Charlie ask for that?" Alina asked, glancing at the flash drive.

"No." Hawk tucked it back into his pocket. "But it was too dangerous to leave it behind."

"If Stephanie's basement gnome is as smart as they think he is, he could probably use it to find out where the money went," she commented thoughtfully. "Lord knows Stephanie could use a break right now."

"I'll consider it."

Alina nodded and fell silent. Her phone vibrated against her thigh, but she ignored it. Damon glanced down at her, his eyes dark and unreadable.

"It wasn't *all* a lie, Viper," he said softly.

She raised her head and Damon caught the flash in her eyes before they became guarded again.

"We both lie," she said with a slight shrug. "I guess now we're even. At least you didn't drug me."

"Lina..." Damon turned toward her, but she held up her hand, stopping him.

"It's done," she told him flatly. "There's no point in discussing it."

"I think there is," Damon muttered, his blue eyes glinting dangerously.

"You're entitled to your opinion," Alina retorted, straightening up. Her entire body hummed with warning, making him think twice about trying to pursue the subject. "Are you leaving town now?"

Hawk studied her for a long moment, his face suddenly unreadable.

"That depends on you," he finally said.

Viper gazed back at him, her eyes cold and shuttered.

"No, Hawk," she said quietly. "It never depended on me."

Michael sighed and pulled his phone out of his pocket. He was sitting on the deck in the darkness, drinking a beer while Angela was still pacing around the living room on her Bluetooth, trying to put out fires at work. Raven perched on the roof of the garage, settled down and watchful, keeping one eye on Michael and the other eye on the trees. He had been there since Michael came outside half an hour before, trying to escape Angela's level of stress inside the house.

Michael glanced at the name on the incoming call and raised an eyebrow.

"Hey," he answered. "Kind of late for you to be up, isn't it?"

"Look who's talking, old man," Blake retorted good-naturedly. "Some of us have work to do, you know."

"Or the appearance of," Michael shot back with a grin, drawing a chuckle from his friend. "What's up?"

"Your girlfriend around?" Blake asked, his voice turning serious.

"Why do you want to know?" Michael answered, frowning.

"Moon's dead," Blake told him. "Someone went in and took out him *and* his entourage. They had a window of maybe eight to ten minutes to get in and out."

Michael stared across the dark lawn.

"And you think it was her," he said, rather than asked.

"She's the only professional I know of in the area," Blake replied. "Not saying it was her, but it's a pretty big coincidence."

Michael sighed, rubbing his forehead. Viper wasn't the only professional in town, but Blake didn't need to know that. Blake already knew too much as it was.

"Even if it was her, and I'm not saying it was, what are you going to do about it?" he demanded. "You can't touch her. She's got protection at levels higher than mine!"

"Hell, Mike, I don't want to do anything about it," Blake protested. "As far as I'm concerned, whoever did it should get a medal. This guy was an asshole and no one could get near him. I'm not shedding any tears over here."

"Then why are we having this conversation?" Michael asked, lifting his beer to his lips.

"I just thought you'd be interested," Blake told him. "Look, Mike, your business is your own. God knows I'm the last one to judge and give advice. But, if you find out it *was* her, do me a favor? Tell her to stop getting involved in FBI investigations. Trying to keep track of the bad guys is hard enough without having to juggle a scary-ass, highly-trained, bad good-guy!"

Michael chuckled.

"You're just pissed that you have paperwork now," he accused him.

"Damn straight I am!" Blake retorted. "I have to go. Stephanie's giving me the evil eye. I'll catch up with you tomorrow."

"Ok," Michael agreed. "Blake?"

"Yeah?"

"Thanks for calling."

After a brief silence, Michael could almost see Blake nod his head.

"No problem, gunny," he replied.

It was nearly three in the morning when Stephanie finally rode the elevator down to the parking garage beneath the FBI building. John had left about half an hour before, unable to keep his eyes open any longer. She shook her head tiredly as she leaned against the side of the elevator.

Splitting her time evenly between the two crime scenes, she had spent most of the time at the hotel running between the Parkview Suite and the roped off driveway. The two musicians had been shot precisely in the head, from the direction of the park. Agents sent into the park reported two light posts were shot out in a corner of the park with a clear view to the front of the hotel. Beyond that, they found no other trace of the shooter.

Up in the Park Suite, the situation was similar. Five dead bodies were the only pieces of evidence to say that a killer had ever been there. Stephanie thought they caught a break when one of the techs found a wireless camera in the wine and cheese basket on the table, but the excitement was short-lived. The camera had already stopped transmitting, making it impossible to find the wireless signal source. Blake had bagged it and tagged it, but Stephanie didn't hold out any hope. Matt wasn't a miracle worker, no matter what they all liked to think. After discovering the miniature camera, Blake went through the suite again, looking for more, and came up empty.

With the one lead gone as fast as it had come, Stephanie returned downstairs where she was met by John, accompanied by the hotel head of security. After reviewing the hotel security footage, John informed her the cameras had picked up absolutely nothing. Moon's killer was invisible.

The elevator lurched to a stop and the doors opened. Stephanie stepped out into the parking garage, stifling a yawn. They had returned to the office so late that she was able to park right next to the elevator, and she beeped her car unlocked as she stepped into the garage.

Kwan was in lock-up, being held until she could interview him. Next door to him was Turi, awaiting transportation down to Washington DC with Blake. Two dangerous criminals were behind bars. Stephanie should be satisfied, but as she opened her driver's door and slid behind the wheel, she wasn't.

She didn't have the virus.

She had Kwan, and Blake was right. Having Kwan was better than having nothing at all, but Stephanie wanted that flash drive. It didn't matter that she was 90% sure who had taken it. 10% of her wasn't sure, and it was that 10% she knew would keep her up all night, worried about who might have access to the virus.

Stephanie stifled another yawn and started the engine, hitting the power locks and putting the car into reverse. She raised her eyes to the rear view mirror and froze, staring at the mirror, stunned.

A flash drive dangled silently from the end of a black, nylon cord.

Alina stood in the darkness, staring out her bedroom window into the night, absently swirling a vodka tonic around in its glass. Raven watched her from his perch, fluffed out and settled in for the night. Michael and Angela had both been waiting for her when she returned. Angela was beside herself and, after venting about terrorists and FBI agents who couldn't stop a bank robbery, she finally took herself off to bed three glasses of wine later. Michael, on the other hand, was strangely quiet all night, content to watch her with his hazel-green eyes.

Alina sighed and raised the glass to her lips. Something was on his mind, but he showed no indications of wanting to mention it. Whatever it was, he appeared willing to let it go unspoken. She wondered if it had to do with Damon and their conversation the other night. Alina sipped her drink, then her hand stilled as a thought occurred to her. Her eyes narrowed and she lowered the glass slowly. Of course! Moon! Blake probably called Michael to tell him about Moon. Michael would immediately assume she had been involved. He knew what she did. He knew she killed men like Moon.

Alina's lips twitched and she raised her glass again. *Oh Gunny, if you even knew half the truth your mind would spin*, she thought to herself. Shaking her head, she sipped the last of her drink and set the empty glass on the windowsill. *It wasn't me this time.*

The smile faded from her lips and Viper gazed out into the darkness, feeling hollow somewhere in the vicinity of her gut.

Hawk was gone.

He hadn't said good-bye. He didn't need to. The look in his eyes as she had turned to leave the parking garage was one she knew well. She saw it each time they parted company and went their separate ways. When she reached the stairwell door, Viper had turned her head to glance back. Even now, staring out into the night, she didn't know why she looked back. They never looked back. Ever.

Damon had been getting into the van, one hand on the steering wheel and one hand on the door. As she glanced back, he turned his head. Over the length of the parking garage, they had stared at each other silently. Alina's breath caught in her throat now, remembering the plummeting feeling of despair that had crashed over her as she looked at Hawk, one long leg already in the van, getting ready to drive away from her.

Alina spun away from the window and headed for the dresser impatiently. She pulled open one of the drawers, yanking out a pair of running pants. Raven watched as she disappeared into the walk-in closet around the corner, between the bedroom and the master bath. He blinked his shiny black eyes and continued to watch until she emerged a few moments later, dressed in the pants, tank top, black hooded jacket and running shoes. Not wanting to run the risk of rousing Michael, she crossed to the window and threw it open, sliding up the screen and swinging one leg out. Raven yawned and stretched his wings, walking to the end of his perch and watching as Viper disappeared out the window. Blinking, he launched off the perch and followed her out.

Alina landed on the deck softly and vaulted over the banister to land on the lawn, restless energy making her movements quicker than they should have been at two-thirty in the morning. After a quick stretch, she made sure her knife was secured on her ankle, then took off running into the trees. Raven followed, soaring over the tree tops, easily keeping his mistress within sight of his hawk vision.

Viper ran through the woods, leaping over underbrush and fallen logs in stride, her blood pounding in her ears and her heart rate settling into a steady cadence. She ran to clear her mind of the memory of the two men she shot, two more pieces of her soul ripped away. She ran to forget the image of Hawk getting into a van to drive away. She ran to try to get away from the hollow feeling of loneliness eating away at her gut.

But, most of all, Viper ran to try to erase the memory of the slow, sexy wink Damon had given her before she turned and disappeared into the stairwell.

Chapter Thirty-Nine

"What the hell do you mean, they're gone?!" Stephanie exclaimed, her voice loud enough to be heard by John and Blake, waiting outside Rob's office.

Blake raised an eyebrow and sipped his coffee.

"Is she always that quiet when she's in a closed meeting?" he asked John idly.

John grinned.

"Only when she doesn't like what she's hearing," he answered.

"She's a real spitfire, isn't she?" Blake asked, leaning against the wall.

"You have no idea," John murmured.

"Any idea what that's all about?"

"Nope."

They both listened to a deep, even tone inside the office, unable to make out what Rob was saying.

"Is something missing?" Blake asked after they had tried, unsuccessfully, to eavesdrop for a few moments.

"Apparently, but she didn't say what," John told him. "She went down to autopsy to see Larry and came flying back up like a bat out of hell. All she said as she passed me was, "They're gone!""

Blake sipped his coffee and studied John thoughtfully.

"Now what on earth could be missing from autopsy?" he wondered.

John shook his head.

"I don't know," he said. "That's why I'm standing here, trying to hear what they're saying."

Blake grinned and fell silent, but after a few more minutes, all they could hear was Rob's low, even tone before it went silent. Blake glanced at John.

"You don't think she killed him, do you?" he asked with a grin.

Next Exit, Dead Ahead

"I didn't hear a gun shot," John retorted.

The office door flew open then, startling both men, and Stephanie drew up short, looking at them in surprise. John had the grace to flush, but Blake just grinned and sipped his coffee, meeting her gaze blandly.

"What are you doing?" she demanded.

"Listening," Blake replied.

Stephanie opened her mouth to blast him with a scathing response, but ended up chuckling instead.

"Did you hear anything?" she asked.

"No."

Stephanie glanced over her shoulder and motioned for them to follow her. She turned and strode away from Rob's office, past her desk, and toward the elevator.

"Where are we going?" John asked as the trio stopped outside the elevator.

Stephanie pressed the button and looked at them.

"I want to show you something," she told them.

Blake raised an eyebrow. He glanced at John, who shrugged, and the elevator doors slid open. They followed Stephanie in and, a few moments later, found themselves standing in the middle of Larry's domain.

"Do you see anything wrong?" Stephanie asked them.

John frowned and looked around hopelessly. Larry emerged from a door in the back, shaking his head when he saw them.

"Any luck?" he asked Stephanie.

She shook her head.

"I don't understand," John said, looking at the metal tables, all filled with cloth-draped bodies.

Blake was a little quicker and started going from slab to slab, checking the clipboards. Larry watched him, then glanced at Stephanie.

"You haven't told them?" he said under his breath.

She shook her head.

"Where are Lorenzo and Ramiero?" Blake demanded after checking all the slabs.

"That's the question of the day," Stephanie replied.

John sucked in his breath.

"*That's* what's missing?!" he exclaimed. "Two bodies?!"

"No. *Six* bodies," Stephanie answered. "All the Cartels."

Blake strode back to Stephanie, the teasing laughter wiped from his face.

"Where the hell are they?"

"Gone," she informed him grimly. "Their remains, all the evidence recovered from their remains, and all the records were removed last night."

373

"By WHO!?" Blake roared.

"The CIA," Larry answered, pulling a plastic apron on over his scrubs. "I sent Stephanie up to Rob to see if anything could be done. Apparently, my work load is now six less. Not to worry though. I still have enough to keep me busy for the next few weeks."

John stared at Stephanie.

"What does the CIA want with six cartel soldiers?" he asked.

"I don't think it's necessarily the soldiers they want, as much as the evidence that went with them," she replied.

Blake stared at her.

"What are you saying?" he asked softly.

Stephanie glanced at Larry, who chuckled and waved his hand dismissively.

"Don't mind me, my dear," he told her, heading to the far slab. "I'm just the one who cuts them up. I don't care about the politics that put them here."

Stephanie smiled despite herself and looked at Blake.

"You already know what I'm thinking," she told him quietly, the smile fading from her face. "You realized it yourself last night when you saw Moon."

Blake's brown eyes met hers, his face unreadable.

"Well, would you care to fill me in?" John demanded. "Apparently I'm the only one here who doesn't have a clue."

"Lorenzo and Ramiero were shot with .22 caliber rounds," Blake said slowly, not taking his eyes off Stephanie's. "Last night, when I examined Moon, I said it looked like the same round."

John whistled.

"And now they're gone," he breathed, understanding dawning. He looked at Stephanie. "You think it was the Black..."

"No!" Stephanie said sharply, cutting him off, unable to pull her gaze from Blake's. "I don't."

Blake's lips curved slightly.

"The Black Widow?" he asked, his voice low and filled with amusement. "That's what you guys call her?"

John stared at him in consternation.

"How..." he began, then stopped, turning to Stephanie. "Oh, you need to explain."

Stephanie glanced over to the other end of the room where Larry hummed as he pulled the cover off Philip Chou, paying them no attention.

"Blake knows about Viper," she told John quietly. "He found out about her in August."

John looked at Blake.

"Is that true?" he asked.

Blake smiled faintly, watching Stephanie.

"Well done," he commended her. "What gave me away?"

"Viper," she answered with a rueful smile. "She said she owed you."

Blake threw back his head and laughed.

"Did she now?" he chortled.

"Ok, look, I'm feeling really stupid right now," John interrupted. "If she owes him, why did her agency take his cartel bodies?"

Blake sobered at the reminder of the missing bodies.

"I don't know," Stephanie lied, glancing at John.

Blake cast her a sharp glance and Stephanie resisted the urge to cross her fingers behind her back. She returned her gaze to him and caught her breath. He knew she was lying. She could see it in his eyes.

"If you don't think she killed Moon, then what *do* you think?" John demanded with a frown. "The CIA doesn't just take evidence on a whim. At least, not on a regular basis. Well, at least not usually from the FBI," he tried to clarify, his voice trailing off.

Blake grinned and slapped John on his shoulder.

"Welcome to Washington," he told him.

"I think the CIA was behind this whole thing from the beginning," Stephanie answered John's original question in a low voice. "They made sure everyone who came close to Kwan was warned off, except us. We have two musicians with classified military files dead after trying to kill Kwan, shot by a sniper we can't find. We have the same caliber pistol killing two cartel soldiers and the head of a North Korean terrorist regime, and now the evidence linking the one with the others is gone. And all of this centered around a virus capable of causing global economic collapse. Frankly, I think we were played from the very beginning."

"And you don't think the Black Widow had anything to do with it?" John demanded, raising his eyebrows in disbelief. "Steph, babe, listen to yourself."

"Oh, I think she was involved," Stephanie said with a nod. "I just don't think she was the one sent to kill Moon."

John ran a hand through his hair.

"Then who was?" he asked.

Stephanie shrugged.

"We'll never know," she replied.

"Well, I call this a bunch of bullshit," John announced.

Blake grinned and glanced at Stephanie thoughtfully.

"Anything involving that agency is usually heaped with the stuff," he told John. "We're lucky to get out of this with our jobs. Usually, when they run the kind of operation Stephanie's describing, the only ones left standing in the end are them."

"Not to sound naïve, but I didn't think Viper's department was like that," John murmured.

Stephanie looked at him grimly.

"Oh, I don't think for one second her department was behind this," she told him. "In fact, I think they're the ones who saved our asses."

Blake watched the armored transport van roll out of the parking garage, headed for Washington with Turi secured inside. As it turned and disappeared from view, he turned to look at Stephanie.

"Agent Walker, it was definitely interesting," he said, holding out his hand.

Stephanie laughed, grasping it.

"I tried to warn you when we first met," she told him. "Do you still think easy is boring?"

Blake grinned, his brown eyes meeting hers.

"Maybe something in between next time," he admitted, releasing her hand. "I have to admit, though, you have some pretty powerful friends in your corner."

Stephanie looked up at him.

"So do you," she replied softly.

Blake nodded, pulling his keys from his pocket and turning toward the black SUV parked a few feet away. He hesitated, then turned back.

"You know who killed Moon and the Cartel soldiers, don't you?" he asked, lowering his voice.

Stephanie met his brown gaze and smiled slightly.

"Have a safe trip, Agent Hanover," she said.

Blake studied her for a long moment before his lips curved into a slow smile.

"If you're ever in DC, give me a call," he told her.

Stephanie answered his smile with one of her own.

"I'll do that," she replied.

Blake nodded and turned back toward the SUV. Stephanie watched as he climbed into the driver's seat and started the engine. With a wave, he pulled out and rolled up to the exit of the parking garage, turning to follow the transport vehicle.

Turning back toward the elevator, Stephanie found herself grinning.

Next Exit, Dead Ahead

Blake Hanover had turned out to be nothing like what she expected, and much more discerning than anyone else. Pressing the button for the elevator, Stephanie stepped inside and turned to face the doors as they slid closed. Blake knew she was protecting an assassin.

He would learn, in time, these particular assassins were worth protecting.

Somewhere in Mexico

Martese Salcedo scowled and slammed down the telephone with such force that the items on the desk jumped. He pushed back his chair and got up, striding to the window of his office angrily. Staring out the bay window to the swimming pool below, he watched as his young wife dove into the water. He didn't see her, or the dozen or so other bikini-clad women who were lounging around the pool.

They had lost the virus. Worse, they had lost seven seasoned and veteran soldiers.

And now Jenaro himself was missing.

How had this happened?

La Cabeza swung around from the window and stalked across the room to a table with a bottle and glasses. Pouring himself a shot of tequila, he tossed it back angrily and poured himself another.

Jenaro had told him that this man, this invisible ghost they called the Hawk, was in New Jersey. He had also told him he had him under control.

Tossing back the second shot, Martese slammed the glass down and returned to his desk. Obviously, Jenaro didn't have him under control. Not at all.

A knock fell on the door and he called to enter impatiently. A maid opened the door silently and entered, carrying a tray with the mail and a box. She set the mail on his desk and then held out the box.

"This came by Federal Express a few minutes ago," she told him.

Martese raised an eyebrow and took it, waving her away. She turned to leave and he tossed the overnight package onto the desk, turning to his laptop while she left. Once the door closed softly behind her, however, La Cabeza slid the box toward to him. He pulled out a switchblade from his pocket and sliced through the heavy tape sealing the box. It was heavy, and he wasn't expecting any deliveries. The return address was Philadelphia, Pennsylvania. Had Jenaro sent something back he didn't want to carry over the border?

Tossing the knife aside, Martese opened the box, frowning when he came across heavy, black plastic sheeting. He pulled it open.

"Dios Mio!"

He shoved himself back from his desk, staring into the box in horror.

Jenaro Gomez stared up at him.

Martese wiped a meaty hand across his lips, his hand trembling as he stared at the head. There was no note. Just the head.

Slowly, his shaking stopped and La Cabeza took a deep breath. Getting up from the chair, he walked over to the window again and stared outside.

Jenaro had been so confident he could catch the Hawk and pay him back for killing the former La Cabeza. Martese had wondered at the wisdom of engaging such a formidable assassin at a time when their forces were already stretched thin. They were trying to rebuild the Cartel out of chaos. Jenaro, however, had been adamant. In a moment of good humor, Martese gave his permission.

Now, Jenaro's head sat in a box on his desk.

La Cabeza shook his head and rubbed his neck. If this Hawk could get through all the soldiers with Jenaro, and then get Jenaro himself, he was indeed a formidable foe. Lapsing deep into thought, Martese struggled with thoughts of vengeance and the realization that, with the loss of Jenaro and his team, his Cartel was even weaker. After a long while, La Cabeza raised his head and turned away from the window.

The Hawk would not be pursued.

Epilogue

Damon set the thick log on its end on a tree stump and picked up the axe. Gripping it firmly, he swung it up in an arc, bringing the blade down sharply on the wood, splitting it in two. The two halves fell off the stump and he set the axe down, turning to get another thick log from the pile behind him. The sun was starting to set, bathing the backyard with an orange glow. The back deck of his large, rambling farmhouse was about fifty yards away, and two huge bull mastiffs lounged on the varnished wood, watching him adoringly.

Wiping the back of his hand across his forehead, Damon glanced toward the house. He frowned when he saw the cloud of dust coming in from the road. The driveway consisted of a half-mile of dirt, making it impossible for any vehicle to approach the house unannounced. Hawk raised an eyebrow and glanced at his watch. It was too late for UPS and he had sent the farm hands home for the weekend.

Leaning the axe against the fence beside him, Hawk watched as the dogs raised their heads, looking toward the driveway. He returned his gaze to the cloud of dust, his eyes narrowing, watching as it grew closer. A car was traveling at high speed toward the house. Reaching behind him, Hawk pulled out his Beretta and started moving toward the drive, flipping off the safety. One of the sudden gusts of wind that had been ripping across the fields all day blew in from the left and Hawk paused as the clouds of dust around the car swirled away briefly, giving him a glimpse of the vehicle.

He flipped the safety back on and tucked his gun back into its holster, a smile crossing his face. The dogs got up and ambled off the deck, stretching before turning and heading toward the side of the house to see who was coming to visit them. As the car approached the house, it slowed down and the dust clouds lowered, swirling away.

Damon walked out to where the drive met the old barn, stopping to watch as a black Shelby GT 500 pulled past the house, growling as it rolled forward. It came to a stop, the powerful engine humming for a

379

moment before it switched off. Silver racing stripes, now covered in dust, ran the length of the sports car and Damon nodded in approval, his lips curving into a grin.

The dogs barked and started toward the car to investigate as the driver's door opened.

Viper got out, smiling faintly as the enormous dogs barked and headed straight for her. Closing the door behind her, she glanced at Hawk, her eyes concealed behind sunglasses.

"Bull mastiffs," she said.

He grinned.

"Bull mastiffs," he agreed, moving forward. "Meet Jack and Daniel."

Alina grinned and turned to the mastiffs. She held out a hand to each and they promptly shoved their snouts into her palms, tails wagging, snuffling and sniffing her as they pressed forward. The tops of their heads came to her waist and she smiled, rubbing their ears. Damon allowed them to greet her, then called them to heel when they showed no signs of stopping. As Jack and Daniel reluctantly went to his side, Alina brushed off her hands and tossed her hair out of her face, turning to face him. She took in his faded jeans and black teeshirt and her heart started thumping.

"Nice dogs."

"Nice car."

Alina's lips curved.

"It was time," she murmured.

Damon looked at her steadily.

"How did you find me?" he asked.

"It wasn't hard," she answered. "I knew where to look."

Damon's lips twitched and he studied her for a moment.

"You're a long way from Jersey."

"Well, I wanted to see the horses," Alina replied with a faint smile.

Damon let out a bark of laughter.

"Well, then, come with me," he said, holding out his hand.

Alina placed her hand in his and felt his strong fingers close around hers warmly. Damon turned to walk across the small field on the other side of the driveway, entwining his fingers with hers. Jack and Daniel barked and ran ahead, leading the way to a wooden fence in the distance.

"I wondered if I would hear from you," Damon murmured, glancing down at her, his eyes hidden behind his sunglasses. "After a week, I decided you were still pissed. After three, I gave up."

"I had some things to take care of," Alina told him quietly. She hesitated, then continued, "I needed the time to think, anyway."

Damon shot her a look from behind the glasses.

380

Next Exit, Dead Ahead

"And buy a new car?" he asked softly.

Alina grinned and nodded.

"I owe you an apology about the car," she said. "You were right. It *was* time. I just didn't want to let you see that part of my life." She glanced at him and he was silent, listening as they walked. "I've spent ten years separating my old life from this one," she told him quietly. "Everything fits into its appropriate box nicely, except you. The Mustang, it was part of my past, something I've wanted since before I could drive. It's part of someone I don't know anymore. Somehow, having you know about it..."

"Made it real again," Hawk finished for her.

Alina looked at him.

"Exactly."

"I know what you mean," Damon told her. "I feel it now, having you here. We're not used to this, you and I. We're not used to letting people in."

"Then why are you so damn calm about it?" Viper demanded.

Hawk laughed.

"Because I know *you*," he replied simply. "That's all I need to know."

Alina glanced at him, a feeling of warmth washing over her, and she smiled slightly as his fingers squeezed hers briefly. He nodded in front of them.

"There they are," he said softly.

Alina looked into the fenced field, taking in the sight before her. The setting sun lit up the horizon in a breathtaking display of orange and purple, painting the sky in streaks of color. Milling around the large field in small groups were about fifty horses, their colors ranging from black to brown to gray to white. Bathed in the colors of the sinking sun, they appeared magical and regal at the same time.

"These are all yours?" she asked, leaning on the fence and gazing over the field.

"Yes." Damon took off his sunglasses and propped them on his head, leaning next to her while the dogs took off, chasing a rabbit and barking joyfully. "This is just one herd. I have two more."

Alina glanced at him and encountered sparkling blue eyes.

"Wow," she murmured, unable to tear her gaze away from those eyes. "You really are a cowboy."

Damon grinned slowly and reached out to pull her sunglasses off her face.

"Yes, ma'am," he drawled.

Alina caught her breath, her dark eyes meeting his, and smiled.

"I don't know if I can get used to that drawl," she said softly.

His eyes smiled into hers as he slipped his arms around her, pulling her to him.

"I got used to the Jersey accent," he murmured.

"I do *not* have an accent," Alina muttered, her eyes narrowing.

"Whatever lets you sleep at night," he retorted with a grin, lowering his lips to hers.

Alina forgot all about horses, mastiffs, cars and accents as she wrapped her arms around his broad shoulders, her eyes sliding closed. None of it seemed important. All that mattered was his strong arms around her and his heart beating against hers.

It was a long while later before Alina came to her senses to find herself sitting on the fence, her legs wrapped around his hips. She pulled away, her breathing ragged, disoriented about what had brought her back to earth with such a jolt. Damon groaned and lifted his head, his eyes dark cobalt blue. He seemed to realize exactly what had nudged her back to reality and he sighed, looking over her shoulder.

Alina raised an eyebrow and opened her mouth to ask what was wrong when she was *literally* nudged, quite firmly, on her shoulder blades. Spinning around swiftly, she came nose to nose with a black horse.

"Oh!" she exclaimed softly, her eyes widening.

The horse stared at her with warm brown eyes before lowering his head to nudge her again questioningly. Alina giggled, clapping her hand over her mouth at the sound. Her shoulders shook slightly and she looked past the black horse to find about five others crowding behind him, all trying to get a look at her.

"Do they do this with all your lady friends?" she asked, turning to look at Damon.

"I don't know," he answered. "You're the first one they've seen."

Alina laughed as the horse nudged her again in the back. She twisted around on the fence, sitting with her back to Damon, and reached out to stroke its neck.

"What kind of horses are they?" she asked over her shoulder, dropping her hand and watching as the black horse shook his head, causing his mane to flow out majestically behind him.

When Damon didn't answer right away, she turned her head to look at him. He had a smile on his face as he slipped his arms around her waist. Lowering his head, he whispered in her ear,

"Mustangs."

About the Author

CW Browning was writing before she could spell. Making up stories with her childhood best friend in the backyard in Olathe, Kansas, imagination ran wild from the very beginning. At the age of eight, she printed out her first full-length novel on a dot-matrix printer. All eighteen chapters of it. Through the years, the writing took a backseat to the mechanics of life as she pursued other avenues of interest. Those mechanics, however, have a great way of underlining what truly lifts a spirt and makes the soul sing. After attending Rutgers University and studying History, her love for writing was rekindled. It became apparent where her heart lay. Picking up an old manuscript, she dusted it off and went back to what made her whole. CW still makes up stories in her backyard, but now she crafts them for her readers to enjoy. She makes her home in Southern New Jersey, where she loves to grill steak and sip red wine on the patio.

Visit her at: www.cwbrowning.com
Also find her on Facebook, Instagram and Twitter!

Made in the USA
Las Vegas, NV
22 July 2023

75084099R00213